BROKEN
GIRLS

BOOKS BY JOY KLUVER

Last Seen

BROKEN GIRLS

JOY KLUVER

bookouture

Published by Bookouture in 2021

An imprint of Storyfire Ltd.
Carmelite House
50 Victoria Embankment
London EC4Y 0DZ

www.bookouture.com

ISBN: 978-1-80019-647-6
eBook ISBN: 978-1-80019-646-9

To my mother, Rosalie

CHAPTER 1

Thursday

'I'd say she's been out here for about five or six days at least, judging by the state of her. She's coming out of the bloating stage now,' said Dr Nick White. 'But I'm sure your entomologist over at the forensic lab will be able to tell you more when she examines the maggots.' He held up a clear pot. 'I've got some ready to go to the lab. Would you like a closer look at the body, Detective Inspector Noel?'

DI Bernie Noel turned her head slowly towards the corpse, willing her stomach to settle. This was the part of the job she hated the most. She could cope with skeletonised remains but not decomposing ones. The sickly sweet smell would stay with her now for the rest of the day. She wasn't looking forward to the post-mortem, especially as the pathologist liked to make her squirm.

She raised her eyes to look at the dead woman a few yards away. Hidden by the red and orange leaves that had fallen around her. Long dark hair. Her face disfigured, especially around the lips, leaving her with a permanent, gruesome grin. Gold hoop earrings clinging to her chewed ears. A short red dress, smudged with dirt and split. Scratches and cuts on her bare, dirty feet. Red stilettos had been recovered further away. A couple of rings were hanging on slender fingers.

'Any ID on her?'

'No, nothing that I've found so far.'

Bloating, insect activity and other scavengers had disfigured her face so facial identification would be difficult and, more importantly, distressing for the identifier. DNA or dental records would be their best chance for a match to any missing women.

Bernie nodded towards the pot. 'I think the entomologist will want to come out and collect her own samples. There might be some things she needs in particular.'

White paused. He wasn't known for admitting when he was out of his depth. 'Of course.'

Bernie saw, rather than heard, the pathologist huff; his shoulders going up and down. She steeled herself to look more at the body but the billowing feeling in her stomach warned her against it.

'I'm going to send Matt to take down details. And I'm sure the photographer has taken lots of stills.'

'Detective Inspector Noel, if you're going to make DCI one day, you have got to be made of sterner stuff. Now, look at this young woman. You need to get angry on her behalf so that you can find the person responsible for doing this and get justice.'

Bernie narrowed her eyes. 'So definitely murder then?'

'Yes. Unless she strangled herself.' He pointed to her neck. 'Her hyoid bone is broken. I can feel it.'

Bernie looked one more time and instead of seeing a corpse, she tried to imagine a young, vibrant woman in a red dress, out enjoying herself. There had been no reports of missing women in the last few days yet she had lain here almost a week.

How has no one missed you? The anger Nick White had spoken of was beginning to build. *I'll find who did this to you, I promise.*

Vomit burned Bernie's throat as she retched by her car. That was breakfast gone. She'd managed to hold on until she was away from the scene as she didn't want any disapproving looks from White.

Opening the driver's door, she pulled out an almost empty bottle of water and took a swig, swirling it around her mouth and then spitting it out. Leaning against the car, Bernie looked up. Clouds skittered across the autumn sky, being chased by a westerly wind. She could smell the dampness in the air – rain was on the way. It would be a relief after the recent but surprising autumnal warmth. The white tent was hastily being erected. For some reason the pathologist preferred to do his initial examination in the open air; maybe he was more sensitive to the smell than he liked to admit.

Bernie closed her eyes but swiftly opened them again. The victim was still there, imprinted on her retinas. She wondered how the young woman had ended up in the woods, close to the railway. She was fairly certain she was young, judging by the dress she wore. Had the murder happened there? Possibly. Soil samples would help with that. If she had been dumped, why had there been no real attempt at burial? Just covered with leaves and some of those had probably fallen directly onto her from the tree canopy above. There was no proper road nearby, only a track that led to a farm. The farmer's teenage son was still in shock after discovering the body. DC Matt Taylor was interviewing him. With Matt being only twenty-five, she thought the boy would open up to him more. Her right-hand woman, DS Kerry Allen, had contacted the forensic experts and was starting to trawl through Missing Persons' records. All Bernie needed to know now was who the senior investigating officer would be and whether she would be given free rein to run the case, since Detective Chief Superintendent Hugh Wilson was at home recovering from a hernia operation and would not be back for a couple of weeks.

A car rumbled along the bumpy farm track. She looked up. The Forensics vans and four-by-four vehicles had coped fine but the sleek, shiny cars of MCIT had struggled. It was the latter now heading towards her. She groaned inwardly as she glimpsed the man in the passenger seat – DCI Patrick Worth, or DCI Worthless, as he was more commonly known amongst the rank and file. Pedantic and pernickety were the two words that came to mind when Bernie thought about him. Even if he let her run the case, she would be bound by his rules. Was it worth the effort? But it was too late now. Bernie had seen the body and Dr Nick White was right – she had to get justice.

CHAPTER 2

'Ah, Detective Inspector Noel. First on the scene. Shall we walk and talk?'

Bernie nodded. Her stomach was churning and the last place she wanted to go was back to the body. But there was no choice.

'So what do we have?' asked DCI Worth.

Bernie gave him a sideways glance as they walked across the field. She looked at his weasel-like face, with a thin pencil moustache that was probably quite dapper in the 1950s but looked ludicrous in the twenty-first century. His views on women came from the fifties as well. He was close to retirement but was showing no sign of slowing down. She had to make a good impression if she was going to keep the case.

'Body is of a female, possibly young. She's decomposed quite quickly so facial recognition will be difficult. In fact, finding any distinguishing marks isn't going to be easy. But there is some jewellery – earrings and rings. Soil samples and entomology are going to be crucial with determining whether she was killed here or not and when.'

Despite being shorter than her, Worth's stride was long. Bernie made sure she matched it.

'I'm sure Nick White has already dealt with that.'

Bernie swallowed. 'It's better if they take their own samples. DS Allen's already rung them.'

DCI Worth suddenly stopped and gave Bernie a sharp stare. 'This is a murder scene, not a freak sideshow where anyone is invited. Detective Chief Superintendent Wilson may be foolhardy enough to let you loose on a murder case but I'm the senior investigating officer here and if you want to be my deputy, then you play by my rules. Understood?'

'Yes, sir.' Bernie attempted to keep her voice as normal as possible while she seethed inside. 'Why don't we see the victim, sir, and then you can make the decision?'

Worth smiled, showing nicotine-stained teeth. 'Good, that's better. We'll make a fine officer of you yet. Now, are we nearly there?'

'Yes, sir, the outer perimeter cordon is just past those trees. We can suit up there.'

Bernie allowed the DCI to go ahead of her. She was tempted to say, 'I'm already a damn fine officer, thank you very much' but held back. She'd already riled Worth. She wasn't about to push her luck.

Bernie had been right about the enclosed tent intensifying the smell of the corpse. The stench was overpowering as she lifted the flap to let DCI Worth through.

'Nick, good to see you. What have we got here then?' asked Worth.

'Good to see you too, Patrick. I would shake hands but, you know.' Dr White lifted a stained, gloved hand. 'Victim is female, I would say young but I'll need to confirm that. My first thought is strangulation as her hyoid bone is broken. I can feel it but will confirm once I've opened her up.'

Bernie was glad White had made her look at the body earlier. Her stomach wasn't somersaulting as much the second time around.

'We're past the time frame for normal indicators for time of death such as rigor mortis so we'll need the story from these little fellas.' The pathologist pointed at the maggots. 'What time is your entomologist turning up, DI Noel?'

'Do you think that's strictly necessary, Nick?' Worth asked.

White's eyes flickered towards Bernie. Was it sympathy she saw in them?

'To be fair, Patrick, the entomological evidence is going to be crucial here. Not just for time of death but also to determine if she was killed here. Same with soil samples. Much better to have experts in court that came out to the scene.'

'Hmm. Well, you must have what you need, Nick. In the meantime, we have to think about how this poor woman got herself into this predicament.'

Bernie could feel her blood boiling. *This poor woman hasn't done anything to get herself like this.*

'Underwear?' Worth added.

'Intact, at first look. But I will check for sexual assault when I get her back to the morgue.'

'And the attacker? Any ideas?'

'Judging by the break of the bone, I'd say this was a man. The hyoid has literally snapped. That takes a lot of strength through the hands and arms. Not impossible for a woman, though, if she's using a ligature.'

'Hmm, I see. Well then, DI Noel, I think we'd better get back to the station and rally the troops. I'm sure we can leave Dr White and the crime scene investigators to do their jobs. No doubt your entomologist...'

'Dr Phyl Bridger,' said Bernie.

'Oh, is he good?'

'*She* is, sir.'

'Really? When I was a lad, girls used to run away from anything creepy-crawly.'

'Dr Bridger has her degree and doctorate from Cambridge and now teaches at Bristol University. She's one of the best in her field and this young woman deserves the best, don't you think, sir?'

DCI Worth tensed. Bernie knew she was walking a tightrope.

'DI Noel is right,' said Dr White. 'A standard forensic postmortem isn't going to be enough here, Patrick. We need these experts to unlock this woman's story. I can't do it alone.'

Worth nodded. 'All right. Let's go back to the station and rustle up some manpower… oh, and womanpower too, of course.'

Bernie resisted the temptation to roll her eyes.

They were almost back to the cars when DCI Worth said the words Bernie had been waiting to hear.

'Well, DI Noel, I would like you in future to run major decisions past me first, particularly ones with a financial implication, but I would like you to be my deputy for this investigation. Am I right in thinking you have only one detective sergeant and one detective constable in your team?'

'Yes, at present. The plan is to recruit some more when DCS Wilson returns to work.'

'Then we must get in some other officers. A couple more DCs, perhaps, and you'll be needing a family liaison officer for the relatives – when we find out who she is. I have a chap in mind; he's very good. In fact, I think you've worked with him before. DS Anderson.'

Bernie's stomach dropped. *Oh God, no.*

CHAPTER 3

Bernie was aware of the door to the Major Crime Investigation Team briefing room opening and closing. She looked at Kerry who gave a slight nod. Two, maybe three steps and he'd be breathing on her neck. They'd managed to avoid each other the last few months with DS Anderson being seconded to Avon and Somerset Police to help with the large gambling case they'd uncovered in May. She still felt bad about standing him up for lunch and going instead to view her cottage. There had been a moment when she'd been tempted to take things further and break her rule of not dating a colleague but she couldn't get past what Louise Anderson had said about her ex-husband in a phone call – charming but manipulative. She may have to work with him but she wasn't going to let him into her personal life.

'Ma'am.'

His Glaswegian accent had softened slightly since she had last seen him. She turned round, fixing a smile on her face.

'DS Anderson. It's good to have you back.'

'Is it?' He raised one eyebrow.

'As part of the team, yes.' She worked hard to keep her face as neutral as possible. 'DCI Worth is just about to start the briefing. Please take a seat.'

The chairs were arranged in orderly rows as opposed to their normal haphazard arrangement. The DCI stamping his authority on furniture as well as the team.

Worth cleared his throat before speaking. 'Right, ladies and gentlemen, let's get started. Firstly, a few introductions. My name is DCI Patrick Worth. I'm sure you've heard of me before. I have a reputation for running a tight ship.'

Oh dear God. A man who believes his own hype. Bernie heard a laugh being stifled by a cough. It was her sergeant, Kerry Allen, but she didn't dare look in case she started laughing too.

Worth paused before continuing. 'I've drafted in a few others to help. DC Alice Hart and DC Mick Parris have worked with me before and you already know DS Dougal Anderson, our family liaison officer, who'll be working on the main investigation until we find the victim's relatives and he transfers to them.

'And so to our victim. Female, white, not sure of age yet but believed to be in the fifteen to twenty-nine age range. Red dress. Underwear intact. Red shoes a short distance away from the body. Earrings and a couple of rings. But no bag, no ID. And unfortunately, no clear face left to identify.'

Without warning, Worth tapped a key on a laptop and a photograph of the decomposed woman's head appeared on screen. Bernie heard a sharp intake of breath. She looked at DC Alice Hart, with her mousy hair and delicate features. She had turned pale and had her hand over her mouth.

'Might be best to move on to the next image, sir.' Bernie jerked her head in Hart's direction.

'Yes, of course.'

Bernie winced as she saw the bloated torso with maggots everywhere. She got up and held the door open for Alice as she went flying out of the room.

Worth tutted. 'Does anyone else need to leave?' He paused for a few seconds, waiting for any answers. 'Good, then we'll continue. Until we hear back from our forensic experts, which, fortunately, DI Noel has already started to sort out…'

Bernie knew he wasn't praising her.

'…we won't be any closer to identity. I believe DS Allen has been looking at missing persons?'

Kerry stood up. She stared at DCI Worth and the photo behind him on the screen, unfazed by both. 'Yes, sir. I have five possible leads at the moment but I'll wait for the post-mortem report before I do any more. Although the jewellery may help.'

'Thank you, DS Allen. Dr White has suggested she may have been outside for perhaps five or six days but, of course, that doesn't mean she died at that time. She may have been held somewhere else and killed there before being dumped. She may have been in a freezer for the last six months for all we know.'

Not if those dirty feet are anything to go by.

'Obviously,' Worth continued, 'we can't get an image out in the media of her but a vague description and a picture of the dress would be a start. We'll get DC Hart to look at that when she gets back – find out where the dress is from and look for an online picture of it we can use. Same with the shoes. If you could jot that down, please, DI Noel.'

Bernie held in a sigh; she hadn't realised Deputy SIO was a secretarial position.

'In fact, I was hoping Jane Clackett would be here for this meeting. I did ask her to come along. Media coverage is going to be crucial to this investigation.'

'I'm sure we can pass on all the relevant details to her,' said Bernie, wondering if Jane from the press office had deliberately not turned up. Although not the best of friends, they were united over their dislike of DCI Worth.

Worth scowled. 'Even so, if I ask someone to a meeting, I expect—'

There was a knock at the door and a thin woman dressed completely in black, with a sleek black bob and bright red lips came into the room.

'I'm sorry I'm late, DCI Worth,' said Jane Clackett.

'Have you come straight from a funeral? Is that why you're late?' asked Worth.

Jane's eyes narrowed as she took the seat next to Anderson 'I'm late because I've been dealing with the press about a tip-off for a dumped body. Apparently the boy who found her wasn't as completely traumatised as you may have all thought because he was perfectly capable of tweeting the local rag. So, again, I'm sorry I'm late but I've been doing my job, *sir*.'

Bernie covered her mouth to hide her smile. Only Jane would be brave enough to take on Worth.

'I was just explaining, Jane, that media coverage is going to be crucial in helping us.'

'But of course, DCI Worth. And I'm already on to it. I've told Clive Bishop over at the *Salisbury Journal* he'll be the first to know details when we're ready to release them.' She gave him a winning smile and then turned it round to Anderson.

'And it's lovely to see you back, Dougie. We've missed you.' Jane crossed her black-clad legs slowly. A few months ago that would have annoyed the hell out of Bernie but now she felt they were welcome to each other. Both schemers and manipulators – they were the perfect match.

Bernie wanted to laugh as she saw Anderson shift uncomfortably in his chair. She also sensed Worth's impatience.

'We need to get a move on now. We don't have time to waste. DCs Taylor and Parris. I want you to check out CCTV. Look at stations on that line. Had she been on a train and then followed and dragged into that wooded area? Maybe she accepted a lift? Had she been to any bars and clubs? Today's Thursday so look back to the weekend and Thursday and Friday of last week as well.

'DS Allen, use the jewellery to narrow your search on Missing Persons but let's also be aware this woman may not have been reported missing yet. Maybe her friends and family think she's away. So, Jane, as soon as we know more about the clothing, I want you to release that info. I'm going to stay here and coordinate things until it's time for the post-mortem. Nick White is planning on doing that later today. He'll text me the time.'

'Sir? What about me?' asked Bernie.

'Yes, me too,' said Anderson.

'Well, you two can go and have a little friendly chat with the teenager who found her and remind him why we don't like the press being tipped off.'

CHAPTER 4

Anderson headed towards his car.

'No. We'll take mine,' she said. 'You don't know where you're going.'

He paused, gripping his car keys in his hand. He turned round slowly.

'I believe there's a little something called satnav. I wasn't sure how good your wrist is these days, since we haven't spoken for a while.'

Bernie hated Worth for pairing them together.

'It's fine,' she lied. Her wrist had been smashed with a hammer by a suspect five months before. She still got the occasional twinge, something that should pass if she did her physio exercises – as if she had the time. 'Besides, satnav is a bit hit and miss round here. Makes more sense for me to drive.'

Anderson continued the stand-off. He hated backing down.

'*Detective Sergeant* Anderson, we really do need to get going.' She pressed the key fob and the doors clicked open. She sat in the front seat and waited. She looked in her rear mirror as he walked slowly towards her car. Despite herself, her body still lurched when he opened the door and got in. The attraction hadn't faded completely. She closed her eyes for a few seconds.

'Ready to go, *ma'am*?'

Bernie opened her eyes and nodded. She started the engine and then pressed the button to wind down the window. She needed the air.

They drove in silence. Bernie expected Anderson to quiz her about the case and the scene but, instead, he stared out of the window. He was probably memorizing the journey so he would be able to come back without her. They drove underneath the railway line that ran close to the scene.

'Not far now,' she said after they'd been driving for twenty minutes. 'The problem is getting round all these fields.'

'Does the farm we're going to belong to Ron Willis?'

'No, Ron's farm is north of the railway. We're south of it here. It's a small farm with pigs. That's all I know. Matt dealt with the family.'

'Clearly not well enough if number one witness went and blabbed to the press. Bloody kids these days – living their lives on social media.'

Bernie laughed. 'Careful, you sound like a grumpy old man.'

'Not really. I prefer living in the real world, not the virtual one.'

Bernie thought back to the social media search she had done on Louise Anderson. She'd found her on Facebook. There wasn't a single reference or photo of her husband until the divorce came through. And even then she didn't mention him by name. 'It's done,' she had written, 'I never have to see him again.' Bernie thought maybe it was less about living in the real world for Anderson and more about not wanting to leave damning evidence behind.

She flicked the indicator switch and then turned right down a small track.

'This is the Moffatts' farm. Craig is the son. He's fifteen. From what Matt told me, he'd been walking the dog when he found her.'

'If she's been there for several days, why didn't he find her before?' asked Anderson.

'He's been ill for over a week. A bad stomach upset. First time this morning he felt well enough to go out. I guess this will set him back a bit.' She looked across at Anderson as they pulled up outside the red brick farmhouse. 'Please let me handle this. I know what you're like.'

Anderson feigned surprise. 'I don't know what you mean.'

'Oh yes, you do. You're too abrupt at times. You can take notes.'

A dog barked as they approached the door – a large German Shepherd chained to a post on a long lead. An odour of manure and pigs lingered in the air and Bernie heard grunting from a few yards away.

'I want to see the scene after this,' said Anderson.

Bernie looked down at his designer suit and shoes and smirked.

'Just as well the rain was light earlier. We have to trek across a field first before heading into the woods.'

She knocked at the blue front door, paint peeling to reveal red underneath. A tired-looking woman in scruffy clothes opened it. Bernie showed her warrant card.

'Mrs Moffatt? I'm Detective Inspector Noel and this is Detective Sergeant Anderson. I know you saw one of my colleagues earlier but we need to ask Craig a few more questions. May we come in, please? We'll need either you or your husband to be with him.'

The woman sighed. 'I suppose so. John's feeding the pigs so I'll do it. But Craig's still in shock. I think he's going to need counselling.'

The woman led them into a darkened lounge where a teenage boy lay on a brown leather sofa, a blanket up to his chin.

'He can't stop shivering. He was already ill but this has set him back badly,' said his mother.

Bernie thought of her own reaction after seeing the body. She didn't think the lad was making it up. But if he was this bad, how did he manage to tweet the newspaper?

They sat on two matching leather chairs, either side of the sofa. Both were cracked and faded. Bernie took the seat nearest the boy's head.

'Craig, I'm Detective Inspector Noel but you can call me Bernie, if you prefer. I know you spoke to another officer this morning but we have a few more questions if you can cope. If it gets too much then we'll stop. Is that OK?'

Bernie saw a slight nod of the head.

'Right, can you tell me what happened this morning?'

Craig coughed a little. 'Erm, I've been ill but this morning I felt well enough to walk the dog. That's my job. Normally I'd take him before school but as I wasn't going in today, I took him a bit later.'

'So what sort of time?'

'It was about eight o'clock.'

Bernie saw Anderson writing down notes in his notebook.

The boy coughed again. 'I usually take him over to the woods. He likes to chase the squirrels up the trees. Anyway, this morning, he was going loopy. He kept running off and then barking. And then he'd come back to me and do it all again. I knew he'd found something, probably a dead animal, but I didn't think too much about it. I'm still not feeling that strong; I didn't want to clamber through the bushes. And then he came back with a shoe. A woman's shoe.'

Craig paused. He put his hand to his mouth. His mother disappeared and quickly returned with a bucket and a glass of water.

'Just in case, love.' She turned to Bernie. 'He's kept nothing down since this morning.'

Bernie nodded. 'It's all right, Craig, take your time. Maybe try a sip of water.'

A few minutes passed and then Craig, very pale, continued.

'Then Blaze ran off, barking madly, so I went after him. And then I saw—'

Craig grabbed the bucket and heaved. His mother stroked his head and murmured, 'It's OK love, it's OK.'

Bernie looked across at Anderson. She gave a little shake of the head. There was no way he had tweeted the newspaper. She gave Craig a bit more time to recover.

'Well done, Craig. You've had a terrible shock. If it makes you feel any better, I'm not great seeing these things either. I'm just wondering, and you might be able to answer this, Mrs Moffatt, are you aware of anyone coming down here at night, or even during the day over the last week or so?'

Mrs Moffatt shook her head as did Craig. 'We've not noticed anyone we weren't expecting and the dog would probably have heard. He barks when anyone comes. We got him because someone tried to steal some of our pigs.'

'If you do think of anything then just let us know. One other thing. Craig, you're clearly not well. Have you been on your phone today?'

The boy looked puzzled. 'No. I've been here on the sofa since this morning. My phone's been on charge in my room.'

'So how did you manage to tweet the *Salisbury Journal* about finding the body then?'

'What? I haven't done anything like that.'

Bernie turned her head at the faint sound of scurrying in the hallway. She glanced at Mrs Moffatt, who sighed.

'Wait a minute.' Craig's mother got up and went to the lounge door. 'Laura Anne Moffatt. Get in here now.'

Bernie saw a sulky-looking girl with a high ponytail sidle round the door.

'Have you been on Craig's Twitter account again?' asked her mother.

Laura looked down at the floor. 'Maybe,' she muttered. 'Why?'

'Why? Because this police officer wants to know.'

Bernie saw Laura's eyes flicker towards her and then Anderson. The girl's gaze stayed on Anderson.

'How old are you, Laura?' asked Bernie.

'Twelve.'

Bernie sighed. The girl looked older. 'And do you know how old you have to be to be on Twitter?'

'Thirteen.'

'And do you know why that is?'

The girl dragged her eyes away from Anderson to Bernie, a smile on her face.

'Yeah. Our form tutor, Mr Gardener, had one of your lot come into school to give us a lecture.'

'Hey,' said Mrs Moffatt. 'Don't be rude to the *detective inspector*.'

Laura's eyes met her mother's. She glanced down and fiddled with her necklace, stroking the owl pendant.

'I tweeted it. I thought it was cool.'

'Well, it wasn't,' said Bernie. 'Thankfully, someone at the paper got in touch and it was removed. But we have no idea how many people may have seen it. This is a murder investigation, Laura. It's very important to preserve evidence and we're careful about what we release to the press. We don't want to alert the person responsible unless we have cause to do so. Do you understand?'

The girl nodded, her eyes downcast.

Bernie looked back at Craig. The skin in his face had gone slack. She reached out and felt his neck for a pulse. It was erratic.

'Anderson, get an ambulance. If he's not keeping anything down he might be dehydrating.'

Mrs Moffatt came over to her son. 'Oh, Craig. I hadn't realised you were so bad.'

'Don't worry, Mrs Moffatt. The paramedics will put a line in and start him on fluids. Is your husband around?'

'He's out in the field. I'll call him.' She dashed out of the room.

Bernie looked at Laura, still skulking by the door.

'Laura, do me a favour. Get rid of any social media accounts you might have. Wait a year and then sign up again and make sure your mum is a friend.'

Bernie checked Craig's pulse again. She wasn't surprised he was in such a state. The image of the young woman in the woods would stay with them both for quite some time.

CHAPTER 5

Bernie helped to shut the ambulance door and then waved goodbye to Mr Moffatt and Laura as they followed in their car. The dog barked as they left.

'Oh God, what's going to happen with the animals?' she asked.

'I heard Mr Moffatt on the phone. He's got someone coming over. Now they've gone, can we please go over to the scene?' asked Anderson, impatience in his voice.

Bernie wondered what it was like to be demoted; for your natural instinct to lead to be curtailed. Anderson was still ill at ease with being a sergeant rather than an inspector.

He'd already started to walk across the field, towards the police vehicles. More had arrived since earlier that morning, including the pathologist's black ambulance. It wouldn't be long before the body would be moved.

She walked quickly to catch up with Anderson. The light rain had given way to warm sunshine. Summer had, unusually, continued into October. She regretted not leaving her jacket in the car. She'd be warm in the forensic suit, her third one of the day.

They suited up at the outer cordon and were signed into the crime scene log. Uniform were searching the surrounding area looking for anything of significance. They walked a little way on a path and then Bernie led Anderson off-track past trees and bushes until they could see the white tent ahead of them.

Anderson lifted a gloved hand to his nose. 'Ugh, I can smell that from here.'

'Wait until you get inside the tent.'

Bernie heard a familiar voice as she approached – Dr Phyl Bridger. Bernie had attended a lecture Phyl had given to police in the summer and had then spent a couple of hours afterwards discussing the merits of forensic entomology with her over a cup of coffee. She pulled back the tent flap.

'Phyl, I thought I could hear you. I would say it's nice to see you but…'

A woman with rosy cheeks and glasses looked up. 'Yes, I know what you mean. One day our lives will cross in a more pleasant environment. Like a pub. In the meantime, I have a whole host of little helpers here.' She pointed to an array of pots with various insects and larvae.

'Do you think you'll be able to help with time of death?'

'Well, temperatures are above the seasonal norm at the moment, so I think things have accelerated a little from what you would expect to get in autumn. I'll know more when I get all my samples back to the lab and I can look at the weather data.'

'But if you were to hazard a guess now?'

'Bernie, you know better than to ask me that.' Phyl Bridger waved a finger in mock anger. 'However, based on the warmer weather and the fact she wasn't buried, I would say around five or six days, but don't quote me on that just yet.'

'That fits in with what Nick White thought too. So maybe last Friday.'

Anderson coughed behind her.

'Oh sorry, I forgot to introduce Detective Sergeant Anderson. This is Dr Phyl Bridger, our entomologist.'

They nodded at each other.

'Where's Nick White?' asked Bernie.

'He's gone for a break,' said Phyl. 'He'll come back when I'm finished. It won't be long before we move her.'

'A break sounds good, ma'am.'

Bernie turned to Anderson. His olive skin had paled. Photos were one thing; actually seeing – and smelling – the body was another. 'Shall we go and join the search then?'

Anderson gave a slight nod of the head. Bernie was relieved she had coped well. The last thing she wanted to show was weakness in front of him. Her immunity to horror was obviously improving.

Anderson stayed silent until they reached the inner cordon. Then he pulled down the hood of the white suit and breathed out noisily.

'Oh God, that was horrible,' he said.

'I know. It's the third time I've seen her. I suppose I'm getting more used to it.'

'But we shouldn't get more used to it. That's the whole bloody point. If we lose our sense of shock at such a horrific crime, then we won't feel the need to find the bastard who did it.'

'I didn't mean it like that.'

'I know you didn't. I'm sorry. I'm just angry that someone has done this to her and left her to rot like rubbish.'

A train trundled past a few hundred metres away from them. Bernie caught glimpses of it through the trees and bushes.

'So close to the line and no one saw her,' said Anderson.

'She was covered in leaves. And besides, most people these days are glued to their phones. Or maybe reading a paper or a book. And if this happened at night…'

'Then no one would have seen,' finished Anderson. 'And if the Moffatts didn't hear anything then it's unlikely she came in this way. There has to be another path into this wood. Right, let's go.'

'Go where?'

'To find the other side of the wood, of course.'

Bernie stared at him. The colour had returned to his face along with a look of determination.

'You're wasted in Family Liaison,' she said.

Anderson shook his head. 'Tell me something I don't already bloody know.'

Their white suits were catching on brambles and their shoe covers were in danger of falling apart. After wading through the undergrowth for about ten minutes, they finally came into a clearing. There was a more discernible path now that would lead them through more trees.

'You OK?' asked Anderson.

'Yes, although these booties have seen better days. Should have brought another pair with me.'

'It looks as though there may be a bigger path at the end of this one. Are you happy to keep going?'

Bernie couldn't quite believe what Anderson had just asked. She wasn't going to let him out of her sight. He'd only go and solve the whole crime if she did.

'Of course I bloody am. The sooner we find another way in, the better.'

They tramped on through with Anderson leading. He held back bushes that were straying onto the narrow track so they wouldn't ping back at her.

The trees were closing in above her. Although some leaves had fallen, there were still enough to blot out the autumn sun. The temperature had dropped in the shade and Bernie found herself shivering. Keeping her jacket on had been the right decision after all. The air was rich with mulch which tickled her nose and she stuck her tongue to the roof of her mouth to stop a sneeze.

After a few more minutes, they came to a metal farm gate and, beyond it, a bigger path. Bernie and Anderson climbed over and looked left and right.

'I'm guessing the right takes us along fields,' said Anderson, 'but the left should take us to the railway line. Is there an unsupervised crossing like the one near Otterfield?'

'I don't know,' said Bernie. 'Only one way to find out.'

They turned left and walked for a few more minutes to the end of the small wooded area.

'Well, look at that,' said Anderson.

There before them was a bridge over the railway and a narrow roadway on the other side.

'I suppose you might get a car driving along on the road, maybe even a tractor,' said Bernie. 'But not once you cross the bridge. It becomes too narrow.'

'For a car, yes,' said Anderson, 'but not a bicycle or motorbike.'

CHAPTER 6

Bernie held her phone up in the air.

'No, I'm still only getting one bar of reception,' she said. 'Oh wait, it's gone up to two.'

'I've got three,' said Anderson.

Typical.

'Here we go, I've got Maps up. Right, if I press this it should show where we are now… yes, and if I zoom down it'll show us the view from the ground. Yep, that matches.'

Bernie leaned across to look at the picture of the small railway bridge on the phone depicting what she could see in front of her.

'So, where does this road go then?' she asked.

'Well, if we zoom back out… it's quite long and it goes up to this main road here. Didn't we drive this way? There was a farm on the left and this track was on the right. It must be used by the farmer to get to his land. Do you know who it belongs to? Didn't you say that Ron Willis's land is north of the railway line?'

'Whoa, slow down. We don't know for sure she was brought in this way.'

'Let's check it out then.' Anderson started to walk away.

Bernie reached out and grabbed his arm. Even through the forensic suit and his clothes she could feel his muscles. She had a sudden recollection of his arms around her, pulling her in to him.

He snapped his head back towards her and glanced down at her hand. She let go.

'There are protocols to follow, DS Anderson, and DCI Worth will have your hide if we don't follow them. We need to seal off the road properly and search it. And yes, the land on the other side is Greenacres, Ron Willis's farm.'

'So what are we waiting for? We need to go and talk to him and his family.'

'Dressed in our best forensic suits?' Bernie raised her eyebrows. 'Besides, it'll be best if you leave the questions to me. I know Ron a little bit.'

'Then surely that's a conflict of interest.'

'It's a rural community. You can't help but know people. Besides, I only know him to say hi at the pub.'

'The pub in Marchant you sometimes go to for Sunday lunch?' *How's he remembered that?*

'Although I guess you go there more regularly now you live in your little cottage in Marchant with your new boyfriend,' said Anderson.

Bernie felt clammy in the forensic suit. 'How do you know that? Who told you?' She might not have had much contact with Anderson for the last few months but clearly someone had been talking about her behind her back.

'Matty boy, of course. You may have stopped talking to me but he hasn't. We've caught up quite a few times. I know better than to ask Kerry. That one permanently has your back. Anyway, shall we go? And maybe I should ask those questions, don't you think?'

Bernie stripped off the forensic suit and stuffed it into a refuse bag. Anderson had already gone back to the car to make arrangements for having the track sealed off and searched. Bernie needed to hear a friendly voice before she could face him again. She pulled out her phone – the reception had improved.

'MCIT, DS Allen speaking.'

'Kerry.'

'Bernie. How's it going?'

'Bloody awful. Anderson is trying to take over again and he knows what I've been up to these last few months. He even knows about Alex. He says Matt told him.'

'Oh. He might have done. He did say he'd seen Anderson a few times for a drink or a curry. Don't be cross with him. He wouldn't have known not to say anything.'

Bernie kicked at a leaf and sighed. 'I know it's not Matt's fault. Anderson's just being bloody antagonistic about it.'

'Then maybe you should just tell Anderson the truth. Tell him about talking to his ex-wife.'

'And let on I know he's a manipulative, controlling bastard who gave his wife hell? I don't think so.' Bernie put her hand to her head. It was starting to throb. She needed to eat something. 'Have you got anywhere?'

'I've got it down to three possible women now but I need the photos of the jewellery. But as DCI Worth said earlier, maybe she hasn't been reported as missing yet.'

'True. Sorry for ranting. I feel a bit better now.'

'No problem. Get something to eat and you'll feel even better. I'll see you later.'

'How do you know I need to eat?'

'Because you're always ratty when you're hungry.'

Bernie laughed. 'Bye, Kerry.'

Bernie headed back to her car, trying to work out the nearest place to get some food. Was there a garage nearby she could grab a sandwich and some chocolate? She guessed Anderson would need something as well.

'Bernie.'

She turned to see Phyl Bridger a few paces behind her, carrying a case.

'Hi, Phyl. Have you finished?'

'With the scene, yes. I've got enough samples. I can tell you a bit more over the next few days. They're about to move her to the morgue. They've got everything ready.' Phyl Bridger shook her head. 'Such a grim business.'

'Definitely.' Bernie's stomach rumbled.

Phyl laughed. 'I take it you're hungry? I've some snacks in the car if you'd like some.'

'Oh yes, please.'

Phyl's car was close to Bernie's. Anderson was sitting in the passenger seat, talking on his phone.

'Would DS Anderson like something too?'

Bernie looked across at him. She was tempted to say no. 'I'm sure he would. Mealtimes tend to go out of the window on cases like these.'

Phyl opened her boot and pulled out a plastic bag. 'Not the healthiest options, I'm afraid, but it's important to have some emergency supplies. You should probably have a bag in your car.'

Bernie smiled. 'But that would mean going food shopping.'

'Don't you eat?'

Bernie laughed. 'Of course I do. But I have a man who sorts that all out for me. Cooks too.' She pictured all the washing up he'd left for her the previous night. She wasn't sure how Alex had managed to use so many pans.

'Oh, how lovely. Fortunately I have rooms at uni so I have lots of people cooking for me. Although one individual man would be quite nice.'

'You don't have your own place then?'

'No, being a residential tutor gives me somewhere to live and then I can spend my money on exotic trips looking at exotic insects.'

Bernie wanted to ask her more but just then Anderson hooted the car horn.

'Well, someone's definitely tetchy. You better choose quickly,' said Phyl.

Bernie grabbed a couple of packets of crisps and some cereal bars.

'Take the water bottles as well.'

Bernie looked up. 'Are you sure? They're your last two.'

'I've got one in the front. Go on, take them. You can make it up to me one day. Maybe your man can cook us all a meal. Or we can finally meet in a pub.'

Bernie picked up the two bottles. 'Thanks, you're a star, Phyl.'

'No problem. It's important you keep your strength up. How else are you going to cope with the "manipulating, controlling bastard"?' said Phyl, with a wink.

CHAPTER 7

Bernie parked her car as close to the farmhouse as possible. Her nose wrinkled at the smell of manure. But it was preferable to the smell of the crime scene they'd just left.

'So what do I need to know about this family?' asked Anderson.

Bernie sighed. 'Ron is married to Janet. They have three grown-up sons. The farm has been in his family for ages. His father, Stan, is still alive and lives with them. Ron has expanded Greenacres by buying more fields from neighbouring farms.'

'Do you think he wants the Moffatts' land as well?'

'Not that I've heard. And even if he did, I don't think he'd go to such lengths as killing a woman and dumping her on their land.'

'I don't know, stranger things have happened.'

Bernie noticed a curtain twitch downstairs. 'We've been spotted. We'd better go and knock on the door.'

After locking the car, Bernie headed towards the house but she noticed Anderson wasn't following.

'DS Anderson?'

She saw him walking away from the house towards an open barn. *We're here to ask questions, not do a search, you bloody stupid man.*

'Anderson.'

She saw him raise his index finger – one minute, he was telling her. She heard the front door open behind her.

'Bernie?' said a woman's voice.

She turned to see Janet Willis looking confused.

'What's he up to? Is this a social call?' Janet asked, pushing her grey hair away from her face.

Bernie glanced again at Anderson.

'No, not exactly.' Bernie avoided answering the first question.

Janet put her hand to her mouth. 'Oh. Is it Ron or one of the boys? Has something happened?'

'No, it's nothing to do with them. There's been an incident, though, and we just need to speak to some local people in case anyone saw or heard anything. Can we come in?'

Bernie saw Janet's eyes drift to Anderson, who appeared to be examining something.

'I'll just get him.' She walked nearer towards him. 'Detective Sergeant Anderson, the family are free to see us now.'

Anderson dropped the tarpaulin he'd lifted up. He muttered 'motorbike' as he walked past her. She saw him put out his hand for Janet and she knew he would be giving her his winning smile.

'Mrs Willis? I'm Detective Sergeant Anderson. Sorry to intrude but we're hoping either you or someone else in your family might be able to help us with our enquiries.'

The smile had obviously worked as Janet Willis took Anderson's hand and visibly relaxed. *Damn his charm.*

Janet led them into a small front room stuffed with two large sofas and an armchair by an unlit fireplace. The sofas looked new but the armchair was old and shabby and some stuffing was coming out of a split in one of the arms. In the chair sat an old man, his hair a wispy white. His head rested against the back of the chair. One eye was completely clouded over and the other seemed to be following suit. A border collie was sleeping by his feet.

'Bernie.' His voice was raspy and he held out a hand in her vague direction.

She grasped it with both of hers. 'Stan. It's lovely to see you.'

'Wish I could say the same. They've put the cataract op off again.'

'Oh, how annoying.'

He shrugged his shoulders. 'Yes, but what can you do? Just as well I've still got my hearing. Who's the Scottish bloke you've brought with you then?'

Bernie let go of Stan's hand. 'This is Detective Sergeant Anderson.'

Anderson stepped forward to shake Stan's hand in turn. 'Pleasure to meet you, sir.'

Stan laughed. '*Sir*, indeed. Take a seat. Janet, get some tea in, love.'

Janet rolled her eyes. It was clear, even into his late eighties, that Stan was still in charge.

'Janet, you don't have to on our account,' said Bernie.

'Actually, ma'am, I wouldn't mind a cuppa,' said Anderson. 'I've not had one all day.'

'And some biscuits too,' said Stan, 'or cake, if there's any left.'

Bernie mouthed 'sorry' to Janet.

Anderson started to talk to Stan about the farm and Bernie looked round at the photos on the walls. There were pictures everywhere of the family – Ron and Janet's wedding and some with the boys when they were younger. In pride of place over the mantelpiece was a large photo of the whole family – the two older sons, Gareth and Will, were married with children. Ryan was the youngest son at nineteen. Bernie thought of her own little family – just her mother and grandmother now. Although Granny was as distant as ever – emotionally as well as physically. Her grandfather, Pops, had died earlier in the year and Bernie still missed him. Finding her real father had helped to alleviate the pain a little and they were beginning to build a relationship, with Gary helping to paint her cottage. Her mother, Denise, had helped too with the decoration and Bernie sensed a burgeoning relationship between her parents. But Pops had raised her. She understood how much affection the Willis family had for Stan.

Janet came in carrying a tray, laden down with teapot, mugs, plates and a large cake tin. The dog stirred and lifted its nose.

'Oh aye, someone can smell cake,' Janet said. 'Hope you like coffee and walnut. It was made yesterday and there's actually some left for a change. But don't give any to Hollie, no matter how much she begs. It's not good for her.'

As Janet poured the tea, Anderson glanced at Bernie. She gave him a nod.

'Thank you so much for this, Mrs Willis. We've had a very busy day so far,' said Anderson. 'I'm afraid we can't tell you much but there's been an incident which I guess will be on the news later. We've noticed there's a small road opposite the farm here. Does anyone else use that road, apart from yourselves?'

Stan noisily slurped his tea. 'Sorry, teeth are a bit loose.'

Bernie averted her eyes as he pushed his dentures back up.

'So, I'm guessing someone has been up to mischief in the woods,' said Stan. 'I'm not surprised. People have been getting up to all sorts in there for decades, including me.'

Janet shook her head at Stan.

'Dad, I think it may be a bit more serious than people having… hanky-panky in the woods.'

Stan roared with laughter. 'And they say old people are prudes. Well of course, there are drugs too. I once caught Ron, high as a kite, down there. Mind you, that was a long time ago.'

'So,' said Anderson, 'does that mean others do use the road?'

Janet handed a plate with a large slice of cake to Bernie and gave her a fork as well. 'Sometimes. Traffic wise, it's mainly us with the tractor because it's our fields as far as the railway line. Occasionally people drive down it by mistake thinking it's a short cut and then get stuck by the railway bridge. We tend to get more walkers and cyclists who want to use the footpath through the woods. Horse riders too.'

'But that would be during the day?'

'Yes. People don't really go down there at night.'

'What about motorbikes?' Anderson continued.

Janet shrugged her shoulders. 'I guess someone might. To be honest, I don't really pay much attention to the traffic noise, especially at night. I'm a sound sleeper.'

'I noticed there's a motorbike outside. Who does that belong to?' asked Anderson.

So that's what you were doing, thought Bernie.

'It's Ryan's. He's my youngest, only one still left at home.'

'So you haven't heard any other bikes, especially at night, going down the lane?'

Janet shook her head. 'Can't say I have but they all sound the same to me.'

'Pah!' said Stan. 'They don't all sound the same. Ryan's purrs like a cat when he first starts her up. This is his new one. The one before sounded like a tractor. He started off on a moped which was basically a sewing machine on wheels.'

Anderson laughed. 'You obviously know a lot about motorbikes, Mr Willis.'

'Yes, he does,' said Janet. 'And you can guess who encouraged Ryan to get one against my wishes.'

Bernie tapped Anderson on the arm. She didn't want a family row started. He nodded. 'OK. This is a completely different question but have you been in for the last week, in the evenings?'

'Mostly,' said Janet. 'Although we often go to the pub in Marchant. In fact, we're going tonight. There's a pub quiz on Thursday evenings and Ron and I like to go.'

'What about last Friday and the weekend?'

Janet rubbed her head. 'We were out then as well. Went to the pub again on Friday and then to friends on Saturday night to celebrate their ruby wedding anniversary and then over to our eldest on Sunday for tea. It was a busy weekend, which is unusual for us.'

'What about you, Mr Willis?'

'Well, I get left alone here to fester, most of the time.' The dog staggered up and put her head on Stan's knee. 'Hollie keeps me company.' He stroked her.

'Dad. That's not true. You came with us on Sunday and you didn't want to go to the pub last Thursday and Friday.'

Bernie felt her phone buzz in her pocket. She took it out and found a text from DCI Worth. *Where are you? PM set for 1600 hours. I expect you to be there. Bring DS Anderson with you.*

Bernie smiled at Janet.

'Thank you so much for your time,' said Bernie. 'We need to get going, I'm afraid. But you've been very helpful. If you remember anything then just give us a call.'

Anderson eyed up the piece of uneaten cake on his plate.

'I'm sure you'll be allowed to take that with you,' Bernie said.

'Oh, of course. I'll wrap it up for you, Detective Sergeant.' Janet whisked the plate away before Anderson could object. He downed his tea before that disappeared too.

'Do you mind if I use your toilet, please?' he asked.

'Not at all. There's one downstairs. I'll show you.'

Bernie picked up her mug to finish her tea.

'Psst, Bernie!'

She looked up to see Stan beckoning her over.

'What, Stan?'

'Come closer, I've got something to tell you. I couldn't say with Janet in here.'

Bernie crouched next to the old man.

'Janet and Ron go to the pub pretty much every Thursday and Friday. Ryan's been having drag races down the lane while they're out. People bet on them. I normally go to the pub too on a Friday but Ryan asked me to stay home last week, just in case he needed me.'

'Why would he need you?'

Stan shook his head. 'I don't know for certain. But I think he was scared.'

'I could come back or if he wants to come into the station…'

'No, no. It'll need to be off the record somehow.'

'What do you suggest then, Stan?'

'Well, if you're caught meeting secretly, that would look suspicious. In plain sight might be better. Any good at pub quizzes?'

CHAPTER 8

Bernie pulled up outside the morgue. She sighed deeply.

'If it's any consolation, I don't like these things either,' said Anderson.

Bernie gave him a weak smile. 'No, they're not much fun. Of course, it will all depend on whether Nick White behaves like a prick or not.'

'Bernie…'

'We should go in, DS Anderson. We're late.'

The post-mortem was already under way. DCI Worth was in the viewing area. Bernie was surprised he wasn't closer to the action.

'Here you are, at last.'

'Sorry, sir. Got stuck in a bit of traffic on the way over,' said Bernie.

'Anything to report?'

'Yes, sir,' said Anderson. He filled Worth in on what they'd discovered that afternoon; in particular, the other way into the wood.

Bernie's throat itched as she remembered what Stan had said. Until she met Ryan, though, and spoke to him, she couldn't be sure the motorbikes were connected to the murder. She coughed.

'Yes, DI Noel? Do you have anything to add?'

'Oh, no, sir. Just the smell of this place. It tends to catch in my throat.'

The smell of antiseptic was strong, serving the dual purpose of cleanliness and covering the stench of death. Bernie gritted her teeth and looked at the view before her. The body on the steel table had been cleared of its extra inhabitants.

'Nice of you to join us,' said Nick White. 'Right, carrying on. I'm confirming my initial thoughts for cause of death. Under closer examination, it is clear that the hyoid bone is broken, so COD is asphyxiation due to strangulation of some kind. Initially I wasn't sure if this was manual or by ligature but there are faint marks spaced along the neck, indicating fingers. A ligature is more likely to cause a consistent line. I've yet to find any other wounds but I'll keep looking.'

'What about sexual assault?' asked DCI Worth.

Nick White glanced towards the viewing area. 'I'll take swabs, oral as well, but because of the state of the body, my preliminary examination is inconclusive. Even if we do find traces of semen, either on the body or her underwear, we can't be sure it was rape. It could be consensual; it might not even be the killer.'

'So, do we have anything?'

Nick nodded. 'Yes. Firstly, the dress. There's a label. It's from Primark so hopefully we can get a picture online.'

'Actually, that might be tricky. They don't have an online store in this country as such. They have a website showing their lines but they've probably already moved on to their autumn and winter collections. I could be wrong but we may have to go to them direct. I'm sure they'll oblige, though, given the circumstances,' said Bernie.

'Oh, well,' Nick White said, 'we still have fingernails. Lovely and long although a couple are broken. There may be trace evidence under them along with the soles of her feet. In fact...' White lifted up the bagged hands to look. 'There are quite a few deposits under the nails. Definitely soil but possibly a bit of material there too. If we're really lucky she might have the DNA of her killer if she scratched him.

'We have the jewellery too. In terms of identification, we can measure to get height; she obviously has brown hair. But until we have something we can match DNA with, or dental records, we have no idea who she is.' Nick White looked at Worth. 'I'm really hoping it won't get to this point but we may have to consider a forensic artist. Don't you know someone, DI Noel?'

'Yes, or rather Matt does. I'll give him a call now. I'll do it outside, reception is a bit better out there.' She glanced at Worth. It was obvious he wasn't happy about paying for a forensic artist.

Bernie made her way to her car as quickly as possible. She was relieved to smell fresh air again, albeit tinged with car fumes. She leaned against her car and called Matt Taylor.

'Ma'am?'

'How's it going, Matt?'

'Oh God. I hate going through CCTV. Nothing as yet. Until we have a few more specific details on our victim, it's hard to pinpoint anyone in particular.'

'It looks as though the red dress is from Primark so if you can get Alice on to that, please. By the way, have you spotted any motorbikes?'

'Motorbikes?'

'Yes. Maybe circling the area. Picking anyone up. That sort of thing.'

'I don't think so. But I'll check with Mick.'

'Good. I was actually ringing to ask you to email the details for your forensic artist friend to Dr White. Hopefully we won't need them but good to have them as back-up.'

'Sure. I'll email now.'

'Thanks. I'm not sure how late we'll need to work tonight. It'll depend on DCI Worth. But if we're out by eight this evening, do you fancy going to a pub quiz at my local?'

'A quiz? Tonight? Why?'

'Because you're the only one on the team who's been to uni so I'm hoping to put your brain to good use. Plus you love a good quiz. Tell Kerry as well.'

'No, I meant why do you want to do a pub quiz this evening?'

Bernie paused. 'Because it's been a totally shit day and it's not going to get much better in the next few days. I thought we could all do with a break. A pub quiz would be fun.'

'A quiz?' said a Scottish voice behind her.

Bernie spun round to see Anderson.

He smiled. 'I'm definitely up for that.'

CHAPTER 9

'You want to do what?' asked DCI Worth.

Bernie resisted the urge to look down at her feet and forced herself to keep eye contact with her senior officer as he sat behind the desk. He had commandeered DCS Wilson's office.

'I want to take the team to the pub. It's been a hell of a day. And it would be good for the new officers too; get to know them better.'

DCI Worth shook his head. 'We have just begun a murder investigation. It may be good for team morale but it won't look good to the public. I'm planning on recording a short piece for the news. Jane's sorting it out as we speak.'

Bernie bit the corner of her lip. She knew she would have to come clean. 'OK, sir, I'm going to level with you. I need to meet a possible new informant at my local pub tonight. It's quiz night. If it looks as though we've turned up to join in, then I have a reason to be there. And if there are any problems, I have back-up.'

Worth tapped a pen against his lips.

'What kind of information are we talking about?'

'Illegal motorbike racing and gambling. It's possible they were racing the night of the murder. They may have seen something.'

'They were nearby?'

'Yes. On the road that leads to the woods.'

'Then you must be careful. Nick White has come back to me. The material he spotted under the victim's fingernails looks as though it may be leather. Your informant may have been involved.'

Bernie thought back to what Stan had said about his grandson, Ryan, that he was scared.

'I don't think he's involved but I'm guessing he may have seen something. He's worried. Hence this has to be off the record.'

Worth grimaced. 'That's not my preferred method but we need all the help we can get at the moment. I can't make it appear that I've sanctioned you going to the pub though. I'll let you all go at seven thirty. There isn't much more we can do at the moment anyway. What you do after that and who you ask to go with you is your decision. But I want you to report back to me. Is that clear?'

Bernie smiled. 'Of course, sir.'

The Marchant Arms was bustling. Bernie had been before on quiz nights and she knew almost the whole village turned out for it, as well as others from further afield. She hadn't had to worry about taking the two new officers with her – DC Alice Hart and DC Mick Parris. As soon as they were told they could go, they were out of the door.

'They've both got kids,' explained Kerry. 'In fact, Alice has only been back from maternity leave for a couple of months. She was rather desperate to get home.'

Bernie had hoped Anderson would change his mind about coming but he was now at the bar with Matt, getting the drinks in and ordering chips.

'So how was your day with Mr Grumpy Pants? Did it improve after I spoke to you?' asked Kerry.

Bernie tapped her fingers on the table. 'No, not really. He insisted on talking to the Willis family. Said it would be a conflict of interest if I did.'

'To be fair, he's probably right about that. Is Alex coming tonight?'

Bernie's tapping got faster. 'No. I think I managed to put him off. Told him not to worry about coming over.'

'Is he ever going to move in properly with you? He's got a fair amount of stuff at yours.'

Bernie shook her head. 'I know. The place is getting a bit messy. I don't remember asking him either. It's just kind of happened. Not sure I'm ready for him to be there all the time though. Don't think his mother is either. She really doesn't like me. Besides, I have another reason for him not coming over tonight. I have to keep him and Anderson apart.'

'Oh dear, Bernie, does this mean that you've not had the past lovers talk?'

Bernie suddenly stopped tapping and started clenching and releasing her fist. 'Yes and no.'

'And what exactly does that mean?'

'It means he's told me about his two previous girlfriends and I've been very selective about my past. And Anderson wasn't a lover, after all. He wasn't anything really.'

'But he would have been if his ex-wife hadn't rung you.' Kerry smirked.

'Thank God she did.'

'Bernie, has it ever occurred to you—'

'Here you go, ladies. One orange juice for Kerry, who's driving, and one large red wine for you, ma'am, who only has to stagger across the road.' Matt smiled.

'Thanks, Matt,' said Bernie. 'And how many times do I have to tell you, call me Bernie when we're off duty.'

'Sorry, ma'am… I mean, Bernie.'

Anderson brought two more drinks over. 'I've registered the team. We're "The Boys in Blue".'

Kerry glared at him.

'What? They all know who we are.'

'It's not that. Half the team is female. Honestly.' Kerry rolled her eyes.

Anderson gave a smug grin. 'I can change it to "Lads and Lasses in Blue" if you like.'

'No,' said Bernie. 'Just leave it.'

She took a large mouthful of wine and started scanning the pub for the Willis family. She'd only seen Ryan a couple of times. He was a skinny lad with dark hair and acne scars, very different from his older and burlier brothers. She'd heard them teasing him about being the runt of the family. They had seemed good-natured but Ryan had not appeared impressed.

The pub was busy so it wasn't easy to see from where she was sitting but she didn't want to draw attention to herself by standing. A few people moved away from the bar and she saw Stan at a table on the other side of the pub. Janet was next to him. She looked around trying to find Ron and spotted him by the bar. Permanent red cheeks and a large nose that she knew was due more to rosacea than weather and drinking. He was a big man, like his two older sons. Bernie wondered if jokes were made about Ryan's paternity but then she remembered one of the photos she had seen earlier at the farm. Ron and Janet's wedding photograph with, she assumed, their siblings. A rake-thin man was standing next to Janet. Her brother perhaps. So maybe Ryan took after his uncle.

And now she saw him, a little further down the bar, leaning over, trying to chat up the young barmaid. She saw him tapping a packet of cigarettes on the bar. Good, she thought, he'll have a reason to go out.

Sue, the landlady, appeared with four large bowls of chips on a tray.

'Now, I didn't know what you wanted in terms of condiments, so I've brought salt, vinegar, ketchup, brown sauce and mayonnaise,' she said. 'Quiz is starting in five minutes.'

'Thanks, Sue,' said Bernie. 'You make the best chips.'

Anderson reached for the ramekin dish with the brown sauce. 'Glad she brought this. But who wants mayonnaise with their chips?'

'Actually, me,' said Bernie, as she stuck a chip into the creamy white sauce and blew on it before putting it in her mouth. It was crunchy on the outside but beautifully soft on the inside.

'And I thought I knew you,' said Anderson.

Bernie decided to ignore the look in his eyes.

She had eaten almost half her chips by the time the quiz started. The quiz master was Paul Bentley, the local vicar and a good friend of hers. He smiled broadly at her.

The first round was Sport and she left Anderson and Matt to argue over who was right while she kept an eye on Ryan. He was still sitting at the bar, cigarette packet in his hand. His left leg was twitching, as though he was getting ready to go.

'OK, everyone, that's the end of Sport. Swap your sheets with the team to your left and I'll give you the answers.'

The noise level in the room increased as papers were passed around. Ryan got up and left. He was heading for the beer garden. Bernie counted to thirty in her head and then picked up her bag.

'I'm just popping to the loo,' she said quietly to Kerry. She'd already told her DS the real reason for attending the pub quiz.

'Don't be too long. Music is up next and you're good at that.'

Bernie nodded. 'If I'm not back in ten, you might want to check I'm OK.'

She walked across to the toilets and feigned going in. The answers were being read out and everyone's attention was elsewhere. Bernie took a quick glance back at the crowded pub and then slipped through the door marked Beer Garden.

CHAPTER 10

The glowing tip of his cigarette was the only clue to his whereabouts in the dark. The sounds from the pub were muffled. Bernie shivered. She'd left her jacket inside. It would have looked odd if she'd taken it with her.

'Ryan?'

'Yeah. Bernie, right? That's what Granddad said to me.'

'Yes.' She drew closer until she could see him sitting on a bench. She sat down next to him.

'Stan said you might want to talk to me.'

A trail of smoke drifted out of Ryan's mouth.

'Maybe.' He put the cigarette back in his mouth and inhaled. Bernie glanced down. A couple of stubs lay on the ground. *Has he smoked those already?*

She sat quietly, just waiting. It was a technique she used in interviews sometimes. It soon paid off.

'I like to ride bikes – motorbikes, I mean. Normally, on Thursday and Friday nights, I organise races up and down our private road. It's quite narrow and full of potholes so it makes for an exciting race, especially in the dark.'

'But you haven't organised one for tonight?'

'No. I'm worried *he's* going to turn up.'

'Who?'

'I don't know. I don't know his name, he never said. And no, I didn't get the registration either. The plate was filthy. But he was riding a BMW, a beast of a bike. Wish I could afford something like that.'

Bernie was aware of Ryan turning towards her; could hear the excitement in his voice.

'You know, it's the kind of bike you feel pulsing in your chest as you ride it. It's so powerful. The rest of us didn't stand a chance really. Cleaned us out Thursday and Friday night.'

'So he had a great bike and won all the money. How does that make him scary?'

'Because of *her*.'

'Her?'

'The girl he had with him. He offered her as winnings. And I don't mean a quick snog. What kind of bastard boyfriend does that?'

An idea formed in Bernie's brain.

'What did she look like?'

'I don't know. She kept her helmet on all the time with the visor down. He even turned that into a game! Said we wouldn't know if she was a minger or not but his taste in bikes should tell us about his taste in women.'

'Can you tell me anything about her? What was she wearing?'

'I'm not sure of the colour because it was dark and she stayed away from the bike lights but she was definitely wearing a dress and heels. I remember thinking it was a bloody stupid outfit to wear. She had a leather jacket but looked cold. She was shivering a bit but now I'm thinking maybe she was shaking. Cos she knew what he expected her to do. She was scared.'

Bernie's heart was racing. 'What night did this happen? And did someone win her?'

'It was Friday night and I don't know. I left. Made me feel sick. I know most of the others did too. But at least one person must have stayed because I heard another race. They didn't come back though. Normally we go to the railway bridge, turn round and return. They must have carried on through the woods and fields.'

'None of the others have said anything to you about it?'

'No. I don't know who raced him.'

'What about the man?'

'Dressed completely in black. Plain black helmet with visor. Again, like her, he didn't take it off.'

'What was his voice like? Accent?'

'Deep. Friendly at first but more menacing on Friday night. Not local but I couldn't tell where he was from. The helmet muffled his voice.'

'Did she speak?'

'No, nothing.'

'Was she there both nights?'

'No, just Friday.'

Bernie put her hands over her mouth. Her heart was leaping around now. She couldn't help but imagine what this young woman had gone through. And was it the same young woman in the woods? It seemed too much of a coincidence for it not to be her.

'There was something he said that was, well… really bad.'

'Go on.'

'He was really disappointed that most of us didn't want to do the final race. Said it was a shame as he'd hoped to make it a regular occurrence.'

'Were those his exact words?'

'Yeah. He was quite well spoken. I feel really bad now. I should have come to you sooner. I saw it on the news on the TV here. A body in the woods. You think it's her.'

'I can't comment on that. He didn't say her name at all?'

'No. He just called her "babe".'

*

Bernie went back in first. Ryan said he would follow in a few minutes. The warmth of the pub suffused her the moment she opened the door and she walked quickly to the toilets to make it look as though she had come from there. Paul was reading out a music question.

'And the last one for this round is a very appropriate one really – what is dairy farmer Michael Eavis famous for?'

Starting Glastonbury, duh. Too easy, Paul. She was almost back to their table when she froze. Sitting opposite Anderson was Alex. Anderson's olive skin and darker, almost black, intense eyes were in contrast to Alex's boyish good looks. Bernie had a feeling Alex wouldn't look like a man until he hit his forties.

Alex turned and saw her.

'Bernie.' He stood and hugged her, his lips brushing her cheek.

Anderson stared at them, not bothering to disguise his annoyance.

'I thought you weren't going to come over,' she said.

'Well, I wasn't but when I saw the news about that woman, I guessed you'd had a rotten day and I didn't want you to be on your own. You didn't say you'd be here.' He stroked her cheek.

'You actually watched the news?'

'Well, Mum had it on. It was that DCI Worth you've mentioned before. What is it you call him, DCI *Worthless*? Anyway, I've just got here. I'm going to get a drink, do you want another?'

Bernie glanced at her half glass of wine. 'No, it's fine. I don't want to have too much tonight.'

'OK. I'll be back in a minute.' Alex turned back to the table. 'Anyone else want another?'

'Yes,' said Matt. 'I'll come with you.'

'I'm all right,' said Kerry, 'but I do need the loo. You'll have to do the marking, Anderson.' She shoved a sheet of paper in his face.

Bernie sat down in her newly vacated seat.

'So,' he said, 'that's Alex.' He grabbed a pen and started marking the quiz as Paul called out the answers, pushing down hard onto the paper.

'Yes.'

'Because, I was expecting someone a little more… impressive. I mean, how old is he? Twelve? Is he even allowed in a pub? Where did you meet?'

Bernie closed her eyes. 'He's twenty-six. And if you really must know, he was the estate agent who sold me my cottage.'

Anderson shook his head. 'Hmm. He looks like an estate agent. So he's six years younger than you?'

'Yeah. Call me a cougar if you want.'

Anderson put the pen down. 'Does he know about me? I don't think he does because there didn't seem to be any recognition when we were introduced by Matt. Kerry, on the other hand, had a face like thunder. Maybe Alex and I should get to know each other.'

Bernie stood up and grabbed her bag and jacket.

'Don't be so stupid. There's nothing to tell. Alex?' He turned his head. 'Let's go. I'm not feeling so good.'

She stood up and looked down at the piece of paper in Anderson's hands. 'They've got that last question wrong. Michael Eavis is the founder of Glastonbury, not a member of The Wurzels. I'll see you in the morning.'

CHAPTER 11

Friday

DCI Worth looked gravely at his team. Weak sunshine trickled into the large briefing room via the gaps in the white plastic Venetian blinds.

'We're almost at the twenty-four-hour mark and we're no further forward than we were yesterday. I only agreed to letting you go home last night because we had so little to go on. So I hope you all had a good night's sleep because we will keep working now until we get some answers. I hope that's understood.'

Bernie stifled a yawn. She hadn't slept well. It hadn't just been the young woman on her mind. Anderson had been at the forefront. She had barely responded to Alex as he had tried to make love to her.

'Not tonight, love. It's been a shitty day,' she had said and then turned her back.

She had left the house before he'd even woken up this morning, in work at six o'clock to write up her notes from her conversation with Ryan.

'You may have seen on the news last night,' continued Worth, 'that I gave a statement. We've had some information that has come in since which may have a bearing on the case. DI Noel, if you'd like to tell us more.'

Bernie stood up to face the team in front of her. They all looked a little worn down even though the really hard work hadn't started yet.

'So,' she began, 'we've had an anonymous tip-off about motor-cyclists in the area last Thursday and Friday evenings. One of the motorcyclists had a young woman with him. The witness reported she was wearing a short dress and heels – colour unknown. She also had on a black leather jacket and black helmet but kept the visor down at all times. The witness didn't see the biker and the woman leave but thought they had gone in the direction of the woods, over the railway bridge and up the track.' Bernie paused. 'Thanks to DS Anderson, we closed that track yesterday for searching. We don't know for certain if our body is the same woman but we need to consider the possibility that she might be.'

'Or they're potential witnesses,' said Matt.

'Exactly. But there is one more thing that suggests this may be our woman. The motorcyclists were racing. The man with the woman offered her as winnings.'

'That's awful,' said Kerry.

'It is,' said DCI Worth, 'especially as the witness has said the man had hoped to make this a "regular occurrence" – his exact words. Did he mean with the same girl or does he have others at his disposal? So, DC Taylor and DC Parris – back to CCTV for you. Start looking for any cameras in that area – particularly any speed cameras or ANPR – and for any motorbikes. DI Noel has the make but unfortunately not the model or the registration number. Even so, just having an image to go on will help us out. I believe the woman was only with him on the Friday evening. Is that correct, DI Noel?'

'Yes, sir.'

'DC Hart. Dress and shoes. Where are you up to on that?' asked Worth.

Alice Hart's cheeks coloured. 'Erm, dress is from Primark. Not sure about the shoes. I'm visiting a store in Swindon this morning and just waiting for a photo from Forensics to take with me. I know it's a long shot but maybe someone will remember her.'

'Can't you take one of the photos from the scene? We have those already.'

Alice blushed more deeply. 'The dress is still on the body in the photos, sir. I can't really show that to members of the public.'

Bernie stole a glance at DCI Worth. She couldn't believe he had suggested such a thing.

'No, of course not.' Worth lowered his gaze slightly. 'Chase up Forensics ASAP. We need a decent image to release to the press. DS Allen – missing persons?'

'Narrowed it down to a few, sir, but to be honest, I'm not convinced it's any of them.'

'And your reasoning for that?'

'Small parameters being off. Since Dr White sent me the height and age approximations, no one has fitted exactly. Originally we thought she might be in the higher end of the fifteen to twenty-nine-year-old scale but according to Dr White, her pelvis suggests otherwise so it seems she was fifteen to nineteen. Some of the women are the right height but too old, or right age range but too tall. I think you were correct, sir, when you said yesterday that maybe she hasn't been reported yet.'

DCI Worth slowly nodded his head. 'All the more reason to get some information out to the public.'

'The jewellery is interesting, though, the rings in particular,' said Kerry.

'In what way?' asked Bernie.

'I haven't had the full report but the guy looking at them thinks they might be a wedding set and although it's not impossible she's married, she is very young. Once I have photos, I'm going to do a search, in case they're stolen.'

'That's good,' said Worth. 'Well, rather than wait, chase up what you need and get cracking. DI Noel, could you sort out the search team, please? DS Anderson can help you. I'll be in my office if anyone needs me.'

While the others started work, Bernie picked up the shift list to see who might be available to join the crime scene search. Anderson tapped her on the shoulder. His face was sullen and he looked as though he had had as much sleep as her.

'This "witness", did they use Crimestoppers?'

Bernie stepped away. 'I'm not at liberty to tell you that.'

'So, you didn't meet this person at the pub when you went to the toilet then? Because you were gone for a while. I'd hate to think you used us all last night when we could have been here working.' He lowered his voice. 'I think I need to go and have a chat with young Ryan Willis. He has a motorbike.'

She saw his dark eyes searching hers, trying to read her.

'No, we've dealt with the Willis family for now. The DCI said you were to help with the search. Maybe you should go and lead it. Get some fresh air. A break from the station might do you some good.'

'Fine.' Anderson strode off.

It'll do me some good too, thought Bernie.

CHAPTER 12

An aroma of coffee and sweat hung over the office. The sun was now blasting through the blinds and Bernie opened a couple of windows to get some fresh air. She was sleepy and it looked as though the others were feeling the same.

It was getting close to lunchtime and Bernie was getting fed up playing the waiting game with Forensics. She sauntered over to Matt and Mick who were glued to the computer monitors in front of them. She hadn't really had a chance to talk to Mick other than a cursory hello and welcome to the team. He was short and stocky with brown, curly hair. Bernie had winced at the creased tan leather jacket he had worn the day before. She liked her team to look smart and professional, not Starsky and Hutch. She guessed Matt must have said something because today Mick was in a suit, albeit a slightly shabby one. Mick looked like he was pushing forty and Bernie wondered why he was still a DC. But then she remembered he had kids; maybe he preferred to have less responsibility at work.

'So, Mick, anything?'

Mick blew noisily out of his mouth and shook his head. 'No. DS Anderson showed us the area on Google Earth and we traced where the bikes might have gone. But there are no cameras on those roads at all. They're all small.'

Matt paused the tape he was looking at. 'There's always the possibility the bikes were wheeled back down the track as well. But again, no cameras in that area.'

'Shit,' said Bernie.

'Ma'am?' said Mick.

'Yes?'

'If the woman was wearing a leather jacket and a helmet, where are they now?'

Bernie thought for a moment. 'Good question. If they belong to our mystery man then he may have taken them with him; not leave any incriminating evidence behind. Although I don't know how easy it would have been. We've certainly not recovered anything like that yet but it's something we need to look out for. I'll text Anderson and let him know. If there are no cameras in the immediate areas then fan out and look in town. Finding this guy is number one priority now.'

'That's what we're doing,' said Matt. He sighed. She knew he hated this kind of work but it was essential. He much preferred being out and talking to people. He was good with witnesses.

'You're both doing a great job. I'm going to pop out to the baker's to get some lunch. What do you want? My treat.'

'Cheese and pickle sarnie, please,' said Mick.

'Hot sausage roll,' said Matt.

Bernie laughed. 'I can't guarantee it will still be hot by the time I get back. I'll get cakes as well.'

She turned round to see Kerry tapping away at her computer. 'What do you want, Kerry?'

Kerry carried on typing, without looking up, clearly engrossed in whatever she was doing. 'Veggie cheese and tomato, please, in a roll. And definitely a cake too. Thanks, Bernie.'

'You got something interesting there, Kerry?'

Kerry glanced up. 'Possibly, but not completely sure yet. I should know more by the time you get back.'

*

Bernie had mistimed the lunch queue. A line of people snaked its way out of the shop and onto the pavement. Mainly office workers, and dressed in her normal black trouser suit and white shirt, Bernie blended in perfectly. She listened in to snippets of conversation from the women in front of her.

'Did you see that bit on the news last night?'

'What bit?'

'They've found' – the woman lowered her voice – 'a body, by the railway between Pewsey and Westbury.'

'Oooh, no, I didn't see that. Did they give any more detail?'

'No. Just said the body of a young woman. It's awful, isn't it?'

'God, yes. Just not safe round here any more.'

Bernie wanted to smile but managed to resist. This was the safest place she had ever lived in. She knew people were always more shocked in areas where crime wasn't as common. When she had worked in the Met, bodies were found pretty much every day – suicides, accidents and natural causes as well as murder. A face flashed before her. Eyes staring as life seeped away. A teenager's life ending before it had even really begun.

Bernie's hand instinctively moved to her left side and the scar that was beginning to itch. She felt a gentle nudge from behind.

'Could you move over please? There's a lady with a double buggy who wants to get past.'

Bernie snapped back to her surroundings.

'Oh, sorry.' She realised the queue had moved up into the shop. Her hands were clammy. She walked forward, wiping her hands on her trousers as she stood in the doorway. The owner spotted her and waved her in.

'Detective Inspector, nice to see you. I'll serve you next.' The woman looked flushed and little beads of sweat glistened on her forehead. She finished serving her customer and then called Bernie over.

Bernie pointed at the others in front of her. 'These people are ahead of me.'

'Oh, don't worry about that. None of you mind me serving the detective inspector first, *do you?*'

Bernie felt embarrassed as she stepped out of the line and went up to the counter. She heard a few mutterings but decided to ignore them. She gave her order.

As the woman made the sandwiches, she said, 'I suppose you're investigating that woman who was on the news last night.'

Bernie smiled as sweetly as she could. 'You know I can't tell you that.'

'Oh, I don't want any details, if that's what you think. I'm very squeamish. No, I just thought you might want us to do breakfast for you again.'

Bernie gave a genuine smile this time as she remembered all the goodies the bakery had sent during a missing child case earlier in the year.

'That's very kind of you but you don't need to. You were so generous back in May and we don't want you losing out on money.'

The woman packaged up the last sandwich. 'Well, if you change your mind, just let me know. Now, what cakes would you like?'

Bernie sat back in her swivel chair and sank her teeth into a chocolate éclair. It was delightfully squidgy and she remembered one of the nuns at school who had taught her cooking. 'Today, ladies, we're going to make eclairs. The Chambers Dictionary describes them as "long in shape but short in duration".' Bernie smiled at the memory of the very patient Irish nun who had made it her mission to get her making edible meals. 'Bernadette Noel,

I swear you will be skinny all your life if you don't learn how to cook. And you won't get a husband either.'

Thankfully, Alex was a good cook and Bernie had noticed her clothes were starting to get a bit snug. She finished the éclair, licked her fingers and downed the rest of her coffee. Matt and Mick were tucking into their lunch as they continued to watch CCTV footage. Kerry hadn't touched hers yet as she appeared to be having an in-depth conversation with someone on the phone.

'OK. Get back to me ASAP when you know more. Thanks,' said Kerry. She put the phone down.

Bernie wandered over to her. 'Sounded interesting.'

'It was. Can I?' Kerry pointed to the cheese and tomato roll in front of her.

'Sure, go ahead. You can tell me in a minute.'

'Thanks. We've run out of milk at home so only had a banana for breakfast.'

Bernie knew Kerry's partner, Debs, worked as a nurse, and their long shifts often left little time for grocery shopping.

'God, that's better. I was so hungry,' said Kerry once she'd had a few mouthfuls of her roll, wiping tomato juice from her chin. 'Right. I've been on the phone to the forensic lab. Do you want the good news?' She took a swig of water from an insulated bottle. 'Remember the rings? They've found two sets of DNA on them. One of them has a diamond and apparently diamonds are very good at harbouring skin cells. They're working on the sequencing now. But better than that, the ring with the diamond is engraved. "To H love R".'

Bernie felt a flutter in her chest. 'And?'

'And I'm about to put the details into the system and see if we get a hit. I think my hunch may be right. I think the rings are stolen.'

*

'Here we go,' said Kerry.

Bernie turned in her chair. 'You got something?'

Kerry looked up from her computer and smiled. 'A report filed three weeks ago of stolen rings from one Mrs Harriet Fox.'

Bernie got up and walked over to read the report on Kerry's computer. 'Hmm, interesting. She's in Salisbury.'

'It does look a likely match – "To H love R" engraved on the band of the diamond ring is written in the theft report. Do you want to go now?'

'Yes. Get the address and we'll go. I'll just tell DCI Worth what we're doing.' Bernie was halfway to the door when she stopped. 'Actually, Kerry, I'll get the address. You tell the DCI. This is your work, you should get the credit.'

'Thanks.'

Bernie went back to her seat as Kerry left. Mick Parris stared at her from his desk. 'You all right, Mick?'

'Yes. I'm just not used to seeing a DI pass the glory on. My normal one claims everything I find out.'

Bernie beamed at him. 'We work as a team here. Anything you find gets credited to you. If you spot anything while I'm out then text me but tell the boss as well. He'll only get all uppity if you don't.'

Bernie wrote down the address and telephone number for Harriet Fox before grabbing her bag. It wasn't long before Kerry was back. Her cheeks were pinched pink.

'What's up?' asked Bernie.

'Bloody *Worthless*! Apparently he thinks it would be better if *he* goes with you, rather than me.'

Bernie gave Kerry a sympathetic look. 'Oh, Kerry, I'm sorry.'

'Huh,' said Mick. 'You won't take the glory but it's OK for him to do it.'

Kerry shrugged. 'I'll get back to chasing up Forensics. If I'm really lucky, the report on the maggots will be ready.'

CHAPTER 13

Bernie watched the countryside whizz past. She'd offered to drive but Worth had a 'man' for that. She thought it was a complete waste of the young PC's time to be ferrying the DCI around. No one spoke. She thought about how different it would have been with Kerry – having a good natter and gossiping. She might even have told Kerry about Anderson and her differing emotions. A part of her still felt tempted by him but she knew she was better off with Alex. She remembered Kerry had started to say something to her about Anderson at the pub but had been interrupted by the drinks arriving. She would have to check back with her.

Worth cleared his throat. 'Now, Bernie.'

She turned her head away from the window. 'Yes, sir.'

'I'm sure you've realised we have to tread carefully with Mr and Mrs Fox. Currently, they think we've only come about the rings.'

'Won't they think it a bit odd that a detective chief inspector and a detective inspector have turned up to deal with a theft?'

'Possibly not, initially. Do you have the photographs?'

Bernie pulled out her phone and found the email Kerry had sent. She'd had the good sense to just send the photos taken at the lab of the rings. She wouldn't have blamed Kerry, though, if she had snuck in a scene photo of the rings on a lifeless hand. 'I have them, sir.'

'Good. And when the time is right, I want you to be the one to tell them the girl found wearing them is dead.'

Bernie looked at Worth in surprise. 'She may have nothing to do with the theft. They may have been given to her by the real thief.'

'I'm not so sure. The report said the bathroom window was left open. She was petite so maybe she did break in. Let's see what this couple can tell us first.'

Bernie sat in a very upright chintz armchair, the kind of chair that an embittered maiden great-aunt might have. She was tempted to pull out the cushion from behind her back as it was pushing her forward. Mr Fox was on a more modern sofa. Bernie was relieved he didn't actually resemble a fox. In his forties, with short, premature salt and pepper hair and a round face, there was a jolly feel to Rupert Fox, though right now he seemed strangely twitchy. Harriet Fox, sitting next to him, was more mouse-like, with light brown hair and beady eyes. Neither seemed terribly relaxed to have two police officers in their lounge, particularly as for them it was meant to be an update on stolen jewellery.

Bernie glanced at Worth who gave her a nod. She was to kick off the questioning, apparently.

'So, Mr and Mrs Fox, we gather you made a report about some stolen rings.'

Harriet Fox gave a nervous nod. 'Yes. They went missing about three weeks ago.'

'In the report, you mentioned you had left the bathroom window open.'

'Yes,' said Rupert Fox. 'We think that's how someone got in.'

Bernie thought his reply sounded a bit rehearsed. *Insurance fraud?*

'I see. At the time, the CSIs didn't find any physical evidence to link this crime with a particular person. We have now found some rings that may be yours.' Bernie pulled her phone out of her pocket and opened the photos from Kerry. 'If you could have a look at these, please, and tell me what you think.' She passed the phone over to Harriet.

Mrs Fox flicked through the photos. 'Yes, it looks like them. The solitaire diamond ring is my engagement ring from Rupert. It has an engraving inside, "To H love R". Since having the children it doesn't fit me so I keep it in a box along with my mother's wedding band. Both went missing.'

Harriet handed back the phone.

'It does sound like they could be your rings. If you have any photos of you wearing them then that would be useful but equally, we can do a DNA test to prove they're yours.'

'A DNA test? Really?' asked Rupert Fox. 'Why go to such trouble?'

Bernie inwardly cursed herself, and Worth too. She wasn't ready yet to tell them but it couldn't be avoided now. 'I'm so sorry to have to tell you this, but they were found on the body of a young woman discovered in woodland yesterday morning.'

Harriet's eyes widened. 'Oh God, no.' She looked at her husband and then back at Bernie. 'No. She can't be.'

Bernie noticed Rupert Fox squeeze his wife's knee but it was too late. Harriet Fox had already said too much. 'Who, Mrs Fox?'

Harriet covered her face with her hands. 'No, no, no.'

'Mr Fox? Do you know who this young woman might be?'

He nodded slowly, his eyes staring at the floor. 'It might be our former au pair – Rosa Conti, from Italy. She's nineteen and has long dark brown hair. Quite petite. In fact, she doesn't look her age, she looks younger. Which is unusual these days – girls normally look older, don't they? Lottie and Tamsin adored her but...'

'But what?' asked Bernie.

'Harriet let her go.'

Mrs Fox looked up at the sound of her name. 'I had to. I caught her… entertaining a man in her bedroom when she should have been looking after the girls. They were downstairs watching TV and she was upstairs…' Harriet shook her head. 'I sacked her on the spot. You can understand my reaction, can't you? She was very upset, begged me to let her stay and I almost gave in because she was so good with the girls, but at the time I was sure I was right.' Harriet Fox grabbed her husband's arm. He didn't express the same shock as his wife.

'Mr Fox, are you OK? You don't seem surprised.'

'I'm not. I heard DCI Worth on the news on the radio last night talking about the body and when you said your names, I knew it wasn't just about the rings. We suspected she might have taken them but didn't know for sure. That's why we didn't mention it in the report. Poor, poor girl.'

'We haven't actually identified her yet but from the description you gave, Mr Fox, and the fact she was wearing your rings, it seems quite likely.'

'I suppose you need one of us to identify her, don't you? I'm not sure I can but maybe Rupert?' Harriet turned to her husband, her eyes moist. 'What do you think, Rupe?'

Rupert nodded his head. 'If I have to.'

Bernie swallowed. There was no way anyone could facially identify the body.

'That won't be necessary, Mr Fox, but thank you for the offer. Our preferred method of identification, in this particular case, is DNA, or dental records if she had registered with a dentist here. Did Rosa leave anything behind at all? Any clothes, toothbrush or hairbrush?'

Harriet shook her head. 'No. She took those things. Any junk that was left I threw away. And she hadn't yet gone to the dentist.'

Bernie thought for a moment. 'But you haven't thrown out the mattress, have you? The one on her bed?' she asked.

'The mattress? No.'

'Good.' Bernie turned to Worth who had been strangely silent. Maybe her giving the bad news had been a test, a rite of passage he expected her to go through. 'Sir, I suggest we get Forensics down here ASAP and scan the mattress and the rest of the room.'

Worth nodded. 'I agree.'

'What? Why?' asked Harriet.

'Because there may be some bodily fluids still present on the mattress that will provide us with DNA,' Bernie said.

Harriet looked appalled. 'But this is silly. Rupert can identify her. There's no need to have a Forensics team in my house. What would the neighbours think?'

'Mrs Fox, I hate to say this to you,' said Bernie, 'but the young woman has been dead for a while and it's no longer possible to facially identify her. We have to use DNA. And taking any samples from the mattress is our best bet. Who knows? The man she was entertaining may be the killer and he may have left his DNA behind.'

Rupert Fox paled before her. In a small voice he said, 'I'll show you her room.'

Bernie stood on the landing and looked into the empty bedroom. It was large with a double bed. Painted white, there were little blue marks on the walls, indicating that posters had been put up at some point. Had Rosa done that? Tried to personalise her blank room, make it her own? Bernie had to stop Rupert Fox from going in.

'Best if you stay out of here until after Forensics have been, Mr Fox. We'll have to take DNA samples from you and your wife for elimination purposes and also to confirm your wife's rings. Did your two daughters go in here as well?'

He shook his head. A film of sweat glistened above his top lip. Bernie looked at him carefully, a suspicion growing in her mind.

'Mr Fox, as it's just you and me up here, is there anything you want to tell me?'

Rupert Fox wiped the sweat away with a trembling hand.

'Mr Fox?'

Rupert kept his eyes on the floor. 'Umm, my wife goes to yoga classes on Wednesday evenings and then she goes for a drink afterwards. She's out for a few hours.'

'I see. And your daughters?'

'They're in bed, their rooms are in the loft. They're six and four. Quite small still. We had them a little later in life.'

'OK. And Rosa?'

Rupert coughed. 'Rosa... and... I... well...'

'Mr Fox, are you trying to tell me that we're going to find your DNA on the mattress in Rosa's room?'

Rupert nodded, his eyes still glued to the floor. He whispered, 'Yes.'

Bernie inwardly sighed. 'Where were you last Thursday and Friday?'

Rupert finally raised his eyes. 'During the day I was at work. I'm a chartered surveyor. And in the evenings and overnight I was here, at home.'

'And can anyone corroborate that?'

'Yes, there are five colleagues I work with and Harriet was here.'

Bernie was buzzing with other questions she wanted to ask but thought it would be better to do so at the station.

'Once the Forensic teams arrive, I'd like you to come back to the station with me to answer some more questions and make a formal statement.'

More sweat was forming on Rupert Fox's face. 'Yes, OK.'

'I take it your wife doesn't know.'

He shook his head.

'My job is to find a killer, not play marriage guidance counsellor. However, I suggest that after you have made your statement, you have a conversation with your wife because I can't promise to keep this quiet. Is that clear?'

Rupert Fox sniffed and wiped away more sweat. He nodded.

Bernie turned away from the man who had slept with a woman young enough to be his daughter. Was it a mid-life crisis? In which case, was there a sports car in the garage? Or a motorbike?

CHAPTER 14

Bernie pressed the buttons on the recorder.

'This is Detective Inspector Bernadette Noel with Detective Sergeant Kerry Allen, interviewing Rupert Fox in connection with the murder of a young woman. Mr Fox is here as a witness currently and so does not have any representation. However, if at any point in the interview that situation changes, then Mr Fox is entitled to a legal representative. Is that clear, Mr Fox?'

Rupert Fox nodded, his arms crossed tight over his body.

'For the recording please?'

'Yes, I understand.'

Bernie smiled. 'Right, Mr Fox, I'd like to start with when Rosa Conti first arrived. When was that?'

'Hmm, she came at the beginning of the summer holidays, so around the end of July. Harriet, my wife, went back to work in the spring and she couldn't get time off for the whole summer so we decided to get an au pair. We went through an agency that a friend had used.'

'What's the name of that agency?'

'Wiltshire Au Pairs, I think. Harriet will know. She arranged it all.'

Kerry, sitting next to Bernie, jotted everything down in a large notebook.

Bernie leaned forward. 'So, initially, you were Rosa's employer. Did that relationship change?'

Fox looked up at the ceiling. 'Yes.' His voice cracked.

'What did it change to?'

'We became lovers.'

'When did this change happen?'

Fox covered his mouth with his hands. He was trembling.

'Mr Fox? When did you first have sex with Rosa?'

He mumbled something.

'For the purposes of the recording, we need to hear what you're saying. Can you please take your hands away from your mouth?' Bernie kept her voice as calm and as neutral as possible, even though she wanted to yell at this man she suspected had abused his position as an employer.

'Beginning of September. It was a Wednesday evening. Harriet had gone to yoga. The girls were in bed. I came upstairs just as Rosa came out from the bathroom after having a shower. She had a towel wrapped round her. I apologised for seeing her like that but she just smiled. She went to her room and… smiled again. She left the door slightly open. I should have just gone to my bedroom to get the book I was planning on reading but instead I went to her door and pushed it open. She was completely naked, the towel was on the floor. I'm very ashamed of what I did… of what we did.'

'Was that the only time?'

'No. It happened about three more times, always on a Wednesday evening. Sometimes we'd shower together and have sex in the bathroom or in her room. Never mine and Harriet's. Rosa, well, despite her age, she was very experienced. She did things that Harriet would never dream of doing.' He wiped his face with his hand and sniffed. 'I sound like a pervy old man, don't I? Mid-life crisis maybe. Should have bought a Porsche.'

Yes. Bernie waited. She knew Fox wanted to say more.

'Rosa suggested we film one of our sessions. I really wasn't happy about that but she said she would delete it after we watched it back. And I saw her delete it. But there must have been another camera because a few days later, I received an email with an attachment. It was a video of us but filmed from a different angle. And there was a demand for money. I was going to have it out with her but it was the same day Harriet found her with another man in her room. And Harriet sent her packing immediately. When Harriet couldn't find her rings, I guessed what had happened.'

'And that's why you didn't mention Rosa's name in the initial report and said the window was open.'

Fox nodded. 'I couldn't risk her sending the footage to Harriet. I thought it best to let her keep the rings as payment.'

'Did you see or hear from Rosa again?'

'No, nothing.'

'And where were you last Thursday and Friday?'

'At work during the day – Fox and Turner's Surveyors. And at home at night. Harriet was there. And the girls.'

'Do you still have the email containing the footage?'

'No. I deleted it. Twice.'

'What kind of email address do you have?'

'Google.'

'Did you delete it online as well?'

Fox stared at Bernie. 'No. I didn't think of that. I just got it off my laptop.'

'Then we're going to need your laptop and access to your email. It may be possible to retrieve it. We need to see if we can trace the address.'

He seemed to visibly shrink.

'What else are we going to find on your laptop, Mr Fox?'

His eyes were down again. 'It's all adult stuff but… Harriet wouldn't approve.'

'OK, Rupert. We're going to stop there for the moment. The time is seventeen twenty-five hours.' Bernie pressed stop on the recorder. 'If you can wait here for a few minutes, please. I'm going to send another officer in to stay with you. Would you like anything to drink?'

Fox shook his head.

'So what do you think?'

Bernie and Kerry were sitting at Bernie's desk, going over Kerry's interview notes.

'Gut reaction… he didn't do it,' said Kerry decisively. 'He would have taken the rings back. However, until we see the footage from the email and what else is on his laptop, we can't completely rule him out.'

Bernie nodded. 'I agree, he wouldn't have left the rings unless he was disturbed. That email is crucial and we'll have to see if Harriet can provide an alibi, work colleagues too. And we need to get in contact with the au pair agency to get next-of-kin details. I guess the family will be in Italy.'

'That'll be right up Anderson's street, being half-Italian,' said Kerry. 'I guess he can speak it fluently.'

'He'll probably ask to go over. Give the news in person,' said Bernie. 'To be fair, he may have to. If we can't get a good enough sample from Rosa's room, we're going to need DNA from her parents.' She shook her head. 'What a mess.'

'I hear you've brought someone in? Can I put this out to the press?'

Bernie turned round. Jane Clackett was standing in the doorway of the main room for MCIT.

'You'll need to check with DCI Worth about that. As you've said before, the press is "not my thing",' said Bernie.

'Ouch! Did I really say that about you?'

Bernie raised her eyebrows by way of an answer.

'I might have said it before we were friends,' Jane conceded. 'Where can I find the DCI?'

'He stayed at the house to oversee Forensics.'

'Really? That doesn't sound like him.'

A thought flashed through Bernie's mind. Jane was right. Worth never did anything himself if he could delegate it to a junior – he didn't even drive himself, for God's sake. Why *had* he been so keen to go to the house instead of Kerry?

'No, it doesn't, does it?' she said.

She picked up her phone to call Matt. She'd sent him to Salisbury to help.

'Hi, Matt. Are you at the house?'

'Yes. I've just arrived.'

'Can you tell DCI Worth to come back please? Tell him you've come to replace him and that we need Rupert Fox's laptop.'

'What? I can't tell a senior officer that.'

'Yes, you can. Tell him I sent you so that he can come back to headquarters. Decisions need to be made back here.' Bernie paused. 'And have a look to see which CSIs are at the house. If Lucy is there, discreetly ask her if Worth did any of the searching.'

She hung up before Matt could say anything else. 'Kerry, we're going back to Rupert Fox to ask a couple more questions, off the record. Jane, hold fire for the moment.'

Jane smoothed back her jet black bob and smiled. 'You're the boss. But be careful. You don't want to get done for witness intimidation.'

'I'll be careful,' said Bernie as she marched down the corridor back to the interview room. Anger bubbled up. She threw the door open, much to the surprise of Fox and the officer inside.

She looked at the PC. 'If you could leave us for a minute, please.'

Kerry scuttled in, trying to keep up with Bernie. She sat down opposite Fox but Bernie began to pace. She pointed to the recorder.

'I'm not going to put this on for a moment. I have a few more questions for you, off the record. Do you know DCI Worth? Have you ever met him before today?'

He shook his head but his eyes said something else.

'Do you belong to any clubs, Rupert?'

'Umm, well, I… go to the gym and I'm a member at the golf club.'

Rupert looked startled. Bernie wasn't sure if it was her sudden arrival or her questions. Still standing, she placed her hands on the table and leaned forward towards Fox.

'Mr Fox, do you understand how close we are to arresting you for the murder of Rosa Conti?'

Rupert swallowed and began to tremble again. Bernie thought he might be sick.

'You… you don't have any proof.'

'Maybe not yet. But we do have one hell of a motive. You'd better hope to God that Forensics don't find your DNA on her body.' Bernie pushed herself back up from the table. 'Finish your tea, Mr Fox. We'll be back later after we've had a look at your laptop. It'll be in your interest to give us full access to it. Perhaps you could write down your login details, with passwords, please.'

Kerry pushed the notepad towards Fox and gave him a pen. He eyed it warily.

'If you want to go home this evening then you need to write it down. Otherwise, I'll just pass your laptop over to our tech guys and they will hack into it and go through every single file and all your search history. Am I making myself clear?'

Rupert Fox picked up the pen and began to write. 'I'm willing to cooperate with you but I'd really like my solicitor now.'

Bernie's phone buzzed as she and Kerry walked back to MCIT. She pulled it out and saw it was a text from Matt.

Spoke to Lucy. She said she saw Worth looking at the laptop in Fox's study. He closed the lid down quickly. Said he was checking to see if it was on. Does that help?

'Yes! Well done, Matt.' Bernie tapped back her thanks.

'What? Has he found something at the house?'

'Sort of.'

Bernie pulled Kerry into the ladies' toilets and showed her Matt's text.

'I think I know where you're going with this but you need to be careful,' said Kerry. 'What are you going to do about it?'

'Not sure yet. It's standard practice to check if devices are still on. If I can't prove Rupert Fox knows old Worthless, and that Worthless only came with me to have the chance to tamper with the evidence, then I have nothing. And if the DCI has any sense then he won't have wiped everything, if he has touched the laptop.'

'Fingerprints?'

'He'll have worn gloves. He's not stupid. He'll have left the email footage, I'm sure, but the other things that Rupert mentioned?' Bernie shook her head. She felt like kicking the wall. Had Worth really been the only DCI available to take on the investigation? Or did he already know about the young woman in the woods? Bernie's heart fluttered with unease. How could she do her job if she didn't trust her senior officer?

CHAPTER 15

'So what's the plan?' Kerry asked.

They were back in MCIT.

'Well,' said Bernie, 'we need to get someone in ready to look at the laptop when it arrives. Could you do that, please? Mick, can you look into the au pair agency, please? We're going to need next-of-kin details. Where's Alice? She's been out all day.'

'Sorry, ma'am, I forgot to tell you Alice rang in to say she had to go and pick up her baby from nursery. He's sick,' said DC Mick Parris. 'But she has emailed some pictures of red dresses from Primark and one of them looks like a match. They said they serve hundreds of people a day so can't pick out a particular customer who bought this outfit. Do you want to see?'

Bernie looked at the photo of the short red dress on a mannequin, designed to cling to a body. She swallowed slowly. She remembered something she had heard on a training session – find out how the victim lived and you'll find out how he or she died. The clingy red dress and her behaviour, as told by Rupert and Harriet Fox, showed a possible side of Rosa. But was it the truth? Had the mystery biker chosen her outfit that night? Had she really suggested to Fox that they video their sex session or had there only been one video all along, designed to protect Rosa from him? Maybe it wasn't as consensual as Fox was making out.

'That looks likely. Send the photo to Forensics for comparison. Hopefully, as it's Saturday tomorrow, Alice will be back in.' Bernie paused before asking her next question. 'Has DS Anderson been in contact at all?'

'Not much. He called in about fifteen hundred hours and said he had nothing to report.'

'I might just give him a ring.'

Bernie pulled out her phone and found his contact details. She hoped he was in a better mood.

'Anderson, DI Noel. Just wondering how it's all going?'

'Yeah, still here but not much found. Apparently there was a big litter-picking campaign down the main pathway last weekend. One of uniform said his wife was involved. So anything of interest may have gone.'

'They obviously didn't go into the woods then. Probably just as well.' An image of Craig Moffatt, the young lad who'd found the body, floated into her mind. She made a mental note to check up on him and see if he was out of hospital.

'We're going to stop at eighteen thirty and then I'll come back. Anything happening your end, ma'am?'

Bernie thought of Rosa and the Italian connection. 'Possible ID for our victim. Rosa Conti, Italian. Do you speak Italian?'

'*Parli italiano*?'

'I take it that's a yes then.'

'Of course. You don't get away with having an Italian mother and not learn the language.'

'Well, if it turns out Rosa is our young woman, then we're going to need your linguistic skills to talk to the family. We're working on next-of-kin details at the moment.'

'We'll talk about it more when I come back. Please don't contact them before I arrive.' He hung up.

'I wouldn't dream of it,' Bernie muttered.

*

Anderson and DCI Worth arrived back at MCIT within minutes of each other. Bernie thought she knew what had taken the DCI so long but decided to keep her question for later. Now, Worth was asking for a full briefing.

'So, where are you holding Mr Fox?' Worth asked.

'In an interview room. He's currently only a witness, not a suspect,' replied Bernie.

'It's not great we're holding him at all. I'm assuming this hasn't gone out to the press, Jane?'

'No, sir. And if it did, I would phrase it as "a man helping us with our enquiries".'

'Hmm, might be better to say nothing at all.'

'With all due respect, sir—' Bernie started to say.

'DI Noel, Mr Fox has alibis for the time period we're looking at and no criminal record. Nor does he have a motorbike. I checked during the search,' said Worth.

'Until we see the email, we don't know anything for sure about Rupert Fox, sir. I'm assuming you've brought the laptop back with you.' Bernie knew she was out of line but she held her ground. If she was right about Worth and Fox knowing each other, Worth would have to back down at some point. She saw his mouth twitch.

'I did bring the laptop. I gather someone is setting it up for us as we speak.'

'Yes, sir,' said Kerry. 'Tom Knox. He's recently started as a digital media investigator. Bit of a computer whizz, by all accounts. He's connecting it to the interactive whiteboard so we can all see.'

'Good, moving on then…'

And moving away from Rupert Fox.

'…what about next of kin for Rosa Conti?'

Mick Parris raised his hand. 'I've been dealing with this, sir. We have contact details for her grandparents. Apparently her parents died in an earthquake a few years ago and she'd been living with her paternal grandparents in Florence until the summer when she came here. When Rosa left the Fox household, the agency owner tried to contact them but she had problems getting them to understand. She said her Italian is a bit rusty but also the grandparents seemed a bit deaf. So—'

'Don't worry about that,' said Anderson, 'I speak fluent Italian and I'm happy to go over there if need be.'

I bet you are, thought Bernie. Free holiday, right? Or find that one bit of evidence that cracks the whole case.

'Not sure we have the budget for that. Rather a lot has been spent already on Forensics.' Worth looked pointedly at Bernie. 'I'm sure our fellow Italian officers will do a great job of looking after the Contis and collecting the necessary DNA samples. Much better if you can do a call with the local police, perhaps even video.'

There was a tap at the door and a young man with short, wavy blond hair popped his head round.

'Ah, are you Tom?' Worth asked.

'Yep, that's me. Laptop is ready for whenever you want to see it, sir,' he said.

'Well, there's no time like the present. Let's see what this email has to offer.'

Everyone got up from their seats. Bernie still felt a niggling sensation about Worth and Fox. She tried to remember if there had been a flicker of recognition between them, anything at all. She held Jane Clackett back as the others left the room.

'Quick question, the DCI did a slot for TV last night, correct?'

'Yes, it was on the local news.'

'What about the radio? Did he record something for that?'

'No. It just went out as part of the normal bulletin. I listened to it and then watched the TV. I always do to make sure everything's all right. Why? Is there a problem?'

Bernie shook her head. 'No, no problem. I just thought someone said they heard Worth on the radio – they must have meant the TV.'

Bernie let Jane go ahead of her out of the door. She smiled. *Got you, Rupert Fox.*

CHAPTER 16

Bernie cringed at the grainy images on the screen. It was like watching a very bad porn film. Rupert Fox may have been genuine but Rosa was clearly playing a part. The other camera that Rupert mentioned could be clearly seen.

Wrong about that then. But it still could have been Fox's idea rather than Rosa's.

'Sir,' Mick Parris raised his hand, 'could the wife have set this up to catch him out?'

'It's a possibility,' said Worth.

Bernie forced herself to look closer. 'No, I don't think so. Look, freeze it there.' The footage was paused. 'See, Rosa is looking up at the camera. It's only quick but she knows it's there. And the look in her eyes is different.' Bernie shook her head. 'I'm not sure what. Unhappy? Fed up? But when she looks at Rupert Fox, she's smiling. Carry on, although I'm beginning to feel I've seen enough.'

The clip continued. Bernie wanted to avert her gaze but knew she had to be on the lookout for clues.

'You know,' said Worth, 'we're assuming this is Rupert Fox but can we be one hundred per cent sure? Mrs Fox said she caught Rosa with another man. Maybe this is him.'

Bernie looked across at Kerry and gave her a knowing look before replying. 'Rupert Fox was convinced it was him.'

Worth was tapping a pen against his mouth. Bernie wondered if it was a habit or stress-related. She noticed the nicotine-stained fingers and teeth but no smell of cigarette smoke. Had he recently given up smoking?

'Maybe,' he said.

The clip was almost finished when the man turned his head and there was a clear shot of Rupert Fox's face.

'I think that settles it, don't you, sir?'

Worth paled. 'Yes, it's clearly him. Try and find out where that email came from. DI Noel, my office now, please.'

Bernie's stomach fizzed. She'd goaded Worth enough for a confrontation. He clearly didn't want it to be public.

She was barely through the door when Worth rounded on her.

'Detective Inspector Noel, while I respect you as a colleague, I will not put up with these jibes and digs at me. If you have something to say, say it now.'

Bernie clenched her hands into fists. She didn't particularly want to air her suspicions but knew she had to. 'I'm concerned you may personally know Rupert Fox and, if so, then that would jeopardise the case.'

'And what evidence do you have for that?'

'Fox said he heard you on the radio but you didn't do a sound-bite for the radio, only a clip for TV.'

'So? He got it wrong, he meant the TV.'

Bernie dug her fingernails into her palms. She shook her head. 'No, sir, he said he recognised your voice. If he'd seen you, he would have said he recognised your face.'

'Maybe he was out of the room but heard the sound.'

Oh, you've got an answer for everything.

'And what makes you think I know him?'

'DS Allen had found the link with the Foxes but you chose to come along. You made the call to the family. You stayed behind to wait for Forensics. As the SIO, I would have expected you to have delegated that task to me or another officer.'

'Surely if I knew Rupert Fox, I would have brought him back to headquarters to take his statement. And how do I know him, anyway?'

Bernie stared at DCI Patrick Worth. She knew she had to choose her words carefully.

She softened her tone slightly. 'Perhaps you know him from a club?'

Worth's eyes narrowed. 'A club? What sort of club?'

'Maybe a... golf club.'

Worth began tapping the pen again. As Bernie had thought, this action was stress-related – he was about to try and hide something.

'I see. It's come to this, has it? Are you so threatened by me and my authority that you're reduced to throwing accusations around?'

'Sir, I'm not accusing you—'

'Oh but you are, DI Noel, you are. I'm tempted to throw you off the case right here and now but you're a good officer when you put your mind to it. I think it would be good to canvass the local area in Salisbury tomorrow. See if any of the neighbours knew Rosa at all. Check out the clubs, bars, cafés, et cetera. I'm sure you can manage that with a few of the team.'

'What? No, sir, I'm needed here. I have questions I want to ask Rosa's grandparents, particularly about her time with the Fox family—'

'I've made my decision. You can leave my office now, DI Noel. Feel free to go home.'

Bernie gave a terse nod and walked out of the door, closing it behind her. She unclenched her fists and saw the nail indentations on her hand. It was only then she realised Worth had neither confirmed nor denied that he knew Rupert Fox personally.

*

Bernie repeatedly kicked the toilet cubicle door.

Kerry came into the loos and looked at Bernie.

'What are you doing?'

'Kicking the door.'

'I can see that. Why?'

'I'm pretending,' Bernie said, her breath coming quickly, 'that it's Worth's head.'

'And do you feel better yet?'

'No.'

Kerry sighed. 'Well, you may want to stop before you break your toes or the door or both. Come on, calm down and talk to me.'

Bernie stopped and felt her toes throb. She looked at Kerry. Her clear blue eyes exuded calmness. Bernie took a deep breath.

'He wants me to go to Salisbury tomorrow. Ask around about Rosa.'

'And? That's quite an important job to do.'

'Yes, I know. But I want to be here, talking to the Italian police, maybe even Rosa's grandparents. I have questions.'

'Let me guess – Rupert Fox?'

Bernie nodded.

'Well then, write them down and give them to Anderson. He can ask them. In fact, it might seem less incendiary if he did it rather than you.'

'Like he's going to help me.'

'Actually…' Kerry paused.

'You were going to say something about Anderson last night at the pub and then you stopped. Spit it out.' Bernie folded her arms and leaned against the sink.

Kerry wrinkled her nose. 'I think maybe my source on the police grapevine I listened to was a bit biased against Anderson. He knew the other officer that Anderson had hit. I've heard some good things about him lately. Really good. You know me, I'm always the first to support women but maybe his ex-wife is the real manipulator here.'

'Perhaps. But she sounded very convincing to me.' Bernie rubbed her face. 'Worth also told me to go home.'

Kerry put her hand on Bernie's arm. 'Then go. Alex will be pleased to see you. Get some sleep. We've got a lot of walking to do tomorrow.'

'We?'

'I'm coming to Salisbury with you. And I am totally going to beat you on steps walked.'

Bernie laughed. 'How are you going to manage that then if we're together?'

'Short legs. I'm at least one and a half strides to your one.'

They both laughed.

'Oh, Kerry, you know how to cheer me up. Right, I'll go home and see Alex. Poor guy – I've been neglecting him a bit recently. See you in the morning.'

CHAPTER 17

Saturday

Alex stirred next to her as the alarm went off.

'What time is it?' he murmured.

'Six thirty. Sorry. I have to work today. Where were you last night?'

The house had been in darkness when Bernie had returned home from headquarters.

'Figured you'd be late so I went out with the lads. It got a bit manic and someone poured a beer over me. I had to shower when I got back.'

'Thought I heard you in the bathroom.'

'Sorry for disturbing you.'

'It's all right. I was too tired to talk.'

Alex rolled onto his side to face Bernie. He reached out to stroke her arm. 'I was quite tempted to wake you up properly last night. It's been a while.' His hand moved onto her breasts and then worked down. 'Do we have time now?' He kissed her neck.

Bernie knew she ought to get into work early but she was enjoying what Alex was doing. 'We have time.'

Bernie stuffed the last piece of toast into her mouth. 'Got to go. Oh, if you've got to wash last night's clothes, can you stick the bedding in too, please?'

'Yeah, sure. I've got football this morning so I'll stick my kit in and do it all together afterwards.'

'Great, thanks. I have no idea what time I'll be home today. I'll text you later.'

Although it was good to spend time with Alex, Bernie was on the back foot going into work. She wanted to write some questions for the Contis that Anderson could pass on to the Italian police. In particular she wanted to know if Rosa had told her grandparents anything interesting about the Foxes. Or had she told anyone else? Getting access to her emails would be priority. She had her notepad and pen ready for the briefing but hoped to jot down a few ideas in between Worth's comments.

'Thank you all for coming in bright and early on a Saturday morning,' said Worth. 'Today, we need to do our best to find out as much as we possibly can about Rosa Conti. DS Anderson and myself will liaise with the police in Florence. We'll be asking them to speak to Rosa's grandparents and collect DNA samples and dental records. DS Anderson has already made initial contact.

'I've asked DI Noel to look into Rosa's life in Salisbury. I've already spoken to Mrs Fox this morning. She's still in shock but would like to help as much as she can. She's willing to talk to you this morning so I suggest you go there first before asking around the town.'

Bernie looked up in surprise. She couldn't quite believe Worth was allowing her to go back to the Foxes after her comments the previous evening. 'Really?'

Worth nodded. 'Yes. Having ruled out Rupert Fox, it's important we get back to the essential task of finding out more about Rosa.'

Bernie looked down at her notepad so Worth wouldn't see her face. *You might have ruled out Rupert Fox but I sure as hell haven't.*

Worth glanced at his watch. 'We need to get a move on as our Italian counterparts are an hour ahead and expecting us very soon. DC Hart – Rosa's clothes. You've found out about the dress but what about the shoes?'

Alice flushed. 'I'm still working on the shoes. Forensics have come back to me and said they're very good quality and likely to be expensive.'

'Keep looking into it. DS Anderson, where did you get up to yesterday with the search?'

Anderson coughed a little. 'Other than plenty of tyre tracks, we didn't find anything else of interest. I didn't find out until nearly the end of yesterday that there had been a litter-picking session along the track last weekend. So any evidence may have already gone.'

'How infuriating. Shame they didn't venture into the woods as we might have found our victim a lot sooner.' Worth looked at his watch again. 'DI Noel, I'm going to leave you to divvy out the jobs for the rest of the team. DS Anderson, shall we go to my office?'

'Yes, sir. I'll be there in a few minutes.'

'Right, the rest of you carry on and we'll have a check-in at twelve hundred hours.'

Bernie quickly scribbled down some of the questions she had for Rosa's grandparents and the Italian police as Worth left the room.

'Anderson, I'm sure you have it covered already but just a few thoughts.'

He took the notepad, read it and smiled, before handing it back. 'Great minds think alike. I'll catch up with you later.'

Bernie stood up. She was now regretting spending that time in bed with Alex as she hadn't had a chance to prepare what tasks needed doing. Thinking on her feet was her only option.

'Right. Alice – these shoes. Do we have a decent photo of them that could be shown to the grandparents? It's more likely she bought the dress here but maybe she brought them with her.'

'Yes. I can send it to the DCI.'

'Good.' Bernie looked at the others. 'Matt and Mick, I guess you're still drawing a blank on the motorbike on CCTV?'

Matt nodded. 'Yes, ma'am. We can keep trawling but we're assuming he has some idea where the cameras are.'

'Hmm.' Bernie thought about the questions she'd written down for Anderson, and one in particular – how had Rosa stayed in touch with her grandparents? 'I think what's important here is not what we have, but what we don't have. A mobile phone. An address for where Rosa went after she left the Foxes. She must have been living somewhere.'

'Presumably with the motorcyclist,' said Kerry.

'Possibly but perhaps she'd made some friends and was bunking with one of them.' Bernie thought for a moment. 'I wonder if she knew any of the other au pairs from the agency. Where's it based, Mick?'

'Salisbury as well.'

'Right, in that case, Mick and Matt, I want you to go to Salisbury to talk to the woman who runs the agency. She must have a photo of Rosa even if it's from a copy of her passport and she might know if any of the other au pairs knew her. If there are any, check them out. Then, assuming you can get a photo, I'd like you to go round the pubs and bars in Salisbury. Also, see if any of the nightclubs are open – but that might not be until after lunch.

'Kerry – you and I will go and see Harriet Fox and see what she has to say. Then we'll move on to the neighbours.

'Alice, if Rosa's grandparents don't recognise the shoes then it might be she did buy them here after all. As it seems likely she got the dress in Swindon, could you go to the designer outlet village please? There might be a shop there that sells them. Kerry and I can check in Salisbury too. Could you send me the photo as well?'

Alice pulled out her mobile. 'Sure, I'll Bluetooth it to you now.'

'Great. I know the DCI said check in at twelve but we'll have to call in. So if you can let me know where you're up to by eleven fifty that would be helpful.'

Bernie's phone pinged and she looked down at the photo that had just arrived. 'Thanks, Alice. Wow. Those are some shoes. I have to admit I didn't look that closely at them at the scene.'

Kerry leaned in. 'Ooh! If I wore those, I'd be nearly as tall as you.'

Bernie laughed. 'You'd have to wear stilts to be nearly as tall as me! Sorry, Kerry, that was mean. How high are they?'

'Ten centimetres,' Alice replied.

Matt looked over Bernie's shoulder. 'God, those look—'

'Oi,' said Kerry, 'no sexist comments, please.'

'No, of course not. I was going to say they look dangerous. You could take someone's eye out with those.'

Bernie looked at the shoes again. Bright red leather with tall, silver stiletto heels. 'That's a good point, Matt. Why didn't she use them against her attacker? Or maybe she did. The shoes weren't with the body. Perhaps she threw them at him. Mick, what do you think?'

She held out her phone to him.

He paused before speaking. 'Well, at the risk of sounding sexist myself...'

Kerry groaned.

'No,' said Bernie, 'let's hear Mick out.'

'Well, I'm thinking a man might have paid for them if they're really expensive. I doubt she would have earned much as an au pair. And maybe he liked the look of them.' Mick blushed. 'Personally I don't care what shoes my wife wears but some men like that sort of thing.'

Bernie looked at Kerry. 'Maybe a man like Rupert Fox? I think we need to find out what his missus has to say.'

CHAPTER 18

The drive to Salisbury was slower than expected. Weekend road-works delayed them, plus shoppers and day-trippers clogged the roads closer to the city. As Worth's driver had taken them the day before, Bernie roughly knew the route to the Foxes and was able to divert down some of the quieter roads.

She pulled up outside their house, taking in more detail this time; the day before, her mind had been full with a possible ID for the victim. The house was detached and didn't seem large from the front but Bernie remembered it was a bit like a Tardis – small on the outside but huge inside as it extended back and up into the loft. The city centre wasn't too far away and the famous Salisbury Cathedral spire could just be seen. Bernie looked up and down the road. The other houses were similar, either detached or semi-detached, with neat driveways and gardens. It was a quiet area, not overly affluent but definitely middle class.

Harriet Fox opened the door as they approached. She gave a taut smile. 'I was waiting for you.' She stood back and let them in. 'Rupert has taken the girls swimming. We thought it best they were out of the house and you've already interviewed Rupe.' She grimaced.

Bernie decided to not respond directly to the last comment. Not yet anyway. 'This is my colleague, DS Kerry Allen. DCI Worth said you wanted to talk to us.'

'Yes. Come through to the kitchen and I'll make some coffee.'

Bernie and Kerry followed Harriet Fox into a large, modern extension with a kitchen on one side and an informal seating area on the other. The sofas here were a lot more welcoming than the hard armchair Bernie had sat in the day before.

Harriet busied herself with making coffee and Bernie thought it was more to do with calming her nerves than actually needing a drink. 'How do you like your coffee?' she asked.

'White with one sugar,' said Bernie, 'and Kerry's white, no sugar. Thanks.'

The room was immaculate and if it weren't for the children's drawings up on the fridge, Bernie would have assumed that no children lived here. She guessed their toys were in another room.

Harriet put a tray down on the coffee table in front of them and handed them each a mug.

'You have a lovely house,' Kerry said.

'Thank you, it's taken quite a while to get it like this.' Harriet sat down on the sofa opposite and sipped her coffee. 'We may as well start. Get it over and done with.' She avoided their gaze.

'All right,' said Bernie. She nodded at Kerry who put her mug down and pulled out her notebook and pen. 'Let's start with when Rosa arrived. When was that exactly?'

'Thirtieth of July. Just after we got back from holiday. I'm a legal secretary. I only went back to work earlier this year, partly to help pay for all this.' She gestured around the room. 'But I also wanted to get my brain working again and have some space from the girls. I didn't particularly want to put them into summer camps for the whole holiday and a friend recommended the au pair agency. It seemed ideal as the school run was a bit of a struggle too. There were a few girls to choose from and we went with Rosa. I can't speak a word of Italian but I love Italy – the scenery, the atmosphere and the food. She was from Florence, which I adore, and she claimed to be a good cook.' Harriet took another sip of coffee.

'I'm guessing she wasn't,' Bernie said.

'No, dreadful. And her English wasn't as good as we expected either. She picked it up pretty quickly though. I think the girls helped with that. And as I said yesterday, she was very good with them. They adored her. We haven't told them yet. I'm hoping we won't have to.'

Bernie glanced at Kerry. 'We'll probably announce her ID when it's confirmed. Can I ask, did Mr Fox tell you about his interview?'

Harriet put the mug down on the coffee table and began to rub her fingers against her thumbs. She kept her head down. 'Yes. He told me everything. I promise you, though, he was here that Friday evening – all night.'

'Did you have any idea at all about him and Rosa?'

Harriet gave a brittle laugh. 'No, despite some of the mums on the class WhatsApp group making some jokes. Obviously they saw Rosa on the school run from September and they put up the usual clichéd remarks – "Better watch your husband, Harriet." I ignored them, to my cost.'

More Rosa's cost than yours, thought Bernie. You're still here. She took another sip of her coffee. 'How much did you pay Rosa?'

Harriet lifted her head, a little startled at the change of direction. 'Um, we paid five hundred pounds a month to the agency and then they paid the wage to her. I'm guessing they took a cut. Obviously she had bed and full board here.'

'And did she stay here every night?'

'To begin with, yes. Then she started to make friends and she was often out all night on Friday and Saturday evenings. We didn't expect her to work weekends. She would go clubbing and stay over with a friend.'

'Male or female?'

'At the time I didn't know but I now suspect it was a man.'

Bernie put her mug down and pulled her phone out of her pocket. She opened the photos and found the picture she wanted. 'Would Rosa get ready here first? Do you recognise these shoes?' She handed her phone over.

'Oh yes. She got those sometime in September, I think. No idea how she managed to walk in them, let alone dance.'

'Not your kind of thing then.'

'God, no. I've never worn heels.'

'Do you know where she bought them?'

Harriet shook her head. 'No. They looked expensive. I did wonder at the time how she managed to afford them. It's not like she was saving her money. She was spending most of it, mainly on clothes, make-up and toiletries.' She picked up her mug but then put it down again. 'Oh God, do you think Rupert gave her the money? I mean, they were… doing it by then. Is that what you think?'

Bernie picked her mug up again. 'We don't know. The dress she was found in was very cheap in comparison to the shoes. It may be nothing at all but we have to look at the possibility that someone else paid for them.' She spotted Kerry jotting down 'financial check on Fox'.

Harriet was still rubbing her thumbs and fingers together.

'Something else I'd like to ask about is Rosa's mobile phone. I'm assuming she had one.'

Harriet nodded, her eyes slightly glazed.

'Do you have her number? We've not managed to locate her phone yet.'

Harriet looked at Bernie. 'Her number? Yes, it's on my phone. I'll just get it.'

She got up and left the room.

Bernie looked at Kerry and whispered, 'What do you think?'

'Very nervous. And she's had time to think.'

'Exactly. Can you send a text to Alice to say the shoes were definitely bought locally?'

'Sure.' Kerry pulled out her mobile as Harriet came back in the room.

'Here you go. Just so you know, I texted her last night. In case it's not her who's… I said I was sorry and asked her to reply. There's been no response.'

Bernie took the phone from Harriet and jotted the number down on Kerry's notepad. 'Thank you. That's very helpful. Don't suppose you know which phone company she was with?'

'No, but I do know she changed to a SIM-only contract when she arrived here. She wanted a UK number and was on a three-month trial with us so it made more sense to do that.'

'And you've no idea where she went after leaving you?'

Harriet shook her head again. 'No. No idea.'

'What about the man you said you caught her with? The reason you told her to leave.'

Harriet's cheeks coloured. 'Oh, yes. I suppose she may have gone to him.'

'Can you give us a description?'

Harriet's blush deepened. 'No, not really. I didn't exactly see his face. I'd rather not describe what I saw. But he was white, tall and had dark hair. I told her to pack her bags and leave. I took the girls out and by the time we got back, she'd left. As I told you before, I hadn't realised about the rings until the next day. Of course, I now understand why Rupe wanted to keep her name out of it.' She shook her head. 'I'm so sorry. If I'd known I was putting her in danger by sending her away, I would never have told her to go. Do her grandparents know yet?'

'DCI Worth and another of our officers are in touch with the Italian police now. They'll be told today. Do you mind if we have another look at Rosa's bedroom? I know the CSIs have finished with it.'

'Yes, of course.'

Bernie and Kerry followed Harriet back to the hallway and up the stairs. She indicated to the bedroom at the front.

The room was large with a double bed. Opposite it was a wardrobe and shelving unit combined.

'Did Rosa bring much with her?'

'No, very little. She bought most of her things here.' Harriet sighed. 'I feel so awful. She was only nineteen. Still a child in so many ways. She even had a teddy bear that she kept on the shelf over there.' She pointed to the middle shelf on the unit.

Kerry stood by it and then turned to look at the bed. 'Right here? Did she bring that from Florence?'

'No. She got it here. The girls wanted to play with it but she said no. Said it was a special bear given to her by a special friend.' Harriet covered her face with her hand and gave a sob.

Bernie glanced at Kerry. It was time to go.

'Thank you for your time, Mrs Fox,' she said. 'We may have to ask you some more questions at some point. In the meantime we're going to ask your neighbours if they saw who Rosa left with.'

'Oh God. Do you have to?'

'Well, yes. This is a murder investigation. Someone brutally killed Rosa.'

Harriet looked at the floor. 'Of course. Go ahead and ask.'

Bernie was tempted to say she didn't need permission but she needed to keep on the good side of Harriet Fox. She was sure this conversation would be relayed back to Worth at some point. 'We'll just get our things and leave you in peace. I'm sure you'd appreciate a bit of space before Mr Fox and the girls get back.'

They trooped back downstairs and downed the rest of their coffees.

'Oh, before we go, do you have a photo of Rosa?'

'No, I don't. She didn't like having her photo taken which is odd because she is… was such a pretty girl. And she definitely didn't want me to mention her on social media.'

Interesting. Bernie held out her hand. 'We'll be in touch.'

Harriet shook Bernie's hand. 'Let me know if there's anything I can do for her grandparents. We were supposed to be looking out for her. We failed.'

Bernie raised her hand as Harriet Fox shut the door.

As they reached the pavement, Kerry said, 'Are you thinking what I'm thinking about that teddy bear?'

'Oh yes. It definitely had a camera in it.'

CHAPTER 19

Bernie had hoped for some nosy neighbours but most were out. She was about to signal to Kerry it was time to leave when her DS waved her over from the other side of the road. Bernie joined her.

'Ma'am, this is Olivia. She remembers Rosa leaving.'

Bernie looked at the teenage girl before her, probably about seventeen, still in her PJs and dressing gown, even though it was almost eleven thirty. Bernie smiled. 'What do you remember?'

'I don't know what day it was. It was two or three weeks ago. But I saw her come out of the door with a large suitcase and some bags. Then this black car turned up and she put her stuff in and left. I thought it was a cab but it might not have been.' Olivia pushed her dark, unbrushed hair out of her face. Kerry had obviously woken her up.

'Did you see the driver at all?'

Olivia thought for a moment. 'No, not really. He was on the side closest to the pavement and stayed in the car which I thought was a bit weird. Cab drivers normally help you with your stuff, don't they?'

'They normally do. What about before this? Had you seen much of Rosa from when she arrived in the summer?'

Olivia pulled a face. 'I'd seen her around but I didn't go out of my way to make friends. I used to babysit for the girls but Harriet told me she didn't need me now she had Rosa. She cost me money.'

Someone else who thinks Rosa cost them something. 'I see. Is there anything else you remember from that day? Maybe the make and model of the car? Or any part of the registration?'

Olivia shook her head. 'No idea about cars. But thinking about it, there was some shouting maybe an hour or so before she left. It was Harriet and then she got in her car with the girls and drove off.'

Kerry pulled out her notebook and pen. 'Did you see anyone else leave the house?' she asked. 'A man, perhaps?'

'No, I wasn't looking all the time. I was doing my homework.' She pointed to the upstairs front window. 'That's my room.'

Bernie looked up. It was opposite Rosa's. The road was quite wide and the driveways fairly long but it might still be possible to see across. 'Can you see into Rosa's room from yours?'

'I wasn't spying on her, if that's what you mean.'

'No, not at all. I was just wondering.'

The girl sighed. 'Yeah, to begin with, especially if she had her curtains open and light on. But she must have spotted me looking cos she then started pulling her curtains quite early, before it got dark. Can I go now? I've not had breakfast yet and Mum told me I had to be dressed before she got back from the supermarket.'

'Yes, of course.' Bernie pulled a business card out of her pocket. 'Give me a call if you remember anything else.'

'OK. Is Rosa in trouble or something?'

Bernie was surprised Olivia was only asking now. But she wasn't about to say without confirmation. 'We're not sure yet. Thanks for your help.'

They headed back to the car and got in. It was almost time to check in with the others. Bernie looked at her phone to see if anyone had been in touch. There was an email from Anderson.

'Right, what have we got here then? Great, a photo of Rosa.' She showed it to Kerry. Staring back at them was a smiling, pretty young woman with long dark hair, dressed in jeans and a T-shirt.

'Harriet was right – she was pretty. I'm guessing she doesn't look like that any more,' said Kerry.

Bernie sighed. 'No, she doesn't. But at least we have something to show now. I wonder if Matt got a photo from the agency. This would be a much better one to use.' She was about to ring him when Alice's name came up on the screen. Bernie answered the call.

'Hi, Alice. What have you got for me?' She put it on speakerphone.

'I found the shoes. You were right about the outlet village. Even better, one of the shop assistants remembers Rosa. As soon as I showed her a photo of the shoes she knew straight away who I was referring to. Was able to describe her. Apparently Rosa was really excited about the shoes. Unfortunately there's no CCTV footage as it was over a month ago and they only keep it for a month. She told me Rosa had said her boyfriend had given her the money for them. They were two hundred and sixty-five pounds, down from five hundred and sixty. She paid cash, and there was a man waiting outside for her. White, tall, dark hair, she thinks, but had a baseball cap on.'

'That's great work. Have you asked security at the centre if they have CCTV footage?'

'Yes. Same thing. Keep it for a month then get rid of it unless there's an incident and it's needed for us.'

'Damn. That's not helpful, but great you found the shoes. Confirms what Mick said earlier. It was a man who paid for them. Can you go back to headquarters and write that up, please? I'm going to catch up with Mick and Matt and see where they're at. Good work, Alice.'

'Thanks, ma'am. I'll see you later.'

Bernie looked at Kerry. 'That's good news. And one less thing we have to do here.'

'Shame. I was looking forward to trying on some heels.'

'You still wouldn't be taller than me.'

They both laughed.

'Seriously though,' said Bernie, 'this guy that's been mentioned might be our motorcyclist. And likely Rosa was with him after she left the Foxes. Let's see if Matt and Mick have got anywhere.'

Bernie called Matt.

'Hi, ma'am. Haven't got much, I'm afraid.'

'Tell me what you do have.'

'Rosa didn't get much pay. Four hundred pounds a month that the agency paid directly to her.'

'Whoa. Harriet said she paid the agency five hundred. How many au pairs do they have on their books?'

'Not sure exactly but quite a lot. At least fifty. Do you want us to check out the legality?'

'Leave it for now. Not really our department but we can pass it on if need be. What about friends?'

'She did connect with a couple of the other au pairs over the summer but from September onwards she didn't see them. The owner rang them up and we spoke to them. They both said the same thing – a man came on the scene and Rosa just dumped them.'

'Interesting. What about her passport?'

'The owner did have a copy of it but it's a few years old so she looks quite young. Don't know if it'll be much use.'

'Don't worry. Anderson has sent a photo from the grandparents. I'll forward it on to you.' Bernie glanced at her watch. It was getting close to twelve. 'You and Mick can take lunch now if you want. I'll call the DCI and let him know where we're all up to. Then Kerry and I can come and help you and Mick with the pubs and bars. I'll text you in a bit. Oh, and you can tell Mick he was right – it was a man who paid for the shoes. Alice found the shop. Catch you later.'

'OK. Bye, ma'am.'

Bernie looked at Kerry. 'I suppose I ought to call the boss next.'

'That's the politest you've ever been about Worth.'

'Probably because I've had some time out from him.'

Worth answered after two rings and Bernie relayed what the team had found out.

'So Kerry and I are going to join Matt and Mick in the city centre and see what we can dig up.'

'Good. Sounds like some progress has been made, albeit small. I'll make use of Alice once she's back. I'd like you all back here for five o'clock for a briefing.'

'Yes, sir. I'll pass that on to the others. See you then. Oh, how's it going with the Contis? How did they take it?'

'I'll inform you all at the briefing.'

'Yes, sir.' Bernie ended the call. *Shutting me out again.* She reached for her seat belt. 'Huh! Small progress indeed. Let's see if we can find anywhere to park and then grab some lunch,' she said. 'And then you can beat me on steps, little one.'

'Oi! You do know I can throw you over my shoulder, don't you?'

Bernie laughed. 'I know.'

CHAPTER 20

Saturday lunchtime was not the best time to be asking questions. The pubs and cafés were full and staff rushed off their feet. Quick glances were followed by shaking heads. By three o'clock, they'd all had enough.

They sat on a bench opposite the cathedral. The sun was shining and the green was full of people – tourists taking photos of the spire, children running around and others sitting quietly, taking in the full majesty of the cathedral.

'How tall is the spire?' Mick asked.

'One hundred and twenty-three metres,' Matt replied.

'Blimey, that was fast.'

Bernie laughed. 'Matt is our quiz expert. If you're doing one make sure you have him on your team.' Bernie looked at the expansive building in front of them. 'Do you think Rosa ever came here?'

'Maybe. Not sure the staff here would remember though,' said Kerry. 'Plus, she was probably Catholic.'

'Actually, I found a Catholic church on Exeter Street and went in,' said Matt. 'The priest didn't recognise her.'

'Considering what she'd been up to, you'd have thought she'd pop in for confession,' said Mick.

Bernie looked at him. 'Seriously? From what we're finding out, we have a young woman who's been manipulated by men. Even you said it was probably a man who'd paid for the shoes.'

There was silence.

'Sorry, ma'am.'

'Apology accepted. You might have said it the wrong way, Mick, but it's possible she may have gone to another Catholic church. There must be more than one round here.'

Bernie pulled out her phone and did a quick search. 'Oh wow, there's one two streets away from the Foxes. Far more likely she went there. Right, we have an hour before we ought to leave to get back for the briefing. Kerry and I will check out the church and you two can go and see if any of the nightclubs have opened yet to get ready for tonight.'

The church was on a quiet suburban street. Bernie and Kerry got out of the car and headed up the path.

'Can I help you?'

They turned to see a short man, with greying hair, in a black suit with a dog collar.

Bernie smiled. 'Hello, Father.' She held up her warrant card. 'I'm DI Noel and this is DS Allen. We were wondering if you could help us with something.'

He bowed his head slightly in greeting. 'I'm Father Adrian – I'll help if I can. I don't have long. I have a mass to do at another church in a couple of hours and I need to set up.'

'It won't take long. We were wondering if you've ever seen this woman in your congregation.' Bernie held out her phone.

The priest studied the photo far closer than the staff in the pubs and cafés. 'No. I don't think I have seen her at mass. She may have come in for confession but obviously I wouldn't know that for certain.'

'She's Italian.'

'Oh! Rosa?'

'So you do know her?'

'Not exactly. I know of her. She was with the Foxes. Harriet comes here for mass on a Sunday.'

'What about Rupert Fox?'

The priest shook his head. 'No. Not his thing. I know Rosa was staying with them as an au pair but Harriet told me last week that she'd left.'

'Did Rosa come to confession?'

Father Adrian hesitated.

'So she did come to confession,' said Kerry.

The priest raised his hands in a sorry gesture. 'Once. I can't possibly tell you what she said. It's between her, me and God.'

'Can you at least tell us when she came here?'

Father Adrian scratched his head. 'It must be at least three weeks ago.'

Bernie bit her lip as she weighed up what to say next. Rosa's ID wasn't officially confirmed but most likely would be in the next twenty-four hours.

'Father Adrian, I fully appreciate you can't tell us Rosa's confession. I'd also like you to keep quiet what I'm about to tell you. A young woman was found murdered on Thursday morning. It's not confirmed yet but we believe her to be Rosa. Does your confidentiality about the confession still stand?'

The priest covered his mouth with his hand and shut his eyes for a few seconds. Bernie wondered if he was praying. He pulled his hand away.

'Oh, the poor child. Does Harriet know?'

'Yes. She may want to talk to you but she doesn't know we're here. It would be better if she comes to you.'

Father Adrian nodded quickly. 'Yes, of course.'

Bernie pulled out a card. 'Here's my number.'

He paused before taking it. 'I'll need to seek advice about Rosa and come back to you. I risk excommunication if I reveal her confession. But something I think I can say, is that she was very frightened. Frightened for her life.'

CHAPTER 21

Bernie pondered on what Father Adrian had said on their way back to headquarters. Who had Rosa been scared of? Rupert Fox? Her new boyfriend? Or someone else altogether?

'Penny for them,' said Kerry.

'What? Oh, I was thinking about what the priest said.'

'Me too. And what Harriet said about social media and no pictures. Have we looked for any accounts for Rosa yet?'

'No, without a photo it was a bit pointless. Definitely worth doing now. Do you know if Tom's in today?'

'I don't think he is. We might be able to get him tomorrow though. You want him to check out her phone number.'

'Yes. It would be good to know who she was texting and calling.' Bernie glanced at the clock on her dashboard. It was four forty-five p.m. They were only five minutes away from headquarters. 'I would consider getting him in now but I don't think Worthless would be too happy. Wouldn't like the additional cost. Actually, that's just reminded me. Both Harriet and Olivia said that Rosa had cost them something. Not sure what to think about that.'

Kerry shifted in her seat towards Bernie. 'Yeah, me neither. With Harriet, you could argue that Rosa had some responsibility there but Rupert Fox is the main culprit. And as for Olivia, Rosa didn't know she'd put someone out of a job. Let's hope Anderson's managed to find out more.'

*

The chairs were still in their neat rows in the briefing room – Worth's personal touch. Bernie really missed Detective Chief Superintendent Wilson and his somewhat chaotic nature.

'Someone's been busy with the chairs,' she muttered. She caught Anderson's eye.

'It was me. Under instruction. Waste of my time.' He shook his head.

'Not a good day then?'

'I'll tell you later.'

Worth clapped his hands. 'Right, now that we're all here. Let's start.'

They all took a seat. Jane had joined them too.

'Thank you for all your hard work today. It may seem we haven't got very far but we're starting to build up a picture of Rosa Conti. From what DI Noel told me earlier, there was definitely a man on the scene, apart from her "relationship" with Rupert Fox. Did you find anything else this afternoon?'

Bernie told the team about meeting Father Adrian and what he had said. 'Of course, it might be that Father Adrian isn't allowed to tell us but I'm hoping in this instance that he'll share what Rosa said.'

Worth paled a little. Bernie wondered, if the priest decided to disclose Rosa's last confession, would it cast a bad light on Rupert Fox?

The DCI coughed. 'We'll have to see. Catholic priests can be real sticklers for the rules. What about in Salisbury itself? Any luck with the clubs, et cetera?'

Moving on quickly again. 'Kerry and I didn't find anyone but Mick and Matt checked out the clubs this afternoon.'

Mick shook his head. 'No joy there. They were only just opening to get ready for tonight so mostly bar staff and cleaners in. No one recognised her from the photo. Thought it more likely the bouncers would know. We've passed the photo on to Salisbury police and they're going to ask on patrol this evening.'

Worth tapped his pen against his mouth. 'Hmm. Bernie, Harriet definitely said Rosa went clubbing?'

'Yes, sir. Said she didn't normally come home. Maybe it wasn't in Salisbury.'

'Perhaps.' Worth sighed. 'I think it's fair to say that DS Anderson and myself have had a fairly traumatic day. Dealing with a victim's family is never easy but harder still when they're in a different country. I want to thank DS Anderson for his help today. Without his language skills, it would have been very difficult.

'Rosa's parents were killed in an earthquake about three years ago and she'd been living with her grandparents since then. She was fairly troubled as a result and her behaviour became unruly, particularly in the last year. Her grandparents thought that coming to the UK to be an au pair would be good for her. She would be in a family environment, learning a language, gaining life experience in a safe place. Understandably, they're devastated. Rosa was their last close family member.'

Worth lowered his eyes for a moment. As much as Bernie had wanted to be on the call, she now thought she had dodged a bullet. She glanced at Anderson. His face was solemn. It clearly hadn't been easy.

Worth looked up and continued. 'Inspector Gabriel De Luca is our contact with the Florence police. He's taken DNA samples from Rosa's grandparents and an Italian lab is going to process them and send the results to our Forensics team, hopefully by the end of play tomorrow. Likewise, he's asking the family dentist for dental records. He's also going to look into Rosa generally for us.

'Right, I think that's it for now. Jane, we'll wait for DNA results before issuing anything to the press. And I've asked Tom to come in tomorrow to look at Rosa's telephone number.'

'Social media accounts too, sir,' said Bernie. 'It might be that Rosa was actively avoiding them.'

Worth glared at her. 'Yes, of course. Thank you for the reminder. Please write up your notes for HOLMES and then go home. Looking at the roster for tomorrow, I'm not expecting DC Hart or DC Parris to come in. DC Taylor and DS Allen, you're due to be in. And DS Anderson and DI Noel, you have a rest day too.'

'Sir, I'm more than happy to work my rest day and take it later next week,' Bernie said. 'The super normally lets me.'

'I am not the super. Take your rest day.'

'But, sir—'

'That's an order, DI Noel. Let's get cracking with those notes and maybe we can all have an evening at home with our friends or family.'

Bernie was fuming as everyone got up from the chairs and headed back to the main office and their desks. She was used to working rest days in the early stages of a big investigation. Now wasn't the time to reduce the team. What was Worth playing at?

Bernie glanced at her watch. It was gone five thirty. She figured she'd be in for another hour. She pulled out her phone and texted Alex.

Hoping to be home for seven. Do you want me to pick up some take-out?

Bernie started to type up her notes. She hated how victims were reduced to words on a screen. Surely Anderson and Worth had found out more about Rosa, about her character.

'Anderson.'

He turned round at his desk to face her. 'Yes, ma'am.'

'The DCI didn't give a particularly full account of his time today. Did you get more from Rosa's grandparents?'

'Some, yes.'

'Then why didn't he say so? It feels like I'm being shut out here. Being sent on house-to-house enquiries rather than talking to the family, and now told to take my rest day.'

'Look, I don't know what his motives are but I'm happy to fill you in. Do you want to go for a drink after this?'

Bernie's phone pinged. 'I promised Alex I'd go home. That's probably him now.' She opened the text, expecting to see Alex's choice of takeaway.

Sorry. Cos I hadn't heard from you I've gone out on the lash with Ali. I might stay over at Mum's. See you tomorrow?

Bernie was annoyed. She'd told Alex she'd text him but he'd gone ahead and made new plans without her. She looked at Anderson. 'Alex has gone out so I'm free after all.'

'Good. Do you want to make it dinner then? I know a great pub. It's a bit further out but I'm happy to drive. That way you can have a drink. Looks like you need one.'

Bernie laughed. 'Thanks for that.'

'Well? You can either get the low-down from me over a very nice dinner or you can watch Saturday night TV in your PJs scoffing pizza. Your choice.'

The thought of spending Saturday night alone wasn't very appealing. 'OK. You're on.'

CHAPTER 22

Bernie popped home first to shower and change. She was sticky from walking around Salisbury. She sighed when she saw that Alex hadn't stripped the bed. He'd put his dirty football kit in the washing machine with his clothes from the previous night but hadn't switched it on. He'd obviously forgotten before going out. She changed the bedding and bundled it into the machine with her suit. Even if Alex wasn't going to be there tonight, it would be nice to get into a clean bed and hopefully have a lie-in. As cross as she was with Worth for making her take a break, she looked forward to not getting up early.

A car horn tooted outside. Bernie looked out and saw Anderson. She waved to him. A quick check in the mirror and she was ready to go.

'You look... different,' he said as she got in the car.

'What? Like a normal person?' Bernie laughed. 'Actually, it's a relief to wear jeans and a top. And you were right earlier, I probably would have changed into my PJs if I'd stayed home. So where're we going?'

'Over towards Chippenham to a little hamlet. Lovely pub by a small river. It's very popular. And as lovely as the Marchant Arms is, this one is a little bit better. Although Sue still does the best chips.'

*

Anderson was right about the pub. It was definitely a step up from the Marchant Arms and worth the longer drive to reach it. A real gastropub with gastro prices. Bernie wondered if she could afford it. The pricey steaks were a definite no but there was a nice-looking chicken and ham pie on the menu.

As a late booking they'd been pushed out into the beer garden but Bernie didn't mind. There was a slight chill in the air but an outdoor heater was keeping her warm as she sat next to the little brook, waiting for Anderson to return with the drinks. She was glad he'd offered to drive as she really needed a glass of red. Worth was pushing her to the edge.

Anderson appeared a couple of minutes later.

'Sorry it took so long. They're busy tonight. Do you know what you want to eat?'

'Yes, I think so. Do you have to go back in?'

'Yes, but that's fine. I figured you really needed a drink and I wanted to make sure the wine was good first.'

'Oh, you're one of *those* people. Hang on – you tasted my wine?'

Anderson laughed. 'Not in that glass. Try it.'

Bernie took a sip. 'Wow. That's lighter than I was expecting. It's really good.'

'Italian.'

Bernie laughed. 'Well, that explains it. It's probably the wrong wine to go with it but I'm going to have the pie.'

'Good choice. I'm going to have a steak.'

'They're not cheap.'

'No, but my half of the house has come through. Got a bit of cash to splash.'

'So you've been here before then?' Bernie asked.

'Yeah, a few times. I like to get out and about on my days off. It's good to clear my head.' Anderson picked up his orange juice. 'Cheers.'

Bernie clinked her glass with his. 'Cheers. And thanks again. For suggesting this. So how was your day with old Worthless?'

Anderson's face softened a little and half a smile appeared. 'I can see why you call him that. Despite what you may think, I'm not his lackey.'

Bernie laughed. 'I'd never suggest that. You're no one's lackey. Did he say anything about me?'

Anderson's lips tightened briefly.

'Well?' she said.

'Only that you'd gone off on one yesterday evening. That you had no basis to question Rupert Fox the way you had.'

'Did he speak alone with Fox after I left?'

Bernie was sure she knew the answer already.

'Yes, for a few minutes. I saw him give Fox his card. Told him to ring if he or his wife thought of anything that might help.'

Bernie shook her head in disbelief. 'You're giving away a lot of stuff. Why are you helping me?'

'Because you stood up for me back in May with DCS Wilson. I'm returning the favour.'

Bernie half-laughed. 'So we're quits after this then.'

'Contrary to popular belief, I don't hate you, Bernie. Far from it.' Anderson sighed. 'If you're happy with Alex, then I'm happy for you. Truce?'

Bernie looked at Anderson, his eyes drifting briefly to hers. She already knew it was better to have him with her than against her. 'Truce. Go and put the food order in and then you can tell me about Rosa's grandparents.'

While they waited for their food to arrive, Anderson added more detail to what Worth had said earlier. 'Rosa was in a bad way when she arrived at her grandparents. She'd been injured in the earthquake – hit on the head. In fact they wondered if that's why she'd changed so much from being a sweet girl to aggressive teen.

Doctors ruled it out, though, and thought it more likely she was suffering from PTSD. Plus she got in with the wrong crowd. She was never actually arrested but the police did give her a couple of warnings. She was starting to settle, though, as she got older. Got a job in a hotel kitchen before deciding to work as an au pair. It was her idea.'

'Really? Worth made it sound as though it was the grandparents' idea.'

Anderson paused. 'Yes, you're right. Ah, I think they were saying that when you rang so he missed it. I'll tell him on Monday.'

Bernie was barely aware of her meal being placed before her, she was so engrossed listening to Anderson.

'Enjoy your food.'

Bernie snapped to. 'Oh. Thank you.' She waited for the waitress to leave before saying anything. 'So what was the hardest part of today?'

Anderson cut into his steak. 'I think having to tell them by FaceTime. It's hard enough giving that news as it is but when you can't be in the room,' he shook his head, 'it's the worst.'

'Maybe it's better I wasn't there, then.'

'I'd have preferred you to Worth. At least you know to be sensitive. There was one point when Rosa's grandmother was sobbing. I promised her we'd get justice for them. Her reply was heart-breaking. She said, "Justice won't bring her back." I nearly lost it at that point too and Worth wanted me to ask more questions. I told him we had to wait for her to stop crying. He just didn't get it.'

'Were you able to find out anything else helpful?'

Anderson ate a bit of his steak before answering. 'I think what's most interesting is hearing how you all described Rosa in comparison to her grandparents' description. Yes, she had gone off the rails a bit, but she didn't go clubbing that much and she was a bit of a tomboy. Loved to wear jeans and trainers. They almost laughed when I showed them the shoes. Almost. I'm guessing she hid things from them. Didn't want them to know the kind of clothes she was really wearing. Can't be easy living with your grandparents.'

Bernie gave a wry smile. 'I grew up with mine.'

'Really?'

'Yes. My mum had me at fifteen. She lived there too until I left home to go to police training at nineteen. She couldn't afford a big enough place for both of us in London. I used to wear heels that high as well. I was over six foot in them.' Bernie looked down at her food, a painful memory surfacing. 'Pops used to joke about me "tap-tapping" down the road in my "silly high-heeled shoes", but my grandmother called me "Giant". Believe it or not, that was one of her nicer names for me.'

'She sounds lovely. Personally, I prefer taller women. Much easier to kiss. Don't get a crick in my neck.'

Bernie glanced up. There was a mischievous look in Anderson's eyes. She shook her head. 'Honestly.' She was tempted to ask if Louise, his ex-wife, was tall but decided against it. 'Is there anything else? Did you ask about contact with Rosa?'

'Yes, she emailed them once a week to tell them what she was doing. She wrote about taking the girls swimming, going to the park, feeding the ducks down at the river – the usual sort of thing. She mentioned about going to Longleat too, and seeing the lions. Gabriel De Luca, the police officer – he's really good by the way, excellent English – is going to request access to her email account to see who else she was in touch with.'

Bernie nodded. 'That's good. But one thing that's bugging me – Father Adrian said Rosa was frightened for her life. That doesn't sound like the girl you're describing. So whatever's happened to scare her, must have happened here. But what? Did Rupert Fox threaten her?'

'Or, if Ryan Willis is telling the truth – the motorcyclist boyfriend?'

'Very likely. I'm sure Ryan is telling the truth but he's definitely not told us everything yet.' Bernie took another bite of her pie. 'Oh, this is getting cold. Less talking, more eating.'

Anderson gave her a warm smile that caught her by surprise. Bernie didn't want to admit it but she was having a good evening.

Although she was sure she had no room after the pie, the dessert menu was calling.

'I'm just going to pop to the loo. Be back in a minute.'

The bar and restaurant were very busy and she had to push past a few people before she saw the sign for the toilets. She headed in that direction and then suddenly stopped. A waitress nearly collided with her.

'Oh, sorry.'

The woman tutted as she walked past and placed a large plate with three tasting-size desserts on it in front of a couple. The man was facing away from her but she still recognised him. He picked up his spoon, delved into a chocolate brownie and then fed it to the young woman opposite him. Bernie felt sick and rushed quickly towards the toilets.

Thankfully, the ladies' was empty as Bernie locked the cubicle door. She sat down and tried to regain her composure. Had he seen her? Or had he been too focused on the pretty woman in front of him? Bernie swallowed down the acid rising from her stomach and finished in the toilet. She was just washing her hands when the door opened and the young woman she'd seen walked in. She smiled at Bernie.

'Are you OK? You look a bit peaky.'

Bernie nodded. 'I'm fine. Eaten a bit too much.'

'Me too. Made the mistake of going for the sharer puddings. But they're so delicious. It's all right though – my boyfriend will finish them off.' She leaned against the sink next to Bernie.

'Actually, I shouldn't complain. It's a special meal tonight. Our one month anniversary. To be honest I thought he'd forgotten but then he called me up late afternoon and said he'd booked a table.'

Bernie remembered the text she'd sent earlier in the day and the reply she'd received back.

Sorry. Cos I hadn't heard from you I've gone out on the lash with Ali. I might stay over at Mum's. See you tomorrow?

Bernie plastered a smile on her face. 'That's nice. I'm Bernie, by the way.' She scanned the young woman's face for recognition. There was none.

'I'm Alison. Ali to my friends. Anyway, I really need the loo.'

'Of course, good to meet you.'

As she opened the door, Bernie knew what she had to do and she only had a few minutes.

She slid onto the chair opposite Alex.

'Shit,' he said.

'What? The desserts? They look pretty good to me.' Bernie picked up a spare clean fork and cut a piece of sticky toffee pudding. 'Mmm.' She chewed and swallowed before speaking. 'Banana in there as well. Lovely. Definitely not shit. Oh, of course you don't mean the puddings. You mean the fact that I've caught you out. Funny how you never explained all those times you were out with "Ali" that *he* was actually a *she*. Your one month anniversary, apparently.'

Tears pricked at her eyes but she wasn't going to give Alex the satisfaction of crying in front of him. And she certainly wasn't going to beg him to stay.

'I'll have your keys back now, please. Quickly, before Ali comes back. She seems a nice girl and I don't want to embarrass her.'

Alex fumbled in his jacket pocket and pulled out some keys. 'I'm sorry.'

'Bit late for that. We'll sort out later when you can get your stuff. Bit busy looking for a murderer at the moment, as you well know.'

Bernie grabbed the keys and left quickly. As she reached the door to the garden, she looked back. Ali had just come back from the toilet and was smiling at Alex. She bit her lip and opened the door.

Anderson looked up as she approached. 'You OK? You were gone for a while. Do you still want dessert?'

'No, not really. I'm not feeling so good. I'd like to go home, if that's all right with you.'

'Sure.' Anderson stood up and touched her arm. 'I'll just pay.'

Bernie reached for her bag. 'Of course. I'll find you some cash.'

'It's fine. We'll sort it out later. I'll be back in a minute.' He pulled out his car keys and threw them to her. 'Wait in the car if you want.'

She watched as he walked to the pub door, hoping he wouldn't see Alex inside.

It seemed ages before Anderson returned but Bernie knew from looking at her watch it'd only been five minutes. He took her hand without looking at her.

'You saw him then?' she asked.

'Yes.'

'Did he see you?'

'No, I don't think so. I'm sorry, Bernie. I know how that feels.' He squeezed her hand and looked across at her. 'Let's get you home.'

CHAPTER 23

They were silent on the drive back. Bernie was doing her best to not think about Alex. Instead, Louise Anderson came to the forefront of her mind. She thought about Kerry's earlier comment that maybe it was Louise who had been the real manipulator. She knew she had to tell Anderson what his ex-wife had told her back in May.

Anderson pulled up outside her house. 'Would you like me to come in? Make you a cup of tea? I really do know how this feels,' he said.

She nodded. 'I know you do. Yes, please. There's something I'd like to talk to you about.' She fumbled in her jacket pocket for her keys and fished out Alex's. 'Oh, shit.' The key-ring had a picture of a chalk white horse that she'd bought especially for him. She sniffed.

Anderson took them from her. 'I'll open up.'

Five minutes later, Bernie had her feet tucked under her on the sofa. She picked up the hot mug of tea Anderson had made and curled her hands around it. 'Thank you.'

'No problem.' Anderson sat down in an armchair. 'What do you want to talk about? I think we can leave the case until Monday.'

She shook her head. 'Not the case. I want to explain what happened. Why I didn't turn up for lunch that time.'

Anderson got up from the armchair. 'I don't need to hear it.'

'Yes, you do. Hear me out. Back in May, I had a phone call. It was Louise, your ex-wife.' She waited to see how Anderson would react. He slowly sat back down.

'All right. What did *she* want?' he asked gruffly.

'She wanted to know where to send some of your things. Asked if she could send it direct to headquarters.'

'Bullshit. I'd asked her to send anything to my mother.'

'That's what she asked me.' Bernie drank some of her tea. 'But she also said something else. She asked me if I had any female officers on my team. She asked if I would keep an eye on them because… apparently, you're a dangerous man. You controlled and manipulated her and made her life hell.'

Anderson rubbed his face with his hands. 'And you believed her?'

'I didn't know what to believe.'

'But instead of coming to see me and ask me, you went off and threw yourself at an estate agent instead.'

'It wasn't like that. And besides, I didn't get together with Alex until after the sale was completed. Not that any of that matters now.'

'Maybe not but you still ignored my texts and phone calls. God, I wish you had come to me straight away, Bernie. Let me tell you about Louise. She's a precious little princess. What Louise wants, Louise gets – an only child used to getting her own way. I'm one of five – I grew up knowing how to share. Louise didn't. She couldn't bear to share me with anyone. Not my family and definitely not the job. Hated the long hours. I stupidly thought things would settle down after the wedding but no, she even hated our honeymoon. She wanted to go to the Maldives but I couldn't afford that and it was too far to travel. I wanted to show her where I'm from. I took her to Florence.'

'Your family's from Florence, like Rosa?'

'Originally on my mother's side, yes. I thought she would love it. I hired a car and we drove around. I took her to the mountains, to the beach, round Florence but... she hated it all. I saved up and took her to the Maldives the following year. But I still didn't get it right. Apparently I booked the wrong hotel. She wanted the five-star hotel that I couldn't afford. I was never good enough for her. If anyone is controlling and manipulative, it's Louise.'

Bernie waited. She was unsure what to think and say.

'And then, just to show me that I really wasn't good enough for her, she went and shagged a colleague of mine. And I hit him. And that's why I was transferred. I didn't sense any atmosphere when I went into the pub to pay so I'm guessing that, unlike me, you didn't lose the plot tonight.'

Bernie nodded her head. 'I was very tempted to. But Ali seemed like a nice girl and clearly had no idea who I was. Dougie, I've been thinking a lot more about that phone call. I can't help but think now that Louise was talking directly to me, warning me off you. But how did she know?'

Anderson looked at her. His face was flushed.

'Oh shit, I think I told her. But I didn't say your name. She texted me, the day after we... had that moment. She wanted to try again.' He shook his head. 'I've fallen for that one before, I wasn't going to go back. Told her I'd found someone else. Another officer who understood the pressures of the job, understood me. She must have worked it out somehow.'

Bernie felt her heart beat faster. 'You told her that? But we'd only known each other about a week at that point. And most of the time we were arguing. Still are.'

'I know. I don't normally believe in that "love at first sight" crap but with you... God, Bernie, you have no idea what you do to me.'

There was a longing in his eyes. His feelings towards her hadn't changed. Bernie put her tea down and stretched out her legs. Her body was sending out signals she recognised all too well.

'Ask me,' she said. The words were out of her mouth before she'd even realised. Maybe it was the shock of Alex's disloyalty. Or the wine. Or maybe she was finally admitting to herself her true feelings for him.

'Ask you what?'

'What I would have said, if there hadn't been a phone call from Louise.'

'And what would be the point? I should go.' He stood up.

Bernie stood too. 'Ask me.' Her brain was trying to send out frantic messages to stop but her body and her heart overruled it. She stepped closer to Anderson until she was right in front of him.

'Dougie, ask me.'

She saw him hesitate and then saw the intensity in his dark eyes.

'What would you have said?'

'Yes.' She reached out and caressed his cheek. His stubble was rough under her thumb.

'Bernie, you've had a shock tonight. This isn't a good idea.'

'Ssh. No more talking.' Her hand slipped to the back of his neck and she pulled him towards her to kiss him.

CHAPTER 24

Sunday

Bernie knew it was morning without even opening her eyes. Birds were singing and people were talking outside. Soon the bell at the church would start to toll, calling the village to the service. She squinted. Sunlight leaked out from the edges of the heavy curtains. She was lying naked on her back, the duvet wrapped tight around her. He was sleeping next to her, his breath gently rising and falling.

Her phone buzzed. She ignored it. Anderson stirred slightly next to her. Bernie held her breath. She wasn't ready for him to wake up and had no idea what to say. She had done what her body had told her to do and it had been very good. It had never been like that with Alex. She refused to feel guilty. He'd been cheating on her for a month.

The phone buzzed again. Was it a text? *God, I hope it's not Mum.* She opened her eyes. Turning slowly away from him, she reached for her phone.

CALL ME ASAP. It was from Kerry. A text in block capitals meant urgent. And if Kerry was asking Bernie to ring, it meant Kerry could receive a phone call but couldn't be seen to make one.

Worthless. Something's happened but he doesn't want me contacted.

She slid herself out from under the bedclothes and found her knickers and top on the floor. If Anderson woke up, she wanted to be at least partially dressed.

She crept into the bathroom and closed the door before making the call.

'Hello?'

'Kerry? It's me, Bernie.'

'Oh hi, can you wait just a second, please?'

The phone was muffled. Bernie looked in the bathroom mirror. Her make-up was smudged. There hadn't been an opportunity to remove it the night before. A few seconds later, Kerry was back.

'Sorry about that. I had to leave the room I was in.'

'What's going on? Have you got a suspect? Have you arrested someone? Is it Rupert Fox?'

'Whoa, slow down. Nothing like that. We're no further forward with Rosa. But you need to come in.'

'But it's my rest day and you just said you're no further forward.'

'We're not. It isn't Rosa. I'm at the Moffatts' farm.'

Bernie grabbed a facial wipe and started to clean the smudged mascara from her light brown cheeks.

'Oh no. Is Craig all right? I thought he was getting better.'

'No, not Craig. He's on the mend. It's his sister, Laura. She's missing.'

Bernie's heart sank as she pictured the sulky pre-teen girl. 'What happened?'

'She was supposed to be spending the night at a friend's house while her parents stayed late at the hospital with Craig. Her mother remembered it's church parade today for Guides so she rang the friend's mother early this morning to say she would come and pick Laura up.'

'Let me guess, the friend's mother said she wasn't there.'

'Yep. So Mrs Moffatt dialled nine nine nine and we've been put on it. And she's going loopy and asking for you.'

'Where's the DCI?'

'He's here, trying to placate her. Said there was no need for me to ring you.'

'Well, you haven't. I rang you. Do I really need to come in? Isn't she with another friend?'

She threw the wipe in the bin.

'No. The friend's mother managed to get out of her daughter that Laura had gone to meet someone. A boy she'd met online.'

'Oh shit. Check for social media accounts, probably Instagram. I'm fairly certain she has one. OK. I'll get ready and grab something to eat. I'll aim to be with you within the hour.'

'Thanks. See you soon.'

Bernie hung up. She looked at herself in the mirror. She didn't look any different but felt it. She needed to make a decision about Anderson. *But not now, Laura needs me.* She opened her bathroom cabinet, pulled out a strip of pills and found the one marked 'Sunday'. She popped it out, put some water in a plastic mug and swallowed it down.

She bent down to splash cold water over her face and flinched as two hands moved under her top and cupped her breasts.

'It's OK, it's only me,' said Anderson as he nuzzled into her neck.

'Well it's not going to be anyone else.' She reached for a towel to dry her face, trying to ignore Anderson's hands moving down both sides of her waist and him hooking his thumbs into the top of her knickers to roll them down.

'Stop,' she said.

'Really?' He kissed her neck.

'Really. I have to go to work.'

Bernie looked again at the mirror, at Anderson standing behind her, naked. She couldn't read his face. Disappointment? Confusion?

'Why? We've both got a rest day.'

'Remember Craig Moffatt, the teenager who found Rosa?'

'What about him? Oh God, he's not dead, is he? He didn't look good when we sent him off to hospital.'

'No, he's doing better but his sister, Laura, has gone missing. Apparently she went to meet someone she found online.'

'God, what is it with these girls? Why do they think these guys go after them? And why do you have to go?'

'Mrs Moffatt has asked for me specifically. Kerry said she's going mad with worry. I have to go.'

Anderson pulled his hands away. 'I see. What about us?'

Bernie turned round to face him. 'You said last night you told Louise you'd found someone who understood your job and the hours you have to work. I need the same.'

'Point taken. But…' He brought his hands up to hold her face and kissed her. 'I don't want to wait another five months. You have to decide what you want.'

Bernie looked into his eyes and saw concern there. Anderson was more vulnerable than he liked to admit to. 'I know.'

CHAPTER 25

DCI Worth glowered at Bernie. She didn't bother to return his stare and instead kept her eyes fixed on Laura's mother.

'I've tried all her friends, well, all the ones I know about. She went to secondary last year and it's not the same as when they're in primary. You don't get to know the friends and their families.'

'Mrs Moffatt…'

'Please, call me Caroline.'

'Caroline, do you know what social media Laura has, other than Instagram? Or are there any websites or games that she goes on? Ones that allow you to chat with other people online?'

Caroline Moffatt slowly shook her head. Her eyes were red-rimmed. Kerry had said she'd spent the last couple of hours crying but now her face was dry, as though she had run out of tears.

'I don't know. I said she could have Instagram but she wasn't to follow anyone she didn't know.'

Bernie looked across at Kerry. 'I'm assuming that her phone—'

'Has been checked, yes, DI Noel, we have done that. It's not here so we assume she took it with her. It's switched off,' Worth cut in.

Bernie couldn't ignore him any longer. 'Just re-checking all avenues, sir.'

Worth gave a long sigh. 'A word outside, please.'

Bernie placed her hand gently on Caroline's arm. 'I'll be back in a few moments.'

Worth was standing by the open front door. Threatening black clouds were overhead, just waiting to deluge them.

'It really wasn't necessary for you to give up your rest day.'

'With all respect, sir—'

Worth raised his hand, indicating Bernie to stop talking. 'But since you are here, it makes sense for you to continue with this investigation. You already know the family. So, you will carry on here with DS Allen and I will go back to headquarters and deal with the murder case.'

It took Bernie a moment to understand what Worth was saying.

'Wait a moment, you're kicking me off the Rosa Conti investigation?'

'Of course. You can't dedicate yourself to both.'

'But, sir—'

'Bernie, you've given up your Sunday lie-in to take control of this so, by all means, take control. Keep me informed.'

Worth started to walk away.

'If we haven't found her by tomorrow, I'm going to need Anderson as FLO.'

DCI Worth turned back. 'Oh, I think I can put DS Anderson to much better use, don't you? But I agree that the Moffatts need support. Why don't you contact the local vicar and his wife? Isn't that what you did when Molly Reynolds went missing?'

Bernie watched as her senior officer sauntered away to his car. She was aware Kerry had joined her.

'Did he just kick you off a murder case?' she asked.

'Yes, he bloody well did. And you too.'

Bernie opened the door to Laura's room. At first glance, it seemed like a normal almost-teenager's room with posters of pop groups on the wall and a dressing table strewn with used cotton wool balls, make-up and hairbands. The duvet cover had bright white, prancing unicorns on a pink background and Laura's school bag lay on top of it, her exercise books spilling out.

'Do we know if she took clothes with her?' she asked Kerry.

'Yes. She seems to have taken a few things with her, including clothes and toiletries. Her hairbrush has gone, as well as her toothbrush.'

'Damn. They're our usual DNA checkers. I see now why old Worthless hasn't issued the Child Rescue Alert. She planned to go. Shit.'

'Do we need to take her bedding?'

'We're going to have to now. For DNA if nothing else. And maybe those used cotton wool balls as well. Has the rest of the farm been searched?'

'First thing I did when I got here.' Kerry wrinkled her nose. 'The pigsty stank. Needs cleaning out.'

'You offering?'

'No, I am not. I can't tell you how uncomfortable I felt being around those pigs knowing what will happen to them.' Kerry shuddered.

'So, we've done what we can here for now. Let's get Forensics over to check out this room.' Bernie glanced at her watch. It was nearly eleven. She'd left Anderson eating breakfast and had given him Alex's keys to lock up and then put back through the door. Far from being the awkward morning-after, it had seemed natural to have him there. He'd even offered to come in as well.

'Might be better if you don't,' she'd said. 'Kerry will wonder how you know and she's better than a sniffer dog when it comes to sussing out secrets.'

'Earth to Bernie.'

She snapped to. 'What?'

'You were miles away,' said Kerry. 'And you had a smile on your face. I can guess what you were up to last night.' She winked. 'Anyway, I asked you if we should go and see this friend of Laura's. Her name's Daisy.'

'Yeah. That seems like a good idea. I'll just check if anyone can come and stay with Caroline first. Then we can go.'

Bernie didn't want to admit it but Worth's idea of Anna Bentley, the vicar's wife, helping out was actually a good one and it turned out she wasn't averse to missing her husband's sermon when Bernie called her.

'I've heard it once already when he was practising. Trust me, I don't need to hear it again.'

Bernie smiled. 'Thanks. We have to head off now but we'll come back later.'

Daisy lived in Bishop Cannings, a village north-east of Devizes with a mixture of chocolate box thatched cottages and more modern housing. Bernie was surprised to see that Daisy's family lived in one of the thatched cottages. It was normally retired city dwellers who bought those.

'Very quaint,' she said.

'Yeah, look out for low beams. Don't want you knocking yourself out.'

Bernie grinned. 'You won't have that problem.'

'Oi.'

'You started it. Come on. Hopefully Daisy can tell us where Laura is and then I can go home for the rest of the day. What's their surname?'

'Flint.'

A woman with bright red hair opened the door. Bernie wondered if it was dyed until she spotted a girl behind her with the same colouring.

'Mrs Flint? I'm DI Noel and this is DS Allen from Wiltshire Police. I believe Caroline Moffatt called you this morning about her daughter. Could we come in and ask some questions please?'

The woman looked worried. 'She hasn't turned up then?'

'No, not yet.'

'Come through. Mind the beams,' she said over her shoulder, leading them into the lounge.

Kerry smirked.

'Right, kids, out of here, please.'

Mrs Flint turned off the television and ushered two young boys out.

'I was watching that.'

'You can watch it later. Daisy and I need to have a chat with these nice ladies.'

The younger boy, aged about five, looked at Kerry and sniffed. 'You smell like a pig.'

'Aaron! Say sorry immediately.'

'But she does. Really.'

'Upstairs to your room – now.' Mrs Flint turned to Kerry. 'I'm so sorry. I don't know where he got that from.'

Kerry smiled. 'Actually, the Moffatts have a pig farm and I was searching there earlier, so he might be stating a fact rather than being rude. Don't worry.'

Daisy stood in the doorway. Her mother beckoned her in.

'Please sit down, officers. Oh, just move the clothes and the toys. Sorry. It's a bit of a mess in here.'

Bernie glanced around the lounge. It was a hotchpotch of furniture with nothing matching at all. Toys were scattered around the room but it was lovely to see in comparison to the stark neatness of Harriet Fox's house. 'Don't worry. We won't take up too much of your time.'

Kerry pulled out her notebook and pen.

'So, Daisy,' said Bernie. 'What did Laura say to you?'

Daisy lowered her eyes and twisted a strand of her long red hair round her finger. 'Um. She messaged me Friday afternoon and asked if I could cover for her. Say she was staying the night at my house.'

'Did she tell you why?'

The hair twisting continued. 'Said she was meeting a…' Daisy mumbled.

'Speak up, Daisy! The police officers can't hear you.' Mrs Flint smiled apologetically.

'She was meeting a boy.'

'Do you know where?'

Daisy shook her head quickly. Too quickly. Bernie thought she knew more but probably didn't want to say with her mother present – and as Daisy was a minor, she couldn't ask Mrs Flint to leave. *So frustrating.*

'Has Laura mentioned this boy before?'

'Not to me.'

'But she might have done to other friends?'

Daisy shrugged. 'Don't know.' She kept her eyes down.

Bernie glanced at Kerry. They were getting nowhere. 'OK, Daisy, Mrs Flint. We'll leave it there for now. If you remember anything else or if Laura gets in contact with you, then please ring us.' Bernie handed a card over.

'You'll let us know if Laura comes home.'

'Yes, of course, Mrs Flint. You can let your boys come back in now.'

As they left, Daisy's little brother followed them outside. 'I'm really sorry for what I said.' He looked sheepishly at Kerry.

'That's all right. I was at a pig farm earlier so I do pong.'

He pointed to Bernie's car. 'If you're police, why haven't you got a real police car?'

'Not a real police car?' Kerry pretended to look shocked. 'We have lights. And a siren. Do you want to see?'

'Yeah!'

Mrs Flint hurried after her son as he followed Kerry. 'Don't touch anything, Aaron.'

Bernie took the opportunity to speak to Daisy quietly. 'I know you might not want to say things in front of your mum. While she's distracted, is there anything else you want to tell me?'

Daisy shook her head.

Bernie wasn't convinced. 'OK. You can send me a text if you remember anything. Your mum has the card.'

The noise of the siren ripped through the air, the lights flashing too.

'So, Aaron, is that good enough for you now?' Bernie asked.

His eyes lit up. 'Can we go for a drive? Please.' He was in the driver's seat, turning the steering wheel.

Bernie shook her head. 'Not today. We have to go back to work now. Maybe another time. Perhaps we could even come to your school one day and do a talk.'

'Hooray!'

'Come on, Aaron. We need to let the officers go now. Thank you.'

'No problem, Mrs Flint.'

Kerry turned off the lights and the siren and Bernie got into the car. They waved to Aaron and the rest of the family as they drove away.

'You're going to make me do that talk, aren't you?' Kerry said.

'Yep. You let a five-year-old get in my car with his sticky fingers.' Bernie wiped her right hand on her trousers.

CHAPTER 26

'Matt, I need your help with something.'

DC Matt Taylor turned round at his desk. 'Sorry, ma'am. DCI Worth has given me lots to do. Not sure I'm going to have time.'

'What?' Bernie was exasperated. 'I need you to put out some social media alerts for Laura Moffatt.'

'I'll do it,' said Kerry.

'Oh no, you won't.' Matt shook his head. 'Give me the info.'

'What's wrong with me doing it?'

'Because last time you went way over the 280 character limit on Twitter and still missed out some info.'

'Oh yeah. I forgot that.' Kerry laughed.

'Thanks, Matt. Kerry, let's work out what we need to do next.' Kerry sat down next to Bernie.

'Right, plan of action. Lucy has texted to say she's at the Moffatts' so we know we have Forensics under control. Matt will deal with social media. If Tom's around I'd like him to look at Laura's Instagram account.'

Matt called over his shoulder. 'He's in but dealing with the Rosa Conti case. He's looking at her phone number and trying to get access to her calls and messages.'

Bernie sighed. 'Worth definitely won't free him up then. I'm guessing Jane's not in today either.' She thought for a moment. 'I'd still like to issue the Child Rescue Alert but I'll have to go through

Worth to get it.' She shook her head. 'We're going to need more before he agrees to it. Kerry, you said you searched the farm. Did you search the woods?'

'No. There's no reason to believe she went into the woods. Far more likely she headed to the main road to either meet someone or get a bus.'

'I think we have to look there anyway just to rule it out.' Bernie looked at her watch. 'It's just coming up to one o'clock. We'll get the social media alerts sorted out and, Kerry, maybe you can start looking at Laura's Instagram. Look for any clues. I'm going to chat with Tom to see if he can request full access. We need to get into her direct messages.'

Bernie headed down to the basement. The Digital Media Investigation team was newly established and temporarily housed in the only free space at headquarters. As it was a Sunday, only Tom was in.

'Afternoon, Tom.'

He looked up from his computer. 'Oh, hi, ma'am. I didn't think you were in today.'

'I wasn't supposed to be. I've come in for the Laura Moffatt case.'

'Oh yes. I looked at her mobile number earlier. It's switched off but I've applied to the phone company for the data. Should get that through tomorrow.'

Bernie pulled a chair up next to him. 'We're going to need access to her Instagram account as well. Kerry found it just before I came down to you.'

Tom sucked in his lips. 'That's going to be tricky. We need pretty high authority to get a warrant. Be much easier if the family have some idea about the password.'

'Mother says she doesn't know. Don't suppose there's any other magic you can weave?'

'Hack? Are you asking me to break the law, ma'am?' Tom grinned. 'In theory, yes, I can probably get in fairly easily. But in reality, no. Any evidence we did gain would be inadmissible in court. I'll let you know when I hear from the phone company. Maybe we'll get something from that.'

'OK.' Bernie pointed to the computer monitor. 'Are you working on Rosa's number now?'

Tom nodded. 'Yes. Although I'm going to need DS Anderson's help tomorrow. What I've found out so far is that she had the SIM-only account here in the UK but I now know the security IMEI handset number and that shows me another telephone number in Italy. So I'll need him to write an email for me so we can ask for her data. I could use Google translate but there are some specific things I want to ask for and I'd rather get the Italian right.'

'Good idea. Or it might be easier for Anderson to ring the Italian police and ask them to do it. Talk to him tomorrow and see what he thinks. What about social media accounts?'

'That's my next job. I've already done a quick search and there are a hell of a lot of Rosa Contis. Having the photo will help though. I'll let you know if I find anything.'

Bernie stood up. 'Best to send it through straight to DCI Worth. I'm the lead on the Laura Moffatt case now.'

'Oh right. Wait a minute. Should I have told you that stuff about Rosa?'

'Probably not.' Bernie winked. 'But thanks anyway.'

'Kerry, got anything for me?'

She looked up from her monitor. 'I can see who Laura's following and I'm just starting to work my way through it. Could Tom help at all?'

'Not yet. He'll need a warrant for Instagram and he's not hopeful about it. Thinks it would be better to ask the family again.

So stop that for the moment. Let's go back to Caroline Moffatt. Maybe she'll remember something about her daughter's password now. And we can check out the woods and the track. I know you didn't go there this morning but did you go out there at all for the search after Rosa was found?'

Kerry shook her head. 'No. I was working here, going through the Missing Persons files.'

'OK. Let's see what your eagle eyes can pick up.'

CHAPTER 27

Caroline Moffatt was asleep when they arrived.

'She fell asleep about half an hour ago. I'd rather not wake her unless it's important,' said Anna. 'She's in such a state.'

'No, it's fine. Thank you for looking after her. We're going to search the woods and then we'll come back later.'

Bernie led the way over the field and into the woods as she had done with Worth and Anderson only a few days before. They trampled through undergrowth before spotting the inner cordon tape. Bernie stopped and pointed.

'Over there, by that small mound of earth, that's where Rosa was.'

Kerry shook her head and blew slowly out of her mouth. 'But she wasn't buried.'

'No, she was on top of the earth, with some leaves covering her.'

Bernie glanced up at the trees. The leaves appeared to be changing colour rapidly now as autumn advanced. The earlier storm clouds had moved away so thankfully the ground wasn't muddy.

'And this track where the motorbike races took place, where's that?'

'Follow me.'

Bernie trudged through the brambles until they found a narrow pathway. They hadn't gone far when Kerry stopped.

'What's that smell?' she said.

'What smell?'

'Something really rank. Something very dead.'

'Oh God,' said Bernie. 'It can't be her.'

Kerry shook her head. 'No, this isn't recent. It smells cheesy.' She veered off the path, sniffing as she went.

'I don't know why we use cadaver dogs when we have you,' said Bernie. 'I'm going to nickname you "bloodhound" after this.'

She followed Kerry into the tangle of bushes and brambles. After a few minutes, Kerry stopped and pointed at a black and white mound.

'Look, over there. Something very dead.'

Bernie reached for her phone to take photos.

'It's a badger, I think,' said Kerry. 'There must be a sett around here. It's probably worth speaking to Rural Crime.'

'Why?'

'Badger baiters. They dig out the setts, take the badgers and get them to fight with dogs. Spectators gamble on how well the dogs will do. It's horrendously cruel to the badgers, the dogs too. This badger may have died of natural causes but probably worth checking it out. Looking at the state of it, it's been here longer than the body.'

'That would explain why the body decomposed so quickly.' Bernie looked over her shoulder. 'The blow flies were already in the wood. They must have found her very quickly, especially given how warm it was then. Could there be a connection with our mystery biker?'

'You never know. Something to consider. Rural Crime will be able to tell us more. Or, rather, DCI Worth, since we're off the case.'

'I'm sorry, Kerry. It's all my fault.' Bernie paused. 'Why wasn't this badger found during the search of the area?'

Kerry shrugged. 'Don't know but you still had the smell of the body and, by all accounts, that was pretty bad. It might have all just mingled together.'

'But if this wasn't found, what else has been missed? Come on. Let's go to the track and see what your fresh eyes spot. This is why I send you out on the searches normally.'

They made their way back to the path, taking photos to help Rural Crime find the badger later, then carried on through the woods and climbed over the metal gate that separated the woods from the track.

Bernie pointed to the left. 'That way leads back to the main road and it's where Ryan Willis and his mates were racing.' She pointed to the right. 'That way is just a bridle path really, and there's a T-junction at the top. There are lots of tyre tracks. Motorcycles or bikes. Won't be easy to isolate them.'

Kerry looked both ways. 'Hmm, let's go to the right.'

Steep banks either side of the track, with trees overhanging, created a tunnel effect. A slight breeze rustled through the copper and amber leaves. Bernie could hear a knocking sound.

'What's that?'

'A woodpecker. God, Bernie, you're such a townie.'

'Says the girl from Manchester.'

'Ha! True. But I was already visiting Debs here regularly before finally making the move last year. I'm slowly becoming a country girl.'

They continued uphill, the track steeper than Bernie first thought, becoming darker and more tunnel-like as steep banks rose higher on either side. She looked down at the ground. As well as the mud, there were bits of old red brick and stones, suggesting it was once a more substantial lane.

'Look up, Bernie. This is amazing. And very eerie.'

Bernie raised her eyes and saw trees perched precariously on the top of the sides of the track, their tree roots visible in the banks.

'I'm guessing it's some kind of sandstone,' said Kerry, 'so it's eroding.' She turned round slowly. 'This is stunning. Can't believe I've never been up here before.'

Bernie nodded. 'Me neither. A real shame it's such a horrible case that's brought us here. I don't think I'm ever going to forget when I first saw her.'

A sound of a dog barking close by interrupted their conversation. Bernie didn't think it was the Moffatts' dog. This one was less aggressive.

'Has this path been closed off?' said Kerry.

'It should have been.'

A chocolate Labrador approached them, nose to the ground, a woman in her early sixties holding a lead a few steps behind.

'Good afternoon,' said Bernie. She reached into her jacket for her warrant card.

'Afternoon,' replied the woman.

Bernie showed her warrant. 'I'm Detective Inspector Noel. This pathway has been closed off for an investigation.'

'Oh, I'm so sorry, I didn't know. There wasn't anything up at the top saying so.'

'The tape has probably come loose,' said Kerry. 'I'll go and have a quick look.' She jogged off up the path.

'Can I ask if you walk here a lot?' Bernie noted the woman's muddy wellies and waterproof jacket.

'A few times a week.'

'And what about in the last week and a half?'

The woman shook her head. 'Afraid not. I've been away and this is our first walk here in about two weeks. Sorry I can't help you more. You'll be gone before it gets dark, won't you?' She lowered her voice. 'This lane is haunted, you know.'

Bernie raised her eyebrows. 'Really?'

'Oh yes. A few hundred years ago, Seymour Wroughton, the owner of the big house that used to be here, drove his carriage down this lane too quickly and it overturned. He broke his neck. At night, especially on Sundays, you can hear the sound of the horses' hooves and their whinnying. And a man screaming. We know this place as Wroughton's Folly now but it also used to be called Maggots Wood.'

Bernie suppressed a giggle but the woman seemed in earnest. 'Why Sundays in particular?'

'Because it happened on a Sunday. So if you don't mind, I'll be on my way.'

'Please carry on. We'll leave very soon. Thanks for the warning.'

Bernie watched as the woman whistled to her dog and then walked away, trying to decide if she was a crackpot or not. She heard Kerry jogging back towards her.

'Well?'

Kerry stopped to catch her breath. 'Yes, the tape was down. I've tied it back up now.' She nodded at the woman. 'Anything useful?'

'No, not really. She's been away for a couple of weeks. Although there was one thing.'

'Oh yes?'

'Apparently this lane is haunted.'

'I'm not surprised. There are a lot of ghost stories in Wiltshire – not that I believe them. Anyway, there's something I want to show you. It's just up here on the right. No one has mentioned this at all in the search reports.'

They walked further up the track. More trees looked as though they were about to slide down onto the path. Rich green ferns peppered the lower part of the banks. Anderson had been right. There was no litter around and nothing they could tie to either Rosa or Laura.

'Here,' said Kerry.

'What am I looking at?'

Kerry sighed. 'You're always looking down. Look up.'

Bernie surveyed the trees and their tangled roots. Her eyes widened.

'There's a hole in the bank up there.'

'Follow your eyes down.'

Bernie smiled. 'There's a rope. I've not heard anything about this.'

'No, me neither. I think I'd better take a look.' Kerry found the end of the rope and gave it a little tug. 'Seems to be holding firm.'

'Be careful.'

Going hand over hand on the rope, Kerry climbed slowly but steadily up the bank. Within a few moments, she had reached the entrance to a largish hole. She found a foothold and let go of the rope with one hand. She reached into her jacket pocket and pulled out her phone. A light came on and Kerry looked intently into the darkness of the hole. After about thirty seconds, she looked down at Bernie and smiled.

'Wow. This is a proper small cave. I need a better torch but we've definitely got something up here.'

'What?'

'Well, it's a bit hard to tell but it looks suspiciously like a jacket and a motorbike helmet to me. And possibly a few bats too.'

CHAPTER 28

'I was just about to go home for a late roast lunch. What's so important, Detective Inspector Noel?'

Even with slightly dodgy reception, Bernie could hear impatience in DCI Worth's voice. She imagined him standing in his office, coat on and ready to leave. Although knocking off at close to four p.m. on Sunday wasn't really the right thing to do.

'DS Allen and I thought we ought to check the woods near the Moffatt house, just in case Laura was hiding out there.'

'Really? You think she would go to the woods where her brother found a body?'

'Need to look at all avenues, sir. Anyway, we're on the track on the other side of the woods, where we think the motorbikes were, and Kerry has found something. There's a large hole near the top of a steep bank. There's something inside it.'

Bernie winked at Kerry. She loved stringing her senior officer along.

'Well, spit it out.'

'It's very dark in there but Kerry's fairly certain she can see some clothing in the hole. It could be the dead girl's missing motorbike jacket and helmet.'

'Good God. What? But nothing of interest was found on that track so I decided there was no point continuing.' Worth sounded flustered.

Did he deliberately curtail the search?

'I wouldn't have spotted it either, sir. That's why I always put Kerry on search duty. She sees things no one else does. There's a rope that helps you get up to it. Unless you look carefully, you wouldn't notice it as it's lying next to some of the exposed tree roots. I was wondering if you could send Rural Crime out to us. They have a four-by-four that will get up that bumpy lane by the Willis's farm. It'll be quicker than one of us going back to the Moffatts' and driving the car round.'

'Does it have to be done now? Couldn't we leave it until the morning?'

'We could but we'd have to put an officer here overnight to secure the scene.'

Worth sighed. Bernie knew he was weighing up the cost of taking an officer off main patrol.

'All right, but you can ring them yourself, surely.'

'Except it's not my case any more, is it, sir?'

Kerry had a smirk on her face.

'I mean, really, you should come down and deal with this but I'm happy to secure any evidence for you, if you like,' said Bernie. She knew he was squirming on the other end of the phone.

'Well, I have just told my wife that I'm on my way home.' He sighed. 'It might be better if you deal with this for now. I'll call Rural Crime for you.'

Bernie mouthed 'yes!' to Kerry. 'Of course, sir, I'm happy to help.' She ended the call.

'Oh God.' She laughed. 'It must have killed him to let me do this but he was about to head home. He really didn't want to miss his roast.'

The sun was obscured by clouds and the temperature lowered.

'I hope they get here soon,' said Bernie. 'Don't want to meet the ghost.'

'You don't believe in all that crap, do you?'

'Crap? I'll have you know that the ghost train's my favourite ride at the funfair!' She laughed. 'Nah. But it does feel a bit creepy down here.'

They lapsed into silence as they waited. Kerry's phone pinged.

'Rural Crime should be here in about ten to fifteen minutes. I just need to confirm location,' she said.

Bernie rubbed her arms. 'It's starting to get cold now.'

'It is. Hopefully they won't be too long. Anyway, what did you get up to last night?'

Bernie sighed. On the one hand she didn't want to say anything but on the other she had to talk to someone and there was no one better than Kerry. 'I did something really stupid.'

'Oh shit, Bernie. What?'

'I slept with Anderson.'

'What? How? Where was Alex?'

Bernie shook her head. 'You know Alex has this friend called Ali he goes drinking with.'

'Yeah, I think you've mentioned him.'

'*Her.* Turns out Ali stands for Alison rather than Alistair. And they just happened to be in the pub that Dougie and I were in last night. It's one I've not been to before.'

'OK. Back up. Why were you and Anderson in a pub last night? And don't think I haven't noticed that you just called him Dougie.'

'We went out to dinner to discuss the case. We were seated outside and I went in to use the loo. And that's when I saw Alex with this woman. He was feeding her dessert. Then I met her in the toilets and she said it was her one month anniversary with her boyfriend.'

'One month? God. I understand you were hurt but that doesn't mean you then sleep with Anderson. Why did you do it?'

'I don't really know... No, that's not true, I do know. There's just something about that man that drives me crazy. I told him about

Louise calling me so he explained their relationship and you were right. It was the other way round – she was the controlling one.'

'Oh, Bernie. Who started it? You or him?'

Bernie looked down at her feet and nudged a leaf. She didn't want to face Kerry at that moment. 'Me.'

'And did you do that because you wanted to get back at Alex or because you have genuine feelings for Anderson?'

Bernie sniffed. 'I'm not sure. I was so angry with Alex but it didn't feel like revenge. It actually felt really natural. Like it was meant to be.'

'Now you sound like a greetings card. Do you want to be with Anderson?'

Bernie glanced up but kept her eyes away from Kerry. The clouds were darkening. She almost wished the ghost driving his horse and carriage down the track would turn up, just so she didn't have to answer the question.

'Bernie?'

'God, Kerry, I don't know. Maybe.'

Kerry placed a hand on Bernie's arm. 'You need to make a decision.'

Bernie nodded. 'I will, just… not yet. I need to find Laura and finish the case and, despite what Worth says, I need to find Rosa's killer too.'

'Oh, Bernie, there's always a case to finish with you. And what about Anderson? How does he feel?'

'I'm pretty certain he wants to be with me. I'm wondering if I can cope with his intensity though.' Bernie heard the low rumble of an approaching car. 'Think the cavalry has arrived.'

'Yeah. I'll go down and get them,' said Kerry. 'We'll carry this conversation on another time.'

Bernie watched as Kerry disappeared down the track. The trees crouched over her, the branches whispered in the breeze. A shiver ran down Bernie's spine. At that moment, she could believe the track was haunted. The thought of hitching a ride on a runaway carriage seemed like a good idea.

CHAPTER 29

Bernie jolted around in her seat in the Rural Crime police vehicle as they drove down the bumpy track back to the main road.

'God, this is bad,' she said to Kerry. 'How on earth do those guys race their motorbikes along it?'

'They must know it well,' Kerry answered.

Bernie thought for a moment. *How could a stranger just turn up and beat them all?* 'I think I might have to speak to Ryan Willis again. It doesn't make sense that a person new to the area could win all the races if he didn't know the lane. So either he's a local or he had opportunity to practise somehow. And the cave? How would someone new to the area know about that? I don't think Ryan has told me everything. Maybe we should formally take him in.'

'Bernie, you're off the case, remember? You need to concentrate on Laura Moffatt now.'

'It's not like you to give up on something.'

'No, but it's too late to save Rosa. We could still find Laura though.'

Bernie sighed. She glanced at her watch. It was almost six p.m. It had taken longer to secure the evidence than she thought it would. Fortunately, the officer from Rural Crime had everything that was needed for Kerry to climb safely up into the cave. Bernie was glad Kerry had gone up – the thought of going into a small, dark space brought her out in goose bumps. But Kerry had been right and they now had one black leather jacket and one black motorcycle helmet, bagged, ready for Forensics. Bernie didn't expect she would get a thank you from Worthless but she hoped Kerry would get a mention at least.

The police vehicle continued to lurch down the track.

'Ma'am,' said the Rural Crime officer, 'I couldn't help but overhear what you just said about the motorbike racing.'

'Do you know about it?' asked Bernie.

'A little bit. There was a complaint a few months ago about the noise. I had a little chat with Ryan Willis. He agreed to cut it back. As far as I could tell, it's just a few local lads having a race and small amounts of cash passed between them. It didn't seem worth it to take it any further.'

'Bit of a shame you didn't,' said Kerry.

Bernie nudged her.

'What?'

'You know what.' Bernie knew it wasn't fair to blame the officer. 'Do you know of anyone else using the lane?' she asked.

'I guess you mean for illegal purposes. There was a problem with badger baiting a while back.'

'Oh yes, we saw a dead badger in the woods. We took photos of where it is.'

'Really? If you could send them to me that would be great. We arrested most of the people involved so hopefully this one's just a natural death. Although thinking about it, we missed a couple of lads when we raided the baiting. They were on a motorcycle but the passenger took his helmet off so we had to stop the pursuit. Too dangerous to continue. Can't risk them crashing if one of them isn't wearing a helmet.'

'Did you get the registration?'

'Covered in mud.'

Bernie remembered what Ryan had told her about the motorbike – the registration plate was dirty. Could the two be connected?

They finally reached the top of the lane.

'Thank God for that,' said Bernie.

'Where to now, ma'am?'

'Turn right. We need to go back to the Moffatts' farm for my car.' Bernie looked across at Kerry. 'Probably ought to have a check on Mrs Moffatt as well. See if she's remembered anything for Laura's password.'

Bernie's phone buzzed. She pulled it out of her pocket. It was a text from a number she didn't recognise.

Laura said she was going to Salisbury.

Bernie closed her eyes. She wished Daisy had told her this earlier. But if she had, they would have missed out on finding the motorcycle helmet and jacket.

As they approached the Moffatts' house, Bernie recognised the vicar's car outside. Paul Bentley had joined his wife.

Anna opened the front door. 'Is there any news?'

'No, I'm afraid not. We came back to check up on Mrs Moffatt and collect my car.'

Kerry popped her head round Bernie. 'Hello, Anna.'

'Hi, Kerry.'

'We need to speak to Caroline,' Bernie said.

'Of course, come in.'

Caroline Moffatt was curled up on the sofa her son Craig had been on just a few days before. Paul Bentley looked up expectantly as they walked in. Bernie shook her head and mouthed 'no news'.

Caroline barely raised her head. Bernie knew from experience that parents handled this situation in lots of different ways and Caroline Moffatt was heading downhill fast. There were questions Bernie wanted to ask about Laura's password and the motorbikes

– in particular, had Caroline made the complaint about the noise? She beckoned Paul Bentley over.

She whispered, 'Does she need a doctor?'

Caroline was clearly in no state to be answering questions.

Paul kept his voice low. 'Not at the moment. She went a bit hysterical when I first arrived. She thought I was bringing bad news but we managed to calm her down. It doesn't help that John has to stay with Craig at the hospital in Salisbury. He was about to leave when Craig was sick again. They haven't told him – they don't want to make him worse.'

Bernie thought for a moment. 'I understand that but I'm wondering if Craig knows anything that might help. Her password, for one. Kerry was able to see Laura's Instagram account but we really need to get into her DMs. We've heard she was supposed to be meeting someone she connected with online. That news hasn't been put out to the press yet. It will be in the morning though.'

Bernie wasn't looking forward to her chat with Jane Clackett. She looked again at Caroline. Her eyes were starting to droop.

'Will you and Anna stay until Mr Moffatt gets back?'

Paul nodded. 'Yes, our diaries are fairly clear for the next few days. We're at your disposal.'

Bernie placed her hand on Paul's arm. 'Thank you. We ought to make you honorary police officers.'

'Funny you should say that. I was thinking about setting up a Street Pastors team for Devizes for Friday and Saturday nights. Thought it might benefit the local police if there were a few extra people out on the streets willing to help those in trouble.'

'Well, thankfully, it's not too hairy in Devizes, although it's a good idea. There's more need for it in the larger towns, like Swindon, Trowbridge and Salisbury.'

'I know some of the people involved in Salisbury. That's where I got the idea from.'

A thought triggered in Bernie's mind. 'Do you have a contact number for them?'

'Well, yes, I do. Why?'

Bernie looked across at Kerry and then back at Paul. 'I'm really trusting you with this information, Paul.'

The vicar nodded. 'You know you can trust me, Bernie.'

'One of Laura's friends said she was going to meet this man in Salisbury. Maybe, just maybe, one of those street pastors saw Laura.'

And maybe Rosa too.

By the time Bernie had dropped Kerry home, it was after eight p.m. MCIT had been deserted when they'd logged in the evidence Kerry had found. Both Matt and Tom had sent emails detailing what they had done so far. The social media alerts had received little attention due to it being a Sunday, and the phone companies would be in touch on Monday. Bernie updated the alerts to mention possible location and Kerry emailed Laura's photo to the CCTV team in Salisbury and let them know they'd be there in the morning. Bernie had also emailed Phyl Bridger to let her know about the badger they'd found. She hadn't been sure if it was relevant or not but better to let Phyl be the judge of that.

They had both wanted to stay longer but there was little more that could be done.

'We might as well go home and get some sleep. Come back to this fresh in the morning,' said Bernie.

She opened her front door and immediately smelled her clean washing. Had she hung it up before she left? She didn't think she had. Which could only mean one thing – Anderson had done it. She wasn't too sure how she felt about that.

He'd left her a note on the kitchen table.

Saw your suit in the machine and thought you might need it for the morning.

It was sweet of him to think of her. Also hanging up were Alex's football kit and the clothes he'd claimed he got covered in beer. Far more likely he was washing off Ali's perfume. Same with the shower.

She sat at the little kitchen table and remembered the day she moved into the cottage back in August. Alex had turned up with a bottle of champagne that they had downed far too quickly and, in a drunken haze, had ended up in bed. It should have stopped there. They got on OK but had little in common. Maybe that's why Alex had looked elsewhere.

And then there was Anderson. Kerry was right. Alex's infidelity shouldn't have sent her into someone else's arms. But it had and she needed to make a decision. Now wasn't the time though. She focused on Rosa and Laura. They needed her more, which meant getting some sleep. Bernie made a cup of tea. Grabbing some biscuits, she headed up to bed.

CHAPTER 30

Monday

'Right. Let's get cracking on this and bring Laura Moffatt home,' Bernie said to Kerry.

'You're chipper this morning. Did you get some good sleep?'

'Surprisingly, yes.'

Bernie looked round the office. DCs Matt Taylor and Mick Parris were working at their computers. Despite only being in MCIT for a few days, Mick's desk was already cluttered and Bernie wondered if his house was the same. Alice Hart hadn't yet turned up and Worth was in his own office. Anderson was downstairs with Tom.

'Right,' Bernie said, 'first priority is to check out CCTV in Salisbury, especially near the bus stops in the town centre. That's the only way she could have got there.'

'Unless he picked her up along the way.'

'There is that. But in the meantime, if you can get in touch with the guys over at the CCTV centre and let them know we'll be there soon and then contact this street pastor Paul Bentley told me about.' Bernie pulled out her phone and jotted down the contact details Paul had sent. 'I'll go and deal with *Ms Clackett* in regards to media coverage. Laura's been missing two nights now. We have to escalate this. I don't care what old Worthless says.'

'I thought you were getting on better these days with Jane?'

Bernie screwed up her face. 'Yeah, but you never know when she's going to turn back into a vampire.'

Bernie knocked on Jane's office door and waited. She knew to her cost that Jane hated people barging in on her.

'Come in… Oh, Bernie. Sit down. What can I do for you?'

Bernie resisted the urge to pinch herself. It was only recently that Jane had started being nice to her. She still wasn't quite used to it.

'I've come because of the missing girl, Laura Moffatt. It was her brother who found the body in the woods.'

'Oh God, yes. I thought the surname was familiar.' Jane shook her head. Her sleek black bob swished with it. 'Such a nasty business. And how awful for this family. Right, so what do you want me to do?'

'Well,' said Bernie, 'not much has been done so far. Alerts have gone out on social media and some news websites have picked it up. I think we need to expand this now. She did take clothes and toiletries with her so we know she meant to go, rather than it initially being an abduction. However, it's always possible that it's an abduction now. She may want to leave and isn't able to do so or…'

'Or she's dead.' Jane's lips were a tight, red line. 'We have to consider that, Bernie.'

Bernie closed her eyes and sighed. 'I know. But I can't think of her in that way yet. Kerry and I are going to head over to Salisbury and see if we can find any CCTV footage.'

'Let me know if you do and I'll add them to the press release. I'll get on to Clive Bishop at the *Salisbury Journal* as well and ask for a big splash.'

'So you're getting on better with Clive now?' Bernie had once heard the journalist call Jane the Wicked Witch of the West – but not to her face.

'Needs must. I'll get on to it now. There's nothing I can do about Rosa Conti until she's formally identified.'

'Think we're due to hear from Forensics today.'

'That'll be good. Maybe DCI Worth will get his butt into gear then.'

'What do you mean?'

'Well,' Jane leaned forward, 'in my experience of dealing with murder cases, he isn't doing nearly enough in terms of getting the press involved. Which is unusual for him. He's normally such a stickler for these things. I told him so as well.'

'I bet that went down well.'

'Oh yes. Told me to get out. The sooner he retires the better.'

'When's that?'

'Next year. He's already got himself a lovely new house in Pewsey to retire to. In the meantime, we still have to put up with him. Anyway, I'd better let you get on.'

Bernie smiled. It was Jane's subtle way of telling her to go. As she left she thought about what Jane had said. It was interesting to note she wasn't the only one thinking Worth wasn't doing a very good job.

CHAPTER 31

Bernie drove over to the church where one of the leaders of the Street Pastors was based, having dropped Kerry off to view the CCTV. There was no point them both watching it and they had to make up for lost time. Laura had now been missing for thirty-six hours.

Bernie knew a bit about how the teams operated but had never spoken to any of them, it was generally Community Policing that worked with them. When she found herself on an industrial estate she thought the satnav had made a mistake. But then she saw the sign for the church and managed to park out front. From the outside, the building looked similar to the other commercial units – boxy and grey – but the inside was quite unexpected. There was a main hall where comfortable chairs were laid out facing a stage with musical instruments set up, including a drum kit. Very different to the church in Marchant with its aging organist banging out hymns each week. To the side was a coffee shop. She wasn't quite sure where to go when she saw a smiling woman wave to her from behind the counter.

'Hi,' said the woman, 'would you like some coffee? Maybe something to eat?'

Bernie looked at the cakes and thought again about her waistline. 'A latte would be nice but I've actually come to meet David Nicholson. He's expecting me.' She pulled out her warrant card. 'I'm Detective Inspector Bernie Noel.'

Bernie expected the smile to diminish but instead it got bigger.

'Oh yes, he did say an officer would be coming. I'm Gillian. Please take a seat and I'll get him for you. I'll bring your coffee over as well.'

Bernie looked around the shop. There were a couple of older women sitting together, otherwise it was empty. She chose the table furthest away from them and Gillian at the counter. If she was going to have to talk in the coffee shop, then she didn't want to be overheard.

Her phone buzzed. A text from Kerry.

Found Laura on CCTV. Definitely came in by bus.

Bernie texted back as she listened to the whirrs and whooshes of the coffee machine. The women murmured quietly, their heads down. She wondered if they were praying rather than chatting. A couple of minutes later, her latte appeared, along with a hot sausage roll and a large chocolate brownie.

'Oh, I hadn't asked…'

'I know. But I know what you officers are like. You never get to eat properly. They're always ordering pizza on those real-life cop programmes. You're OK with sausage? I can get you something else instead.'

'No, this is fine. Thank you.' Bernie reached for her purse.

'Oh, no charge. On the house. David will be with you in a couple of minutes.'

Bernie's stomach juices gurgled appreciatively. With no Alex at the house to make sure she ate, she had run out of the door without eating breakfast. She tucked into the sausage roll, pastry flakes falling onto her plate. She had almost finished it when she saw a tall, slim man striding towards her.

'Detective Inspector Noel? I'm David Nicholson, leader of this church.' He held out his hand.

Bernie was conscious of her greasy hands. She wiped them with a napkin before shaking his.

'Sorry, I've just had one of your lovely sausage rolls. Thank you for meeting with me.'

'Not at all. And I'm glad you enjoyed your food. I asked Gillian to make sure you had something.'

'Well, thank you. It's a lovely little café.'

David Nicholson smiled. 'Yes. It's quiet now but in an hour it will be bustling with lunchtime trade from the estate. But you're not here to talk about that. Paul Bentley has told me a few things. We take it in turns to run the Street Pastors teams but my wife and I were on over the weekend. I did Friday and she did Saturday.'

'Oh, I see. Is your wife here?'

'No, she's at work but I have rung her. She doesn't remember anyone reporting seeing a young girl hanging around. It's normally the young adults coming out of the clubs who are too drunk to find their way home who need our help. And the homeless. If we had spotted a twelve-year-old girl out at that time, we would have called it in.'

Bernie pulled her phone out and showed Nicholson a picture of Laura. 'This is her. With make-up on and the right clothes, she might have looked older. And we know now that she definitely came to Salisbury on Saturday afternoon. We've found her on CCTV. I've left my sergeant back at the CCTV centre to track her movements.'

Nicholson stroked his chin before looking over to the woman behind the counter. 'Gillian, can you come over, please?' He turned back to Bernie. 'Gillian was out on the streets on Saturday night. It's a long old shift, you know – ten p.m. to four a.m.'

Gillian appeared. 'Everything all right? Do you want another coffee? Anything for you, David?'

'No, we're all right for the moment. Pull up a chair, Gillian. The inspector would like to ask you some questions.'

The smile was still fixed on Gillian's face but there was a nervous twitch with one of her eyes.

'It's OK. You're not in any trouble.'

'Phew. Someone once made a complaint about me when I tried to help them.'

'Don't worry, it's nothing like that.' Bernie pushed her phone across the table towards Gillian. 'Have a look at this photo. Did you see this girl at all on Saturday night?'

Gillian picked up the phone and studied the picture. She slowly shook her head. 'No, I don't remember seeing her. And I'm sure one of the others would have said something if they had. We're all pretty experienced at spotting the underage ones who are trying to get into clubs. Sorry. But we'll definitely keep an eye out for her.'

'Yes,' said Nicholson. 'If we can have a copy of the photo then we can make sure that's distributed through the local churches and the Street Pastors.'

Bernie's chest tightened. 'I hope to God we'll find her before next weekend.'

'Yes, of course. But we can ask our congregations to look out for her in the meantime. I'm sorry we couldn't help more. We'd better let you get back to your sergeant.'

Bernie drained her coffee, looking again at Laura's photo. She didn't want to think of all the possibilities, including the one Jane Clackett had mentioned. She didn't want to see another dead girl.

Gillian appeared from behind the counter with two paper bags and a takeaway coffee. 'I thought your sergeant might be in need of refreshments too. So there's another sausage roll and an extra brownie.'

'Thank you.' Bernie didn't have the heart to tell Gillian that Kerry was vegetarian. She picked up her phone as there was another photo she wanted Gillian to look at, even though Worth had kicked her off the case.

'I know you didn't see Laura on Saturday but have you ever seen this girl?'

Gillian put the bags and the coffee down on the table. She took the phone. 'Hmm. I don't think so but she does look familiar. Oh wait, no, I thought it was Rosa but it's not.'

'Rosa?'

'Yes, won't forget her in a hurry. She wore the most amazing red shoes but she was so drunk she couldn't walk in them. I gave her a pair of flip-flops.'

Bernie swiped to the photo of the shoes. 'These ones?'

'Yes, that's them. I saw her another time when she wasn't drunk and we chatted about her family and a friend called Ria. She asked me to pray for them. But I definitely don't recognise this girl.'

CHAPTER 32

Bernie hurried into the CCTV centre as fast as she could without spilling the coffee. Kerry was sitting next to a man with a scruffy beard, watching a screen for any sightings of Laura. She put the bags and coffee down and paused to take breath.

'You all right?' asked Kerry.

'Yes… I legged it up the stairs, the lift had just left.'

'You could've waited.'

Bernie shook her head. 'No, I couldn't. I have news.'

'The street pastors saw Laura?'

'No. Rosa. Well, maybe. She didn't recognise the photo of her but she knew the shoes. Said the woman who wore them looked a bit like Rosa. In the photo the Contis sent, Rosa doesn't have any make-up on and she's dressed very casually so I imagine she might look different all done up. The woman I spoke to, Gillian, saw her a couple of times. She had a chat with her and Rosa asked Gillian to pray for her family and a friend called Ria. I've passed it on to Matt.'

'That's good news.' Kerry pointed to the coffee. 'For me? I'm gagging for a drink.'

'Yes. Gillian also gave me a sausage roll for you and a brownie.'

'Oh, that's very kind but…'

'I know,' said Bernie. 'But I didn't feel like I could ask for something else after she'd already been so generous. How are you doing here?'

Bernie could see Laura on the screen, walking past shops.

'Bernie, this is Gerald, and he is a marvel. He found Laura very quickly and it's like he can anticipate where she'll go next. She keeps looking around her, as though she's searching for someone. She came in by bus. I've contacted Salisbury police and they're going to send uniform out to find the bus driver and look at their CCTV.'

'Good. Thanks, Kerry. That'll allow us to concentrate on Laura here. And well done Gerald for finding her so quickly.'

Despite the beard, Bernie noticed Gerald's face redden.

'Thanks. When you've been doing this job as long as I have you notice all sorts. I spot fights before they start. And lost kids are pretty easy. As Kerry said, she kept looking around.' He clicked on a clip. 'She took a phone call just after five p.m. and then went into this clothes shop here. Um, I don't mean to be cheeky but if there's a sausage roll going free…'

Kerry opened one of the bags, peeked inside and then passed it over. 'Please, be my guest.' She turned to Bernie. 'I'm really confused. I thought you had gone to a church.'

'I did,' said Bernie as she pulled up a chair. 'They have a coffee shop. Gillian works there. She was out with the Street Pastors team on Saturday night and is sure that no one saw Laura.'

Kerry and Gerald continued eating as they waited for Laura to leave the clothes store. More people entered and left. Five minutes turned into ten. Laura still hadn't left the shop.

Bernie's phone buzzed. It was a text from Anderson. They hadn't actually spoken yet after the events of the weekend.

Tom said you were going to ask Laura's family about her password details. Thought Craig might have some idea. If it's OK with you I can visit him in hospital now. Still waiting for Rosa's ID so nothing much doing here.

Bernie turned away from Kerry as she answered. She didn't think Anderson had Worth's permission to do this but she wasn't about to say no. They really needed more people to help find Laura.

That would be helpful, thanks. He's more likely to know than his mum.

She looked back at the monitor. 'Is there a back way out of this place?' asked Bernie.

'I'm not sure,' said Gerald. 'If there is, it's unlikely to have CCTV.'

'Spin forward a little,' said Kerry.

The video juddered in front of them but there was still no sign of Laura. Gerald paused it.

'What do you think? Did she stay in the shop for ages? Did she go out of the back? Or…' said Gerald, 'did she change her clothes?'

'That's a good point. Can you rewind it, please?' asked Bernie.

Gerald put it back to the point that Laura went into the shop. They all watched carefully as people left. No one looked like Laura.

'Wait. There,' said Kerry.

Gerald paused. There was a big group of girls coming out. Was there an extra girl with them?

'She might be attaching herself to this lot. She must have seen the cameras. Kids are so much more clued up these days,' said Kerry.

The group wandered down the street. One of the girls had a cap on. She swung a bag onto her back.

'There,' said Kerry. 'She had that bag with her when she got off the bus.'

'Follow those girls, Gerald. You said she received a phone call. Don't we have the phone records, Kerry?'

'Yes, but that's a different phone. The last call made on her normal mobile was to her mother. Then it got switched off.'

'Oh jeez, he gave her a phone. That's really not good. We've got to get into her Instagram account. Anderson texted to say he's going to see Craig to find out if he knows.'

Kerry gave her an enquiring look.

'By the way,' said Gerald, 'I'm recording all this for you so you can take it back to headquarters.'

'Thanks, that's really helpful,' Bernie said. 'We'll then have a choice of shots to release to the press.'

They continued to follow Laura for quite a while as she ducked into different shops and latched on to various groups of people.

'She really is doing her best to stay hidden, isn't she?' Kerry said.

'Maybe she was instructed to do so. Especially if she has another phone. We've no idea what's being sent to her.'

At seventeen twenty-five on the recording, Laura went into a café. They stared at the screen for five minutes but nothing really changed.

'Can you fast forward, please, Gerald?' Bernie asked.

They watched carefully but there was no sign of Laura leaving.

'Are there any cameras behind this parade of shops?'

Gerald shook his head.

'So our only hope is there might be some private CCTV behind the store.'

'I'm afraid so,' said Gerald. 'I'm sorry I can't help more.'

'Oh God, you've done loads. We're very grateful. Maybe we should go and check out this café. What do you think, Kerry?'

'Yes, absolutely. Now?' Kerry jotted down the address of the café.

'I'll keep checking this for you,' said Gerald, 'and then I'll send all the visuals over to you at headquarters.'

'Thanks,' said Bernie.

'And if there's anything else you want me to check out then just let me know.' He scribbled something on a piece of paper. 'This is the direct line through to here plus my mobile if I'm not in.' He smiled as he gave it to Kerry. She murmured her thanks.

As the door swung shut behind them, Bernie said, 'I think you've pulled there.'

Kerry gave her a hard stare. 'That's not even remotely funny.'

'Oh, come on. He's a sweetheart. Just not for you.'

CHAPTER 33

Finding parking around the café proved to be hard. In the end, Bernie abandoned the car on a single yellow line and stuck a 'police' sign in the windscreen. She hoped it would be enough to deter any parking wardens. They walked back to the café they were looking for. The weather was pleasant enough but a cool breeze signalled that autumn was firmly in charge. Bernie pulled her suit jacket across and did up the buttons.

The café was called The Little Teapot. A bell tinged as Bernie pushed open the door. A middle-aged woman with red-framed glasses looked up from behind the counter and smiled.

'Good afternoon. Table for two?'

'No, thanks. I have some questions actually,' said Bernie. She held up her warrant card. 'I'm Detective Inspector Bernie Noel and this is my colleague, Detective Sergeant Kerry Allen. And you are?'

'Oh, Barbara Finch. I own this place.'

'Mrs Finch, we believe this girl came in here on Saturday.' Bernie flicked through her phone and found the picture of Laura.

'Oh.' Barbara Finch pushed the glasses onto the top of her head and peered at the photo. 'I'm not sure. We were very busy on Saturday. We had a promotion on so lots of extra customers.'

'It would have been around five twenty-five p.m.,' said Kerry. 'We have CCTV footage showing her come in but not leave.'

'Not leave?' Barbara looked puzzled. 'I'm not sure how that's possible.'

'Do you have a back door to the shop?'

'Yes, it leads out onto a small service road.'

'Do you have CCTV out there?' asked Bernie.

Barbara shook her head. 'No, I don't. But some of the other larger shops might. I don't understand it… Oh, wait… I popped up to the loo. Left my daughter in charge. She helps out on Saturdays. I would only have been gone five minutes though. It was nearly closing time anyway.'

Bernie looked at Kerry. Five minutes would be long enough for the daughter to let Laura out the back.

'Can we see your back door, please?' asked Bernie.

'Yes, of course.'

Barbara Finch locked the front door and turned the sign round to 'closed'. She then pulled back a curtain behind the counter and led them down a short corridor to a back door, passing a kitchen on the way. Outside was a small parking area with one car and two large wheelie bins. Bernie stayed with the café owner as Kerry jogged quickly up and down the service road.

'We're in luck. CCTV at a couple of shops in both directions. If she came out this way then we'll be able to spot her,' said Kerry.

'I don't understand what's going on here,' said Barbara.

Bernie gave a brief smile. 'I'm sorry. I can only tell you so much but this girl has gone missing. And the last place we saw her on CCTV was your café. We're going to need to speak to your daughter.'

Bernie waited for Barbara Finch's daughter to arrive while Kerry visited the shops that had CCTV overlooking the service road. She glanced at her watch – two fifty p.m. – and checked her phone again. There was a message from Anderson.

Got possible password from Craig for Instagram. Going back to HQ now to see if it works. See you later.

She tapped back quickly.

Great. Thanks.

She was aware that she and Anderson needed to have a conversation, the sooner the better.

'Katie should be here in a few minutes,' said the woman. 'She normally comes here straight from school and does her homework upstairs until I close up.'

Bernie looked up at Barbara. She seemed a bit twitchy, fiddling with a pen, twisting it round and round with her fingers.

'How old is she?' asked Bernie.

'Fifteen.'

'In that case, you'll need to be present when I speak to her. I'm afraid you may have to shut again.'

The woman gave a slight nod of the head. 'That's fine. It tends to be a bit quiet on a Monday. I was thinking of going half-days on Mondays anyway, use the time to catch up on ordering and the accounts, so it's not a problem.'

Bernie thought Barbara was nervous, telling her things she didn't really need to know.

'Oh, here comes Katie now.'

Bernie turned to see a tall teenage girl with bountiful brunette hair cascading down her back. She had model features and looked a lot older than fifteen.

The bell rang as the door opened.

'Hi, Mum. Is everything OK? You look a bit odd.'

'Umm, Katie, love, this is a police officer. She'd like to ask you a few questions.'

Bernie watched Katie to see her reaction. She saw the same puzzlement her mother had shown.

'Hello, Katie. I'm Detective Inspector Bernie Noel. Don't worry, you're not in trouble. I want to ask you about a girl that came in here on Saturday around five twenty-five p.m.'

Bernie pulled out her phone and showed the picture of Laura to Katie.

'Do you remember seeing her?'

The girl stared at the phone and then slowly nodded her head. 'Yes. She was a bit cagey. I told her it was too late to be ordering anything. We shut at five thirty. Mum had gone upstairs to the loo. But she said she didn't want anything to eat or drink, she needed help. There were some girls after her and she asked if there was a back way out of the shop. She seemed so scared I took pity on her. So I let her out the back.'

Bernie put her phone away and took out her notepad and pen.

'In what way did she seem scared?'

Katie thought for a minute, her eyes drifting briefly to the floor. 'Well, her voice was quiet and she just seemed a bit shaky. She kept looking around as well, looking out of the window. She was definitely on edge.'

'Can you remember what she was wearing or if she had anything with her?'

'Umm… she was wearing jeans and had a dark jacket – maybe black. Her hair was up in a very high ponytail, like in the picture… Oh wait, she took her hair down and tied it loosely just before she left. So it was tied at her neck rather than on top of her head.' Katie took hold of her own hair and demonstrated.

'Why do you think she did that?' asked Bernie.

'I don't know. Maybe she was trying to change her appearance because of the girls.'

'Did you see these girls or did anyone come in asking for her?'

'No.'

'And when she left, which way did she go?'

'I don't know. I heard the bell on the door ring so I rushed back.'

Bernie smiled. 'You're doing really well, Katie. Have you ever seen this girl before?'

'No. It's the first time but I'm sure I'd recognise her again. Has she done something wrong?'

'No, she hasn't done anything wrong. She's gone missing and we're trying to track her movements. You've been really helpful.'

The girl's eyes widened. 'Oh no. I hope I wasn't the last person to see her. Oh, she had a bag with her – a rucksack. It looked quite heavy. She kept pulling it up onto her shoulders, as though it was uncomfortable.'

Bernie delved into her pocket and pulled out a card. 'This is my number. If you think of anything else, no matter how small, just contact me. If I can't answer, leave a message and I'll get back to you ASAP.'

Bernie met Kerry by the car. A plastic bag containing a ticket fluttered underneath one of the windscreen wipers.

'Oh bloody hell, that's all I need. Can't they read?' said Bernie.

Kerry grimaced. 'I'm afraid I have more bad news.'

Bernie grabbed the ticket and unlocked the car.

'One of the cameras is a dummy one,' said Kerry as she got in the car. 'One shop has only one tape so they overwrite it each day.'

'What?'

'It's a small shop. There was one other and I have the tape for that. But if Laura didn't go that way then we're stuffed.'

'Well, we know now she did go out the back. The café owner's daughter let her out. Laura told her some girls were after her. But she doesn't know which way she turned. Where is the shop with CCTV in relation to this one?'

'As you stand out the back, with the café behind you, it's to the left.'

'So, if she went to the right…' said Bernie.

'Yep, we don't have footage.'

'So, I take it you haven't looked at the tape then?'

'No. They were too busy in the shop to play it.'

Bernie grinned. 'But I know a man who can help us. Time to call your latest boyfriend, Kerry.'

CHAPTER 34

Gerald took the tape and popped it into the machine.

'What time was it again? Around five twenty-five p.m.?'

'Yes, please, Gerald,' said Bernie.

The screen flickered in front of them as the picture fast forwarded to the right time. Gerald hit play just before five twenty-five p.m. They all watched but nothing changed on the screen. No one walked past. Gerald put it on the slowest fast forward setting. A figure appeared.

'Stop,' said Bernie. 'Who's that?'

They saw a man pull out a packet of cigarettes and light one. After a couple of minutes, he flicked the cigarette away and walked out of shot.

'Looks like a shop worker having a quick fag break,' said Kerry.

'Might be worth looking into. He might have seen or heard something,' said Bernie. 'Keep spinning forward. Even if we don't see Laura, there may be other potential witnesses.'

The picture moved forward but no one else appeared.

Bernie rubbed her forehead. She could feel a headache brewing. She desperately needed a drink of water.

'I guess our only option at the moment is to see if we can find the guy who had a quick smoke at work,' she said.

'There is something else we can try,' said Gerald. 'We're assuming now that Laura turned right and walked down the service road. I can start searching for cameras in that area and see if I can pick her up.'

'If you're able to work a bit longer, that would be great, thanks,' said Bernie.

'I don't mind working late. If it helps find her, then it'll be worth it, won't it?'

'I guess it's going to be a late night for all of us,' said Kerry. She pulled her phone out. 'I'd better let Debs know. For once, we thought we had a free evening together.'

'Sorry.'

Kerry moved away.

'Debs?' asked Gerald.

'Her partner,' said Bernie.

'Oh.'

If Gerald was crestfallen, Bernie couldn't tell. He kept his eyes on the monitor.

Her own phone buzzed in her pocket. She pulled it out. Matt was calling her.

'Hi, Matt. Have you got something for me?'

'Not exactly. The DCI has called an urgent meeting. You need to come back to headquarters now. It starts at five p.m.'

The car crawled along with the rest of the rush hour traffic.

'I wonder what this meeting's about,' Kerry said.

'No idea. Although, I haven't heard anything yet about Rosa's ID.'

'Why have we been invited then if we're off the case?'

'Why indeed.'

Bernie thought about Gillian's reaction to the photos earlier. She recognised the shoes more than Rosa. And then there were the comments from Rosa's grandparents about her being a tomboy. Something wasn't right. She edged the car forward.

'This is all we need. It takes about fifty minutes in good traffic to get back to Devizes. It's going to be well over an hour at this rate,' said Bernie.

'Unless…'

'Unless what?'

'You do something a bit naughty,' said Kerry.

'Blues and twos?'

'Well, I'm sure it won't be the first time an officer has bent the rules a little bit on that score.'

'It is tempting… but probably shouldn't. Can you look again to see if Matt has got back to you?'

Kerry checked her phone. 'No. We really can't be late. Apart from Worth going apeshit at us, Jane might nab your seat next to Anderson.'

Bernie gave Kerry a withering look.

'Hey, what's that for? With Alex out of the way, there's nothing stopping you two now.'

Bernie huffed loudly. 'You've changed your tune. You were telling me off yesterday.'

'It was a shock. I've had a chance to think about it. You'd be good together. Of course, you'll probably argue all the time.'

'There's no guarantee we're going to end up together. It might have just been a one-night stand.'

'Do you really think that?'

'I don't know what to think. Oh… shut up and let me drive.'

The traffic lights turned green and Bernie inched the car forward, only for the lights to turn red as she approached.

'Sod it. Pretend to take a call and then talk to me,' said Bernie.

'What?'

'What did you say? There's an emergency up ahead and our presence is required?'

Kerry giggled and put her phone to her ear.

'Yes, ma'am, we're needed right away.'

Bernie hit the lights and siren and sped away.

CHAPTER 35

They all sat round a large table in a meeting room. The whole team was there – Matt, Kerry, Anderson, Mick Parris, Alice Hart – along with Jane, Tom, Nick White, Therese from Forensics, Lucy the CSI, and Phyl Bridger. DCI Worth had saved a seat next to him for Bernie. She couldn't decide if this was a good thing or him keeping an enemy close by.

'Well, as we're all here now, let's begin,' said Worth. He looked at Bernie and then Kerry. 'DI Noel and DS Allen – I know you're working a different case now but since you were involved at the beginning, you may have something to add.' He turned his attention back to the rest of the room and took a deep breath. 'You may have noticed there's been a delay in the identification of our dead woman in the woods. Nick, Phyl, Lucy and Therese will be giving us an update of the forensic evidence. We'll go over what we know about her. Feel free to take notes and if you have any thoughts, please raise your hand. Nick, perhaps you'd like to start with the post-mortem results.'

Bernie glanced at the pathologist. Dressed in a smart suit, as opposed to his usual scrubs or forensic coverall, he looked quite different. Greying wavy hair softened his hard face. *Almost human.*

'Thank you, Patrick. I have detailed copies of the report here. I think some of you may have to share, sorry.' The papers were passed round the table. 'I'd like to draw your attention to a few things. Firstly, cause of death. The victim was asphyxiated, strangled manually and her hyoid bone was broken. Because of decomposition, certain things remain inconclusive. I haven't discovered any other wounds and I wasn't able to find any evidence of sexual assault but that doesn't mean nothing happened – it's simply inconclusive. However, I can tell you that our victim was, most likely, sexually active. I found an IUD in her uterus. Which in itself is interesting. Most young women prefer the Pill.

'Now, the dental records. Unfortunately, our forensic dentist couldn't make this meeting but I have his report. It's his conclusion that the dental records sent by the Italian police do not fit with our victim, *unless* she had had some dental work done in the last year, including two implants. The X-rays in the records are over a year old. But,' he shook his head, 'it's not looking likely. I think Therese can tell us more.'

Therese looked up from the report, pushing her glasses onto the top of her brown, bushy hair, and rested her gaze on Worth. 'Do you want the good news or the bad news?'

'Bad news.'

Therese picked up a report. 'Well, I've been working on the DNA results for the last two days. I had to go back to the Italian lab to double check. Our victim's DNA doesn't match Rosa Conti's grandparents. So, there are three possible options. Either, Rosa was adopted or her father wasn't her biological father, or, and this is far more likely, our victim isn't Rosa Conti.'

A murmur went round the table. Bernie looked at Anderson. He shrugged.

'So, what's the good news?' asked Worth.

'The good news is that the leather jacket and helmet have our victim's DNA all over it, and that of an unknown male. His DNA is also on her dress. He's not in our database. But we will have something to check by if you arrest a suspect.'

Bernie closed her eyes briefly. She was aware Worth was unnervingly still next to her.

'Before we reconsider ID for the victim, Dr Bridger, do you have anything that you'd like to say about your results?'

'Yes, I do.'

Bernie smiled at Phyl.

'Taking everything into consideration, it looks as though the victim was killed or placed in that spot on the Friday evening, six days before she was discovered, as originally thought. Decomposition has been rapid but warm temperatures and the body being exposed have increased it. Plus, I examined today a badger found by DI Noel and DS Allen. In my opinion it had already been dead several days before the victim, and was a fairly immediate source of blowflies.'

Worth nodded, his hand with a pen creeping towards his mouth. 'Thank you, Dr Bridger. Nick, Lucy – you both worked at the scene. Do you think she was killed there?'

Nick White nodded. 'Yes, I think that's far more likely.'

'I agree,' said Lucy, flicking her ash blonde fringe out of her eyes. 'On her body, we've only found vegetation and soil matter that matches the area, particularly under her fingernails and on the soles of her feet.'

'So,' said Worth as he put his pen on his chin, 'she was probably murdered there but isn't Rosa Conti. So, what then? Rosa gave the rings to our unknown woman and the Foxes' au pair is off gallivanting somewhere else?'

Bernie remembered something else Gillian, the street pastor, had said – 'She asked me to pray for her friend, Ria.'

'No, sir, I think our victim was Rupert and Harriet Fox's au pair.'

'Detective Inspector Noel, the evidence now suggests that the victim isn't Rosa Conti.'

Bernie knew it would sound mad to the others but the DNA results confirmed her suspicions. 'And she's probably not. But I do think she was the au pair for the Fox family.' She glanced across to Anderson. 'Do you remember what Rosa's grandparents said to you about her? She was a tomboy who didn't go clubbing. And she never wore high heels. You said yourself that the woman we were describing didn't match what you were hearing from the family.'

Worth looked at her, puzzled. 'You're talking nonsense.'

'No, sir, I don't think I am. Haven't you ever had a time when you look at someone and think they're someone else? Sometimes you have to look twice to realise your mistake. But that tends to happen when you know someone really well. But what if you only have a photo to go on? Rupert and Harriet Fox and the agency probably only had a passport photo of Rosa. I think Rosa swapped identities with a woman she knows and who looks similar to her. And that woman came here to the UK. Gillian said that Rosa asked her to pray for her friend, Ria. What if our victim is actually Ria?'

Worth sat back in his chair and folded his arms. He appeared to be thinking. Bernie was aware of the tension in the room. She knew she was right.

'You know,' said Anderson, 'there may be something to this, sir. Inspector De Luca told me about some of Rosa's friends and he mentioned one called Ria. She had a juvenile record. One of his colleagues who knows the girls referred to them as *terribili gemelli* – terrible twins. I thought he meant about their behaviour – that's what it normally means in English. But what if he meant more than that? What if they look alike too? Would you like me to ring Inspector De Luca now, sir?'

'Wait until the end of the meeting,' said Worth. 'There are quite a lot of things we need to think about in regards to these two young women. When, where and why did they swap? Was it really just because Rosa didn't want to be an au pair? It seems a bit extreme.'

Bernie thought about the dentist report and the Catholic priest she spoke to. 'Maybe this isn't about Rosa escaping but Ria. Two dental implants suggests the victim's teeth were possibly knocked out. Father Adrian said the young woman he spoke to was scared for her life. Perhaps Rosa swapped with Ria to keep her friend safe and that's why she agreed to be an au pair. And if so, where's Rosa now? If someone has got to Ria, has he caught up with Rosa too? And does he ride a motorbike?'

Worth tapped his fingers on the table. Bernie thought he was probably flummoxed by the results and was trying to hide it.

'I think we need to speak to Ryan Willis again. And this time, I'll do the interview.'

CHAPTER 36

They all filed back to the office. Matt edged towards Bernie.

'I've got something to show you,' he said. 'DS Anderson passed on Laura's possible password. Her brother was right. It's "craigisanidiot" – all lower case and ones for the I's. And her email address is littlemissmoffatt@gmail.com. I've sent that to Tom for him to check out but I thought I'd start with the Instagram account Kerry found yesterday.'

Bernie and Kerry gathered round Matt's desk. He opened up a tab on his computer.

'Here it is. Her age says that she's fifteen.'

Bernie shook her head. 'Silly girl.'

Matt started to scroll down the timeline. 'It's mostly teenage chatter on here. Sharing stories about pop groups, TV programmes and films. She has over three hundred followers from various countries. I find it hard to believe she knows all of these people. There are a lot of teenage boys. Of course, how many of them are actually teenagers remains to be seen.'

Matt clicked on to the photos. 'She likes to take a lot of selfies.'

Bernie took a sharp intake of breath. Laura looked much older in the photos and her clothes were quite provocative.

'What haven't you told us yet, Matt?' she asked.

Matt tapped on the keyboard. 'It's the direct messages that are really interesting. Or should I say, disturbing? There's one guy in particular, called Luke Davidson – assuming that's his real name.'

'Unlikely,' murmured Kerry.

Matt opened the thread and scrolled back up to the top. 'Best you read it from the beginning.' He got out of his seat and let Bernie sit down.

She started to read. It all seemed innocent to begin with. He liked what she had written about a film. He asked her questions about her favourite things. Oddly enough, they seemed to share similar tastes in almost everything. 'Isn't that funny?' he had written. 'We're so alike.'

The messages went on and subtly began to change. He liked a photo of her in a Christmas jumper, then a party dress and then a bikini. He told her how pretty she was and how he would love to meet her someday. 'Wouldn't that be fun?' he had suggested. He told her he was seventeen.

Laura was enthusiastic in her replies. Lots of emojis littered her messages. 'You make me laugh,' she had written. And then, as his messages had changed, so had hers. 'No one understands me like you. I wish I could spend the whole day with you.' 'And the night,' Luke had replied.

She started sending him photos. Lots of make-up and pouty lips. Her clothes became more revealing. Then another message from Luke.

Hey babe what you up to?

                                        not much, at the hospital

Why r u sick?

                                        no it's my brother

Ur parents there too?

yeah but its ok, they're too busy to notice what im doing

Cool cool

You done that photo for me yet?

> *no not yet I will but idk im not too sure about it*
> *ur not gonna send it to anyone else right?*

Nahh babe of course not!! It's just for me, I loved ur other one ur so pretty I just want to see more of you

I'm free at the weekend babe if you wanna meet up or go to a party or something?

> *yeah id love that! maybe go for a ride on ur motorbike too?*

Haha of course but send me ur photo first

'Shit.' Bernie banged the table with her fist. 'When was this sent?'

'Friday. Have you noticed what he's called her throughout?' said Matt.

Bernie looked again, scrolling up and down. 'He calls her "babe". Double shit. And she mentions a motorbike.'

'Keep going down. There's one more message that you have to read.'

Bernie looked down and read with horror the plan Luke had sent to Laura, the plan where he would meet her in Salisbury. Everything she and Kerry had seen on the CCTV had been planned by Luke, even down to where he would meet her on his motorbike – in the service road behind the café.

*

DCs Mick Parris and Alice Hart were dispatched to pick up Ryan Willis as Bernie voiced her concerns to Worth.

'It might be complete coincidence, this motorbike connection, but considering how close Laura lives to Ryan, I think we need to ask him about it.'

'We? As I said earlier, I will interview him along with DC Hart. He's played you once already. You can watch in the viewing room.'

Bernie wanted to huff but kept her emotions under control. 'Yes, sir.'

Bernie was now waiting for Tom to come upstairs and help with looking at Laura and Luke's accounts.

'What are Laura's messages like with other people?' Bernie asked Matt. 'Did she tell anyone where she was going?'

'Nah. She didn't message anyone else after that last one from Luke. Everything else is teenage chat.'

'So she didn't confide in any of her friends.'

'No, but that's not surprising. Luke talks about keeping Laura for himself. He doesn't specifically say not to tell anyone but he implies enough to suggest this is something special, just between the two of them.'

Bernie paced up and down, rubbing her forehead. The thump had subsided to a dull ache but she knew it wouldn't go without sleep. And that was the one thing they all probably wouldn't get tonight. She pulled out her phone. She had an important call to make before they got started.

'We're in for a late night, guys, so does anyone want pizza?'

Bernie, Matt and Kerry were munching on pizza as they worked when Tom arrived.

'Hi, I think you need my services again,' he said.

Bernie stood up. 'We most certainly do. We've got an Instagram account that needs looking at. We've applied for a warrant and they're supposed to be coming back to us with username and password but haven't done so yet. It's got the highest privacy settings. But we're pretty certain it's a fake account, a front for grooming girls.'

'OK. There are other things I can do until the warrant comes through. I can analyse his account. See what I can find out about him. Might need some of that pizza to help me along though.' He gestured towards the box.

'Of course, knock yourself out. But don't take the last ham and pineapple if you want to stay friends with Matt.'

'Pineapple on pizza? No worries on that score.'

The telephone on Matt's desk began to ring.

'DC Taylor,' he said. 'Oh, right, thanks for letting me know.' He put the phone down and looked up at Bernie. 'Ryan Willis has been brought in.'

CHAPTER 37

Bernie thought Ryan looked very ill at ease. His left leg was twitching. When she saw him do that at the pub, she thought it was because he was getting ready to go out to the garden to talk to her. Now, she wondered if it was a nervous habit. He was tapping the table as well. She thought he probably needed a cigarette.

'Where did you find him?' Bernie asked Mick.

'The Marchant Arms. We tried to be as discreet as possible but he wasn't too keen to come with us. He lashed out and his fist connected with my jaw.' Mick rubbed his chin. 'Still hurts now. Had no choice but to arrest him then. Daft lad.'

No, Worthless is the daft one. Ryan would have come peacefully with me.

They watched the monitor and saw DCI Worth and DC Alice Hart enter the room. Bernie wondered how Worth would handle the interview. It must be a while since he'd done one, she thought.

Worth and Hart sat down. The DCI opened a folder and stared at it for a minute before nodding at Alice. She pressed the buttons on the recorder.

'The time is nineteen forty-five hours. Detective Chief Inspector Worth and Detective Constable Hart are present with Ryan Willis. Mr Willis has declined representation but it is your right to ask for a solicitor at any point. Is that clear, Mr Willis?' said Alice.

Ryan nodded.

'For the recording, please, Mr Willis.'

'Yes.' Ryan looked down at the table.

Alice glanced at Worth. He nodded at her to continue.

'Ryan,' said Hart, 'when my colleague and I came to find you in the pub, you didn't seem too happy to see us. We only wanted to ask you to come to the station to answer some questions. We didn't need to arrest you at that point but by hitting my colleague, you gave us no choice. Why did you hit him?'

Ryan shrugged. 'Don't know.'

'But we only wanted to talk to you. We still do.'

'But that other female copper, you know, the fit one…'

Bernie smiled at Ryan's description.

'…she said I could stay anonymous. I already told her what I know.'

'But I haven't said what we want to talk to you about.'

'Well, it can't be anything else. I haven't done anything.'

'Except for assaulting a police officer.'

A vague smile appeared on Ryan's face. 'I couldn't make it look as though I'm a grass.'

'No. You made yourself look like a suspect.'

'What?' Ryan sat upright.

'Well, lad, you've got yourself in a right pickle now,' said Worth.

Oh God, thought Bernie, he's going with patronising old-school.

Ryan turned his head towards the DCI.

'Throwing a punch at an officer when we only wanted a friendly chat… wasn't very clever. And you're right about one thing. To begin with, we did think we could keep you anonymous but there's been a development. So we need to ask you some more questions, I'm afraid,' said Worth.

Ryan lowered his gaze to the table. He wrapped his arms around himself. His leg was still twitching. Bernie knew what it meant.

'He's not going to talk,' she said to Mick. 'He'd rather take the rap for the assault than speak out.'

She sat back in her chair and rubbed her face with her hands.

'He's our best shot at tracking that biker and finding Laura at the moment and he's not going to bloody talk.'

The stalemate progressed. Both Worth and Hart asked questions but Ryan refused to answer. Bernie was frustrated. She paced the small viewing room. She knew Ryan would talk to her.

'I think we're going to pause for a short break. The time is twenty zero five hours,' said Worth.

DC Hart switched off the recording.

'Perhaps you would like a drink, Ryan. A tea or coffee?' asked Alice.

Ryan finally looked up. 'Coffee, please. Two sugars. And maybe get the fit one to bring it. I'll talk to her but no one else.'

Bernie wanted to punch the air. When Worth gave a sideways glance to DC Hart, she knew how much this must be killing him.

'OK, Ryan. Although I think Detective Inspector Noel would prefer to not be called the "fit one",' said the DCI.

'Oh, I don't know,' said Bernie. She grinned at Mick, who was still rubbing his chin.

CHAPTER 38

Bernie placed a plastic cup with coffee in it in front of Ryan. She pressed record on the machine.

'This is Detective Inspector Noel resuming interview with Ryan Willis at twenty fifteen hours. I gather you want to talk to me.'

Ryan nodded, a slightly sulky look on his face.

'I thought anything I said was just between you and me.'

'It was but there's been quite a significant development. Ryan, I have to ask you this, where were you on Saturday from, say, three p.m. onwards?'

Ryan slurped his coffee and then pulled a face. 'Tastes like shit, man. How do you drink this all day?'

'I don't. We have a higher quality instant up in our kitchen. This is the Custody special. So unless you want more of this crappy coffee for the next twenty-four hours, you'd better answer my question.'

Ryan blew noisily out of his mouth. 'I was working at the farm all day. We were dipping the sheep. Fun job.'

'So, your family can vouch for you?'

'Yes, and some farmhands that Dad took on for the summer and autumn. Why are you asking me this?'

Bernie paused. Should she tell him? She was aware Worth was watching. She decided to take the risk.

'A girl went missing on Saturday. Laura Moffatt. Do you know her?'

Ryan rubbed his nose. 'Vaguely. Her family owns the farm on the other side of the railway tracks. I did hear about a girl going missing. I hadn't realised it was her though. God, that's awful. Maybe she got spooked by the dead girl in the woods.'

'No. We have reason to believe she met someone online. Do you know a Luke Davidson?'

Ryan looked thoughtful as he picked a spot on his cheek. 'No, I don't think so. There used to be a Luke at school but I'm fairly certain his surname wasn't that.'

'OK. What about Instagram? Are you on that? Or any other social media?'

'God, no, I'm not on Instagram. I'm on Twitter though.'

'Why not Instagram?'

'I was for a while but then I came off. Too many old classmates looking me up and writing shit comments.'

'And they don't on Twitter?'

Ryan twisted in his chair. 'Different name on there.'

'You haven't thought about using a different name on Instagram then?'

'No.' He glanced at the table.

'What name do you use on Twitter then?'

Ryan flushed. 'Promise you won't laugh?'

'Not sure if I can guarantee that.'

'It's Wilts Farm Boy.'

Bernie smiled. 'There's nothing wrong with that.' She tipped her head to one side and looked at Ryan closely. 'You like being anonymous, don't you?' She saw a sheen of sweat appear on his face. 'Why is that?'

Ryan rubbed his nose again. 'It's hard being the youngest. People always comparing me to Will and Gareth, especially teachers. I'm not clever or sporty. I don't know any of my followers on Twitter but they like my tweets and reply. I can just be me.'

Bernie found herself feeling sorry for Ryan but then she remembered the ABC of police work – assume nothing, believe no one and challenge everything.

'I want to go back over what you told me about the motorcyclist.'

Ryan took another slurp of the coffee and pulled a face. 'Doesn't get any better as it cools down, does it? I've already told you he was dressed completely in black. I didn't recognise his voice. He had a bird with him. She didn't say anything. Was wearing a black jacket and helmet. A short skirt or dress. In heels. What else do you want to know?'

She desperately wanted to ask him about the cave Kerry had found but knew she needed to keep that info to herself for the moment.

'You raced to the end of the lane but no further. Is that right? Or did you go over the little bridge and up the track?'

Ryan looked at her warily. 'Just to the end of the lane. We don't go onto the track normally.'

'Why's that?'

'It's dark and quite steep.'

Bernie tapped her fingers on the desk. *Does he believe the ghost story?* She looked casually at Ryan. 'Nothing to do with the legend then.'

'Legend?'

'Apparently it's haunted.'

Any cockiness that Ryan had had, appeared to have left him.

'I think that's why you don't go up there at night, isn't it?'

Ryan's sweat was more obvious now. Bernie could even smell it.

'What is it about the track next to Wroughton's Folly that bothers you? Or maybe you know it better as Maggots Wood.'

Perspiration was dripping down Ryan's face, his breath shallow.

'Ryan, are you all right?'

His voice came in gasps. 'I need... to... get out... of... here.'

Bernie pressed the alarm button as Ryan slid to the floor, hitting his head on the edge of the table.

'That went well, then,' said DCI Worth as the ambulance took Ryan Willis away. 'Seems to be a habit of yours, DI Noel. Witnesses going to hospital after being questioned by you. Make sure you write it up in the accident log and then get the room cleaned. He certainly bled a lot.'

Bernie bit her lip to stop herself from speaking out.

'I'll be in my office, should anyone need me,' said Worth.

Bernie felt a poke in her ribs. It was Kerry.

'You OK?'

'Not really.'

'Don't feel guilty about it. It wasn't your fault. It sounds as though you tapped into a memory of Ryan's. Something happened to him on that track. Something bad.'

CHAPTER 39

'Got anything yet, Tom?' Bernie asked.

'Well, considering Instagram is all about photos, he has very few on his account. Apart from his profile pic, which probably isn't him anyway, there are no other personal photos. The ones that are up are mostly of landscapes. I thought they might be of anywhere but Matt reckons they're local.'

'Yeah, definitely. They're off the beaten track but I recognise them, especially this one. There's a similar picture on the board over there.' Matt scrolled down Luke Davidson's page and clicked on a photo.

'Oh my God, that's the track,' Bernie said. 'When did he post that?'

'A month ago. Checking it out perhaps?'

'God, yes. Did he put a comment?'

'Just "out for a ride". Do you think we have enough to convince Worth that the two cases are connected?'

Bernie grimaced. 'Only one way to find out. He can't keep ignoring the evidence when a girl's life is at stake.'

Bernie paused before knocking on the door. It sounded as though the DCI was on the phone. She couldn't quite catch what he was saying but his side of the conversation sounded terse. When she heard the phone click down, she knocked.

'Come in.'

Bernie opened the door.

'Sorry to disturb you, sir, but we've found some more information. It's looking far more likely that Laura's disappearance is connected with our dead woman.'

Worth signalled for her to go on.

'Laura has been groomed online. The "boy" who's been contacting her calls her "babe" and writes about having a motorbike. We've found a message between Laura and "Luke Davidson", detailing where to meet in Salisbury, including where he would pick her up – in a service road behind the place we tracked her to on CCTV.

'I wanted to ask Ryan Willis about what the motorcyclist had said. He called the woman with him "babe". And now, Tom and Matt have just found a photo of the track by the woods on Luke Davidson's Instagram page. I'm sure the cases are connected. In which case, Laura is with a very dangerous man who's already killed once.'

Worth rolled a pen between his fingers.

'Firstly, you got one of my officers to do some work for you…'

'Actually, sir, DC Taylor is one of *my* officers…'

'Please don't interrupt me. Secondly, there were two riders in that final race and we don't have identities for them so we don't know for certain that Laura is with either of them. Thirdly, why are you only telling me this information now? Don't you think it would have been useful to have known this before I interviewed Ryan Willis? We only have his word about this motorcyclist. No one else from the race has come forward. It might not even have happened. He might have made the whole thing up to cover his tracks. Don't you realise that Ryan Willis is now our prime suspect?'

Bernie could see it looked bad for Ryan but her gut instinct told her something different.

'He says he has an alibi for when Laura disappeared.'

'Then you'd better go and check it.'

Bernie glanced at her watch. It was close to nine thirty. 'Now?'

'Yes, now. You can go home afterwards. And you're going to need more evidence that it's the same man for both cases. We have to be one hundred per cent sure before we alert the public. Anything that might suggest a serial offender will cause a massive stir and the press will be over us like a rash. Be aware that I'll be watching you closely from now on.'

CHAPTER 40

Bernie knocked on the farmhouse door. A TV was muted, followed by a shuffling noise inside and a dog barking.

'Who is it?' said a voice, from behind the door.

'Stan, it's me, DI Bernie Noel.'

'Ah, Bernie, wait a minute.'

A key turned in the lock and then the door opened.

'Hi, Stan. I'm so sorry to call late. It's about Ryan.'

'Oh, I know all about Ryan. Janet and Ron have gone rushing over to the hospital. I have to say Janet's a bit cross with you and your lot.'

Bernie sighed. 'I don't blame her. Can I come in, please? I need to ask a few questions and hopefully your answers will help Ryan.'

Stan moved back. 'That's all right. I know you're only doing your job. Since Janet isn't here, I can't offer you a cuppa, I'm afraid.'

Bernie took the hint. 'How about if I make us one?'

'That would be lovely, dear. And there might even be some cake in the tin if you want some.'

'None for me, thanks. But do you want a slice, Stan?'

'Well, if it's not too much trouble.' He winked his good eye.

The fire crackled as Stan poked at it. Bernie set the tea and cake down on a little table next to his armchair.

'There you go, Stan. I've only given you a small bit, though. I don't want to upset Janet.'

Stan tapped the side of his nose. 'Just between you and me. Now, what did you want to ask me?'

'Do you know where Ryan was on Saturday? Particularly in the afternoon.'

'Yes, he was here. We had to dip the sheep. It was a full-on family affair. All the boys were here to help Ron and we've had some Polish chaps helping us too.'

'I don't mean to be rude, Stan, but your eyesight…'

'My eyesight is bad, I know. But there's nothing wrong with my hearing. I was talking with him.'

Bernie smiled. 'OK. But I'll still need a visual confirmation.'

Stan slurped his tea. 'All right. But there's something else you want to know, isn't there?'

Bernie laughed. 'How did you know?'

'You could have confirmed that alibi over the phone. And I think you knew Ron and Janet wouldn't be here. There's something you think only I know.'

'You're uncanny. How did you know?'

'Wisdom of old age. So, shoot.'

Bernie drank some of her tea before she started. 'When I was talking to Ryan this evening, I asked him why he only rode up to the bridge for the race and not over and up the track. He suddenly went very strange and that's when he fainted. Well, I say suddenly, he'd been anxious for a while. I could see it in his body language.'

'Ah,' said Stan. He reached for his plate. 'If you don't mind, dear, I'm going to eat my piece of cake before I tell you.'

Bernie knew what that meant. Stan was fortifying himself to tell her something big, and, as Kerry had suggested, something bad.

She glanced around the room while Stan ate, glad his dentures appeared to be behaving this time. She looked again at the family photos she had seen only a few days before. There were the obligatory school sibling photos and one of Ryan on his own in uniform. He looked such a weed compared to his strapping older brothers. She remembered what he had said before he'd passed out. It wasn't easy being compared to them.

Stan put his plate down and had another gulp of tea. 'Right, my dear. I love all three of my grandsons but… Gareth and Will have always picked on Ryan. They still do now although they always brush it off as harmless banter.' Stan shook his head. 'Not always harmless though. Gareth and Will are two years apart and then Ryan is five years younger than Will. Older two used to love playing over at Wroughton's Folly with their friends. They'd build dens and set traps and have lots of adventures. When Ryan was five, he wanted to go with them. Janet wouldn't let him. He was such a tiny mite but very determined. So, when Janet's back was turned, he went running down the lane to try and find them. Ron used to take him on the tractor out there so he knew where he was going. Anyway, he found them. The boys weren't best pleased. They thought he was showing them up in front of their friends. They let him tag along for a bit but then got fed up with him. So they decided to play hide and seek. Now' – Stan pointed at Bernie – 'Ryan was very good at hide and seek. It was his most favourite game in the world. He and I used to spend hours playing it when he was very little. So, when his brothers suggested it, he was thrilled. I never did find out who it was who showed him the hiding place but someone must have helped him.

'Along the track, the sides go up very steeply. There's a hole on one side, up quite high, called Holy Man's Cave. Gareth and Will used to like going up there and they hooked up a rope so they could get up easily. Someone in that group got Ryan to climb up to the cave and told him to hide in there. Then, they pulled hard on the rope and it came down. Ryan was trapped but he didn't know it. Of course, he wasn't found. He thought he had the best hiding place. But then it started to get dark. There were all sorts of noises and he got scared. And, well, I'm responsible for the next bit, I'm afraid. He was always pestering me for stories and I had told him about the legend, about the track being haunted. Do you know about that?'

'Yes, I was told yesterday by a dog walker.'

'Well, as it got darker and noisier with all the eerie night-time sounds and he couldn't find the rope, he got properly scared. By the time we found him, he was completely traumatised. We had to fix up another rope to get him down. I carried him back to the car. He said to me, and only to me, he'd heard the horses galloping and whinnying and then a terrible crash, followed by a scream. It was weeks before he was right again. His brothers had a big smack that night. I know it's not the done thing these days but it was a wicked thing to do. They swore blind they hadn't put him up there but I'm sure they knew who was responsible. But they never said. They weren't allowed to play there again.'

Stan's good eye was damp. His hand trembled as he wiped tears away.

'It wasn't your fault, Stan.'

'Wasn't it? If I hadn't told him about the legend then he would have been scared still but not as much as he was. He had to sleep in with Janet and Ron for weeks he had such bad nightmares. Janet took him to the doctor in the end. He suggested counselling but Ron wasn't going to have that. I told him if he stuck with me, he'd be safe. So he did. He was my little shadow.'

Bernie rose from her seat and patted the old man on his arm. 'You've done a good job, Stan. Thank you for telling me all that. When I next speak to Ryan, I'll know what to say.'

'Do you have to speak to him again? Can't you leave the poor boy alone?'

'I'm afraid not. He hit an officer. And if my DCI has his way, Ryan will be charged. I'll do what I can but getting someone else to alibi him for Saturday would be useful.'

'OK. Pass the phone over. I'll get you Gareth. He was working with Ryan.'

Bernie gave Stan the phone and he pressed a couple of buttons.

'Gareth's on speed dial five. Makes life a lot easier for me. Oh, hello, Gareth, it's Granddad. I need you to talk to someone for a few minutes... Yes, I know it's late but it's important, I wouldn't ring otherwise... a police officer... about Ryan... OK.'

Stan handed the phone to Bernie. She decided to take the call in the hallway.

'Hi, Gareth, I'm Detective Inspector Bernie Noel. I just have a few questions for you.'

'What's Ryan done now?'

'I can't go into that, I'm afraid, but can you confirm where he was last Saturday?'

'At the farm, all day. We had to dip the sheep. He was working with me.'

'What time did you finish?'

'We started early but I think we finally finished around three p.m. And then we ate lunch. We were starving.'

'And Ryan was there for lunch too?'

'God, yeah. He eats more than the rest of us and never puts on any weight. Bloody annoying.'

Bernie decided to change tack. 'Thanks, that's helpful. Out of interest, do you take part in Ryan's motorbike races?'

'What, the ones he does with his little friends? God, no. Why?'

'It's just something we're looking into at the moment. Must be quite dangerous at night, riding along a road full of potholes and then up the track.'

'Oh, he don't go up the track. The little wuss.'

'Yes, I've heard about the legend.'

'Oh, I suppose Granddad told you what happened. It wasn't Will or me though. Still don't know which one of my friends did it. I'd only just started at secondary so didn't know those boys very well.'

'And Ryan never said which boy had hidden him?'

'No, he was too traumatised and he didn't know his name. None of them admitted to it. I didn't stay friends with them after that.'

'Any of them still around? Names?'

'No idea. It was nearly fifteen years ago and as I said, I didn't stay friends with them. Is that all? I have to get up very early tomorrow so I need to go to bed.'

Bernie thought Gareth was being a bit obstructive but she clearly wasn't going to get anything else from him. 'That's all. Thanks, Gareth.'

She walked back into the lounge and replaced the handset.

'Alibi confirmed?' Stan asked.

'Yes, all confirmed. Now, I'm going to take these things out to the kitchen and wash them up. Then Janet won't know a thing.'

Stan tapped the side of his nose again. 'Just between you and me.'

As Bernie set the cups and plates down in the kitchen, she wondered who had helped Ryan get up to the cave all those years ago and if he rode a motorbike.

CHAPTER 41

Tuesday

Bernie opened her fridge to find it was virtually empty. Alex normally did a grocery shop on a Monday evening. There were a few mushrooms languishing at the bottom, an out-of-date egg and some dodgy milk. The jam jar was almost empty but enough for a scraping. She pulled the last of the bread out of the bread bin. Thankfully, she spotted the mould before she put a couple of slices in the toaster.

'Shit.' She sat down at the table and buried her head in her hands. She'd had a bad night's sleep. Confusing dreams had assailed her. A little boy crying but she couldn't find him. Running through woods, brambles catching and scratching her before falling down and down and down. Pressure had built up on her chest, a tightness around her neck as though being strangled before sitting bolt upright in bed, gasping for air. She felt more wretched than she would have done if she had stayed up all night at work. *So much for fresh eyes.*

Bernie pushed herself up from the table. She was going to do the one thing that would help – a trip to the baker's.

Bernie thought there was a hint of a smile as Worth took a Danish pastry to eat.

'Thank you, Bernie. I'm sure we all need a boost this morning.'

'You're welcome, sir. The baker was asking about Laura. Her daughter goes to school with her. In fact, she asked if we were going to go into school and talk to Laura's friends.'

Worth's eyes narrowed slightly as he bit into his pastry. He chewed a little before speaking. 'We contacted her friends on Sunday before you arrived. No one knew anything.'

'Yes, but it was all a big shock on Sunday. They might have remembered something since then. I thought Kerry and I could go in this morning. In fact, looking in this box, there are far more things in here than I paid for. Might just be the thing to get them talking.'

'Well, before you get them talking, might I suggest another chat with Ryan first? He's been passed fit for interview. If you need me I'll be in my office.'

'Yes, sir.'

Bernie took the bakery box round to the others. 'Tom, Matt, where are you up to with Luke Davidson?'

'Not much further on, I'm afraid. We really need that warrant to come through,' Tom said.

'But we are working on a list of girls he's following and cross-referencing with Laura's followers,' said Matt. 'Hopefully we'll get something before you visit Laura's friends at school.'

'Great. Talk to Jane about the warrant. That woman has powers that go far beyond her job description. Right, I'd better go and see Ryan again. Maybe he'll be more willing to talk now.'

Bernie was just about to leave when her desk phone rang. 'DI Noel.'

'Ma'am, it's Alan Turner in custody. Bad news, I'm afraid.'

'Oh no, what?'

'Ryan Willis has just thrown up. DCI Worth said you'd be coming down to interview him. You'll need to hold off for a while until the doctor's checked him over.'

Bernie rolled her eyes – annoyed that Ryan was ill again but relieved she wouldn't be the one clearing it up. 'Great. Oh well. These things happen. Let me know when the doctor clears him. Thanks, Alan.'

Bernie put the phone down. 'Change of plan. I'll go to the school now with Kerry. Matt, email the list of girls you have so far. In fact, send it to Kerry. She can look through the names on the way over. Maybe a few of them will be at school this morning.'

Bernie and Kerry waited in the front reception area. Unlike the primary schools Bernie had visited, there was no work on display. Just motivational words painted on the walls. She thought the buzzwords were more for OFSTED's benefit than the pupils. The kids didn't care if they were supposed to be 'great thinkers' or 'strong achievers'. They were all counting down the days before they could leave and join the 'real world'. Little do they know, thought Bernie.

As they put on their visitor badges, a man walked towards them. Having checked the school's website before she'd left, Bernie knew he was the head teacher, yet he looked less like a teacher and more like an ageing boy-band member. He held out his hand.

'I'm Pete Travers, head teacher. I would say it's nice to meet you but…'

'Don't worry, Mr Travers, we get that a lot. I'm Detective Inspector Bernie Noel and this is my colleague, Detective Sergeant Kerry Allen. Thank you for seeing us at short notice.'

'It's not a problem. If you'd like to follow me, we can walk and talk. To be honest, I sort of expected you to come yesterday.'

'We had some leads to follow up on yesterday. Have you been able to arrange what I asked for when we spoke earlier?'

'Yes. We've managed to contact all the parents and they're happy for their girls to talk to you. Obviously, as we discussed, there will need to be a teacher in with them. So their form tutor, Mr Gardener, will be present. It was the girls' choice to have him.'

'Are Laura's friends mostly from her form?'

'Yes. We teach in form groups for the first two years and then we stream in year nine, ready for GCSEs. These are her best friends.'

'So, her little gang then?' said Kerry.

'They're called squads these days. Each generation of teenagers finds their own language. And thank you for bringing the food. That's a nice touch. I've managed to get some juice from the canteen. They're through here in the Food Tech room. There's a nice big table for you to sit round.'

Mr Travers opened the door and Bernie and Kerry followed him into the room. Bernie saw four girls sitting at the table, looking very nervous. At the far end of the table was, Bernie assumed, Mr Gardener. Pete Travers' ageing boy-band looks paled into insignificance compared with the young teacher. Slicked-back dark hair, fresh-faced, his shirt clung in all the right places. Not the kind of teacher Bernie had had in her convent school. He stood up to shake her hand and then Kerry's. Bernie resisted the urge to smile too much at him. He was clearly 'first crush' material.

'Hi, I'm Ben Gardener. Thanks for coming in. I've been Laura's form tutor since she started in year seven and I teach her Geography. So I know her quite well.'

'I'm Detective Inspector Bernie Noel. Laura mentioned you to me when I saw her on Friday. Said you'd organised an online safety talk with the police.'

'Yes, that was last year in year seven. I thought it was really important for them to stay safe on the internet. Wait, is this an online thing?'

'I'll explain more in a moment, but in the meantime' – she looked at the girls – 'we've brought some snacks for you. Hope you like Danishes and doughnuts.'

Kerry placed the box on the table. 'Help yourselves,' she said, lifting the lid.

The girls swooped in like gannets.

CHAPTER 42

'Girls, I want you to know you're not in trouble,' Bernie said. 'This is about finding Laura. And I know you want to stay loyal to her. But, not speaking out, not telling us something that might help get Laura back, is more damaging than "grassing her up". Do you understand?'

The girls all nodded.

'OK. Let's start with names. I'm Bernie. And you are?' She turned to the girl on her left.

'I'm Charlie.'

Bernie recognised the next girl. 'Hello, Daisy. We spoke on Sunday.'

Daisy reddened.

The next girl spoke up without being asked. 'I'm Chloe.' She flicked her ponytail back. Bernie noted her black eyeliner. She looked older than the others. And more confident. Bernie nodded at the next girl.

'I'm Emma. Did you get the food from my mum's bakery?'

'Yes, I did. We always get our cakes and sandwiches from there. Best in town.'

Emma gave a sheepish grin.

'Now that we know each other, Daisy, is there anything else you've remembered?'

Daisy's cheeks were now the same colour as her red curls.

'Um... Laura asked if... she could say she was having a sleepover at mine.'

Bernie kept her voice soft. 'When did she ask you?'

'On Friday afternoon. She hadn't come into school because of... well, you know... the body...'

'Oh shit. The body. I can't believe it was on their land,' said Chloe. 'Sorry, am I allowed to say "shit"?'

'Yes,' said Bernie. 'I say it all the time. But maybe we should let Daisy finish.'

'Oh, yeah, sorry. Carry on, Daisy.'

Daisy seemed to be picking at her fingers. 'She sent a message after school. I asked her why and... she said there was a boy who wanted to meet her, in Salisbury. Said he was going to take her to a party.'

'Did she mention how she was going to get home?'

Daisy gave a quick shake of her head.

'Thank you, Daisy. We've managed to get into Laura's Instagram account and we think this boy is called Luke Davidson.'

Bernie heard a gasp. 'Who was that?'

She saw one of the girls slowly raise an arm. 'Me. Chloe.'

'You recognise the name?'

'Yes. I'm friends with him too.'

Bernie looked at Chloe. She looked similar to Laura with the same high ponytail. This wasn't the moment, though, to ask if Luke had directly messaged her. Bernie glanced at Kerry who pulled out her phone to check something. She looked up and gave a quick nod. Chloe's name was on the list of girls that Matt had sent. They would have to speak privately to her but with a parent, not the teacher.

Bernie tried to not give any of this away as she spoke. 'Chloe, did Laura ever mention Luke to you?'

'Yes.' Her voice wavered, her confident manner ebbing away.

'Did you know she would be meeting up with him?'

'Yes.' Her voice was getting quieter.

'Chloe, were you supposed to be going too?'

Chloe sprang from her chair and rushed to one of the sinks where she retched. Kerry went after her. So did Mr Gardener.

Bernie looked back at Laura's friends; their faces were white.

'And this, girls, is why you never, ever meet up with people from online that you don't really know.'

Chloe sat quietly in the back of Bernie's car, Kerry next to her. They'd agreed with her mother they would all meet at headquarters.

They would use the witness questioning room. Soft chairs and a low coffee table made it more informal. There was still a camera, though, and an audio recorder. Drinks could be made in the room and there was a toilet right next door.

As Bernie pulled into the car park, there was a woman waiting.

'That's my mum. She's so going to kill me,' said Chloe.

'No, she won't,' said Kerry. 'She'll be very grateful you had the good sense not to go.'

They were all seated in the witness room, where Bernie explained why they needed to talk to Chloe.

'From what Chloe said earlier to us, she knows something about Laura's disappearance. Having this information will hopefully help us to find Laura. Please, will you consent to this interview?'

Rebecca looked at her daughter in obvious disbelief. 'OK.'

'Kerry, could you start the recordings, please?'

'Sure.' Kerry pressed the button on the camera and then the audio recording.

'The time is eleven twenty-five hours and Detective Inspector Noel and Detective Sergeant Allen are present in the room with Chloe Hampton and her mother, Rebecca Hampton.

'Now, Chloe, what can you tell me about a boy called Luke Davidson?'

Chloe looked nervously around the room. 'He's a friend of mine on Instagram. He's a friend of Laura's too.'

'Chloe, can you just confirm for me your age, please?'

'Twelve.'

'You know that you shouldn't be on Instagram until you're thirteen, don't you? So when you signed up, you would have put a different birth year in. How old does it say you are on Instagram?'

'Fifteen. Laura's the same. We set them up together.'

'When did you get a follow request from Luke? Can you remember?'

'I'm not sure. Maybe six months ago. We were in year seven.'

Bernie saw Kerry writing some notes down.

'And when did he befriend Laura?'

'After me. He found me first and then Laura through me.'

'Did you mind him becoming friends with Laura?'

Chloe's eyes darted about. 'No,' she answered, a little too quickly.

'Are you sure about that?'

'Maybe a bit. She was mad about him. She'd come into school and would be like, "Guess who messaged me last night? He's so lovely." Made me want to puke. He was sending me messages too but I never told her that.'

'What kind of messages?'

Bernie saw Chloe swallow.

'Chloe? You do realise we're going to have to look at your Instagram account and your DMs, don't you?'

'Is that really necessary?' asked Rebecca.

'I'm afraid it is, given the nature of the messages between Luke and Laura.'

'But that's them, not Chloe.'

Bernie turned her gaze to Chloe. 'This is about finding the man responsible and finding Laura. I will be absolutely astonished to find out Luke Davidson is his real name and he really is seventeen.

I suspect he is a lot older and he's a man, not a boy. And Laura is with him now.'

Chloe covered her face with her hands. 'Please don't make me say it.'

Rebecca put her arm around her daughter. 'I can take it. I won't be cross. I'm just glad to not be in Laura's mum's shoes. Come on, love.'

Chloe put her hands down. 'Umm… I sent photos of myself. Topless ones.'

CHAPTER 43

Rebecca Hampton's arms were wrapped around her daughter as they left. Chloe had, very tearfully, taken Bernie through the history of her online relationship with Luke. She handed over her phone and gave her login details for Instagram. She told them there would be messages on there between her and Laura. Ones where she called Laura a bitch for stealing Luke from her.

'I was so horrible to her. If I'd known, I would never had said those things. I hope she's OK,' Chloe had cried.

Bernie had decided that now wasn't the time to tell Chloe she had actually committed a criminal offence by sending the photo to Luke. She would let her mother know at a later date. They certainly weren't going to press charges.

Back in the office, Kerry had Chloe's Instagram page open and was reading the private messages between the two girls.

'It certainly got very heated between them,' she said to Bernie. 'Chloe told Laura that Luke had only invited Laura because she couldn't go. Chloe and her family were at a wedding. There are photos up of it.'

'I bet Laura didn't take that too well.'

'No, she didn't. And then the name calling started. It escalated pretty quickly.'

Bernie looked around the office. Mick, Alice and Anderson were with Worth but Matt and Tom were working for her.

'Right, guys, how are you doing?'

Matt looked up from his desk. 'Jane made a phone call. I don't know what she said but the warrant came through so we're in. While Tom's been trying to track down an IP for Luke Davidson, I've been going through his account. In particular, the DMs.'

'And?'

'Each girl reading them will think they're very personal but in fact, they're all very similar. They follow a pattern. Luke finds out what each girl is into and initially focuses the conversation on that. Then he starts to deviate it slightly. He makes a comment on their appearance – maybe their clothes or hair or say they have a pretty face. Then he turns to their bodies and, well… we all know where that one goes.'

Bernie pulled up a chair next to Matt. 'So, he must keep notes on all of them.'

'He'd have to, to keep up. Tom reckons he'll have other fake accounts too on other social media sites. Twitter, Facebook, Snapchat, WhatsApp…'

'Ah. I have Chloe's phone. She mentioned WhatsApp when she gave it to me. Wait a minute, it's on my desk.'

Bernie grabbed the phone she had put in an evidence bag. 'Tom, do you mind looking at this?'

'Not at all. Do you want me to wear gloves?'

'Yes. I've got some in my drawer.'

She passed the phone and gloves over to Tom. 'Have you had any luck on tracking down his IP address?'

'No, he's a crafty bugger. I think he's using Tor. I know I'm not a profiler or anything like that, but I do know my technology. I reckon this guy has a big set-up, probably at home. He'll definitely have multiple computers and monitors. I'm also guessing he has more than one phone. Now, what have we got here?'

Tom put on the gloves and took the phone out of the bag. 'Do you have a PIN number?'

'Oh yes, I think Kerry has that. Kerry, what's the pin code for Chloe's phone?'

Kerry looked at a piece of paper. 'Zero seven zero seven.'

'Is it her birth date by any chance?' asked Tom. He shook his head. 'Not very sensible.'

'Not sure,' said Bernie. 'Quite possibly.'

'Right. Where's her WhatsApp? Here we go… quite a lot of chatting on here… Right, this is him, Luke Davidson.'

Tom scrolled the messages up until he found the first one. Bernie pulled on gloves and took it from him. She started to read the thread.

'Looks similar to the Instagram messages for the moment. Discussing something they watched on TV… now that's interesting… she's mentioned *EastEnders* but he's replied talking about a character from *Coronation Street*. She pulls him up on it. He tries to cover it by saying he always gets those two actresses confused.'

'Far more likely he doesn't know what she's talking about,' said Tom.

'That makes sense,' said Matt. 'I'm seeing similar things here. He lets them talk about the topic and then gives a brief comment back.'

Bernie continued to read. 'He thanks her for her photos. Says how much he enjoyed them.' She closed her eyes for a moment. 'Oh God, I hate to think what he's doing to Laura.' She started reading again. 'She asks for a photo back. He says he's shy, that his profile pic is the only decent one he's got.'

'Looks a pretty good one to me,' said Matt. 'I feel sorry for the real guy.'

Bernie read on. 'She's persistent. She keeps on asking… shit.'

'What?' asked Tom.

'He sent one. Look.'

She turned the phone round for them all to see. Kerry came and joined them.

'Oh my God,' Kerry said. 'It's a motorcyclist all in black. What's written underneath?'

Bernie flicked down. '"Me in my leathers. Looking forward to riding with you one day." Yuck.' Bernie shuddered.

'Well at least you've got something to show the DCI now. It's got to be connected with our dead woman,' said Kerry.

Bernie rubbed her forehead. 'The DCI made it very obvious I have to have clear evidence. Kerry, can you get on to Gerald, please, and see if he's found any more CCTV footage? And check with Salisbury Police if they've managed to speak to the bus driver. Tom, can you email that photo to me somehow, please? Matt knows the address. And we could do with getting it printed out too. I want to show this to Ryan Willis.'

Matt's desk phone rang.

'MCIT, DC Matt Taylor speaking… oh, yes… OK, she's right here, I'll tell her.'

He put the phone down. 'Looks like you'll get your chance now, ma'am. Ryan's been cleared by the doctor.'

CHAPTER 44

Ryan had a dressing over his forehead, accentuating his sullen eyes and pale skin. He was sitting on the bed in the cell.

'And the doctor definitely said he was OK to be interviewed?' Bernie asked Sergeant Alan Turner.

'Yes, gave him a clean bill of health.'

'Stick him in room five then, please. I'll let the DCI know.'

Bernie walked away from the cells to make the call to Worth. She had contemplated speaking to Ryan first but knew her commanding officer was watching her, just waiting for her to make one false move.

'Sir, I just thought I'd let you know Ryan Willis is fit for interview and will be going into room five in the next few minutes. Are you happy for me to continue speaking to him with you observing?'

Worth sighed. 'Yes, I suppose so. But only in relation to the motorbike race. I will question him further afterwards. And try to keep him in one piece this time.'

Bernie let the barbed comment go. This was the only chance she was going to get to talk to Ryan.

'Thank you, sir.'

'The time is fourteen fifteen hours. This is Detective Inspector Noel resuming interview with Ryan Willis. I'd just like to remind you that you're still under caution. How are you feeling now, Ryan?'

The young man looked slowly up at her.

'Got a banging headache. Not really sure what happened.'

'You fainted and hit your head on the table. But don't worry too much about that now. I'm going to ask you a few more questions but then DCI Worth will be coming in to question you more about your assault on a police officer.'

Bernie pushed a piece of paper towards him. 'When we spoke before, you said the motorcyclist you saw at the race was dressed completely in black. Could this be him?'

Ryan's eyes flickered across the paper. 'Don't know. Could be. Most people tend to look the same when they're dressed completely in black with a helmet on.'

'Please, Ryan. There are some subtle distinctive features about that jacket. I'm not going to point them out though.'

Ryan pushed himself forward in his chair and picked up the photo. He looked intently at it.

'It could be. There are some silver buttons on it but they look more for show than for practical reasons. Motorbike jackets are normally zipped up – much easier to do if you've got gloves on. I can't say for certain as it was dark but I do remember something shining when he walked past headlights – it might have been one of the buttons.'

'Ryan, it would really help us, and help you, if you gave us the names of the others at the race. At the moment, this is unsubstantiated. We need more witnesses.'

Ryan dropped the paper onto the table and shook his head.

'Would it help if I got assurances that you wouldn't be charged for illegal gambling?'

Ryan laughed. 'We barely bet enough to get a Mars bar.'

'Except that last time, Ryan, when something considerably more important than money was exchanged. A young woman is dead. And now a twelve-year-old girl is missing.' She jabbed her finger at the photo. 'And we think he may be connected to both. Think carefully, Ryan. Because my DCI isn't going to be so friendly when he comes to interview you.'

Ryan's hand tentatively went to his head. He winced as he touched the dressing.

'Are you OK?' Bernie asked.

'Yes. It's itchy where they glued my cut. I'll give you one name but only one. He's one of our Polish farm workers.'

The DCI sent Mick Parris to bring in the farmhand. He made it clear he would take it on from there.

'Thank you, DI Noel. You can go back to your missing girl case.'

'But, sir, I'm sure the two cases are linked.'

'I think we still need more evidence.'

Bernie narrowed her eyes as he walked away. She couldn't work Worth out. If the dead woman wasn't Rosa then Rupert Fox was off the hook and there was no need for him to be so uncooperative over sharing evidence. Except no one knew where the real Rosa was. Was there another body somewhere waiting to be found? Her anger was building but she didn't want to vent at her officers. There was only one person who could take it – Jane Clackett.

Jane was furiously typing on her keyboard when Bernie went into Jane's office.

'God, where did you learn to type like that?' Bernie asked.

'A very snobby aunt I used to spend holidays with. She was a PA to a director at a big bank. Told me being able to type properly was the biggest asset a girl could have. Used to make me practise every morning before we could go out anywhere. She was an absolute cow.'

'And was she right? Is typing your biggest asset?'

Jane lifted her hands off the keyboard and looked up at Bernie. 'I have far more talents than typing.' She winked.

'Well, that's true. How did you get that warrant through so fast?'

'Oh, just one PR person talking to another PR person about murder and abduction and how that might look to the public. Now, what else can I do for you? You look riled.'

'I am. I'm furious with Worth but with myself as well. I should have looked at publicity yesterday. How much has Laura Moffatt had?'

'Well, it went out on local news on Sunday but those bulletins don't generally have huge viewing figures. It's gone on local newspapers' websites but won't go to press until later in the week. Went on social media. You want a bigger push though.'

'We've got to. I think we need to get the family in for a proper press conference.'

'I agree. I was ready to do that on Sunday morning but "someone" didn't think it was necessary.'

'And I didn't think to check. I was too busy chasing up leads,' said Bernie. She was aware she was pacing up and down. 'How soon can you set it up?'

'We've missed the lunchtime slot. How about four p.m.? Should make it then for early evening news. Can you sort out the family?'

'Of course. I'll deal with them.'

'Oh, is Tom still working with you?'

'Yep. Why?'

'Just having a few issues with my computer.' The faintest hint of pink appeared on Jane's cheeks.

Bernie smiled. 'It's not really his remit. And I think I need him more at the moment.'

'I'm not sure it's fair you get to hog all the good-looking men round here.'

'Ha! I'm not sure we can class old Worthless as good-looking. See you later.'

Kerry, Matt and Tom were still working when Bernie got back to MCIT.

'I've just spoken to Jane Clackett. She's going to set up a press conference about Laura Moffatt for this afternoon. Ideally, we need to get at least one family member there. I'll give them a call in a minute. But we need to decide how much information to release.'

'Like, whether we mention Laura's plans to meet Luke Davidson or not,' said Matt.

'Exactly.'

'We should name the bastard,' said Kerry.

'I think that would be counterproductive,' said Bernie. 'He'll just shut the Instagram account down. What do you think, Tom?'

He turned round from his computer. 'I agree. It seems to me you have the perfect opportunity to engage with Luke. You have Chloe's Instagram details and access to her WhatsApp. Using Chloe as a front, you can chat to him.'

'Wouldn't that be entrapment?' asked Matt.

'I don't think so,' answered Tom. 'You wouldn't be doing this to entice him into committing a crime. You want him to reveal what's happened to Laura. And by getting him online, I might be able to track him down.'

Bernie thought for a moment. 'I probably should check it first with the DCI but that's a bloody good idea, Tom. Matt, get ready to channel your inner pre-teen girl.'

'What? Why me? Why not Kerry?'

'Because you're the one who's been looking at all these messages. You spotted a pattern between them all. You're good with words. Analyse Chloe's messages – look for speech patterns. Jot down some ideas. We'll look to go live after the news this evening.'

CHAPTER 45

Bernie put the phone down and glanced at her watch. Three o'clock. She had an hour before the press conference.

'Right, that's Mrs Moffatt sorted for later. Apparently, Craig is coming home today so his father will stay with him. I haven't met him yet. Have you, Kerry?'

Kerry looked up.

'Yes, he's a very quiet, private man. Older than her by a good ten years at least. I did think it a bit strange that he went back to the hospital on Sunday morning to be with his son rather than stay with his wife. Craig's definitely the golden child. By the way, Salisbury Police have come back to me. They found the bus driver and checked the CCTV. Laura got on the bus at fifteen fifty hours at Potterne. She spent pretty much the whole journey looking out of the window, just occasionally looking at her phone. Although we now know it was the phone Luke gave her.'

'Yes. Tom, where are we up to with mobile phones?'

Tom turned to face her. 'Laura's is still switched off. No idea about the other one she used. Should hear back from the Italian police later or first thing tomorrow about our murder victim's phone. That'll hopefully give us a name.'

The door to MCIT flew open. It was Worth.

'DI Noel, I've just heard that you've set up a press conference, without consulting me first.'

Bernie stood to face her senior officer. 'Sorry, sir. As the lead for this case, I didn't think I needed to inform you. Plus I know you're busy.'

Worth narrowed his eyes. 'Be careful at this press conference. You're to talk about Laura and only Laura. By the way, we've just charged Ryan Willis with assaulting a police officer and he's been bailed.'

'Oh. And the farmhand, did he corroborate Ryan's story about the motorbike race?'

'Yes, to a certain extent. He left early, before Ryan, so I'm keeping young Mr Willis on my radar.'

It took all of Bernie's strength not to throw something at the door as Worth went out.

'God, that man makes me so mad.'

Bernie worked on her statement for the press conference. She deliberately held back on the Instagram details, and focused instead on the café where Laura had last been seen. Kerry found some stills from the CCTV footage.

At three forty-five p.m., Caroline Moffatt appeared with Jane.

'Thank you for coming,' said Bernie. 'There are a few things we need to discuss. When we go in, I'll read a prepared statement and we'll have up some pictures of Laura. The last place we've tracked her to with CCTV is a café in Salisbury. We're going to show that as well as the photo you provided of Laura. I'd like you to just say a few words, asking for Laura to come home and then I'll take some questions from reporters. Don't be afraid to cry. In fact, there'll be a box of tissues ready. OK?'

Caroline Moffatt nodded.

'I gather Craig is coming home. That's good.'

Caroline bit her lip and she gave a slight nod. 'It's all horrible, though, isn't it?'

Bernie put her hand on Caroline's arm as Kerry appeared. 'Yes. You remember my colleague, Detective Sergeant Kerry Allen, don't you?'

'Yes.'

'Would you like to use the bathroom before you go in? Maybe freshen up a little?' Kerry asked.

'That might be a good idea. I probably look a right state.' Caroline walked away with Kerry, her head down.

'So, you're not going to mention the possible internet grooming?' said Jane.

'Not for the moment. We need Luke Davidson to stay online if we're going to have any hope of catching him. We're going to use Chloe's accounts to contact him.'

'Risky.'

'I know. But we've got to try.'

Kerry came back with Caroline. 'I think we're all ready to go, ma'am.'

'OK. Let's go in.'

A small group of local reporters waited for them in the press room. Bernie's heart sank that there were so few. They desperately needed the coverage. But she wasn't surprised. Obvious abductions of young children always pulled a crowd, but a twelve-year-old, almost thirteen, leaving home with a bag full of things, didn't warrant as much attention. She spotted Clive Bishop from the *Salisbury Journal*. A local reporter all his life, she wondered if he would give her grief.

'Good afternoon, ladies and gentlemen. Thank you so much for coming at short notice. In case you don't know me, I'm Detective Inspector Bernie Noel. I have a statement to give, Mrs Moffatt has a few words to say and then I'll take some questions.

'On Saturday afternoon, sometime after three p.m., Laura Moffatt left her house and travelled from Potterne to Salisbury by bus. We've managed to track her by CCTV to a café, the image should be on the screen. Having spoken to the people who work there, we know that she asked to go out the back way as she said there was a group of girls after her. She left around five twenty-five p.m. We've not managed to find her from that point onwards, although we're still searching.'

Bernie paused and risked a glance at Caroline Moffatt. Her head was down. Bernie was all too aware of the effect of her words.

'We believe Laura was planning on staying out all night. She took a few things in a bag but not enough to suggest she was running away. We're working on the theory that maybe she was going to a party or seeing friends her parents don't know about. We really need to know where Laura went after leaving the café. Who did she meet? Did she actually reach her final destination? Laura was wearing a dark jacket and jeans and her hair was in a ponytail. We need the public to help with any possible sightings. Mrs Moffatt will now say a few words.'

Bernie gave Caroline what she hoped was a reassuring look. Caroline raised her head a little but kept her eyes down.

'I… I just want to tell Laura… that she's not in trouble. I just want her home.' Caroline dissolved into tears.

Bernie always hated these moments. She had to stay professional but she was aware she looked hard, unfeeling, when the very opposite was true.

'I'd just like to reiterate what Laura's mother said. Laura is not in trouble. Her whole family want her back safe and well. I'll take two questions.' Bernie pointed to a young woman she recognised.

'Hi, Gemma Proctor from BBC *Points West*. Laura's been missing for what, three days now. Just how concerned are you?'

'Very,' Bernie answered. 'This is out of character for Laura and from what we've managed to discover so far, it seems as though she was only planning on staying away for one night. Thank you,

Gemma. I'll take one more.' Bernie knew she couldn't ignore Clive any longer, sitting on the front row, waving his arm in the air.

'Yes, Clive.'

'Thank you, Detective Inspector Noel. It's obvious you and the family are concerned. Is that because the body of a young woman was found in woodland last week? Do you think the two cases are connected?'

Bernie hesitated. Worth's earlier words were ringing in her ears. She had to phrase her answer carefully.

'I'm not working on that particular case so I can't comment on it. But, like with all our enquiries, I'm keeping an open mind in regards to Laura's disappearance. We're hoping she'll see the press coverage and get in touch. Thank you, everyone, for your cooperation.'

CHAPTER 46

Caroline Moffatt sat in the witness questioning room. Bernie thought about what Chloe Hampton had told her in this room, only a few hours before. She had deliberately held back on the information in the statement but she knew she had to tell Caroline the truth.

'You did really well in there, Caroline,' said Bernie.

'But I didn't say very much. I just froze.'

'It doesn't matter. You said the most important thing.' Bernie paused. She waited for Caroline to drink some more of her tea before continuing. 'Obviously, when we do a press conference, we tell the media what we want them to know. Sometimes, we have to keep information back.'

Caroline's hand started to shake and she spilt tea down her. 'Oh, that's hot.'

Kerry grabbed some paper towels and Bernie took the mug from Caroline.

'Is she… dead?'

Bernie reached out and took Caroline's hand.

'Not as far as we know. But what we have uncovered, is that we think we know who Laura was supposed to meet.'

Caroline looked from Kerry to Bernie. 'What? Who? Why didn't you say in the press conference?'

'We believe she was due to meet a boy who she knew as Luke Davidson. They had met on Instagram. However, we don't think he's called Luke and we don't think he's seventeen.'

Caroline clasped her hand to her mouth as she gagged.

'There's a toilet right next door. Kerry, could you?'

Kerry quickly led Caroline out.

There was a knock at the door and Jane Clackett came in.

'Sorry to bother you but Clive Bishop is still hanging around. Wants to talk to you.'

The only thing Bernie wanted to do to Clive Bishop was hit him for his insensitivity.

Jane had been right. Clive Bishop was still hanging around. As much as Bernie found him annoying at times, he was also a very good source.

'Clive, what do you want? I have a girl to find and you have a story to write.'

'Nice to see you too, Detective Inspector. I'm sorry if I was out of line. It just seemed too much of a coincidence that one young woman is dead and then a girl goes missing. Especially since the dead woman was found close to the girl's home.'

Bernie frowned. They hadn't released the exact location. 'What makes you think that?'

Clive grinned. 'I'm an investigative journalist. It's my job to find out things.'

'And I thought you were just a reporter on the local rag. Oh no, wait a minute. It was *your* paper that had the tweet about the body.'

Clive waggled his finger. 'Exactly. I find out things. Now, do you want this information or not?'

Bernie narrowed her eyes. 'What information?'

'You know I'm not going to give it up that easily. You're holding
back details about Laura. Is there one little snippet I can have and
I promise not to print it until you tell me I can?'

'You have to give me some idea first.'

Clive laughed. 'You're good at haggling. Two words – Rupert Fox.'

Bernie tried to keep her demeanour the same but her heart
was leapfrogging.

'Why would I be interested in Rupert Fox?'

'Because there was a Forensics van outside his house the other
day. I live round the corner from him. Do you want this info or not?'

Despite Worth's clear warnings, she knew she had to find out
more. She thought carefully. What could she afford to give away?
'When Laura left the shop, she changed her hairstyle. It had been
in a very high ponytail, as you could see in the photo. She tied it
looser, with the hairband at the base of her neck.'

'What did she do that for?'

Bernie shrugged. 'Maybe she wanted to change her appearance.'
But Bernie had already guessed the real reason. It would be hard
to fit a motorbike helmet over a head with a high ponytail. She
wasn't planning on giving that information away, though.

'So, give,' she said, though she could tell Clive wasn't overly
impressed.

'OK. You're asking Rupert Fox the wrong questions. In fact,
you're the wrong team to be asking him questions.'

'So which team should be talking to him?'

Clive merely raised his eyebrows at her.

'Oh God. You can print the hairstyle change now. But that's
all you're getting.'

Clive smiled. 'Fraud team. Have a closer look at his business.
Ask yourself how he managed to pay for all the work done on his
house. And that's all *you're* getting, for now.'

*

Energy pulsed through Bernie's body. There were so many things going on in her brain. She knew she ought to pass on Rupert Fox's name to the Fraud Squad as a person of interest but they couldn't get warrants to look at his accounts without some idea of criminal activity. She was sure DCI Worth was mixed up with it somehow. And if that was the case, then Anti-Corruption would have to become involved. Did she really want that blowing up in her face?

She walked back to the witness questioning room. Caroline looked a little better but not much.

'Please tell me everything you've found out,' Caroline said before Bernie had even sat down.

'Are you sure?'

Caroline nodded.

'OK. It seems as though Laura has been in regular contact with Luke Davidson. They have been sending private messages to each other. Very private. Laura has sent photos of herself, including... topless ones.'

Caroline shut her eyes and gripped the chair arms. 'Carry on.'

'Laura had been invited to a party by Luke. He arranged to pick her up in Salisbury and take her there.'

Caroline opened her eyes. 'Why didn't you say this in the press conference?'

'Because we don't want to alert him. Laura isn't the only girl he's in contact with. Do you know Chloe Hampton from Laura's form at school?'

'I've met her a couple of times.'

'Well, Luke is friends with Chloe as well and there have been similar messages with her. In fact, she was supposed to go to this "party" too but couldn't because of a family wedding.'

'And then you would have had two girls missing. Oh God. I didn't go to the meeting at school last year about online safety. I wish I had now.'

'You can't blame yourself, Caroline. I spoke to Mr Gardener and he told me about the lessons Laura had. Even if you didn't hear about the dangers, Laura did. And we're going to try and use social media to our advantage. We have Chloe's and her mother's permission to use Chloe's accounts to contact Luke.'

'So, you're going to try and capture him that way? And find Laura?'

'That's what we're working on. I have an officer looking into it at the moment.'

'Then message him now.'

'We're going to wait until after the news this evening, when Laura's story is reported. I can't promise you this will definitely work. But it's our best chance.'

Bernie and Kerry waved as Caroline drove away.

'You didn't tell her everything,' said Kerry. 'You didn't mention the motorbike photo that Luke sent Chloe and the possible link to the dead young woman in their woods.'

'How can I? I can't watch her hope drain away.'

CHAPTER 47

'So, Matt, how's your inner pre-teen girl coming along?'

Matt smoothed back his brown floppy hair. 'Pretty good, actually.' He threw a notebook across his desk towards Bernie. 'Have a look.'

Bernie picked up the notebook and read aloud. '"OMG Luke! Have you heard about Laura? She's gone missing. Did she make it to your party on Saturday night?" Is that it? Is that all you've written?'

'No. Turn over. I've made a list of Chloe's favourite phrases on the other side and her patterns of speech, in particular, all the abbreviations she uses. I can't write more because I don't know how he's going to respond.'

'Well, I can tell you right now that she would say, "Shit, Luke!" rather than OMG because she was swearing at school this morning. Think it needs more work, and fast.'

Matt huffed. 'Well, maybe it should be a woman who does it, ma'am.'

Bernie put her hand on Matt's shoulder. 'I'm sorry, you've done a lot of work here. Would it help if you watched Chloe's interview? Hear how she phrases things?'

'Yeah, that might help.'

'Great. Kerry, can you set that up, please, and help Matt with the phrases? Really important to get it right. One false move and he'll be on to us. Now, Tom, how are you doing with Luke Davidson?'

Tom shook his head. 'God, the things he's writing to these girls! Really hope we can catch him later. He's bloody clever. But I'm determined to find that IP address.'

'Ma'am, I have good news.'

Bernie looked up to see Anderson had come in. She was glad he'd stuck to calling her ma'am in front of the others.

'Tom, you're going to be interested in this too. I've had a text from the Italian police officer I've been working with. He's forwarded an email from the phone company. We know who owns the phone that belonged to our murder victim.'

He sat at his desk and opened his email. 'Here we go. I'll translate it. OK, so the IMEI number shows that the phone was registered in the name of... oh, Bruno Manetti. Not a woman.'

'Did Ria, assuming that's her name, steal it? Is that why she changed the SIM as soon as she got here?' Bernie asked.

Anderson read to the end of the email. 'No, she didn't steal it. Well, not from a stranger. From what Inspector De Luca says here, she was Manetti's girlfriend. He assaulted her a while back and he's on bail. Case is due to be heard end of the year. But guess what? He skipped bail three weeks ago and no one's seen him.'

'So when Father Adrian said that she was scared for her life, had this guy made contact with her?' Bernie asked.

Anderson shrugged. 'No idea but it'll be worth checking to see if he's entered the country. I can do that. But the main thing here is that this guy has a long record and is seriously nasty.'

'But he can't be Luke. Our guy's been chatting to Laura and Chloe for six months now.'

'I agree. But could he be the guy who raced Luke? Ryan said he didn't know who raced him. Was there another stranger there that night?'

Bernie rested her head in her hands. None of this was making sense. She lifted her head. 'So what you're suggesting is that our murder victim, believed to be Ria, might not have been killed by Luke Davidson but by this Bruno Manetti? But Laura is with Davidson. So they're not connected at all?'

'Actually, ma'am, I think I might be able to help you with that,' said Tom. 'Do you know Ria's surname, DS Anderson?'

'Yes. Greco. The inspector is chasing up dental records as we speak to confirm ID.'

'So, Ria Greco. Or maybe, Maria G.' Tom pushed back his chair from the desk to show them the screen. 'She and Luke have been messaging.' He scrolled down. 'Quite a few messages here. Basic English but very sexually explicit… and whoa, there's a photo.'

A naked young woman was on the screen. Tom clicked to enlarge it but then covered her body with his hand. 'Does her face look a bit like Rosa?'

Bernie and Anderson both stared at the screen.

'Yes,' Anderson said. 'Can you crop that headshot, please, and I'll send it to the inspector?'

'And I'll send it to Harriet Fox,' said Bernie. 'But we go ahead with messaging Luke. Because I'm sure he has Laura.'

The door to MCIT banged open so hard, Bernie thought it was going to come off its hinges. Worth's face was almost purple with rage.

'I thought I made myself very clear that you are *not* a part of this murder investigation, Detective Inspector Noel,' he spluttered.

Bernie turned round. She was getting fed up with Worth's unpredictable moods. 'I know that, sir.'

'So why did you answer a question about it in the press conference?'

Bernie steeled herself. Although she was getting used to his temper, Worth seemed particularly angry this time.

'I was asked a direct question by Clive Bishop. I said I couldn't comment but was keeping an open mind. In case you'd forgotten, sir, it was Clive's paper that Laura tweeted to about the body being found. We should be grateful he didn't reveal that information. And we *should* be keeping an open mind.'

Bernie paused. She wasn't sure if it was enough evidence to link the cases but she knew she had to pass on the picture they had seen of Luke Davidson.

'Sir, you have asked for more proof that the cases are linked; the evidence is stacking up. Laura has been messaging a man called Luke Davidson she met on Instagram. We've discovered he's been chatting with several girls online, including a girl from Laura's class at school – Chloe Hampton. And also a Maria G who we think might be Ria. Luke encourages the girls to send him photos, very revealing ones, but he's resisted sending photos back. Except for one time, when he sent a picture of himself in a black leather jacket and black motorcycle helmet, with the visor down.'

'And that's the photo you showed Ryan Willis?'

'Yes, sir.'

'You didn't tell me where that had come from.'

'I didn't get the chance to, sir.'

'What's your plan of action?'

'We have Chloe and her mother's permission to use her account to try and contact Luke. I plan to do this with Matt after the local TV news. There should be a story about her.'

Worth was quiet for a minute before speaking. 'We're not looking at entrapment here, are we?'

'No. I'm hoping we can arrange a time to meet but I'm not planning on trying to lure him into suggesting things online.'

'Do you think you can pull this off?'

'I have no idea if we can be a convincing twelve-year-old girl who's pretending to be fifteen but it's our best shot.'

Worth sighed. 'All right. Go ahead. And maybe we do have to keep an open mind. Tomorrow morning we're having an update meeting to discuss everything we have on our dead woman. I'd like you to be in that meeting since you were one of the first on the scene. The chief constable is keen for progress to be made.'

Bernie was itching to smile. *Chief constable wants me in then.* 'Thank you, sir. We'll keep you updated.'

Anderson waited for Worth to leave before speaking. 'You didn't mention Bruno Manetti.'

Bernie gave a wry smile. 'Not my case. Up to you to tell him. Maybe do it later. After we've tried to contact Luke.'

CHAPTER 48

Laura's face filled the screen. Gemma Proctor from BBC *Points West* had done a good job. Bernie wondered if Caroline Moffatt had watched it. It would have been hell for her. She looked around at her team. Everyone was silent during the report. Although she knew they had to maintain a professional distance, a missing child still got to them all. Bernie switched off the TV as the report ended.

'OK, team, here we go. Matt, you've looked at this the most. Which social media site is best?'

Matt walked over to his desk and picked up his notebook. 'Most of the messages have been done via Instagram but the more recent ones have been on WhatsApp.'

'WhatsApp uses mobile numbers, right, Tom? Can't we just ring him and use the signal to get a position on him?'

Tom gave a weak smile. 'Already tried. I did my best "Hello, sir, I'm ringing today to talk to you about the car accident you've had in the last three years." He hung up immediately. WhatsApp uses an internet connection to send messages, either through Wi-Fi or data. So I'm hoping we can find his IP address, especially if he uses the desktop version. We need to be careful though. Chatting to him now might gain some clues but…'

'But what?'

'One false move and he'll know it's not Chloe. Plus, if he's fastidious as I think he is, he might notice that it's not her IP address.'

'What the hell can we do about that?'

'Cover story. She's at someone else's house. I've set up the desktop version on Matt's computer to use. We have protection on our address so Luke shouldn't be able to see where we are. Maybe she could be at her aunt's house and her geeky uncle is a bit paranoid about the government watching him or something.'

Bernie moved her chair next to Matt's. 'Seriously? Is that the best story you can come up with?'

'See if he asks where you are. If he does, then we know he's monitoring her.'

Adrenalin started to pump round Bernie's body. Her stomach felt like it had a snake writhing around in her. She breathed out slowly.

'OK. Matt, you ready to do this?'

Kerry and Anderson stood behind. Tom stayed at his desk, ready to track Luke's IP address.

Matt began typing.

oh shit, luke! did you see the news about laura?

He looked at Bernie. 'Do you think I should write more, ma'am?'

'No. Keep it short.'

They waited in silence. Seconds turned into minutes. The two ticks by the message were still grey.

'Maybe he hasn't seen it,' Bernie said. 'No, wait. Ticks are blue and he's typing back.'

No what happened?

'Carry on, Matt.'

she's gone missing.

Seconds later.

What?! When?!

at the weekend

did she make it to your party?

A longer pause this time.

*No I was supposed to meet her in Salisbury but she
didn't show up so I thought she wasn't coming I feel bad now*

Bernie rolled her eyes. 'How are we supposed to answer that
one?' She looked around her team. 'Tom, are you getting anywhere
with the IP address?'

Tom shook his head. 'As I thought, it's all over the place.'

'Answer him sympathetically,' said Kerry. 'Tell him it's not his
fault.'

Matt began to type.

*ah, don't feel bad not your fault, if it hadn't been for that stupid
wedding i would've come too and then laura wouldn't have been
on her own*

'Luke is typing' appeared at the top of the phone screen.

*Saw the pics on insta. You looked hot in your
bridesmaid dress with those thin straps*

Were you wearing a bra under it?

Matt shook his head. 'He's one sick fuck.'

'I know,' said Kerry. 'Just send back a wink emoji. Actually, do the wide eye one first and then the wink. That's it.'

His response was swift.

Baaabe u don't know what ur doing to me!!

Bernie sat back in her chair. 'I think we do, Luke. I'm going to vomit.'

'But he said "babe",' said Kerry. 'He's typing again.'

Bernie's eyes widened at his response. 'Here we go. He's just written, "Where are you, babe? Want to picture you".' She looked across at Tom. 'Bingo.'

CHAPTER 49

If Luke had twigged something was up, his replies didn't show it. Matt had continued to 'chat' with Luke for another ten minutes before ending the conversation. His request for a photo of Chloe in her bridesmaid dress with no underwear on had finished everyone off.

sorry im gonna be at my aunt's for a few days as mum and dad had a massive row and she's walked out so im stuck here for a bit send u pics when i get home… might get more than one Matt added several wink emojis for good measure.

'Oh God,' said Bernie, 'that man makes my skin crawl. So, what do we do now? Tom, any thoughts?'

Tom looked at his computer monitor before turning back to Bernie. 'I still can't get past his proxy IP. This is driving me nuts now. I don't know if he'll have bought the story about Chloe's uncle being an IT security specialist; we may have offered that up too easily. She wouldn't necessarily know about IP addresses. Probably best to try again tomorrow, maybe before school. Perhaps she hasn't slept well, worrying all night about Laura – try that tack.'

Bernie rubbed her forehead. Her usual headache was coming back. She needed food.

'Have there been any phone calls from the public after the news report?'

'I'll go and check,' said Matt. 'But looking at our accounts there's been a big response on social media. The tweet we put out has had over 700 retweets and on Facebook, there's been about 300 shares and about 150 comments. Nothing concrete from that though. I'll go and check with the switchboard. I asked them to take messages. I knew we'd have to concentrate when chatting to this Luke.'

'Thanks, Matt.'

Bernie looked around the office. Everyone seemed a bit drained after the 'Luke' conversation. 'Think we all need something to eat.'

'Pizza?' said Anderson.

'We had that last night.'

'Oh. I'm happy to run out and get some Chinese or Indian, if that helps.'

'That would be great, thanks. Maybe Indian if that's OK with everyone else. Chicken Korma and rice for me, please. I can give you some money.' Bernie smiled, still aware that they needed to talk at some point. Kerry was keeping schtum for now and no one else had picked up on the friendlier atmosphere between them. Not yet anyway.

'Nah, don't worry about it. My treat. Kerry and Tom – text me your order. I know what Matt will want. Might as well see if the DCI wants anything. Or Alice or Mick.'

'Are they actually still here?'

'Yes, they are. I'll be back soon.'

Anderson nearly collided with Jane Clackett as he left the office.

'Sorry, Jane. Off to get some Indian. Do you want any?'

'No thanks. My office will stink for days.'

'Can we help you, Jane?' Bernie asked.

'I've come to tell you that Laura will be in the hourly local radio bulletins for the rest of today. No need to thank me.'

'Thank you anyway. I've sent Matt to find out about any phone calls after the TV report.'

'Yes, I know some came in. I think my job is done for today. I'll be in bright and early if you need me. Oh, is that Tom over there? Tom, I have a problem with my computer. I wondered if you could have a look at it for me, please, now, perhaps.'

Tom glanced over his shoulder. 'Yeah, I don't do that kind of technical support. I'm here to access computers, find the hackers, cyber security, that kind of thing.'

'Oh Tom, please. My screen keeps freezing.'

'Have you tried switching your computer off and on again?'

Bernie stifled a laugh. 'Tom, just go. She's not going to give up.'

As he headed out of the door, he said, 'If I'm not back in ten minutes, send out a search party.'

Bernie and Kerry burst into fits of giggles.

'Poor Tom,' said Bernie, 'he doesn't stand a chance. Once Jane fixes on a man, he's a goner.'

'And what about you, are you fixed on Anderson?'

'I don't know. I haven't spoken to him yet. There's too much going on at the moment.'

'There's always too much going on.'

Bernie wondered whether or not to tell Kerry what Clive Bishop had said about Rupert Fox. 'True. Actually, I was thinking about Rupert Fox again.'

'Oh, Bernie, no.'

'What?'

'You're obsessed. If our victim is Ria then this Italian guy you were talking about with Anderson seems a more likely candidate for her murder than Fox, so it's got nothing to do with him.'

'And it probably doesn't. But there might be something else. Clive Bishop said something very cryptic to me earlier. He said that we weren't the right team to be investigating him. That Fraud should be looking at him instead.'

'Then pass it over to Fraud.'

'But pass over what? I've got no idea what he's done. I need to look at him more closely.'

Kerry sighed. 'No, you don't. We have a dead woman and a missing girl. That's more than enough to be dealing with at the moment. Plus your complicated love life.'

'God, I know,' said Bernie. 'I don't want to contact Alex but I probably should. If nothing else, he's left stuff at my place that he'll need.' She picked up her phone but put it back down as Matt came in, holding slips of paper.

'Fifty calls. Some are probably nothing but we need to go through them to see.'

He handed a pile each to Kerry and Bernie.

'Where's Anderson?' he asked.

'Gone to get food,' said Kerry.

They started to work their way through. Bernie put to one side any that had Laura in another town or city and looked specifically for Salisbury connections.

'Ma'am, this one looks promising,' said Matt. 'A woman with her small child was nearly hit by a motorbike. There was a passenger on the back who had a bag that looked similar to Laura's in the photo shown on TV.'

'That does sound promising.'

Matt's smile became broader. 'It gets better. The woman said the bike was a BMW. She knows because her partner has one similar. Didn't Ryan Willis say that his mystery motorcyclist rode a BMW?'

Bernie clapped her hands. 'Yes, he did. Can you ring her and see if you can go and get a statement from her tonight, please? And if you can get a definite location, then maybe Gerald can find us some more CCTV footage.' She smiled. 'This has to be enough for the DCI now. These two cases must be linked.'

CHAPTER 50

By the time Bernie got home, Marchant was almost in darkness again. It was kicking out time at the pub and a few of the villagers waved to her. She was physically worn out but her brain was buzzing. The witness statement had been helpful. Although the woman hadn't got the registration number, she'd given enough detail for Bernie to be sure it was Laura. It had been close to the service road behind the shops and the woman had described the rider's jacket as similar to the one Luke was wearing in the photo sent to Chloe. We're closing in, she thought.

As her mind was elsewhere, she almost missed the person sitting in her doorway. A sudden movement, though, caught her eye.

'Who's there?' she asked.

'Sorry, I didn't mean to startle you. I must have dropped off waiting for you to come home.'

She instantly recognised the voice. 'Alex, what are you doing here?'

'I thought I should come and see you. Apologise directly.'

'I see.'

'Please, Bernie.'

Bernie hesitated. She was worn out but like ripping a plaster off a wound, it would be better to deal with Alex now and quickly.

'OK.' She pulled her keys out and unlocked the door.

*

She had always felt comfortable with Alex but there was no denying the awkwardness between them now. He sat at the small kitchen table as she made tea. She opened the fridge door.

'Oh shit, I'm out of milk. In fact, I'm pretty much out of everything.'

Alex held up a plastic bag he had stowed by his feet. 'I thought so. Milk and a loaf of bread.'

Bernie stared at it. 'I shouldn't really but…'

'Take the milk, at least. I hate black tea. And I know you tend to just eat toast when I'm not around. You're totally crap at cooking.'

'I'm not. It's more that I don't have time.'

Alex gave her a sideways glance. She took the bag. 'No, you're right… I'm crap at cooking, along with many other things – like relationships. Having said that, I'm not taking the blame for your mistake.'

Alex shifted uncomfortably. 'And you shouldn't. It's all my fault. I didn't tell you the truth when I said I'd had two girlfriends. Had far more than that. I've always been a bit of a player. My father was the same. And really I should know better because I saw how much it hurt my mum.

'I've known Ali for ages. We went to school together. The pub we were in on Saturday, I saw her there last month. We got pretty drunk, had a snog and I ended up back at hers. To be brutally honest, I have a lot more in common with her than you. And when you said just now that you don't have time to shop or cook – you don't have time for the people in your life either. I'm not blaming you at all but I hardly saw you. You'd creep in late at night and then be gone before I woke up. You'd be better off with that officer I saw the other night in the pub.'

Bernie's head jerked up. 'What? At the pub quiz?'

Alex nodded. 'And again on Saturday. I saw him paying at the bar. I'm assuming you were together.'

'Yes. But in a work capacity. We were discussing the case and I only agreed to go after you said you'd be out.'

'And nothing else happened after that? After you'd seen me with Ali?'

Bernie lowered her eyes.

'I don't blame you. He's a good-looking guy and you're both in the same job. Much more likely to understand the pressure. I'm so sorry, Bernie. I didn't want it to end like this.'

'Me neither. Will you do me one favour?'

'Sure.'

'Don't do this to Ali. She seems a nice girl.'

'God, you sound like my mum.'

Bernie widened her eyes.

'All right. I'll behave better.'

She stood up. 'It's too late to sort your things out now but you'll need to collect your stuff at some point. Although you might want to take your football kit tonight.' She nodded her head towards the clothes horse.

'Oh God, sorry. I meant to strip the bed and put the washing machine on before I went out on Saturday but I forgot. Maybe next weekend I'll take the rest of my things if that's OK with you. I know you're really busy at the moment. I saw the news.'

'Yes. I need to get some sleep before I go back in early.' She glanced at the clock on the cooker. It was after eleven thirty.

'I'll let you get to bed then.'

They were heading towards the front door when Bernie remembered something.

'Oh, I wanted to ask you, do you know a man called Rupert Fox? He's a surveyor.'

'God, yes. He's a bloody nightmare. He does a lot of the mortgage surveys. We all dread seeing him.'

'Why?'

'Because if it's him doing the survey, you can pretty much guarantee that he'll find something wrong with the property and either the sale will fall through, or what happens more often, the vendor ends up dropping the price. Either way, we, as the estate agents, are stuffed.'

'Some might say that's a good thing.'

Alex laughed. 'Yeah, I know – we don't have the best reputation. But at the end of the day, it's the vendor who really suffers here, losing money, and that's not on.'

Bernie closed the door behind Alex. She was tired but her mind was awash with conflicting emotions. She wished Pops was still around to talk to.

But maybe there was someone she could talk to. Bernie reached for her phone as she went upstairs to bed. She sent a text.

Are you still up?

Within seconds, her phone began to ring.

'Hi, Gary. You didn't have to ring. You could've just texted back.'

'If my daughter is contacting me this late, she obviously needs my help.'

'Thanks. Just needed someone to talk to. Alex and I have split up.'

'Oh, that's a shame. Are you sure you want to talk to me about it? Wouldn't your mother be better?'

'No. She'd only go all judgy on me.'

'Why would she do that? What aren't you telling me?'

So Bernie poured out everything that had happened with Alex and Anderson over the previous few days.

'OK. I can see why you came to me.'

'Sorry. Just wanted to talk to a grown-up.'

'Ha! Not sure that's me. But for what it's worth, I think you've done the right thing. And I guess you've got a lot on at the moment. I heard about the girl in the woods. Nasty business.'

'Yes. Not that I can tell you much.'

'Of course. On TV shows it's always obvious, isn't it? Last person who saw the victim.'

'Proving a bit tricky to find that last person. Any other ideas?'

'Is there a butler?'

Bernie laughed. 'And on that note, it's time for bed. Thanks for listening.'

'Anytime, Bernie. Good night.'

'Night.'

Bernie put her phone down and got ready for bed. She smiled, thinking about her father's words. If only this case was as obvious as a TV drama.

CHAPTER 51

Wednesday

They sat in neat rows in the briefing room. Bernie was almost used to it now. Almost. She had her notebook and pen in hand, not just to take the minutes of the meeting but to try and work out the exact links between the two cases. She'd already scribbled down *Luke Davidson, Instagram, Laura, Chloe, Maria G – Ria?* She still hadn't heard back from Harriet Fox about the photo they'd sent but presumably she would contact the DCI.

Worth was late, which was unusual for him. Even Jane was on time although she wasn't entirely happy with Bernie.

'Did you give Clive Bishop additional information yesterday?' had been her opening line to Bernie.

'Morning to you too. I might have given him an extra tiny detail. Very small.'

'Thanks for that. The other journos are spitting blood this morning.' Jane sat down next to Anderson.

Bernie looked at her watch. Worth was now ten minutes late and everyone was getting restless. She was just about to stand up and lead the briefing herself when the DCI appeared.

'Apologies for my lateness. I was on the phone to Harriet Fox. She only looked at her emails this morning. The woman you found on Instagram yesterday – Maria G – was their au pair, although, of course, they knew her as Rosa.' He glanced towards Bernie.

'Looks as though you were correct, DI Noel. I'm sure the Italian police will say the same and confirm her name as Maria Greco and hopefully provide some dental records to prove it.

'Now, our assumption so far has been that the murderer was from here in Wiltshire. But DS Anderson told me last night that the mobile phone Ria was using was originally registered to a Bruno Manetti and they used to be in a relationship. Have you found out any more?'

Anderson opened his notebook. 'Yes, sir. I've asked for a search to be done on his name at all ports going back three weeks. So far, nothing has turned up but we can't rule out him using a fake passport. I'm working closely with the Italians and my aim is to get a positive ID on our victim by the end of today.'

There was a loud ping. Worth glared at Tom as he took his mobile out.

'Sorry, sir.'

'Thank you, Anderson. In the meantime, we need to think about Laura Moffatt. If the two cases are connected then she's in imminent danger. Our priority now is to find her. This motorcyclist keeps cropping up. And the fact we now have an independent witness from Saturday is useful. Who went to see her?'

'I did, sir,' said Matt. He opened his notebook. 'We have a location for where he was seen which DS Allen has passed on to the CCTV centre. So hopefully we'll get some footage very soon. We've got a good description of the motorbike and of the rider and passenger. I didn't show her the photo of Luke Davidson until afterwards. But her description matches the photo.'

'And this "chat" you were having with Luke Davidson, DI Noel, have you had any more contact?'

Bernie looked across at Matt. 'DC Taylor sent a message this morning but he hasn't responded yet.'

'He'll probably come back with a comment that he was at college or something like that,' said Matt.

There was a buzzing sound coming from Kerry's phone. 'Sir, it's Gerald from the CCTV centre. Can I?'

'Yes, of course.'

Kerry answered the phone as she left the room.

'And Tom, you've been looking at the IP address for Luke Davidson,' said Worth.

'Yes, sir. He's using Tor, so it's proving difficult to track him down. But I've just had an interesting email arrive from the mobile phone company about Ria's phone.'

'Go on.'

'Because we knew roughly when Ria had died, I gave them specific time parameters to search for. They've messaged now to say that her phone was switched on and used last Saturday afternoon between three and six p.m., outside the time I'd asked them to look at.'

'What? But she'd been dead for over a week by then,' Worth said.

The rest of the team sat up.

'Does this mean Bruno now has her phone?' Mick asked. 'And there are actually two perpetrators after all?'

Bernie thought for a moment. She remembered what the bus driver had told Salisbury police and what she had seen on the CCTV footage.

'No. I still think it's Luke Davidson,' she said. 'We know that Laura had a different phone on Saturday afternoon. What if he gave Ria's mobile to her and, by doing so, deliberately put suspicion on Manetti? If he was in a relationship with Ria, she might have told him about her former boyfriend and what he'd done to her. We know he's a clever man when it comes to technology. He's not going to give Laura a phone that can be traced back to him.'

Worth was about to answer when there was a loud 'Yes!' from just outside the office door. Kerry popped her head round. 'We've got them on CCTV. Gerald is going to send the recordings over but he's also taken some stills and he's going to email them to me now.'

There was a collective sigh of relief.

'Do you want to put those pictures out to the media?' asked Jane.

'Well, let's see them first,' answered Worth. 'Make sure they're good enough.'

Bernie tapped her pen against her notepad. 'Releasing them may help with contacting Luke. He told us, well, Chloe, that he didn't meet Laura. We could go with the "you lied to me" tack and see how he responds.'

'Hmm, that might work. OK, plan of action. DS Anderson, I want you to contact your Italian counterpart – speed up those dental records. DS Allen, I want to see those photos as soon as you get them. And see if you can get a registration. I think he's probably using false plates but let's at least try. DCs Taylor, Parris and Hart – I want you to keep trawling through all the messages that we have between Luke and the other girls. There has to be a clue in there somewhere. Jane, get a press release ready to send out. Tom, keep trying with the IP address and the internet service and mobile providers. In particular, see if you can get a location for that phone on Saturday. DI Noel' – Worth turned towards her – 'you and I are going to pay one more visit to Ryan Willis. We need all the names of the people at that race.' Worth looked at his watch. 'It's nine thirty hours now. Check in at eleven thirty hours.'

Bernie inwardly winced as she changed gear and a spasm of pain shot through her wrist. She would have to go back to her GP and chase up a physio appointment. She had hoped Worth would have his usual driver but he had suggested she drove instead.

'You know the way there, don't you?' he had said. 'Best if you drive then.'

'What's your approach going to be with Ryan, sir?'

Worth looked across at Bernie. 'He responds best to you. What would you do?'

Bernie swallowed. Was this a trap or did Worth really want to know what she would do? She was still unsure about what to do with the information she'd been given by Clive Bishop, and then Alex's comment. And if Rupert Fox was doing something dodgy, did DCI Worth know about it?

'I think we need to be willing to drop the police assault charge and promise there will be no enquiries into illegal betting, in return for a full list of names of everyone present at the motorbike race.'

'And what if Ryan is the one who raced this man and knows more than he's saying?'

Bernie shook her head. 'No. I don't think so. His grandfather told me about something that happened when Ryan was five. You know the cave where we found the helmet and jacket? Someone, one of his brothers' friends, persuaded Ryan to hide in there. And they left him. It got dark and he was absolutely terrified. He hasn't gone up that track at night since then.'

'You only have the grandfather's word for that.'

'Actually, one of his brothers confirmed it.'

Bernie could see the farm up ahead. A gentle breeze was causing ripples across the small pond by the entrance. She slowed down to avoid a few ducks as they crossed the farmyard.

'We may find Ryan's out in the fields somewhere,' said Bernie.

She parked near the farmhouse and saw Janet, Ryan's mother, come to the door. Bernie could see signs of exasperation on Janet's face.

'What now?' asked Janet, as they approached.

'I'm sorry to disturb you but we do need to talk to Ryan again,' said Bernie.

'He hasn't done anything wrong.'

'Except hitting a police officer,' said Worth.

Janet glared at him. 'You weren't there. You didn't see what happened. That officer goaded Ryan, tried to grab him.' She looked at Bernie. 'Why didn't you come to speak to him instead? He would have gone peacefully with you.'

Bernie kept her face straight although she was desperate to turn to Worth and say 'told you so'.

'I'm here now,' she said. 'Janet, think about Laura Moffatt. We're fairly certain that the two cases are linked.'

A look of horror appeared on Janet's face. 'You mean… the man who killed that poor girl has Laura?'

'Yes, we think so. We have to get all the names of the men racing that night. One of them had a final race with the mystery motorcyclist. He may be a key witness.'

Janet's early defiance melted away.

'All right. I'll get him to come back.'

CHAPTER 52

Bernie and Worth waited for Ryan in the farmyard. There was no offer of tea and cake from Janet this time and they hadn't been invited in either. The breeze was beginning to pick up and Bernie could smell rain in the air, along with manure. A bank of cloud was moving in. Worth had his phone out and appeared to be studying something closely, before looking up at her.

'An email from Kerry. She's sent a still of the CCTV. Looks good enough to me but difficult to read the registration. Although I suspect they're probably false.'

Bernie looked at the picture. It captured the motorbike from behind and it was clear that there were two people on it.

'Kerry's contact is going to keep looking and see if he can get a better image,' said Worth.

'But that would probably be good enough for the moment. Something to put out to the media.'

'Yes. I'll tell Kerry to liaise with Jane and get a statement out ASAP.'

Bernie turned as she heard the front door open. Stan was standing there leaning on a stick, Hollie the dog next to him.

'I know our Janet is cross with you but it's probably about to start chucking it down with rain. I can smell it. Come in. Can't have you getting wet.'

*

Ryan was drenched when he came in to the lounge.

'Do you mind if I get changed first?' he asked.

'No, not at all,' said Worth, 'but we don't have much time.'

'I'll be five minutes, tops.'

Ryan returned a few minutes later wearing jeans and a black T-shirt. His hair was still wet. He sat forward in an armchair, his arms resting on his legs, his back bent over. He kept his head down. He no longer had the dressing on his forehead. The cut from where he hit his head on the table was visible, along with a purple bruise.

Bernie was next to Worth on the sofa and Stan Willis was in his normal chair by the fire.

'Do you want me to leave, Ryan?'

'No, you're all right, Granddad. You can stay.'

Bernie glanced at Worth, who gave his customary nod.

'Ryan,' Bernie began, 'when I saw you last, I said to you we thought Laura may be with the man who came to your motorbike race.'

'Yeah, I remember.'

'We're more certain now. Could you look at this photo please? We've only just received it.' She passed over the DCI's phone.

Ryan took it and stared for a few seconds. 'So, you think this is Laura?'

'Yes. She's only twelve, Ryan.'

'I know how old she is. It could be the same motorbike. It's definitely a BMW. It was dark when I saw it though. I can't be one hundred per cent sure. Like with the photo of the motorcyclist you showed me – I can't be sure it's him. It was dark. I keep telling you.'

'I know, Ryan. But we need more information than that if we're going to find Laura. We need the names of everyone who raced that night. In particular, were there any other new bikers? Sorry to sound melodramatic, but this is about life and death now.'

She watched Ryan's head sink a little lower.

'We're willing to drop the assault charge and we promise to overlook the illegal betting with your race,' said Bernie.

Ryan shook his head. 'It's more than just that. Some of the guys don't have insurance, some don't even have licences… some are under sixteen.'

Bernie looked back at Worth. He sighed but gave a slight nod.

'We can overlook those things too,' said Bernie.

Ryan stayed silent.

'Stan told me a story about you the other day, Ryan…'

'Now, hold on, I told you that in good faith,' said Stan.

'I know. But I think Ryan might be the only one to understand about Laura. To be tricked into thinking something will be fun, only to discover you're trapped. You had a family who came and looked for you. We're Laura's search party. *You* are Laura's search party. If one of those other guys knows anything that could help find her then surely it'll be worth giving us their names.'

Bernie could hear Ryan sniffing.

'Come on, lad,' said Stan. 'You can't muck about when someone's life is at stake, can you?'

Ryan rubbed his face with his hand and finally looked up at Bernie. 'He was the only new guy that evening. I'll get a pen and paper and write down the rest for you.'

Bernie and Worth read down the list of the names as they sat in the car. Raindrops bounced off the bonnet.

'Quite a few names,' said Bernie. 'I know some of them but not all… Oh shit – sorry, sir – Craig Moffatt was there.'

'No apology necessary. I wasn't expecting to see his name either. We'll head there in a moment. I think we need to get the others to go and visit the rest of them.'

'Yes, split them into two teams. Send Anderson and Matt out together and Kerry with either Mick or Alice. Whoever stays behind can search for the addresses of the men we don't know.'

Worth gave her what Bernie thought was an appraising look. 'Yes, that's just what I was going to suggest. You see, when you're not mucking about and being stupid, you're actually a good officer.'

Bernie did her best not to roll her eyes. She turned the key in the ignition and started the engine. 'I'll take that as a compliment, I think. I'm assuming you're going to ring in and give the orders.'

'But of course.'

CHAPTER 53

Despite their destination being only a couple of miles away, the railway line intersecting the land meant they had to drive a long way round. Bernie could hear a dog barking as they drove up the driveway.

'If you're willing, sir, I have an idea as to how to handle this.'

'Go ahead. You managed to get through to Ryan.'

A surly-looking man came out to greet them. Bernie headed towards him, holding out her hand.

'Mr Moffatt? I'm Detective Inspector Bernie Noel and this is Detective Chief Inspector Worth. Could we come in for a few minutes please?'

'Have you found her?'

'No, not yet. I'm sorry. But we would like to talk to you all, as a whole family.'

Bernie looked at the family's anxious faces. It was obvious Caroline Moffatt hadn't slept. Her eyes were sunken, her face pale. Maybe she had reached the stage where she couldn't cry any more and was now completely numb. John Moffatt sat next to his wife on the sofa, his eyes darting between her and Worth. He was a lot older than his wife. Craig was bundled in an armchair with a duvet wrapped round him.

'We have some news,' Bernie said. 'We haven't found Laura yet but we have more of an idea of who she may be with. Mrs Moffatt, did you tell your husband what I said yesterday about Luke Davidson?'

Caroline lowered her eyes. 'No. I'm sorry, John. I couldn't bring myself to tell you. They think he has Laura.'

John's face flared with anger. 'What you waiting for then? If you know who she's with, go and get her!'

'I'm afraid it isn't that simple, Mr Moffatt. We're fairly certain that Luke Davidson is a pseudonym. His profile says he's seventeen but we think that highly unlikely. We've read conversations between them and there's definitely been some grooming happening. I hate to tell you this but Laura has sent explicit photos of herself at his request.'

John thumped the sofa but kept his gaze on Bernie. 'There's more, isn't there?' he asked.

'Yes, I'm afraid so. There's no easy way of saying this but we now have enough evidence to link Laura's disappearance with the murder of the young woman found in the woods on your property.'

Without making it too obvious, Bernie looked across at Craig to gauge his reaction. His already pale face had taken on a ghostly complexion, his eyes wide with terror.

A wail emerged from Caroline and John Moffatt opened his mouth to speak but no words came out.

'I'm so sorry,' Bernie said. 'We're still considering this as a missing child operation at the moment.'

Bernie glanced at Worth who was standing by the fireplace. His eyes were trained on Craig. She knew what she had to do.

'We believe the murder victim had been on your property for a while, and using forensic techniques, we've managed to ascertain that she had been dead for almost a week when she was discovered.

We have evidence to suggest there was a motorbike race that took place on the other side of the woods. We believe she was there.'

Worth gave a little cough. 'Mrs Moffatt, I think you could do with some sweet tea. If you come with me to the kitchen, I'll make you some.' He gently helped Caroline off the sofa and supported her as they left the room.

'Well, that was subtle,' said John Moffatt. 'You obviously want to ask either myself or Craig some questions without Caroline here.'

Bernie nodded. 'You're right, Mr Moffatt. I need to ask Craig some questions. I'd rather do this informally at the moment. Do I have your permission?'

John Moffatt let out a long sigh. 'Yes. I think I know what it's about. You've been riding my motorbike again, haven't you?'

Craig had sunk even lower and only his eyes and the top of his head could be seen from under the duvet.

'Were you at the race, Craig?' Bernie asked.

He gave a glimmer of a nod.

'Speak up, lad,' said his father.

A muffled 'yes' was heard from under the duvet.

'Craig, I need you to pull the duvet away from your mouth. We're talking to everyone in the race and I can promise you that you're not in trouble with us for taking part. I can't speak for your father though.' Bernie was trying to keep it light. 'Was there someone new at the race?'

'Yes.'

'Can you tell me any more?'

Craig's voice trembled. 'He was dressed all in black and had a really big bike. He was winning all the races. I don't know how he managed it as that lane is so full of potholes. You have to know the way.'

'Was he alone?'

'No. He had a woman with him. She had a helmet on so I didn't see her face.'

'Did she speak?'

'No.'

'We've heard there was a final race against this new guy. Do you know who else took part?'

Bernie watched Craig carefully. She saw a tiny shake of his head.

'How did you get back home? Did you ride up the track and through the woods?'

Craig's eyes flickered to his father and then back to Bernie.

'No. I came back the long way on the roads. I won't ride over the railway bridge and up the track in the dark.'

'Why?' Bernie asked.

'Cos of the legend. Ryan told me what happened to him.'

'You stupid lad,' said John Moffatt. He turned to Bernie. 'Craig has permission from me to ride on our land but only when I say so. He's absolutely not allowed to go on the roads. And he's not allowed to take part in races.'

'I see. Have you heard from anyone at the race since then?'

'No. I was ill that weekend with that horrible stomach bug. I was feeling a bit rough that night anyway. I was glad to get away. I don't know who he raced.'

'OK. Did he say anything else? Give anyone his contact details? We heard he wanted to make it a regular thing. He would have to be contactable somehow.'

Craig shook his head again. 'I don't know. He only spoke to Ryan quietly. Otherwise, he was really loud and spoke to us all as a group. Trying to get us to race him. He was quite full of himself, really.'

Bernie was about to ask one more question when John Moffatt interrupted her.

'I think you're done now. This is voluntary after all. You should be out looking for Laura, not hassling my son.'

Bernie stood up. 'I understand that, Mr Moffatt. But in order to find Laura, it's important we gather as much information and evidence as possible. I have one final question. Did this man say the woman's name at all? Or say anything to her that might be useful? Anything at all?'

Craig thought for a moment. 'I don't remember him saying a name. He called her "babe". Oh, but he rode past me later. I was almost home. I stopped so I could wheel the bike down the drive so Mum and Dad wouldn't hear me. He was on his own. She wasn't with him.'

CHAPTER 54

The office was quiet except for the sound of Tom tapping away at his keyboard.

'Any progress yet?' Bernie asked.

'Not on the IP,' said Tom, his eyes glued to his screen. 'But the phone company have come back about this phone registered to Manetti. We already knew it was switched back on last Saturday afternoon with a new number. And they've now confirmed it was in the Salisbury area.'

'That's great news.'

Bernie was about to ask him more when Anderson appeared.

'Ma'am.' He smiled at her.

'Oh. I thought you had gone to check out the racers,' Bernie said, beaming back. They still hadn't spoken about Saturday night but she wanted to, especially as she'd now cleared the air with Alex.

'No. I was still on the phone to Gabriel when the order came in so the others went. However, it's just as well I didn't.'

'Why? Did Gabriel have some information?'

Anderson nodded towards Bernie's desk. 'Let me show you something.'

Bernie sat down and moved some files while Anderson spread some sheets over the desk.

'These are the messages between Luke and Ria. They stopped well over a week ago.'

'Before the race then?'

'Yes. But they've been messaging for a while. And if you go back, she makes reference to wanting to leave her job. Says her employer is hassling her for sex.'

Bernie leaned back in her chair. 'Really? That's not how Rupert Fox portrayed it. He said it was consensual.'

'Not according to this. Luke suggested she should film the next time she's made to have sex and then send it to him.'

'Oh God, this man is unbelievable.'

'No, wait, he also asks for Rupert Fox's email address. If you look here, Ria gives him two addresses – a home one and a work one. The plan was to blackmail Fox.'

'But we know this already,' said Bernie. 'We've seen the footage. We're pretty sure it was filmed from a teddy cam that Ria had in her bedroom.'

Anderson tapped the paper. 'You've seen the video sent to his home email. Maybe a different one was sent to his work address. Perhaps a more extreme one.'

Bernie massaged her throbbing temple. 'We'd need a warrant and old Worthless isn't going to let that happen.'

'You still think they're friends?'

'I'm not sure what it is exactly but something isn't right…' Bernie hesitated. Should she tell Anderson of her suspicions?

'Spit it out.'

She leaned in towards him and lowered her voice. 'Clive Bishop suggested there may be something not quite right about our Mr Fox. And then I spoke to Alex last night…'

'You spoke to Alex?'

Anderson looked worried.

'It's over. I'll tell you more later. We need to talk anyway.'

Anderson raised his eyebrows. 'Good talk or bad talk?'

Bernie smiled. 'Good talk. But we're getting off the point. Alex told me Rupert Fox does a lot of mortgage surveys and he often finds fault in the houses.'

'And?'

'So the buyers then put in a lower offer for the house. Sometimes the vendors take the hit or the sale falls through. What if Rupert Fox is deliberately finding fault and then taking a fee from the buyers?'

'Then that would be fraud.'

'Exactly.'

Anderson looked puzzled. 'So where does Worth fit in?'

'He moved house last year.'

Anderson looked at her for a moment before speaking. 'Do you know what you're implying, Bernie?'

Her stomach lurched. 'I feel sick just thinking about it. Anti-Corruption would have to become involved and that doesn't bode well for my future either.'

'Assuming there is something wrong,' said Anderson. 'You have no evidence at the moment, just a suspicion. Do you think Alex would help? Could he get paperwork together to show us?'

Bernie wrinkled her nose. 'He probably would but not best timing really. I'll text him and ask. So, in the meantime, do we hold fire on a warrant for Rupert Fox's work computer?'

'If it means asking Worth for the warrant, then yes. But I have a contact in Fraud. If we can find evidence of Fox doing wrong then we could pass everything on to them.'

'And Worth?'

Anderson gave a wry smile. 'That'll be up to Fraud to discover, won't it?'

A buzzing sound came from Anderson's pocket. He reached inside and pulled out his phone.

'*Ciao*, Gabriel.' He stood up and walked over to his desk.

Bernie knew she wouldn't understand anything he said so she took her own phone out and sent a text to Alex. She hoped she wasn't being too presumptuous. Although they had parted on friendly terms, she knew she couldn't expect too much of him. She almost finished the text with her customary 'xx' but paused. She left it as, 'Bernie'.

Anderson came back. 'Yes, hold on one minute, Gabriel. My DI needs to hear this.' He switched his phone over to speaker and put it on the desk.

'Hi, Inspector De Luca. I'm DI Bernie Noel. What do you have?'

'*Ciao*, Bernie. Gabriel, please. OK. Let's start with some background. Maria, or Ria, Greco was brought up in a children's home for most of her life. She doesn't appear to have any immediate family so we're still working on next of kin. As a teenager she was arrested a few times and charged once for shoplifting. She pleaded guilty and was given a fine. Since then, as an adult, we haven't seen her until earlier this year. She was assaulted by her boyfriend, Bruno Manetti. It was pretty nasty – he knocked a couple of teeth out. I've contacted Ria's dentist and he's confirmed all the work he did. He will send her records. I'm hoping to send DNA too but it's difficult. Although she gave a sample as a teenager that was removed from the database when she got older. We have her DNA from the assault but it's another team investigating so we have to get permission.'

'So red tape's holding you up,' said Bernie.

'Doesn't it always? But more than that. The mention of Manetti and a phone has got everyone excited. We've been trying to put him away for years as a drug dealer but never managed it. We don't know if Bruno gave it to Ria for safe-keeping or if she stole it. If you find it, please can we have it after you've finished with it? We think there's vital evidence on there.'

'I'm sure we can come to some arrangement, Gabriel, but we haven't found where Ria was staying yet. Do you think he would kill Ria to get his phone back? We know it was switched back on for a few hours on Saturday in Salisbury. I have my own theory on that but Anderson said Manetti has skipped bail.'

'Yes, unfortunately. He left Ria in a bad way so I think he could've killed her or have someone else do it. But I do have some good news – Rosa's emails. When we looked at her sent box we found the emails she had sent to her grandparents. In her inbox, there are emails back from her grandparents and also another email address – no proper name, just a string of letters. It's Ria. She's been telling Rosa what she's been doing as an au pair so that Rosa can then pass that on to her grandparents. Things like places she's been with the children, games they've played.'

'That makes sense,' said Bernie. 'Rosa needs her emails and phone conversations to sound authentic.'

'Yes, that's what I think too. Rosa has emailed a few times in the last ten days asking Ria what she's been up to. She's overdue with contacting her grandparents. She writes, "Where are you, Ria? I need to phone or email my grandparents. They'll be worried. I need to know what to tell them."'

'That suggests Rosa's alive and well somewhere. And hopefully safe.'

'Oh, she's definitely alive. She emailed her grandparents ten minutes ago.'

CHAPTER 55

Bernie knocked on Worth's office door.

'Come in.'

Bernie gave a measured smile as she entered. She no longer trusted Worth but she had to convey otherwise.

'Sir, Tom's had news that Ria's phone was in Salisbury when it was switched back on and we've just heard from Inspector De Luca as well. He's spoken to Ria's dentist who's confirmed the dental work. Manetti knocked them out and they're looking for him for assault. The Italian police are particularly interested in the phone and would like it if we find it. Manetti is a drug dealer and they're desperate to get him on that. We think Ria left Florence because of him. Circumstantially it fits but obviously we need to wait for confirmation before making it public.'

'So our "terrible twins" really did pull off a switch.'

'They did. I've asked Tom to look at Ria's profile on Instagram,' said Bernie. 'She and Luke were messaging. I'm assuming that's OK.'

'Yes, for now.' Worth glanced at his watch. 'Have you heard anything yet from the others? Have they managed to speak to all those racing?'

'I've not heard yet but I'll chase them up.' Bernie eyed the chair in front of her. 'Sir, do you mind if I sit down? I have an idea I'd like to run past you.'

Worth indicated that she could.

'I've been thinking we have a great opportunity to catch our man. We have Chloe's phone so we can contact him. I think it's time for us to tell the public how much danger we believe Laura to be in. Let's hold another press conference. Tell the media that we believe the same man is responsible and show the CCTV footage of the motorbike. Then "Chloe" can message Luke, saying he's a liar and she's going to go to the police.'

Worth waggled his finger. 'You want to lure him in for a meet-up.'

'Exactly,' said Bernie. 'But we'll be there to meet him, not Chloe.'

The DCI breathed in slowly and deeply. 'It's risky.'

'I know, sir. But Tom isn't getting anywhere with finding the IP address. And I don't think we're going to get anything from the racers. We're running out of time for Laura. We have to act now.'

'And you think that dangling a teenage girl in front of him will do the trick?' asked Worth.

Bernie paused. She didn't like the idea of it at all but getting Laura home was her priority. 'We'll make sure Chloe is safe, get her mum to pick her up from school. We'll choose a safe place to meet. And we'll make sure there's enough of us there, including a police motorcyclist if we need to give chase.' Bernie's heart beat faster. She knew it was a risk and would backfire on her if it all went wrong.

Patrick Worth caught her eye with a steely gaze. 'Set it up.'

'Right, everyone, thanks for coming back so quickly. Kerry, anything to report?' asked Bernie.

Kerry shook her head. 'Not really. We spoke to a few of the guys on the list. They all said they left before the final race. I think it's clear no one is going to admit to racing our man. They all know what happened to Ria.'

'I think you're probably right. So we need to try another tactic.' Bernie looked around the briefing room. All the detectives from the team were there plus uniformed officers from Traffic and two specialist motorcyclists. Worth stood at the back of the room. He gave her a nod.

'The DCI and I have been talking and we think it's time to flush out Luke Davidson. Tom has been doing a brilliant job but it's clear this guy knows his tech. So, the plan is to hold a press conference at twelve thirty. We'll mention that we have a possible ID for our murder victim plus the fact we now have evidence linking her death with our missing girl, Laura Moffatt. We'll show the CCTV footage we have of the motorbike. We'll be asking for the press to release this information immediately. Once the public are notified, we'll message Luke using Chloe's account. We're going to try and entice him to meet Chloe, except we'll be there instead. So, Matt, I want you to start thinking about what you're going to write. We'll need to allow a bit of time to get everyone in place so the meet time will have to be after school. The downside is that the traffic will be getting busier. Kerry and Alice, I'd like you to look at the area around Laura and Chloe's school. See if there any quiet side roads that might work well for us.'

DC Mick Parris raised his hand.

'Yes, Mick.'

'Two questions, ma'am. Is it wise to show the CCTV footage? If he knows we're looking out for a motorbike, then he may come by car. And what about this Manetti guy – have you ruled him out?'

Bernie had to stop herself from sighing. *A car. Damn. Why didn't I think of that?*

'That's a good point, Mick. You're right about the car. As for Manetti, we don't know enough about him yet.' Anderson raised his hand. Bernie nodded at him.

'I think,' said Anderson, 'that we just go with "we have new evidence linking the two cases". The important thing is to consider this from Chloe's perspective. If she thinks that Luke is responsible, then she won't agree to meet him. The fact that we're Chloe is irrelevant.'

'I agree,' said Matt, putting his pen down. 'I've just scribbled this. "Hi Luke. Have you seen the news? The police now think Laura's been abducted by a murderer! I'm so scared for her. If she didn't meet with you, who did she meet? I want to go and search for her. Do you want to come too?" Something along those lines. What do you think?'

Bernie nodded her head slowly. 'Yes, that might work. Much better than Luke thinking that Chloe is about to go to the police. We'll go with that.' Bernie glanced at her watch. 'It's eleven forty-five hours. Press conference is in forty-five minutes. That will hopefully be enough time to get the local lunchtime bulletins for both TV and radio. Plus it will go out on the local papers' websites.'

'Ma'am?'

'Yes, Matt.'

'Do you want this on social media too? If we're going to think like Chloe, she's much more likely to see it on Instagram or Twitter.'

Bernie gave Matt a broad smile. 'Yes. Mick, could you look at that, please? I know it's Matt's forte but I need him to focus on contacting Luke.'

Bernie was aware of someone else looking at her, someone who hadn't be given a job yet. Someone who had just saved her butt.

'Anderson, I would like you to start planning how we're going to arrest this man. Work in conjunction with Traffic, particularly focusing on pursuit strategies.'

Worth, at the back of the room, coughed.

'Yes, sir?' Bernie asked.

'I've spoken to the deputy chief constable and we have permission to use the helicopter for a pursuit,' said Worth. 'You know the rules. If there's a danger to the suspect or members of the public, then pull back and let the helicopter take over. We have one shot at this. Let's not balls it up.'

Worth glared at Bernie. That last statement was aimed at her.

CHAPTER 56

'So,' said Clive Bishop, 'you're now telling us that the same man is responsible for the murder of the young woman and the abduction of Laura Moffatt? When I asked DI Noel about that the other day, she denied it. What have you got to say about that?'

DCI Worth shifted uncomfortably in his chair as a mutter passed around the room.

'Well, at the time, we didn't have enough evidence to link the two cases. Now we do,' he said.

'What is this evidence?' asked another reporter.

'I'm not able to disclose that at the moment. We're also close to identifying our murder victim and will hopefully have some news on that soon,' said Worth. 'That's all I have to say at the moment but we would like this news to go out ASAP. When we have further information we'll let you know.'

Worth got up and left a bewildered-looking bunch of journalists behind him. Bernie was about to leave too when Clive Bishop called her over.

He lowered his voice. 'What's really going on?' he asked.

Bernie gave him an innocent look. 'I don't know what you mean. We've given you some info and we'd like you to report it.'

'I know when we're being played,' said Clive. 'You want this out there for a reason.'

Bernie rested her hand lightly on his arm. 'We simply want the public to be vigilant and to stay safe. As the DCI said, we'll let you know when we have more to say.'

She walked away, aware of Clive's suspicious gaze on her. She hoped he would leave it at that. This was the one time she didn't need him snooping around.

MCIT was bustling. Mick had timed the social media release for just after the press conference.

'Ma'am, we're already getting messages in on Twitter, Facebook and Instagram,' he said. 'Most of them are the usual "hope you catch the bastard and cut his balls off" replies. I was wondering if "Chloe" should respond online before messaging Luke.'

Bernie turned to Matt. 'What do you think?'

Matt nodded. 'I think that's a great idea. Will hopefully help with the credibility of my message to Luke in a few minutes' time. I checked with the school what time lunch is. Real Chloe is due back in class in about ten minutes so we need to act fast now.'

'OK, I'll let you get on with it then,' said Bernie. She picked up a cold cup of coffee from her desk and took a few mouthfuls. It was bitter but she needed the caffeine.

'Anderson, how are you doing?' she asked.

'Good. Alice and Kerry have found a good place for a meet up. There's a cul de sac a few roads away from the school. So, with only one way in and out, we should be able to corner him.'

'Have you checked for footpaths?'

His eyes lit up. 'Yes, there aren't any.'

Bernie could sense the excitement on Anderson as he stepped from one foot to another. This was the kind of police work he was used to. He needed to be leading his own team again and if they did become an item, he would have to leave MCIT anyway. She'd put some feelers out for him after this case.

'Good, carry on. The DCI wants a detailed plan by fourteen hundred hours,' said Bernie.

'Ma'am?'

Bernie looked across the room. Matt was signalling to her.

'I've just put up a comment on Instagram. It says, "OMG, I can't believe that some evil bastard has Laura. I'm so scared for her. Praying she comes home safe and well." Does that sound OK? I'm going to message Luke next.'

Bernie quickly made her way over to Matt's desk. She pulled up a chair and sat next to her DC.

'That's fine. You'd better do the message fast if she's supposed to be in lessons in a few minutes.'

Matt pulled up Chloe's WhatsApp on his computer and found Luke. He spoke and typed at the same time. '"Shit Luke! Have you seen the news?! Police think Laura's been abducted…"'

'Wait, would Chloe say abducted? Would "taken" or "kidnapped" be better?'

Matt deleted the word and wrote 'kidnapped' instead. '"Police think Laura's been kidnapped by a murderer! I'm so worried for her I want to go look for her after school. Can you come with me? It'll be quicker on a motorbike."'

'Yes, that's good,' said Bernie. 'Send it now.'

They waited a couple of minutes. Beads of sweat appeared on Bernie's top lip. She licked them away and tasted the salt. If Luke didn't respond then the whole thing would be a waste of time.

The grey ticks turned blue.

'He's typing,' said Matt, loudly.

Everyone stopped what they were doing and listened.

'Yes,' said Matt. 'Here we go. "Babe, you're right, that's so scary but I don't know where we could look. I'm sure the police are looking everywhere."'

'Damn,' said Bernie.

'Don't worry,' said Matt. 'It wasn't going to be easy.' He thought for a second before typing. '"The police are shit! They don't know where to look. Pleaaase Luke it will take me forever if I have to walk."'

'Thanks for the vote of confidence there,' said Bernie.

'Hey,' said Matt, 'I'm just thinking like a twelve-year-old girl.'

Bernie stared at the computer screen, eagerly waiting for the 'Luke is typing' phrase to appear. A few seconds later, it showed and a message appeared quickly.

'"OK babe, just for u. Can meet u after school as I get out of college early today. Where shall I meet u?"'

'What's the name of the road, Anderson?' Bernie asked.

'Potters Close.'

'And what time does school finish, Kerry?'

'Fifteen hundred hours. Tell him to meet Chloe at the close at three ten p.m.'

Matt typed quickly. Luke's response was almost immediate. '"See u then, babe."'

Bernie looked at her watch. 'It's thirteen twenty hours. We have an hour and a half before contact. Let's get going.'

CHAPTER 57

Bernie was about to leave MCIT when her mobile rang. She didn't recognise the number and thought about ignoring it but she'd given her card out to so many people recently she didn't want to risk leaving it.

She answered briskly. 'DI Noel.'

'Hello, it's Father Adrian. Is now a good time for a very brief chat?'

'I'm about to go out but I can talk as I walk to my car.'

'I'll be quick. I'm sorry I haven't called you earlier but I had to take advice about Rosa's confession.'

Bernie decided not to correct him about the young woman's true identity.

'I ended up talking to the bishop and we agreed that I absolutely can't reveal her confession – even in death.'

Bernie inwardly sighed. She thought it would be the case.

'However, other than telling you that she was frightened, I think the other thing I can say, and it does sound a little odd, if you can find her teddy bear then that should help you. I'm sorry I can't say any more.'

Bernie smiled. 'Don't worry, Father. You've said more than enough. Thank you. I must go now. Bye.'

As she walked over to her car, Bernie mentally rearranged her main suspects. Manetti moved into third, with Rupert Fox and

Luke Davidson vying for the top. Was it the man caught by the camera or the one who provided it?

'Everyone's in place. Over.' Anderson's voice was clear on the radio.

'OK. Waiting for visual confirmation. Over.' Bernie put her radio down. She was further up the road from Anderson and the others. Alice was with her. The new DC had proved herself competent but hadn't really impressed Bernie.

'So,' said Bernie, 'is your baby better?'

Alice turned to Bernie, seemingly startled by her DI's personal question. Her mousy hair swayed gently in the breeze from the open window.

'Oh, he's much better, thanks. It was a twenty-four-hour bug.'

Alice turned her head to look out of the window again. Bernie contemplated probing her about Worth, knowing she had worked more cases with him. Bernie hadn't really wanted DC Hart with her. She had wanted Kerry but Worth had ordered her to have Alice.

'I've heard Kerry has a bit of a reputation with martial arts,' the DCI had said. 'Better to have as part of the arrest team. A puff of wind could blow Alice over.'

Bernie had thought him unkind but as she sat next to the young female DC, she thought Worth was probably right. Bernie glanced at her watch. It was 3.08 p.m.

She lifted her radio up.

'This is DI Noel. Any visuals yet? Over.'

She waited as each patrol reported back. There was no sign of any motorbike, let alone a BMW.

'Matt, could you check Chloe's WhatsApp, please?'

A few seconds later, Matt said, 'Nothing here. But if he's going to be late and he's riding then he won't be messaging.'

Bernie watched the digital clock on her dashboard as it flashed away the minutes. Luke was now five minutes late.

'Checking visuals again. Over,' she said into the radio.

Again, there was no sign.

'Ma'am, it's Mick. How long do we wait?'

Bernie sighed. 'Until fifteen thirty hours.' She closed her eyes. She'd gone out on a limb and she could almost sense Worth peeling her fingers off as she desperately tried to hang on. She heard a beep. She opened her eyes to see Alice staring at her.

'The DCI has just texted. He wants to know what's happening.'

So that's why Worth wanted Alice with me, he wanted a spy.

'Tell him we're still waiting for the target. We'll reassess at fifteen thirty hours.'

A few pupils from Chloe's school were walking down the road. The local infant school would be finishing soon and Bernie was keen to avoid a confrontation with small children around. An idea popped into her head. She spoke into the radio.

'This is DI Noel. Just thinking that Luke may be deliberately waiting for the infant school to finish, in case he thinks Chloe has gone to the police. Much harder to give chase with lots of small children around. Over.'

'Anderson here. That's a possibility. He's now ten minutes late.'

Bernie tapped her fingers on the steering wheel but then stopped. Her skin prickled. She knew Alice was watching. Everything would be reported back to Worth.

The minutes continued to flash away until the clock on the dashboard read 15.30. Time to reassess.

'This is DI Noel. Need to reconsider. Matt, anything from Luke on Chloe's phone?'

'Let me just see… no, nothing. Do you want me to message him?'

Bernie held the radio against her cheek for a few seconds before making her decision.

'Message him.'

Bernie's stomach was churning. The thought of going back to headquarters empty-handed was demoralising, especially with Worth there to greet her.

'Ma'am. Message has been sent.'

'Thanks, Matt.'

Bernie's phone buzzed in her pocket. She pulled it out to find a text from Anderson.

You OK?

She quickly typed, keeping her phone tilted away from prying eyes.

No, not really. Think I've got Worth's spy with me.

The radio crackled. 'Ma'am.' It was Matt. 'He's typing back… no! Shit.'

'What?' Bernie almost screamed down the radio.

'Oh God, I don't believe this. His reply is "What you talking about babe? You're already with me."' Matt gasped. 'And he's just sent a photo. He's got Chloe. She's gagged and tied up.'

Bernie parked her car in the school car park and ran into reception with Alice behind her. She'd sent the others out to search the area and Matt had emailed the photo to her and Tom, in the hope maybe he could spot something. She'd felt sick just looking at it. Kerry had the task of contacting Chloe's family. How had Luke Davidson got hold of Chloe when her mum was supposed to be picking her up?

She nearly collided with a teenage girl who was fastening a necklace.

'That's your final warning, Zoe. Next time your jewellery will be confiscated and your parents will have to collect it. You know the rules. Oh!' The receptionist looked slightly alarmed at the sight of Bernie as she held her warrant card out.

'I need to see Mr Travers now.' She was breathing heavily.

'Oh, he's in a staff meeting. I'll see if he can leave—'

'He has to leave it.'

Bernie started to pace up and down. How could she have been so stupid? Somehow Luke must have known it wasn't really Chloe who was messaging him. They were the ones being played. She thought about Clive Bishop. She grabbed her phone and rang Jane Clackett.

'Jane, hi, it's Bernie.'

'Hi, are you all right? You sound stressed.'

'Yeah… I've had better days. Look, I want you to release the CCTV photos of the motorbike. We need that out now. Can you put it on social media too, please?'

'Yes, of course. Was it a no-show?'

'More than that.' Bernie lowered her voice. 'He has Chloe.'

'Oh shit. Does Worth know?'

Bernie glanced behind her. Alice was on her phone. 'I think he's about to find out. I have to go. Talk later.'

She hung up as Pete Travers came through the automatic doors.

'DI Noel.' He extended his hand. 'Do you have news?'

'Yes, but not the good kind. Was Chloe Hampton in school today?' asked Bernie.

'I think so but we can check. Mrs Horley, can you look up today's records please?'

The alarmed receptionist tapped away quickly. 'Yes, she was here for both morning and afternoon registration.'

'And for all her afternoon lessons?' asked Travers.

'Yes. She's marked in for everything. Her mother called about two thirty p.m. to say she'd be late picking her up and asked for Chloe to stay on site until she arrived. I sent a message to her class.'

'What was her last lesson?' asked Bernie.

Mrs Horley looked up from the screen. 'Computing with Mr Gardener.'

Bernie was puzzled. 'Isn't that her form tutor?' she asked.

'Yes,' replied Mr Travers. 'Is there a problem with that?'

'I could have sworn he told me he taught Geography.'

Mr Travers smiled. 'Yes, he does. But he worked in London, in the City, and was, by all accounts, a computer whizz-kid, so he covers IT too, sometimes.'

Bernie's eyes widened. 'What?'

The head teacher stared at Bernie. 'He's very good at computing, especially in security. He's helped with our website. He organises the online safety talks for year seven and their parents. DI Noel, is there something I should know about Ben Gardener?'

Bernie's phone buzzed. It was a text from Kerry.

'Excuse me a moment, please.'

She read the message. *Chloe not at home. Trying to get hold of her parents.*

Bernie tapped the phone against her mouth, wondering what to do next.

'We need to talk to Mr Gardener now and find out what happened to Chloe at the end of the lesson. Can you get him out of the staff meeting, please?'

'He's not in the staff meeting. He messaged earlier to say he had an appointment he'd forgotten about.'

Things were rapidly slotting into place for Bernie. 'How does Mr Gardener get to school?' she asked.

'Well… um, I think he comes by car,' said Pete Travers.

'Although he sometimes comes on a motorbike,' said Mrs Horley.

Bernie turned to the receptionist.

'Don't suppose you know what make it is?' asked Bernie.

'No, I'm afraid not but' – Mrs Horley blushed – 'he does make a rather dashing figure in his leathers. He's got a very snazzy jacket. All black with some special silver buttons down the front.'

Bernie's face dropped, her fears confirmed. She scrabbled on her phone and found the pictures of Luke Davidson, dressed in his biker gear, and then the one with him and Laura on the motorbike. She showed them to Mrs Horley.

'Like this?'

'Yes, that's him and that's his bike.'

CHAPTER 58

Alice contacted the others by radio as Bernie turned the car round and put out the car registration details given to them by Pete Travers. The tyres screeched as they left the car park. She stuck her lights on but only used the siren when other cars didn't move out of her way. They had Ben Gardener's address but it seemed far too obvious to Bernie. Worth was getting the warrant sorted anyway.

She heard Anderson's voice on the radio.

'Close to the location. How do you want us to approach? Over.'

Bernie paused. 'Wait for back-up and the OK from the DCI. I have a feeling Gardener won't be there. But he can't be far away. There wasn't much time between him taking Chloe and the photo being sent.'

Ben Gardener lived on the other side of town. It would normally be a short journey but school traffic was clogging the roads. Bernie resorted to using her horn when the siren didn't appear to be working.

'I suppose it's because we're not in a normal police car,' she said to Alice. 'People don't realise.'

Alice gave a tight smile. 'Always the way when you want to get somewhere fast.'

'DS Allen to DI Noel.'

'Go ahead, Kerry.'

'I've had to leave a message for both of Chloe's parents. I heard Gardener's address and I'm on my way there now with Matt. What's your ETA, ma'am?'

Bernie glanced at her dashboard. It was almost four p.m.

'We're probably about six or seven minutes away. Anderson and Mick are almost there now and waiting for back-up. Uniform should be joining them. It feels too obvious though.'

The traffic was still snarled up and Bernie spotted a broken-down car further along the road. *Oh great, that's all we need.* She thought again about the photo of Chloe. Tape over her mouth, her eyes terrified. She pulled out her phone and looked once more. Something bothered her about it but she couldn't quite work it out.

The cars began to move a little so Bernie put her siren on. Space opened up and within a minute they were past the blockage. She nudged the car to forty mph but was reluctant to do more in a built-up area. The picture came back into her mind and suddenly she realised what was wrong. She slowed down and pulled over.

'Ma'am?' Alice looked confused.

'Need to make a phone call.'

Bernie searched for a number and it quickly connected.

'Devizes Girls' School. How can I help you?'

'Mrs Horley, it's DI Noel again. Did Chloe Hampton pick up her necklace at the end of school?'

'Chloe? No, she's one of the good girls when it comes to jewellery. Make-up, on the other hand—'

'What about Laura Moffatt?' Bernie didn't have time to discuss cosmetics with the receptionist.

'Oh, she's a nightmare. On her final warning. She has a necklace with an—'

'Owl pendant,' Bernie finished. 'Thank you.' She hung up and looked at Alice.

'What's going on, ma'am?'

Bernie showed her the photo. 'I think this is fake. That necklace belongs to Laura. I remember her playing with it when I first met her. Can you get on to Tom and tell him, please?'

'Sure, but how does this help us? Does it mean he hasn't got Chloe?'

'I don't know about that. But it does mean he could still be driving and be nowhere near his home. He only had to send that photo, not tie her up and gag her and then photograph her. And he has a lot of photos of Chloe to choose from. He probably had it already prepared. He knew we'd try something like this. Shit. He's been playing us all along.'

Bernie pulled out into the road as Alice called Tom. She hadn't driven far when the radio crackled.

'Ma'am, this is DC Parris. We're in position and have back-up. Warrant is confirmed. Do you want us to proceed? Over.'

'How much back-up?' said Bernie.

'Four uniforms. And we have a battering ram to force entry if necessary.'

Bernie pursed her lips as she thought it through. It seemed unlikely Gardener would be there with the two girls but there might be vital clues inside to their whereabouts.

'Go in and keep your radio on. I want to hear it all. I'll be with you in about five minutes and Kerry and Matt are on their way too.'

Within a minute there were sounds of banging and voices shouting 'Police!' coming out of the radio. Two loud thumps were followed by splintering wood and fast footsteps. More shouts of 'Police!'

Bernie picked up speed. She imagined her colleagues going from room to room as she heard the noise of doors being opened, with shouts of 'Clear!' She was so focused on what she was hearing she almost missed the turning.

'It's this road, ma'am,' said Alice.

Bernie turned sharply, the car tyres squealing. She saw Anderson up ahead, standing outside a small house. She pulled up outside.

He grinned as she got out.

'Just as well we weren't going for a silent approach, ma'am. I think most of the streets round here heard you coming,' he said.

Bernie noticed the twinkle in his eye. She hoped Alice hadn't.

'What's the story then?' she asked.

'He's not here but we've found a super computer set-up. Think we need to get Tom in to take a look before we move it to headquarters. We've started a more detailed search now. There's a loft and a couple of sheds in the garden. Mick's gone to check them out. I've called Forensics and they're on their way.'

Bernie followed Anderson into the house, snatching a pair of gloves from her pocket. It was a new-build with neutral walls and carpets, more in line with rental properties. Furniture was sparse. The lounge had a brown leather sofa and a large TV opposite it, attached to the wall. A small bookshelf held only a few books.

'Very impersonal,' she said.

'Most of the house is. However, upstairs is the heart of the operation,' said Anderson.

In the back bedroom, a counter, like a long breakfast bar, was fixed to the wall, going from one side of the room, widthways, to the other. Four computer towers and monitors were spread across the top. Unlike downstairs, there were bits of paper with scribbled notes on them, scattered along the counter. Bernie pushed one gently and saw the name 'Maria' on it. Underneath was a list of likes and dislikes. She spotted other familiar names on more scraps of paper, including Laura and Chloe.

'Anderson?' She beckoned him over to see.

'I know. I saw them too. Strange, really – in my head I thought this guy was really methodical, and maybe he is. Perhaps it's all in files on the computers. But to see these torn bits of paper with the girls' names on...' He shook his head.

Bernie wanted to reach out to him but knew she couldn't with Alice standing behind them.

A shout of 'Ma'am' came from outside. Anderson opened the window.

'You need to come and see this,' said Mick, calling up.

Within a minute they had congregated outside, at the end of the small garden. A shed door was open.

'Look what I found,' said Mick. He pulled back a tarpaulin to reveal a motorbike underneath.

'BMW?' asked Bernie.

'Yes,' said Mick.

Bernie glanced around the rest of the shed. Motorbike parts and oil cans lay scattered across the grimy floor. She pulled out her phone and switched on the torch to illuminate the back. There was something vaguely familiar about it but she thought maybe she was imagining it. But then something glinted in the light. Something that appeared to be hanging on a nail in the wooden wall. She gasped. It was a gold chain with an owl pendant. Had Laura left it there for them to find?

'Get Forensics to start here first,' Bernie said.

CHAPTER 59

Bernie assembled her team in the back garden. Tom had texted back, confirming her suspicions that the photo was a fake. She'd noticed nosy neighbours twitching their curtains so she kept her voice low.

'The photo's fake. Chloe's face has been superimposed on Laura somehow. Which means Ben Gardener is probably a lot further away than we first thought.' She flicked through her phone to find the details school had given her. 'We've found out that he drives a black Nissan Note, registration RX62 SJM. Those details have been sent out across Wiltshire and to surrounding areas. There have been no hits yet on ANPR or traffic cams. I suspect he's sticking to quieter roads, assuming he's not already at his destination.'

'So how the hell are we going to find him then?' asked Mick Parris.

Bernie hoped the defeat she felt wasn't showing in her face. 'I don't know. Until we get a hit from a camera somewhere or someone spotting it, we're a bit stuffed.'

Matt pulled Chloe's phone out from his pocket and waggled it. 'Or we could message him?'

Bernie bit her lip. It was tempting. 'No. Not for the moment. I don't want to give him the satisfaction.' Her phone buzzed. She looked at the screen but didn't recognise the number. She answered anyway.

'Detective Inspector Noel.'

'Please tell me he hasn't got my girl. I got stuck in traffic so I couldn't pick her up on time. I tried my husband but he couldn't get there either. I left a message at school. She was supposed to wait for me, just like you said. You promised she'd be safe if we helped you.'

Bernie could hear the desperation in the woman's voice.

'I know, Mrs Hampton, I'm sorry. I don't know for certain but we believe our suspect may have her. She wasn't at your house when we checked and obviously we have her phone.'

'Yes, I know. I've given her mine and I'm using my old one but it's just ringing and then going to answerphone. But she has to have it on silent at school so maybe she can't hear it. Oh God! Where is she?'

Bernie looked at the others. They had all realised who was on the phone. A thought popped into Bernie's head. If Ben Gardener knew that they had Chloe's phone, would he have thought or even had time to search her for another mobile?

'Mrs Hampton, what kind of phone do you have?'

'An iPhone.'

'Don't suppose you have an app—'

Chloe's mum interrupted before Bernie could finish. 'Yes. Why didn't I think of that? Hang on, let me get my iPad… here we go, find my iPhone… yes, I've got it. It looks as though she's heading south towards Salisbury but not on the main roads.'

Bernie briefly closed her eyes. *Thank God.* 'OK, that's good. If you zoom in, you should be able to see the road names and numbers. If you can text those details to me, please. Are you at home?'

'Yes.' There was strain in Mrs Hampton's voice.

'I'm going to send an officer to you who will take over watching the app and then can radio directly to me. We'll get her back, Mrs Hampton, whoever she's with. Speak soon.'

Bernie hung up. 'I think you can all guess who was on the phone and what's happening. Chloe's phone, or rather her mum's, and hopefully Chloe with it, are heading towards Salisbury.' Bernie paused. She looked at her detectives and tried to decide who would work best where.

'Anderson and Mick, you've started here, so I'd like you to carry on with searching the house and deal with Forensics when they arrive. And in particular, look out for anything that might have belonged to Ria, including her phone. Get Tom over to start work on those computers. Once we apprehend Ben Gardener, aka Luke Davidson, we're going to need to know what's on there for when we question him and we don't have time to transport it all back to headquarters.

'Alice, I'd like you to head over to Mrs Hampton. Make sure you have a radio with you…'

Bernie stopped. Alice had a face like a petulant child.

'Have you got a problem with that, Alice?'

'No, ma'am… well, actually, yes. Ever since I got pregnant and had my baby, I've not been allowed to go out on arrests or raids. I've been stuck behind a desk or sent on safe errands and I'm sick of it. I know we all have to do our fair share of paperwork but I didn't join the police to push paper around. I joined because I wanted to make a difference. Sorry, ma'am. Rant over.'

Bernie's eyes widened in new appreciation for her latest DC. 'Well, that was quite a speech. I'm not sure if the DCI would want you—'

'Oh God, he's the worst at keeping me back.'

Bernie smiled. She'd been wrong to dismiss Alice. 'If you want action, then let's give you some. Matt, you go over to Mrs Hampton then. I trust that's OK with you?'

Matt's hand instinctively went to his head where he had been hit with a hammer by a suspect earlier in the year. Bernie knew that feeling. The hammer had also smashed her left wrist at the same time and the normal dull ache was increasing. It wouldn't be long before the scar in her side would start to itch too. She still woke up in the night, a few years on from that incident in London, feeling the stabbing and then wetness running down her skin, although it was now sweat and not blood.

'More than happy, ma'am,' answered Matt.

'Thank you. Kerry and Alice with me then. Everyone get on and hopefully we'll find Chloe and Laura as well.'

Bernie started to leave when Anderson caught her arm.

'Please be careful and make sure you have back-up,' he said quietly.

'I will. I'll ask for officers from Salisbury.' She locked eyes with him. His concern was evident. He would have to change teams.

'I'll be fine.' She pulled away from his hand and ran round the side of the house to her car. Her phone buzzed. She gave it to Alice as they got in the car.

'Open the text please and tell me where we're going,' said Bernie.

Alice's hands trembled slightly as she fiddled with the phone.

'Sorry, ma'am, um… back on A360 now, heading towards Salisbury.'

Bernie turned the engine on. 'Kerry, get on to Salisbury and ask for back-up. They're not to approach but to keep under observation if they find the car before us, which is pretty likely. Think we need to hold back on the helicopter for the moment – it might spook him if he notices it and we don't want him to do anything stupid with Chloe in the car. Then ring the school and ask them to email a photo of the suspect and don't let them pull any of that data protection crap. If they've employed a paedophile then there'll be a lot of questions asked. Get it sent out so that everyone knows who they're looking for. A photo of Chloe too.'

Bernie winced as she put the car into gear and screeched out of the road with her sirens and lights on. She would definitely be triggering the speed cameras.

CHAPTER 60

The countryside whizzed past, the autumnal colours turning into red and gold streaks. Matt was now sending the directions through the radio and Bernie raced towards Salisbury. Rush hour would be in full swing when they arrived and she knew there were pros and cons to that. On the one hand, Ben Gardener would have to slow down, making it easier for him to be spotted. On the other hand, even with blues and twos, she would be slowed down as well.

Bernie heard a phone ringing in the car. She was too busy concentrating to see if it was hers.

'Is that your phone?' she asked Alice.

'No,' said Kerry. 'Mine. Hang on.'

Bernie kept her eyes on the road and only half-listened to Kerry.

'That's great, thanks for letting me know.' Kerry leaned forward from the back seat. 'Good news, ma'am. Our Nissan Note was picked up on CCTV and Salisbury police are now covertly trailing it. We can keep in contact via Control. Do you want me to radio in?'

'Yes, please. Tell them we're about ten minutes away from the outskirts. And find out how many officers they can spare. Thanks, Kerry.'

Bernie glanced briefly at DC Hart, sitting next to her. She was even paler than usual.

'You OK there, Alice?'

Hart gave a vague nod. 'Bit nervous. It's been a while.'

'You'll be fine. Just think of us as Charlie's Angels. And don't let Kerry's petite stature fool you. She's like a bloody ninja. So if you get worried, step back and she'll take over.'

'I heard that,' said Kerry.

'Good. Then you'll know it's a compliment,' said Bernie.

Ten minutes later, they were weaving through the traffic in the city centre.

'Kerry, can you check in with the officer on the ground, please?' asked Bernie.

'Sure. DS Allen to Control. Over.'

'Go ahead, DS Allen.'

'Can you patch me in to our covert officer please?'

'Will do.'

A minute later.

'This is PCSO Vicky Banks for DS Allen. Over.'

'Where's the Nissan Note?'

'It's in a service road behind a row of shops. I have visual now. I saw a man and a girl get out of it about five minutes ago and they went in the back of one of the shops.'

Bernie looked back at Kerry briefly. The words 'service road' had stood out for her.

'Do you know which shop exactly?' Kerry asked.

'Can't say for certain but there's a couple of food shops along here, a card and gift shop and there's a café as well.'

The traffic edged forward and Bernie briefly put her blue lights on to push through the car jam.

'Would that be The Little Teapot, by any chance?' said Kerry.

'Yes, that's the one. What do you want me to do?'

'Stay put for now. Any sign of movement, let us know immediately. How many other officers are there?' Bernie asked.

'Two more officers in a car at the other end of the service road. My car is parked just behind me.'

'OK. We'll be there soon.'

Bernie caught Kerry's face in her rear-view mirror.

'What do you think, Kerry? Coincidence?'

'No. What did that girl say to you again?'

'Katie? She said Laura had come in looking scared and had asked to leave through the back door. I'm now thinking that Laura was following instructions and that Katie was in on the whole bloody thing,' said Bernie. 'Maybe she's another one of Luke's girls.'

'I'm not sure – I'll check the list later,' said Kerry. 'Really, one of us needs to go into the café first but you and I have both been in there.'

In the mirror, Bernie saw Kerry nod her head towards Alice.

'So, DC Hart,' said Bernie, 'you wanted some action. How about a bit of reconnaissance work? Fancy a cup of tea in the café?' She looked at the time. It was nearly five fifteen p.m. 'If I remember rightly, the café closes at half past five. You might be able to get a quick cuppa and maybe ask to use the loo? Have a sneaky look around. There's definitely an upstairs.'

'OK.' From the corner of her eye Bernie could see Alice sit up straighter and square her shoulders. 'I'll do it.'

'Good. We'll keep in contact by phone but make sure you have yours in your pocket on silent and no vibration. We'll hear everything that's happening,' said Bernie. 'Kerry, just check in with Matt about Chloe's phone. Make sure it's in the same spot as the car. We're almost there. I'm going to try and park on the other side of the road from the café but just a bit further back. In fact, I can see a car pulling out of the perfect spot.'

Bernie finished parking as she heard Matt's voice on the radio.

'Yes, the phone has stayed put for a good ten minutes now. I can't see exact location, in terms of shop names but it's definitely in the middle of the row. Does that help?'

'That's perfect, Matt. Thanks. Be careful how you monitor the radio for the next ten minutes or so,' said Kerry.

Bernie looked at Alice. 'Ready?'

'Yes.'

'OK, key word is "peppermint tea". Say that and we'll come in.'

Bernie could just hear voices over the rustling of Alice's coat. They'd connected the call before Alice went over.

'Sorry, I know you're almost closing but is there any chance of a quick cuppa, please?' Although distant, Alice's voice sounded clear.

'Oh, go on then. But I can't do any food now.'

Bernie recognised Barbara Finch's voice.

'Is it OK if I use your loo?'

'No problem. It's just through there, past the stairs.'

'Thanks.'

There was more rustling noise and then Alice's voice was low. 'I'm going upstairs.'

Bernie could hear quiet footsteps. She hoped a boiling kettle in the kitchen would cover the noise of Alice creeping around. Bernie could imagine the DC moving silently up the stairs, her heart pounding with nerves.

There was a creaking noise coming through the speakerphone that sounded like a door opening to Bernie.

'Oi! What are you doing up here?'

It was a man's voice. Bernie looked at Kerry. Her DS nodded. It was Ben Gardener.

'Sorry, I was looking for the toilet.' Alice sounded startled.

'It's downstairs, you dozy mare.'

'Ben, that's no way to talk to our customers.' It was Barbara. 'Sorry, love. I forgot to ask you what sort of tea you want.'

'Oh… I'd like peppermint tea, please.'

Bernie grinned at Kerry. She muted the phone as Kerry spoke into the radio.

'All units, go, go go.'

Bernie and Kerry ran across the road and entered through the front door as uniformed officers came in through the back. They dashed up the stairs to find Ben Gardener holding Alice around the throat with his arm.

'Don't come any closer or I'll break her neck.'

Bernie stopped at the top of the landing, Kerry just behind her with the two other officers. The PCSO had restrained Barbara Finch but she was calling frantically up to him.

'Come on, son, don't do anything stupid now. Let her go. It's over.'

Bernie looked at Ben. 'Son? This is your mother's café? Katie's your sister?' Bernie nodded. 'They're good liars, I'll give them that. Bit late for doing stupid things, though, isn't it? Grooming teenagers online, getting them to send you intimate photos, kidnap and murder too.'

'What?' said Barbara. 'Murder? Who?'

'Not to mention ABH on a police officer.'

Ben looked confused. 'Police officer? I haven't done that.' Bernie noticed his grip loosened slightly.

Alice swung her elbow back into his stomach before grabbing his arm around her neck. She bent over and threw him down to the ground, twisting his arm back and pinning him with her knee. There was a moment of stunned silence. Then Bernie shook herself.

'Wow! Nice one, Alice. Good to see I have two ninjas on the team. Why don't you do the honours?'

'Ben Gardener, I'm arresting you on suspicion of grooming underage girls online, for kidnapping two minors and for the murder of Maria Greco. You do not have to say anything. But, it may harm your defence if you do not mention when questioned something which you later rely on in court. Anything you do say may be given in evidence.'

Kerry stepped forward and cuffed Ben. The two women hauled him upright.

Bernie looked at the two uniformed officers. 'Any chance you could take him back to Devizes for us, please?'

'It'll be our pleasure, ma'am.'

Bernie turned her attention to the three closed doors that led off the landing. Alice pointed to the back room.

'He came out of there and I'm fairly certain he wasn't alone in that room.'

Bernie turned the handle and pushed open the door. She smiled at the two girls huddled together on the sofa.

'Laura Moffatt, how many times do I have to tell you? Stay off Instagram. You too, Chloe.'

Tears streamed down their faces as Bernie gently placed her arms around them.

'It's OK, girls. You're safe now.'

CHAPTER 61

Caroline Moffatt rocked her sobbing daughter back and forth. She glanced up at Bernie.

'And the doctor's sure? She hasn't been… interfered with?'

'No. She hasn't been harmed in that way. Psychologically and emotionally is another matter. Tomorrow, we'll need to take a video statement. That way, when the case comes to court, Laura won't have to give evidence again. The doctor would like to keep her in tonight, just for observation. Then she can go home in the morning.'

Caroline nodded and kissed the top of her daughter's head.

'I'm so sorry, Mummy. I won't ever do that again,' said Laura, her head still buried in her mother's shoulder.

'You haven't called me that since going to secondary school. And I know you're sorry, darling.'

Bernie reached out and lightly touched Caroline on the shoulder. 'I'm going to leave you to it. Will your husband be here soon?'

'Yes. He'll stay the night. Laura's a Daddy's girl really. I'll go back to Craig. He's so relieved she's safe.'

'I bet. How's he doing now?'

'Physically, better. But still quite shocked. Do you ever get over finding a dead body? Especially at his age?'

Bernie remembered her first reaction to seeing Maria Greco. Her stomach lurched just thinking about it. 'It's not easy. We can help arrange some counselling for both your children. I'll see you tomorrow.'

Bernie walked out of the hospital towards the car park when she realised that she didn't have her car. Kerry had taken it back to Devizes with Alice and Chloe.

'Oh shit.'

'Do you need a lift, darling?'

Bernie smiled. She knew that voice. 'I thought I'd left you in charge of the search at Gardener's house,' she said, turning towards Anderson.

'Search is going really well. I was getting in the way and heard on the radio that Kerry and Alice were coming back without you. Figured you'd need a lift back to headquarters. Damn shame that twenty-four hours has already started ticking for Ben Gardener. Otherwise...'

'Otherwise, what?'

'I'd take you home,' said Anderson. He winked.

'I think we should go on a date first.'

'A date? Seriously?'

'Yes. I want a day out and the full works.'

Anderson gave a wicked grin. 'Oh, I can promise you the full works.'

Bernie playfully hit him on the arm. 'I bet you can. Come on. We need to go and deal with Ben Gardener first.'

She took his hand. It felt right – his fingers slotted between hers. They walked towards Anderson's car.

'So, tell me everything you've found out from Gardener's house,' said Bernie.

The roads were fairly empty as they drove back to Devizes.

'Well, Forensics started off in the shed and have taken lots of samples and swabs. Hopefully we'll get something that will place

Laura there. Obviously, we have her necklace and owl pendant. That should have her DNA on it. But we need more than that. On the computer front, we have plenty. Tom managed to get in through a ridiculous bit of luck. Shut down had got stuck on an app so Tom just cancelled it. Oh boy. There's some seriously sick stuff on there. We've only just scratched the surface but there's got to be thousands of images and videos.' Anderson sighed and shook his head. 'I don't understand these guys. But I've saved the best for last. We have Ria's suitcase, her phone and the teddy bear camera. Guess what else was hidden inside the bear?'

'I don't know.'

'The original SIM card for Ria's phone when it belonged to Bruno Manetti. Inspector De Luca is a very happy man.'

'I bet he is. And at the café in Salisbury?'

'Matt's taken charge of the search there. Nothing much to report yet. Gardener's mother and sister are at headquarters, waiting to be questioned.'

'And Gardener himself?'

'Worth is dealing with Gardener for the time being. He's been shoved in a cell while we build the evidence around him. The DCI wants lots of ammunition first so he has no chance to deny anything. We'll probably be able to get an extension, though, as there'll be multiple charges.'

'I'm pretty certain he'll go "no comment" for everything,' said Bernie. 'I think our biggest problem is pinning him for Maria Greco's murder. We're going to need forensic evidence for that which will take time. But with Chloe's statement and Laura's, we should have enough to get him on remand. Assuming the CPS backs the charges.'

Anderson glanced across at Bernie. 'After what I've seen today on those computers, he's definitely being charged.'

*

Worth was pacing the MCIT office as Bernie walked in.

'Finally,' he said.

'I'm sorry, sir. It was important to make sure Laura was OK and reunited with her family.'

'You could have got Alice to do that.'

'Alice was the arresting officer so she had to come back to book Gardener in. She did an excellent job and deserved to do Chloe's interview. Anyway, I'm here now. What's your plan of action, sir?'

Worth coughed.

Have you even got one?

'Well… it seems to me we have enough to go on with the abductions. I've seen Chloe's interview. I suggest you take a look before you interview the suspect.'

'I'm interviewing Gardener? Don't you want to do that, sir?'

There was a shifty look in his eyes. 'No, I want you to do it. I'll watch in the viewing room. I suggest you have DS Anderson with you.'

'Really? You don't want him collating all the evidence from the house?'

Bernie's mind began to tick.

'No, I want him to present the evidence,' said Worth.

'In that case then, it would be good if either Alice or Kerry are watching with you, sir, since they did Chloe's interview.'

The DCI nodded slowly. 'Yes, I'll get Alice in. Now, I suggest you hurry up and watch Chloe's statement and then prepare for Gardener's interview.'

Worth left MCIT just as Anderson came in with two cups of coffee and some packets of crisps.

'Thought you'd need some nourishment,' said Anderson. He nodded towards the door. 'Is the DCI OK?'

'I'm not entirely sure. He seems a bit… jittery. I thought he'd want to interview Gardener himself but he wants you and me to do it.'

'Not Kerry or Alice? They've just done Chloe's.'

'I know. Worth wants Alice with him in the viewing room. This afternoon, I was absolutely convinced she was Worth's spy but I gave her a chance and she came up trumps. In fact, I'd like to keep her on. Mick too.'

'I think they'd like that. Mick was asking if there were any vacancies on the team.'

'Really? The DCI is in for a very rude awakening.'

CHAPTER 62

Ben Gardener stretched and yawned in his seat in the interview room. His shirt pulled tightly across his torso and Bernie could see he was quite muscular underneath. *Such a good-looking man. You could have any woman. Why are you going after teenage girls?* Anderson was right – she didn't understand either.

'You have to admit,' she said, 'it's not looking good for you, Ben. You were found with Laura Moffatt and Chloe Hampton.'

Gardener folded his arms across his chest. 'No comment.'

'I was at the hospital with Laura and her mother. She's in no fit state to give a statement tonight but she should be able to do so in the morning. Chloe, however, was able to give us a statement. Shall I read you some of it?'

Ben glanced across at his solicitor, a man in his forties, who clearly wasn't happy to be at the police station at eleven o'clock at night.

'As I've already told you, my client will be conducting a "no comment" interview,' said the solicitor.

'And as I told you,' said Bernie, 'I'm still going to be asking your client some questions. He's facing some very serious charges, including murder. So if you don't mind, I'm going to carry on.

'This is from Chloe's statement: "I was just about to leave class when Mr Gardener called me back. He said my mum had called school to say she couldn't pick me up after all and I was to go straight home. I hadn't had a chance to check my mum's mobile – I was borrowing it. Mr Gardener said that with everything going on with Laura, he'd be happy to drop me home. I wasn't sure. It didn't seem right really. But he said it was no trouble and on his way. I'm not sure why I agreed but I was feeling a bit nervous with Laura missing. We got into his car in the staff car park. There were no other staff around to see us leave. I think there was a staff meeting. I knew something wasn't right when the car locked. He said it did that automatically and not to worry. But then I realised we were going the wrong way. I asked him to stop and let me out but he wouldn't. He told me to 'relax, babe'. And then I knew. I knew he was Luke.'"

Bernie leaned back in her chair. '"Babe" is your catchphrase, isn't it? Or rather it's Luke's. You used it with all the girls you chat to online. I wonder if it's because you sometimes forget who you're chatting with – there are so many. Detective Sergeant Anderson has been at your house, looking at your computers.'

'Yes,' said Anderson, 'and we've already found a significant amount of intimate photos and videos of teenage girls. And by teenage, I mean under sixteen. You like them young, don't you, Ben? I suppose getting a job as a teacher in a girls' secondary school has been a bit of a perk. Watching all those girls, day in, day out. Did you like it when Laura and Chloe started arguing over Luke? Did it make you feel good?'

Ben Gardener looked at the ceiling. 'No comment.'

'And to think you're the one who talked to them about online safety,' Bernie said. 'Did you find it funny that the girls were listening to your teaching at school during the day but ignoring your advice and talking to your alter ego at night? Bit risky taking your motorbike to school some days, though. Or did you want the girls to guess? Did you want the online adulation to turn into something real? What were you going to do with them, Ben? Leave them to rot in the woods too?'

Gardener looked directly at Bernie, his eyes locking with hers. 'No. Comment.'

Bernie leaned forward, without breaking eye contact.

'The problem is, Ben, every time you say "no comment", that confirms your guilt to me. This is your chance to put your side of the story and you're not taking the opportunity.

'Maybe we should change the subject for a moment. Let's talk about Rosa Conti, aka Maria Greco. Look, she had two names, just like you.'

Bernie glanced at Anderson. He pushed some photos towards Gardener.

'I've seen Maria's Instagram page,' said Anderson. 'She used to be very pretty. Not so pretty any more, is she?'

Ben blinked his eyes and shifted back in his seat.

'Not very pleasant, is it?' said Anderson. 'You should consider yourself lucky that you're only seeing a photo. DI Noel and I saw her first-hand. You see, with photos, what you don't get is the smell. I can't even begin to put into words what that smell is like.'

'Detective Inspector Noel,' said the solicitor, 'is this line of questioning from your sergeant really necessary?'

'Yes, I think so. We're not in court yet. So your objection is overruled. The point we're making is that Maria was left in those woods to rot. Now, while you were clever enough to not take your helmet off, Ben, we have quite a few witnesses who will recognise your motorbike and your leather jacket. It's quite distinctive. And we have the helmet and jacket that Maria wore. They have her DNA on them, and that of an unknown male. All we have to do is check that sample against yours. In fact, Forensics are doing that right now. We were fortunate to find them, though, it was a good hiding place...'

Bernie stopped. Her conversation with Stan Willis began playing in her mind. She propped her elbows on the desk and rested her chin on her hands. 'But you knew it was a good hiding place, didn't you?'

Ben's breathing was starting to quicken. A sheen of sweat appeared on his face.

'You've used that hiding place before. As a child. That's why you knew the track and the woods so well. It was probably just a bicycle you used back then. You hid five-year-old Ryan Willis in that cave and left him there. You see? We're establishing a pattern of behaviour.'

Bernie bit her lip. 'Oh dear oh dear oh dear, Ben. You really are in trouble now. It's one thing to hide a child in a cave, it's quite another to murder a young woman and leave her to rot in the woods until she looks like this.' She picked up the photo.

Gardener suddenly stood up, his chair screeching across the floor. He leaned forward on the table. 'I did not kill Maria. And I wasn't going to kill the girls either.'

'Then who did, Ben? We've spoken to all the people there that evening and they all say they didn't race you. So, it's looking like you are—'

'Check my sent emails.'

'Pardon?' said Bernie.

'Check my outbox on my computer. Everything you need to know is in there. Everything.'

CHAPTER 63

Bernie tapped her fingers on her desk as she waited for Tom to phone her back.

'What's in those emails?' she said as she looked across at Anderson. They were alone in MCIT.

'I have no idea. What do you want to do about Ben Gardener's mother and sister? They're still downstairs in separate rooms. Their statements have been taken by Kerry. His mother's been pretty tight-lipped apparently but Katie's been more forthcoming. She'd had enough of it all.'

'Bail them for now, pending further enquiries.'

'OK. By the way, what was that cave business with Ryan Willis?'

'When Ryan was five, he was hidden in the cave along the track – the one where Kerry found the helmet and jacket. You'd have to know it was there to hide something, particularly in the dark. Both Ryan's brothers swore they hadn't done it. I think if we look more into Ben Gardener, we'll find he went to school with Gareth Willis. I'm sure Ben's mother could help us with that.'

Bernie rubbed her head as Anderson got up to leave.

'Another headache?' he asked.

'Yes.'

'You have far too many of those. You need to get them checked out.'

Bernie pulled her hand away. 'I know already what the doctor will say – cut back on caffeine, get some good sleep and try to relax more. As if I can do that.'

Anderson bent over and kissed her gently on the head. 'You're probably right but it could be more serious, like your blood pressure. I'll keep on nagging you until you go.'

'Fine. Once this is all sorted I'll book an appointment. Now go and sort out Ben Gardener's family.'

Anderson nearly collided with Alice as he opened the door to leave.

'Sorry, sir.' Her face was flushed.

'Are you OK?'

'Yes, I just need to speak to the DI.'

Bernie smiled as Alice came over.

'Well done on Chloe Hampton's interview, you did a good job. And as for how you handled yourself with Ben Gardener, well, I'm seriously impressed.'

'Thank you, ma'am. But that's not why I'm here. Um… I'm not too sure whether to say something or not but…'

Bernie leaned forward in her chair and beckoned Alice to sit down.

'Something's bothering you. What is it?'

Even though they were alone, Alice looked around the room before speaking. 'I was with DCI Worth when you were interviewing Gardener. He was writing a few things down. But when Gardener stood up and said to check his emails, the DCI went pale and left the room abruptly.'

'Did he say anything?'

'Only that he had a few things to take care of. I waited for a few minutes and then went to find him. He was in his office with the door shut but I could hear him on the phone. I might be wrong about this but I thought I heard him say "Rupert". That's got to be Fox, right? Why would he be calling Rupert Fox?'

'Why, indeed?' Bernie stood up and grabbed her bag. 'I can't wait here for Tom to ring me. I know it's just coming up to midnight but do you fancy going back to Gardener's house?'

Thursday – early hours

Tom was scrolling through emails as Bernie and Alice walked in. He glanced up at them.

'Ma'am, I'm sorry I haven't called you back. You have no idea how many emails this guy has sent and received. From what I can tell, Ben Gardener creates something akin to an online porn mag but with underage kids in the photos and some pretty graphic stuff. So he's sending out links to paying customers all the time. He's receiving and sharing videos as well. It's hard to know what to look for so I did a search using "Rosa Conti" and found this email. I need to warn you both, it's not pretty.'

Tom clicked and opened a window. He played the video that appeared. Bernie recognised the room on the screen.

'That's Rosa's or Ria's room at the Fox house. Isn't this the video we've already seen?'

Tom shook his head. 'No. I've already found that one. This video was made a few days later. In the other clip, Ria was more compliant. She's not in this one.'

Bernie watched Ria on the screen, sitting on her bed, reading. Rupert Fox suddenly bursts into the room. Within two strides, he's by her bed, pulling her by her hair, and slaps her hard across the face.

'Bitch. Thought you'd blackmail me, did you? I'll show you.'

Bernie half-closed her eyes as she saw Rupert Fox unzip his trousers.

'Oh God,' she said. 'Please tell me he doesn't.'

'I'm afraid he does,' said Tom, pausing the video.

'And the date stamp?'

'The day she left them.'

'Shit. So she leaves this crappy house and goes to Ben, thinking he'll protect her. Which email address was this sent to?'

Tom minimised the screen to show the outbox behind. 'Rupert Fox's work address. Now I'm guessing he tried to get rid of this email too but as he wasn't very successful with his home email address, I'm hoping he wasn't very thorough with this one.'

'So we need to get a warrant for his arrest and to search his work computer.' Bernie wanted to cheer but didn't dare.

'Er, ma'am,' said Alice. 'Can I have a quick word please?'

The two women stepped out onto the narrow landing.

'Given what I told you earlier, how are you going to get the warrant?' asked Alice.

'Don't you worry about that, leave it with me.'

Bernie sat in her car and was about to ring Anderson when she noticed she had unopened email. She clicked to find there was one from Alex. She opened it.

Hi Bernie.

I checked in our records and I've made a list of houses that Rupert Fox surveyed. I've written down what happened with each house. I've also been in touch with another of our branches. I've attached their list too. They've been suspicious of Fox for a while.

Hope it helps. We need to arrange a time when I can come and get the rest of my stuff. Let me know when's good for you. I know that you're busy. I hope we can still be friends.

Alex.

Bernie was still cross with him but he was trying to help her now. She opened his list first and scanned the houses and names. No one jumped out at her. She looked at the other list and saw a name she recognised.

'Bingo,' she said.

Bernie closed her email and wrote a quick text to Anderson.

We have what we need for warrant for Fox. You know what to do.

CHAPTER 64

Bernie was tempted to drive over to Salisbury but knew it was too far, even in the middle of the night. She waited for DC Matt Taylor to call her at MCIT.

She'd left Alice at Gardener's house with DC Mick Parris and Tom. She thought it safer for Alice. Once Worth knew what was going on, he'd be on the warpath. While she waited, she tried to make sense of her thoughts.

If Fox is capable of rape, does that mean he killed Maria? Was he the mystery motorbike rider who raced Gardener? Did someone mention he had a bike or did I imagine that? No, Worth said there wasn't one at the house but he can't be trusted now.

Her eyes started to droop. She was aware of a commotion outside in the corridor but it wasn't until the door to MCIT slammed open against the wall that Bernie came to with a start.

'What the bloody hell do you think you're doing, woman?'

Bernie blinked quickly and tried to stand up.

'Sir, I don't know what you're talking about.'

Worth stood in front of her. 'You bloody well do. You've sent officers to Rupert Fox's office.'

Bernie, more alert now, stood up to face the senior officer. 'Evidence has come to light—'

'What evidence? You're supposed to be concentrating on Gardener, not pillars of the community like Rupert Fox.'

'As I was saying, sir, evidence has come to light. There's a video on Ben Gardener's computer showing Rupert Fox assaulting and raping Ria. It was emailed to Fox at his work address. I think we have every right to question Mr Fox and to ask him again, where he was the night of Ria's murder. Wouldn't you agree?'

Worth's face turned purple with rage. Bernie was concerned he was going to have a heart attack but then dismissed the thought. He'd consistently protected Rupert Fox. He didn't deserve her sympathy. Bernie's phone buzzed. She looked at the screen. It was Matt.

'Excuse me one moment, sir.'

She grabbed the phone and answered.

'Matt, what have you got for me?'

'You were right, ma'am, he was at his office trying to delete files on his computer. Looks like he was tipped off. He couldn't account for why he was at his office in the middle of the night. We've managed to stop him and have confiscated the computer. Shall we bring him to headquarters?'

'Yes, please, thanks, Matt. See you soon.'

Bernie put the phone down.

'Question for you, sir? How did you know I'd sent officers to Fox's office? You'd expect him to be at home in the middle of the night, wouldn't you?'

Worth's hand immediately went to his mouth. 'I... I heard about it from someone at Salisbury. They rang to check his address with me.'

'Really? Well, that's very odd because it was DC Taylor who led the team and found Fox at his office, not his home. Plus we didn't ask anyone at Salisbury to arrange the warrant.'

Worth took a step back. 'Um...'

'So, sir, I'm going to ask you again, who told you police were at the office? Did Rupert Fox tell you himself? Maybe spotted them out of the window? Will we find a text from him on your mobile?

And how did you know that Gardener had sent an email to Fox in the first place? Have you known all along about the blackmail? Possibly tampered with Fox's home laptop? Have you deliberately attempted to scupper this investigation? What does Fox have on you that you were willing to risk this?'

Worth took another step back. 'I don't have to answer questions from a junior officer.'

'No,' said a voice from behind Worth, 'but you will have to answer mine. So, final chance, how did you know police were at Rupert Fox's office?'

Worth swung round to face Detective Chief Superintendent Wilson.

'I would have liked to have said that you've done a good job in my absence but that clearly isn't the case,' said Wilson. 'You have the option of either answering my question or you can answer to Anti-Corruption.'

Bernie moved round so she could see Worth's face. He was opening and closing his mouth like a fish, uttering no words.

'You see,' said Wilson, 'I was the one who dealt with the warrants. I have to say I wasn't best pleased when DS Anderson woke me up but it was clearly the right thing to do. I am relieving you of this investigation and you are immediately suspended. You will report to Anti-Corruption at eleven hundred hours, later this morning. You're entitled to have representation with you. There are two officers in the corridor who will escort you home.' Wilson folded his arms. 'I trust I've made myself clear.'

Worth was speechless. He gave a small nod and headed towards the door.

After Worth had gone, the super turned to Bernie.

'Well done, Bernie. You moved quickly on this,' he said.

'I've had suspicions for a while but it was only earlier that I realised exactly what was going on. Once Alice told me she thought DCI Worth was talking to Rupert Fox on the phone after listening to Gardener's interview, I guessed Rupert would go to the office to start deleting files. I really didn't want it to happen like this though.'

'Oh, I don't know,' said Wilson. 'Middle of the night, bit more discreet really. Right, you'd better bring me up to speed on all of this and then we can decide how to proceed.'

'I think the wisest thing is to focus on Ria when Rupert Fox is questioned and I think Matt should do that as arresting officer after he's got some sleep,' said Bernie. 'We'll leave the rest to Fraud, assuming there's still evidence on his computer. Honestly, you'd think that surveyors would be as straight as a die. It's normally estate agents that get all the bad press. In this case, it's the other way round. We're fortunate the estate agents have kept the records of all the houses that Fox surveyed and found fault with.'

'Not so fortunate for Worth,' said Wilson. 'Stupid man. Throwing his career away like that so that he could save fifty thousand pounds on his house. Wasn't "worth" it, eh?'

Bernie shook her head. 'Oh, sir.'

'What? I thought it was quite good. Well, time is ticking. What are you going to do with Gardener?'

'Oh, I'm not done with him yet. Fancy sitting in?'

'The time is zero two forty hours and in attendance is Detective Chief Superintendent Wilson and myself, Detective Inspector Noel.

'So, Ben, sorry to wake you up. You'll get your eight hours' break after this but I thought you'd like to know we found a video of Rosa, or Maria or Ria – what did you call her?'

Ben yawned loudly. 'Maria.'

'I see. Where did you meet?'

Ben stared at Bernie and for a moment she thought he was about to say 'no comment'.

'We met at a pub in Salisbury. If I'm there then I kip above the café. I took her back with me. Best shag I've had in a long time.' He sniffed loudly.

Bernie resisted rolling her eyes. 'So, something special then?'

Ben grinned. 'You could say that. She was certainly adventurous. She was very happy to pose for me.'

'You took photos of her and then shared them with your buddies?'

'Yep, but she was over sixteen so it didn't matter. Can't do me for that.'

Bernie didn't want him dwelling on Maria in that way.

'Tell me about Rupert Fox,' she said.

'That scumbag? He'd been pestering her for sex ever since she arrived. The bastard. Then he wanted to film them together.'

'Really? He told us it was her idea.'

Ben shook his head. 'The dead can't speak, can they? She gave in. It was that or lose the job. I came up with the idea of filming it and then blackmailing him.'

'Were you the man that Harriet Fox found in her house?'

Ben looked puzzled.

'Harriet Fox told me she dismissed Rosa, or rather Maria, because she caught her with a man in her room.'

Gardener took a deep breath in and slowly breathed out. 'You didn't watch the whole video, did you? I knew you'd wimp out.' He shook his head. 'It's not nice, though, is it? Seeing a woman get raped. I watched it too. The camera's connected to my computer. I saw it all happen. I jumped in my car and drove over there to pick her up and bring her back to stay with me. But I wasn't the only one to see it. If you'd watched the whole thing then you'd see, right at the end, the door open and Harriet Fox walk in. That's why she told Maria to go.'

No wonder Harriet didn't want to describe the man she'd seen.

'You've got a nerve saying how awful it is seeing a woman get raped, considering the videos and images on your computer,' said Bernie.

Gardener looked down at the floor. 'It's different when it's someone you care about.'

'And those people in your images, no one cares about them? And I doubt you cared about Maria. You offered her as a "prize" in a race. You sold pictures of her.'

'I shared the money with her.'

'And then what? She wanted more of the money? Or maybe she didn't want to do it any more? Is that why you killed her? Did you take Laura and Chloe because you planned to do the same with them?' Bernie leaned forward.

Gardener slowly looked up, his eyes burning with fury. 'I've told you already. I didn't kill Maria. And I was planning on leaving tonight and letting the girls go. I didn't hurt them.'

'Oh really? What about the photo of Chloe you sent, gagged and bound?'

Ben shook his head. 'Fake. When you took Chloe back to the station on Tuesday, I knew what would happen. It was fun stringing you along. I liked the idea of wasting your time, waiting for a suspect that wasn't going to turn up but once I knew Chloe's mum was going to be late, I seized my chance. I was teaching Computing so mocked up the photo while the class was occupied. Easy.'

'We knew it was fake. It wasn't Chloe but Laura. I recognised her necklace. Did you bind and gag her?'

Ben's face hardened. 'I told you – look at my emails. Stop pissing me about and go and check.'

Bernie stared at Ben. 'I think you're just playing for time.'

Ben leaned forward so that his face was level with Bernie's. 'I'm not fucking about here. Go and check the emails again. Because I didn't just see my girl get raped, I saw her being murdered too. It's all on film.'

CHAPTER 65

'Sorry, ma'am. He has so many emails with files attached,' said Tom. 'And I'm having to look at them all to find the right one. You have no idea what I'm seeing here.'

'I'm sorry too,' said Bernie into her mobile. 'There will be specialist officers taking over in the morning. From what you've told me, he's part of a huge paedophile ring.'

'Definitely. OK, I'm going to change my search parameters… right, I've taken Rosa's name out and I'm focusing on dates… hell, there's still got to be over a hundred emails here sent to generic addresses… wait… there's one here with a different subject heading – "I know what you did last night". Email address is a string of numbers so don't know who it's to. I can work on that though. There's a video attached. Do you want me to view it first?'

Bernie hesitated. Tom had seen too much already. 'No. Forward it to me here. I'll let you know if it's the right one or not. Thanks, Tom.'

Bernie rubbed her eyes. They were sore with tiredness. Her stomach was churning at the thought of the video. She couldn't watch it alone. Both Matt and Kerry had gone home to get some sleep before starting interviews in the morning. The search team were continuing at the house. She texted Anderson.

Think we have the right video now. Don't want to watch it on my own.

Her phone pinged a few seconds later. *With you in five.*

Bernie paced the empty office as she waited. Half-drunk mugs of tea and coffee littered the desks along with case notes and photos. It wouldn't be long before the cleaners would be in. She'd have to ask them not to clean this morning. She couldn't risk them seeing things they shouldn't.

Anderson came through the door. His stubble was dark and his eyes were red.

'I bailed Gardener's mother and sister earlier, pending further enquiries. I wouldn't be at all surprised to see them both back at some point to tell us more,' he said. 'Are you ready to see this?'

Bernie shook her head. 'I know I should be tougher than this but…'

Anderson pulled her in. 'If we stop feeling the pain, then we can't do our jobs any more. Why else do we relentlessly seek justice for the victims? If you'd rather I saw it…'

'No,' said Bernie raising her head from Anderson's shoulder. 'We'll do this together.'

They sat down at Bernie's desk and she opened up her email. It was there at the top, marked urgent by Tom. She clicked on the link he sent. A small window opened which she maximised. The screen was filled with a video in night vision. Anderson leaned forward and turned up the sound. Bernie recognised it as the woods by the track. From the angle it looked like the camera was balanced in a tree. There was a rustling noise and then the sound of someone running, breathing hard. A woman came into shot.

'That must be Ria,' said Bernie.

The woman stopped and looked behind her. Her eyes shone bright. She started to move again. There was another rustling sound and a man came in. His back was to the camera. He caught up with her and she fell.

'Turn round,' said Anderson. 'Let's get a look at your face. See if you're Gardener or not.'

'It's not Gardener. This man is slimmer,' said Bernie. *Could it be Manetti after all?*

The man helped Ria up and was then trying to kiss her, his hands moving all over her body. She was trying to push him away. Ria started to scream and the man shushed her. They struggled and fell down together, him on top. She carried on screaming but then the sound became muffled.

'I can't really see, is he covering her mouth with his hand?' asked Bernie.

'I think he must be. Wait, he's saying something,' said Anderson. He turned the sound up more.

'Please be quiet,' said the man. 'I just want to kiss you. We don't have to have sex, even though I won the race. Please, just be quiet.'

Bernie thought there was something familiar about the voice. Definitely not an Italian accent, though.

But Ria wasn't quiet and screamed more. The man's hands moved and there was a choking noise, her legs thrashing… and then, silence.

'There, that's better. You just needed to be quiet. I'm not going to hurt you. I only want to kiss you… why are you staring at me like that? Oh God, what have I done? What have I done?'

The man leapt up.

'Come on,' said Anderson, 'turn around.'

As though the man had heard him, he turned and looked around him, before running off.

Even with the video being in night vision, Bernie instantly recognised him. She covered her mouth with her hand as she gagged.

'The little shit,' said Anderson. 'He's been stringing us along, all this time. You OK?'

Bernie shook her head. 'Give me a minute.' She buried her head in her hands and steadied herself. The normal elation of discovering the culprit wasn't there. She sat up and looked at her watch. 'It's close to four a.m. Shall we go now or leave it an hour? We won't need a full arrest team. I don't think he's going to give us any trouble. Although we'll have to get past his mother first.'

'Whenever you're ready, ma'am.'

Dawn was still a couple of hours away as they drove towards the farm. A patrol car was en route to join them but Bernie wanted to make the arrest as calm as possible, knowing he would come with her. A few birds were struggling to wake the world but most were still roosting in the trees. She was lost in her thoughts, wondering how she had missed the clues. As they approached the farmhouse, a dog began barking.

'So much for a silent approach then,' said Anderson.

They left the car outside and walked towards the front of the house.

'Is that door open?' asked Bernie.

'Yes.' Anderson pulled out his baton. 'Let me go in first.'

Bernie switched her phone torch on. The house was dark but they knew the layout. There was a noise coming from the lounge.

'Someone's crying,' said Bernie.

They went into the lounge and found a woman sobbing on the floor by the fireplace. She held a framed photo of her son in her arms. Bernie gently lifted the woman's face up.

'I didn't know, I swear I didn't know.' Tears streamed down her face.

'Where is he?'

She shook her head. 'I don't know. He left after he told me. I couldn't stop him. He ran out.'

Bernie looked at Anderson. 'I know where he's gone.'

*

The torchlight bounced as they ran. Brambles snagged at Bernie's clothes but she pounded on, Anderson close behind her.

'Are you sure we're going in the right direction?' he called.

'Yes, we need to get to the track.'

'What? I thought he was scared of that place in the dark.'

'He's more terrified by what he's done. Come on. We don't have time to waste.'

They continued running until they reached the track. Bernie looked up it. Slivers of moonlight broke through the tunnel of trees; the branches, like fingers, pointing the way to their suspect. A ghost haunting the lane suddenly seemed more plausible. She heard a noise.

'Did you hear that?' asked Bernie. The air was still around them.

'Hear what?'

'Creaking.'

'It's just the wind in the trees.'

Bernie turned to him. 'Dougie, there isn't any wind.'

They ran up the track towards the sound, Bernie slipping a couple of times on the old bricks. They kept going until torchlight picked something out in the dark. Legs were kicking in the air. Anderson grabbed them and pushed them up.

'Get the rope down!' he shouted.

Bernie swung the torch round to see where the noose was exactly. She caught sight of his face and winced. It was too high for her to reach. He'd used the rope for getting into the cave. She scanned the ground, looking for whatever he had stepped onto to reach that high, but couldn't see anything. Her only option was to get to the noose itself which meant scrambling up the side of the steep bank without the benefit of the rope. She wished now she'd woken up Kerry.

'Come on, Bernie, quickly.'

Putting her phone away, Bernie started to climb up the slope. She tried to find purchase, anything to grab onto, but the sandstone soil came away in her hands. Then, grasping blindly, she found an exposed tree root. She held on and followed it as it snaked up the bank until something skimmed her head. Was it a bat? It took a second to register it was a low branch from the tree. It was moving and she knew that was where the noose must be. Her only option was to break it but that meant letting go of the root. She reached out with one hand to take hold of the branch and then the other. She pushed down on it. Nothing.

'Come on, Bernie. I can't take his weight for much longer.'

'I'm trying!'

Bernie reached up higher with her left hand and felt the top of the bank. She needed to get above the branch to put enough weight on it. Pain ripped through her left wrist as she pulled herself up. Twisting round, she brought her left arm down and pushed on the branch with both hands. The wood started to snap. She pushed harder, putting all her weight through her arms. The branch splintered and gave way. The man fell onto Anderson as Bernie tumbled down. Anderson laid him on the ground and Bernie scrabbled at the rope around his neck, loosening it. She heard the boy gasp and then retch.

'Oh, Craig, why didn't you just talk to me?' said Bernie.

CHAPTER 66

Bernie and Anderson followed the ambulance to the hospital.

'I don't understand it,' said Anderson, as he drove. 'Why did he go and "discover" the body? Why not leave her there?'

Bernie leaned back in her seat. 'Guilt. He obviously didn't have a stomach bug. He was sick because of what he had done. He couldn't hand himself in so did the next best thing – he gave us the body.'

'But all the time and energy and money that's been wasted. If he'd just said, "by the way, I did it", we'd have had this sorted straight away.'

'Maybe. But if he'd done that we wouldn't have caught Ben Gardener or Rupert Fox and DCI Worth would have retired quite happily, knowing he'd got away with fraud. And we would never have…' Bernie turned her head towards Anderson and smiled.

'Well, no, obviously not. Maybe I should shake him by the hand.' Anderson smiled back. 'So, Miss Marple, how does everything else fit in then?'

'Miss Marple? I am not an old maid.'

'I know that. But I bet you have figured this all out, haven't you?'

Bernie put her head on one side. 'I have a few ideas. I think that if we search through Ben Gardener's emails, we'll find more to Craig. I think taking Laura was a warning to Craig about going to the police. And as he admitted, he took Chloe just to wind us up. I may be wrong in all of this but I think Gardener is more of a provider and less of a partaker in the online stuff.'

'Still bloody wrong though,' said Anderson.

'Yes, of course. And he'll go to prison, no doubt about it.'

'But how does this connect with hiding Ryan in a cave all those years ago?'

'Ryan's brother Gareth told me that he and his other brother were punished for what happened to him even though they swore they weren't responsible. Maybe Ben faced the same fate, perhaps worse.'

'So do you think the motorbike race was to wind up Ryan?' asked Anderson.

'Yes. I think the plan was to get Ryan to race up that track. See if he was still scared. But when he refused to take part, Ben adapted the plan. Film and blackmail whoever won the prize. Except it went wrong. Horribly wrong.' Bernie paused.

Anderson glanced across. 'What are you thinking?'

'It was filmed. As far as I'm aware, we didn't find a camera. Ben must have retrieved it. He would have seen her dead. And he still left her there. Poor Ria.' Bernie shook her head. 'Now all we have to do is find the real Rosa Conti.'

'Gabriel is working on that one,' said Anderson. 'Hopefully she can be reunited with her grandparents soon.'

'We need some good to come out of this. I'm not sure how the Moffatts are going to survive. We may have to postpone Laura's statement.'

'But we need that so we can charge Gardener.'

'As you said, there are going to be plenty of charges for Gardener anyway,' said Bernie. 'We need to hear what Craig has to say first.'

'If he can tell us,' said Anderson.

'Yes,' said Bernie. 'We don't know what the damage is yet.'

*

'I'm afraid it's too early to say,' said the doctor. 'He's still unconscious. We'll need to do some brain scans to look for possible damage. He was deprived of oxygen for a while.' He glanced down the corridor at the Moffatt family. 'I'm very concerned about them though.'

'Me too,' said Bernie. 'I've arranged for their local vicar to come with his wife. They'll be in safe hands.'

Bernie walked down the corridor. John, Caroline and Laura were all in tears. Bernie crouched down next to them.

'I'm so sorry. You've been through hell. We can postpone Laura's statement for now.'

Laura looked up. 'No, I want to do it.'

'But we need one of your parents to be there and I don't think that's going to happen for the moment.'

'I could do it,' said a female voice.

Bernie stood up to see Anna and Paul Bentley behind her.

'I don't mind,' said Anna.

'Are you happy for that?' Bernie asked John Moffatt. Craig's father gave a slight nod. 'OK. I'll leave Detective Sergeant Anderson with you and I'll take you back to headquarters.'

'Ma'am, I have a better idea,' said Anderson. 'Laura has to be discharged first so that'll take some time. It's only just gone eight o'clock. You need some food and sleep. The rest of the team are due in at midday. It makes sense for Alice and Kerry to take Laura's statement. We can ask a local officer to come in and wait with the family. We can come back later.'

Bernie was exhausted. Her arms were aching. She hated the idea of leaving the Moffatts though. She felt a hand on her shoulder. It was Anna.

'It pains me to say it but he's right. Go, get some rest. I'll take Laura to headquarters later and Paul will call you if there's any change.' She gave Bernie a kind smile.

Bernie bent down to speak to Caroline. 'When he wakes up, I'll come back. I promise.'

Caroline Moffatt looked defeated. 'If he wakes up,' she said quietly.

'No, Caroline. When. He will wake up,' said Bernie.

Bernie struggled to get her key in the lock, she was so tired.

'Here, let me do it,' said Anderson.

She felt his hands guide her into her cottage and up the stairs. She almost fell onto her bed. As he pulled the duvet over her, she said, 'We're supposed to have a date first, remember?'

'Don't worry, I have no intention of taking advantage of you. Sleep.'

Bernie was asleep before he even left the room.

It only seemed like a few minutes later when Bernie heard her name being called. There was a light touch on her shoulder. She struggled to open her eyes.

'What?' she murmured.

'Craig's awake and asking for you,' said Anderson.

Bernie pushed herself up. Her head was pounding.

'I would say I'd make something for you to eat but there doesn't appear to be much food in your kitchen. I'm going to pop over to the pub and see if they have any sandwiches left.'

'What's the time then?'

'One o'clock. Have a shower. I'll be back soon.'

'Dougie, have you slept?'

Anderson smiled. 'I had a kip on your sofa. It'll be enough to get me through a few more hours.'

*

Craig was pale except for the livid red mark around his neck. Bernie smiled gently at him.

'Hey, you had us all worried earlier,' she said.

'Why did you save me? Why didn't you let me die? It's what I deserve.' His eyes were red from crying.

Bernie took out her phone. 'We should do this formally at the station really but you're not well enough at the moment. I'd like to record our conversation if that's OK with you.'

Craig nodded.

'I've seen the video that Ben Gardener sent you.'

Craig looked confused. 'What? Laura's form tutor?'

'Ah, maybe you know him better as Luke Davidson.'

'Yes. I guess you want to know what happened.'

'Yes. But I need to formally arrest you first.' Bernie pressed record on her phone. 'This is Detective Inspector Noel with Craig Moffatt. Craig, you are under arrest on suspicion of the murder of Maria Greco. You do not have to say anything. But, it may harm your defence if you do not mention when questioned something which you later rely on in court. Anything you do say may be given in evidence. Do you understand?'

Craig nodded his head. 'Yes.'

'OK. The time is fourteen thirty hours. Tell me, in your own words, Craig, what happened that night.'

CHAPTER 67

'I guess I'm a bit of a geek,' said Craig. 'I've always got my head in a book or doing something on a computer. The other boys at school are always going on about all the girls they've been with. They like to wind me up. Nearly every Monday morning they ask if I lost my virginity over the weekend. They know the answer. I haven't even kissed a girl. Never been on a date. I haven't even asked a girl out.

'So at the race that night, when that guy, Luke, offered up his girlfriend as a prize, I said yes. I didn't want to have sex with her... I just wanted to kiss her... I just wanted the boys at school to stop.'

Craig sniffed and wiped his face with his sleeve. 'I didn't think I'd win though. He'd beaten Ryan and he's the best rider. I know now that he let me win. It was a set-up. She seemed quite keen at the beginning. She was laughing and then she started to run into the woods, looking back at me to see if I was following. Honestly, she was laughing. Until I caught up with her. She fell down as I reached her so I helped her up. I tried to kiss her. I... I was touching her as well but... I didn't want any more than that, I promise. She started screaming and I was worried that someone would hear her. So I covered her mouth with my hand but she still made a noise. She struggled and we fell down together. She was still screaming so I put my hands on her neck to stop the sound...'

Craig stopped. His hands moved to his own neck. 'I… I pressed too hard. I didn't know what I'd done until it was too late. I just wanted her to stop screaming.'

He looked up at Bernie, his eyes hollow, his face blanched. 'I didn't mean to kill her. I deserve to die like she did. That's why I did this.' He pointed to the red mark on his neck. 'I deserve to choke and be terrified and…'

Bernie laid her hand on Craig's arm. 'Would you like to take a break?'

Craig shook his head. 'No. I have to tell you everything. It's like I've got to vomit it all up.'

'Is that why you were ill?' said Bernie.

'Yes. I was so sick when I got home. I couldn't keep anything down for days. He sent an email with a video attached. Don't even know how he got my address. I use a number code for it so it's not obvious.'

No, but he had your sister's address. He probably hacked her account to find yours.

'I kept watching it – I couldn't seem to stop myself. He wanted cash.' Craig shrugged. 'I don't have much money and Mum wasn't letting me out of the house so I couldn't empty my savings account anyway. I didn't know what to do. I couldn't pay him and I couldn't confess. So, I did the only thing I could do and "discovered" her body. I study Biology at school but I had no idea…'

Craig gagged and his father, sitting next to him, grabbed a sick bowl. Craig waved it away. Bernie was tempted to take it herself. The memory was still fresh in her own mind.

Craig regained some composure. 'It was worse than I thought. If I'd known, I would have gone out sooner. I'm sorry, I'm really, really sorry.'

Bernie glanced across at John Moffatt. His eyes were fixed on Craig. She wondered which parent had the harder job – the father listening to his son's confession, or the mother hearing about her daughter's abduction. With her son awake, Caroline had gone with Laura.

'Does this tie in with Laura going missing?' she asked.

Craig nodded. 'When we knew Laura hadn't gone to her friend's house like she said, he sent me another email. He told me not to say anything more to you or he'd do to Laura what I did to his girlfriend. And more. Said he'd do more than just kiss her.'

Craig covered his face and shuddered. 'I had to keep quiet. And then you came and asked me about the race and if I'd been there.'

Bernie remembered. 'Did you really see him on his motorbike?'

Craig pulled his hands away. 'Sort of. I ran as soon as I realised what I'd done. Got on my bike and rode up the track. He saw me leave but he must have gone to look for her. When I was wheeling the bike down our drive, I heard him go past. I think he saw me so knew where I lived.'

'And I thought you were scared of your father because you'd taken his motorbike without permission.'

'I was more scared about Laura. He said he'd release her when I paid him a thousand pounds. I emailed him back and said I didn't have that much. I could only give him five hundred pounds. I was going to do that this weekend. I told him I wanted proof she was still alive. He sent me a photo of her tied up and gagged. I have all the emails still.' Craig passed Bernie his phone. 'It's all on there.'

Bernie took it and placed it in an evidence bag. 'Thanks. I'll need the code for it.'

'Two one three two,' said Craig.

Bernie jotted it down in her notebook. 'Is there anything else you want to tell me, Craig?'

He shook his head. 'No, I don't think so.'

'OK. Interview concluded at fourteen forty-five hours.' Bernie switched off the recording.

'What happens now?' asked Craig.

Bernie looked at the teenager. Her heart went out to him. She believed him but justice wasn't her decision to make.

'Well, I'll write this statement up and then you'll have to sign it. We may have further questions as well at some point but you've been quite thorough. I'll get in contact with the CPS and they'll decide the charges.'

'But you must have some idea,' said John Moffatt. 'Surely it's based on your recommendation.'

'It's based on the evidence, Mr Moffatt. We've seen the video that Craig was sent. What he's just told me confirms what we've seen. Until I speak to the CPS, I can't tell you.'

'What about the bastard who took Laura? What'll happen to him?' asked John.

Bernie saw the strain on John Moffatt's face. She wasn't sure how the family would survive but she would do her best to make sure they did.

'Again, I can't tell you until I've spoken to the CPS but… I'm expecting a very long list of charges for him.'

Bernie stood up. 'I'll be in touch. And Craig, DS Anderson and I have no qualms about saving you. It's our job to protect everyone, including you.'

Bernie's shoulders sagged as she walked to her car. Her phone buzzed. She looked at the screen and saw it was Anderson.

'Hey, you,' she said.

'Hey you, too. Do you want the good news or the good news or the good news?'

'There's no bad news? That makes a change. You choose.'

'OK. Firstly, Gabriel's been in touch. Bruno Manetti's been arrested in Rome and is now in custody. We're going to send them the phone ASAP but Manetti's SIM card is already on its way to them. Rosa's been in Spain but is now on her way home. It was as we thought. She wanted Ria to be safe from her ex so gave her the au pair job. She was very upset when she heard about her friend. Alberto and Julietta are relieved though.'

'I bet they are. We probably owe them an apology, scaring them like that. What else?'

'After giving a denial statement last night, Gardener's mother has come back in and spilt the beans on her son. Sounds like he's been an absolute bastard to his mother and sister. They had to go along with what he was doing or he'd hurt them. So that, along with Laura and Chloe's interviews, is enough to charge him with abduction. Lastly, Child Protection have taken over the online stuff but they have found something interesting that might help Craig Moffatt.'

'Oh, yes?'

'A longer video clip from that night. Gardener sent a shorter version to Craig. In the longer one, Ria is laughing and seems to be enticing Craig on. Then she changes character and starts screaming. It was obviously meant to be a set-up all along and from what Gardener's mother said, Ryan Willis was the original target. Although they never told the Willis family, Ben confessed to his parents about hiding Ryan. He got a real beating from his father for it. Clearly wasn't a nice man. Not long after, his parents split up. For some reason, Ben thought it was to do with him and blamed Ryan.'

'Sounds like a messed up kid. There's one thing still bugging me though – Ria's confession. We'll never know which man she was scared of.'

'Probably just as well. If she'd named just one man, we wouldn't have looked at the others. And now they're all facing charges. You can't always know it all, Miss Marple.'

Bernie shook her head. 'Stop calling me that.'

'OK. Is Jessica Fletcher any better?'

'No…'

'How about Christine Cagney? She was damn sexy. Or Make-peace. She was hot too…'

'Oh, Dougie. You are the most infuriating man but I do lo—' Bernie stopped. The words had come out of her mouth without her really thinking about them.

'You do what? Love me? God, Bernie. We've not even had that first date yet.'

She could hear the teasing in his voice.

'I feel the same way too,' he said.

'Please tell me you're not in the office.'

'I'm not. I'm outside.' He paused. 'I guess this means I'm going to have to change teams.'

Bernie bit her lip. She didn't want him to move but knew there was no choice.

'I guess it does,' she said.

CHAPTER 68

Seven weeks later – Early December

The Marchant Arms was covered in Christmas decorations. The landlord and his wife didn't go in for the understated look. The pub was crowded but an area had been reserved for Anderson's leaving drinks.

'I suppose I should give a speech,' said DCS Wilson. All eyes turned to him. 'Detective Sergeant Dougal Anderson…'

Anderson grimaced at his full name.

'…it's mostly been a pleasure having you on the MCIT team these last few months.'

There was a ripple of laughter.

'You've certainly made an impact,' said Wilson. 'In more ways than one. I'm sad to see you go but glad that it's for a good reason. I'm sure that you and Bernie will be very happy together. At least, I hope you will be. She's hell to work with when she's grumpy. So, please, for all our sakes, keep her happy.'

Bernie blushed.

'I'll do my best,' said Anderson.

'Good,' said Wilson. 'Our loss is Serious Organised Crime team's gain. So I'd like everyone to raise their glasses and toast the newly appointed Detective *Inspector* Anderson.'

There were cheers as the team toasted Anderson.

'Well done, mate,' said Matt Taylor, banging him on the back.

'That's Detective Inspector to you, or sir, Matty boy,' said Anderson, laughing. 'Hey, you know what we need – chips! Sue – lots of chips, please!'

Kerry sidled up to Bernie. 'Someone's merry. So, he's moving in before Christmas then? You two didn't muck about, did you? Did you even go on that first date?'

Bernie gave a wry smile. 'Actually, we did. We went to Bath for the day and had a really lovely time.'

'And?'

Bernie sighed. 'He booked a hotel for the night.'

They both laughed.

Kerry indicated to Bernie's glass. 'Get you another? Seeing you only have to stagger home.'

'No, I'd better not. I've got a doctor's appointment tomorrow. Dougie's been nagging me to go and get these headaches sorted out. It won't look good if I turn up with a hangover.'

'No, it won't. And mention your wrist too. You need proper physio.'

'Like I have time for that. I don't have time for anything.'

Bernie sat in the waiting room at the surgery. The doctor was running late. She sighed. She'd only booked an hour off work for this. Flicking through the health magazines, she resisted the quiz to see how healthy she was but did linger over the sex feature.

'Bernadette Noel.'

Bernie looked up to see Dr Forbes smiling at her. She stood up and followed the doctor.

Bernie liked Dr Forbes. In her mid-forties, she ran the practice with one other partner. She was a doctor who loved the local community and was very much part of village life in Marchant. A real 'cradle to the grave' kind of doctor who willingly gave up her time for her patients.

'So, Bernie, what can I do for you today? I so rarely see you here.'

Bernie smiled. 'I know. I'm rubbish at coming to see you. I've been getting quite bad headaches for a few months now. It's not my eyesight as I got that checked.'

'Oh, you've got time to get your eyes checked then.' Dr Forbes smiled. 'I can see here you've not had a check-up for over six months. So we'll do the full works today. Let's start with your blood pressure first.'

Bernie braced herself as the cuff tightened round her arm. She hated that squeezing feeling.

'Hmm,' said the doctor. 'Hundred and forty over ninety – that's quite high. That could be the cause of your headaches. I'm guessing you work irregular hours, drink a lot of coffee and probably not enough water and are generally quite stressed. And don't sleep properly either.'

Bernie smiled. 'Well, yes. I am quite tired.'

'Even so, your blood pressure is still high.' Dr Forbes rummaged in a drawer in her desk and took out a tube. She passed it to Bernie.

'If you could go and do a sample, please.'

'What, now?'

'Yes, now. God knows when I'll see you again, Bernie. As I said, full works today. Off you go.'

Bernie returned a few minutes later and passed the tube back. Dr Forbes unscrewed the lid and stuck a dipstick into it.

'Now, the other thing to consider with your headaches and blood pressure, is your birth control.' Dr Forbes gave a cheeky grin. 'I've seen you around with your new man. I heartily approve. He's very good-looking.'

Bernie's cheeks burned. 'Well, yes. I've been on the Pill for as long as I can remember.'

'When was your last bleed?'

'Late September, I think. I've been taking the packs back to back for three cycles like we agreed. I'm due a break next week.'

Dr Forbes turned back to the urine sample and pulled the dipstick out.

'And you're still taking it?' the doctor asked.

'Yes, every morning, religiously.'

'You've not had any stomach upsets?'

'No.'

'So no diarrhoea or vomiting then?'

'No,' said Bernie. She stopped as a memory surfaced. Next to her car after seeing Ria's body for the first time in the woods. She had vomited. And then a couple of days later, there had been the morning with Alex, followed by the night with Anderson. She looked aghast at the doctor. 'Oh hell. I was sick about a couple of months ago.'

'Well,' said Dr Forbes, 'that would explain it. Looks as though congratulations are in order. You're pregnant.'

A LETTER FROM JOY

Dear reader,

I want to say a huge thank you for choosing to read *Broken Girls*. If you did enjoy it, and want to keep up to date with all my latest releases, just sign up at the following link. Your email address will never be shared and you can unsubscribe at any time.

www.bookouture.com/joy-kluver

I hope you loved *Broken Girls* and if you did I would be very grateful if you could write a review. I'd love to hear what you think, and it makes such a difference helping new readers to discover one of my books for the first time.

This wasn't an easy story to write. As a mother of teenagers, I'm all too aware of the dangers the internet can present. Online grooming becomes more prevalent each day and so it's important to teach our children to be safe online. If you're wondering how to talk to your children then The Breck Foundation is a good place to start.

I love hearing from my readers – you can get in touch on my Facebook page, through Twitter, Goodreads or my website.

Thanks,
Joy

joykluverauthor

@JoyKluver

kluver.co.uk

ACKNOWLEDGEMENTS

I'd like to start with my editor, Therese Keating, and all the rest of the incredible team at Bookouture – it's great to be part of the family. To my agent, Anne Williams – thank you for your continued support.

Thank you to Graham Bartlett and Karen Bate for their police expertise, and also Colin Hart. I've had to use some artistic licence with the story so any police inaccuracies are my own.

To Vicki Goldman and Alex Khan for their unstinting encouragement and an early edit from Vicki. To Rod Reynolds – thank you for reading and giving me advice once more.

Huge thanks to all the bloggers that took part in the blog tour. Having been a blogger for several years I know how much time and energy it takes to read and review so I really appreciate it.

The first draft of this book was written under the guidance of Elizabeth Kay, my tutor at the Malden Centre Writing Class, and critiqued weekly by the rest of the group – John, Viviane, Jean, Mike, Sue, Aleks, Marilyn, Caroline, Loraine and Clare. Thank you for all your help.

I knew nothing about motorbikes when I started writing this. So I'm grateful to Alistair Stewart for his advice and also the staff at J&S Accessories who entertained my questions about motorbike helmets.

As I've included some real places in Wiltshire, it was essential to do a research trip. Thank you to John and Esther Dusting for letting us stay, especially as it was the whole family! The track mentioned in the book is real and when we walked there, we really did meet a dog walker who told us about it being haunted. I have elaborated on it a bit but thank you to Diane Paris for sowing the seed! I've also recently discovered the website hiddenwiltshire. com, which provided more information about the track, so thank you to Paul Timlett.

And finally, to my husband, Phil, and our three children, James, Beth and Hayden – thank you for enduring the research trip, particularly the drive down the potholed lane! At least you got your reward at the bakery.

Made in the USA
Las Vegas, NV
07 March 2022

45199934R00193